If Winter Comes
By
A.S.M. Hutchinson

"...O Wind, If Winter comes, can Spring be far behind?"

—SHELLEY

Foreword

This book contains the complete text of *If Winter Comes* by Arthur Stuart-Menteth Hutchinson, more popularly known as A.S.M Hutchinson. This novel, while not critically acclaimed, was very popular with the masses and was the best-selling book for all of 1922. It was subsequently made into two movies, a silent version and another version with sound during the forties, updated to that time period.

Set in Southern England at the turn of the last century, the book is a work of Social Realism. It was, in many aspects, ahead of its time, dealing with an unhappy marriage, divorce, and suicide. It is the story of Mark Sabre and his descent into a series of disasters. Other interesting characters do present themselves, but all exist only to fill out the main story. Through all the bleakness and despair hope always remains as demonstrated by the quotation alluded to in the title, "*If Winter Comes*, can Spring be far behind?"

-NWC

CONTENTS

PART ONE

MABEL

IF WINTER COMES
CHAPTER I

I

To take Mark Sabre at the age of thirty-four, and in the year 1912, and at the place Penny Green is to necessitate looking back a little towards the time of his marriage in 1904, but happens to find him in good light for observation. Encountering him hereabouts, one who had shared school days with him at his preparatory school so much as twenty-four years back would have found matter for recognition.

A usefully garrulous person, one Hapgood, a solicitor, found much.

"Whom do you think I met yesterday? Old Sabre! You remember old Sabre at old Wickamote's?... Yes, that's the chap. Used to call him Puzzlehead, remember? Because he used to screw up his forehead over things old Wickamote or any of the other masters said and sort of drawl out, 'Well, I don't see that, sir.'... Yes, rather!... And then that other expression of his. Just the opposite. When old Wickamote or some one had landed him, or all of us, with some dashed punishment, and we were gassing about it, used to screw up his nut in the same way and say, 'Yes, but I see what he means.' And some one would say, 'Well, what does he mean, you ass?' and he'd start gassing some rot till some one said, 'Good lord, fancy sticking up for a master!' And old Puzzlehead would say, 'You sickening fool, I'm not sticking up for him. I'm only saying he's right from how he looks at it and it's no good saying he's wrong.'... Ha! Funny days.... Jolly nice chap, though, old Puzzlehead was.... Yes, I met him.... Fact, I run into him occasionally. We do a mild amount of business with his firm. I buzz down there about once a year. Tidborough. He's changed, of course. So have you, you know. That Vandyke beard, what? Ha! Old Sabre's not done anything outrageous like that. Real thing I seemed to notice about him when I bumped into him yesterday was that he didn't look very cheery. Looked to me rather as though he'd lost something and was wondering where it was. Ha! But—dashed funny—I mentioned something about that appalling speech that chap made in that blasphemy case yesterday.... Eh? yes, absolutely frightful, wasn't it?—well, I'm dashed if old Sabre didn't puzzle up his nut in exactly the same old way and say, 'Yes, but I see what he means.' I reminded him and ragged him about it no end. Absolutely the same words and expression. Funny chap ... nice chap....

"What did he say the blasphemy man meant? Oh, I don't know; some bilge, just as he used to about the masters. You know the man talked some rubbish about how the State couldn't have it both ways— couldn't blaspheme against God by flatly denying that all men were equal and basing all its legislation on keeping one class up and the other class down; couldn't do that and at the same time prosecute him because he said that religion was—well, you know what he said; I'm dashed if I like to repeat it. Joke of it was that I found myself using exactly the same expression to old Sabre as we used to use at school. I said, 'Good lord, man, fancy sticking up for a chap like that!' And old Sabre—by Jove, I tell you there we all were in a flash back in the playground at old Wickamote's, down in that corner by the workshop, all kids again and old Puzzlehead flicking his hand out of his pocket— remember how he used to?—like that—and saying, 'You sickening fool, I'm not sticking up for him, I'm only saying he's right from how he looks at it and it's no good saying he's wrong!' Rum, eh, after all those years.... No, he didn't say, 'You sickening fool' this time. I reminded him how he used to, and he laughed and said, 'Yes; did I? Well, I still get riled, you know, when chaps can't see—' And then he said 'Yes, "sickening fool"; so I did; odd!' and he looked out of the window as though he was looking a thousand miles away—this was in his office, you know—and chucked talking absolutely....

"Yes, in his office I saw him.... He's in a good business down there at Tidborough. Dashed good. 'Fortune, East and Sabre'... Never heard of them? Ah, well, that shows you're not a pillar of the Church, old son. If you took the faintest interest in your particular place of worship, or in any Anglican place of worship, you'd know that whenever you want anything for the Church from a hymn book or a hassock or a pew to a pulpit or a screen or a spire you go to Fortune, East and Sabre, Tidborough. Similarly in the scholastic line, anything from a birch rod to a desk—Fortune, East and Sabre, by return and the best. No, they're the great, the great, church and school-furnishing people. 'Ecclesiastical and Scholastic Furnishers and Designers' they call themselves. And they're IT. No really decent church or really gentlemanly school thinks of going anywhere else. They keep at Tidborough because they were there when they furnished the first church in the year One or thereabouts. I expect they did the sun-ray fittings at Stonehenge. Ha! Anyway, they're one of the stately firms of old England, and old Sabre is the Sabre part of the firm. And his father before him and so on. Fortune and East are both bishops, I believe. No, not really. But I tell you the show's run on mighty pious lines. One of them's a 'Rev.', I know. I mean, the tradition of the place is to be in keeping with the great and good works it carries out and for which, incidentally, it is dashed well paid. Rather. Oh, old Sabre has butter with his bread all right....

"Married? Oh, yes, he's married. Has been some time, I believe, though they've no kids. I had lunch at his place one time I was down Tidborough way. Now there's a place you ought to go to paint one of your pictures—where he lives—Penny Green. Picturesque, quaint if ever a place was. It's about seven miles from Tidborough; seven miles by road and about seven centuries in manners and customs and appearance and all that. Proper old village green, you know, with a duck pond and cricket pitch and houses all round it. No two alike. Just like one of Kate Greenaway's pictures, I always think. It just sits and sleeps. You wouldn't think there was a town within a hundred miles of it, let alone a bustling great place like Tidborough. Go down. You really ought to. Yes, and by Jove you'll have to hurry up if you want to catch the old-world look of the place. It's 'developing' ... 'being developed.'... Eh?... Yes; God help it; I agree. After all these centuries sleeping there it's suddenly been 'discovered.' People are coming out from Tidborough and Alton and Chovensbury to get away from their work and live there. Making a sort of garden suburb business of it. They've got a new church already. Stupendous affair, considering the size of the place—but that's looking forward to this development movement, the new vicar chap says. He's doing the developing like blazes. Regular tiger he is for shoving things, particularly himself. Chap called Bagshaw—Boom Bagshaw. Character if ever there was one. But they're all characters down there from what I've seen of it....

"Yes, you go down there and have a look, with your sketch-book. Old Sabre'll love to see you.... His wife?... Oh, very nice, distinctly nice. Pretty woman, very. Somehow I didn't think quite the sort of woman for old Puzzlehead. Didn't appear to have the remotest interest in any of the things he was keen about; and he seemed a bit fed with her sort of talk. Hers was all gossip—all about the people there and what a rum crowd they were. Devilish funny, I thought, some of her stories. But old Sabre—well, I suppose he'd heard 'em before. Still, there was something—something about the two of them. You know that sort of—sort of—what the devil is it?—sort of stiffish feeling you sometimes feel in the air with two people who don't quite click. Well, that was it. Probably only my fancy. As to that, you can pretty well cut the welkin with a knife at my place sometimes when me and my missus get our tails up; and we're fearful pals. Daresay I just took 'em on an off day. But that was my impression though—that she wasn't just the sort of woman for old Sabre. But after all, what the dickens sort of woman would be? Fiddling chap for a husband, old Puzzlehead. Can imagine him riling any wife with wrinkling up his nut over some plain as a pikestaff thing and saying, 'Well, I don't quite see that.' Ha! Rum chap. Nice chap. Have a drink?"

CHAPTER II

I

Thus, by easy means of the garrulous Hapgood, appear persons, places, institutions; lives, homes, activities; the web and the tangle and the amenities of a minute fragment of human existence. Life. An odd business. Into life we come, mysteriously arrived, are set on our feet and on we go: functioning more or less ineffectively, passing through permutations and combinations; meeting the successive events, shocks, surprises of hours, days, years; becoming engulfed, submerged, foundered by them; all of us on the same adventure yet retaining nevertheless each his own individuality, as swimmers carrying each his undetachable burden through dark, enormous and cavernous seas. Mysterious journey! Uncharted, unknown and finally—but there is no finality! Mysterious and stunning sequel—not end—to the mysterious and tremendous adventure! Finally, of this portion, death, disappearance,—gone! Astounding development! Mysterious and hapless arrival, tremendous and mysterious passage, mysterious and alarming departure. No escaping it; no volition to enter it or to avoid it; no prospect of defeating it or solving it. Odd affair! Mysterious and baffling conundrum to be mixed up in!... Life!

Come to this pair, Mark Sabre and his wife Mabel, at Penny Green, and have a look at them mixed up in this odd and mysterious business of life. Some apprehension of the odd affair that it was was characteristic of Mark Sabre's habit of mind, increasingly with the years,—with Mabel.

II

Penny Green—"picturesque, quaint if ever a place was", in garrulous Mr. Hapgood's words—lies in a shallow depression, in shape like a narrow meat dish. It runs east and west, and slightly tilted from north to south. To the north the land slopes pleasantly upward in pasture and orchards, and here was the site of the Penny Green Garden Home Development Scheme. Beyond the site, a considerable area, stands Northrepps, the seat of Lord Tybar. Lord Tybar sold the Development site to the developers, and, as he signed the deed of conveyance, remarked in his airy way, "Ah, nothing like exercise, gentlemen. That's made every one of my ancestors turn in his grave." The developers tittered respectfully as befits men who have landed a good thing.

Westward of Penny Green is Chovensbury; behind Tidborough the sun rises.

Viewed from the high eminence of Northrepps, Penny Green gave rather the impression of having slipped, like a sliding dish, down the slope and come to rest, slightly tilted, where its impetus had ceased. It was certainly at rest: it had a restful air; and it had certainly slipped out of the busier trafficking of its surrounding world, the main road from Chovensbury to Tidborough, coming from greater cities even than these and proceeding to greater, ran far above it, beyond Northrepps. The main road rather slighted than acknowledged Penny Green by the nerveless and shrunken feeler which, a mile beyond Chovensbury, it extended in Penny Green's direction.

This splendid main road in the course of its immense journey across Southern England, extended feelers to many settlements of man, providing them as it were with a talent which, according to the energy of the settlement, might be increased a hundredfold—drained, metalled, tarred, and adorned with splendid telegraph poles and wires—or might be wrapped up in a napkin of neglect, monstrous overgrown hedges and decayed ditches, and allowed to wither: the splendid main road, having regard to its ancient Roman lineage, disdainfully did not care tuppence either way; and for that matter Penny Green, which had ages ago put its feeler in a napkin, did not care tuppence either.

It was now, however, to have a railway.

And meanwhile there was this to be said for it: that whereas some of the dependents of the splendid main road constituted themselves abominably ugly carbuncles on the end of shapely and well-manicured fingers of the main road, Penny Green, at the end of a withered and entirely neglected finger, adorned it as with a jewel.

III

A Kate Greenaway picture, the garrulous Hapgood had said of Penny Green; and it was well said. At its eastern extremity the withered talent from the splendid main road divided into two talents and encircled the Green which had, as Hapgood had said, a cricket pitch (in summer) and a duck pond (more prominent in winter); also, in all seasons, and the survivors of many ages, a clump of elm trees surrounded by a decayed bench; a well surrounded by a decayed paling, so decayed that it had long ago thrown itself flat on the ground into which it continued venerably to decay; and at the southeastern extremity a village pound surrounded by a decayed grey wall and now

11

used by the youth of the village for the purpose of impounding one another in parties or sides in a game well called "Pound I."

At the southwestern extremity of the Green, and immediately opposite the Tybar Arms, was a blacksmith's forge perpetually inhabited and directed by a race named Wirk. The forge was the only human habitation or personal and individual workshop actually on the Green, and it was said, and freely admitted by the successive members of the tribe of Wirk, that it had "no right" to be there. There it nevertheless was, had been for centuries, so far as anybody knew to the contrary, and administered always by a Wirk. In some mysterious way which nobody ever seemed to recognize till it actually happened there was always a son Wirk to continue the forge when the father Wirk died and was carried off to be deposited by his fathers who had continued it before him. It was also said in the village, as touching this matter of "no right", that nobody could understand how the forge ever came to be there and that it certainly would be turned off one day; and with this also the current members of the tribe of Wirk cordially agreed. They understood less than anybody how they ever came to be there, and they knew perfectly well they would be turned off one day; saying which—and it was a common subject of debate among village sires of a summer evening, seated outside the Tybar Arms—saying which, the Wirk of the day would gaze earnestly up the road and look at his watch as if the power which would turn him off was then on its way and was getting a bit overdue.

The present representatives of the tribe of Wirk were known as Old Wirk and Young Wirk. Young Wirk was sixty-seven. No one knew where a still younger Wirk would come from when Old Wirk died and when Young Wirk died. But no one troubled to know. No one knows, precisely, where the next Pope is coming from, but he always comes, and successive Wirks appeared as surely. Old Wirk was past duty at the forge now. He sat on a Windsor chair all day and watched Young Wirk. When the day was finished Old Wirk and Young Wirk would walk across the Green to the pound, not together, but Old Wirk in front and Young Wirk immediately behind him; both with the same gait, bent and with a stick. On reaching the pound they would gaze profoundly into it over the decayed, grey wall, rather as if they were looking to see if the power that was going to turn out the forge was there, and then, the power apparently not being there, they would return, trailing back in the same single file, and take up their reserved positions on the bench before the Tybar Arms.

IV

Mark Sabre, intensely fond of Penny Green, had reflected upon it sometimes as a curious thing that there was scarcely one of the village's inhabitants or institutions but had evidenced little differences of attitude between himself and Mabel, who was not intensely fond of Penny Green. The aged Wirks had served their turn. Mabel had once considered the Wirks extremely picturesque and, quite early in their married life, had invited them to her house that she might photograph them for her album.

They arrived, in single file, but she did not photograph them for her album. The photograph was not taken because Mark, when they presented themselves, expressed surprise that the aged pair were led off by the parlour maid to have tea in the kitchen. Why on earth didn't they have tea with them, with himself and Mabel, in the garden?

Mabel did what Sabre called "flew up"; and at the summit of her flight up inquired, "Suppose some one called?"

"Well, suppose they did?" Sabre inquired.

Mabel in a markedly calm voice then gave certain orders to the maid, who had brought out the tea and remained while the fate of the aged Wirks was in suspense.

The maid departed with the orders and Sabre commented, "Sending them off? Well, I'm dashed!"

Half an hour later the aged pair, having been led into the kitchen and having had tea there, were led out again and released by the maid on to the village Green rather as if they were two old ducks turned out to grass.

Sabre, watching them from the lawn beside the teacups, laughed and said, "What a dashed stupid business. They might have had tea on the roof for all I care."

Mabel tinkled a little silver bell for the maid. Ting-a-ling-ting!

V

The houses of Penny Green carried out the Kate Greenaway effect that the Green itself established. Along the upper road of the tilted dish were the larger houses, and upon the lower road mostly the cottages of

13

the villagers; also upon the lower road the five shops of Penny Green: the butcher's shop which was opened on Tuesdays and Fridays by a butcher who came in from Tidborough with a spanking horse in front of him and half a week's supply of meat behind and beneath him; the grocer's shop and the draper's shop which, like enormous affairs in London, were also a large number of other shops but, unlike the London affairs, dispensed them all within the one shop and over the one counter. In the grocer's shop you could be handed into one hand a pound of tea and into the other a pair of boots, a convenience which, after all, is not to be had in all Oxford Street. The draper's shop, carrying the principle further, would not only dress you; post-office you; linoleum, rug and wall paper you; ink, pencil and note paper you; but would also bury you and tombstone you, a solemnity which it was only called upon to perform for anybody about once in five years—Penny Green being long-lived—but was always ready and anxious to carry out. Indeed in the back room of his shop, the draper, Mr. Pinnock, had a coffin which he had been trying (as he said) "to work off" for twenty-two years. It represented Mr. Pinnock's single and disastrous essay in sharp business. Two and twenty years earlier Old Wirk had been not only dying but "as good as dead." Mr. Pinnock on a stock-replenishing excursion in Tidborough, had bought a coffin, at the undertaker's, of a size to fit Old Wirk, and for the reason that, buying it then, he could convey it back on the wagon he had hired for the day and thus save carriage. He had brought it back, and the first person he had set eyes on in Penny Green was no other than Old Wirk himself, miraculously recovered and stubbornly downstairs and sunning at his door. The shock had nearly caused Mr. Pinnock to qualify for the coffin himself; but he had not, nor had any other inhabitant of suitable size since demised. Longer persons than Old Wirk had died, and much shorter and much stouter persons than Old Wirk had died. But the coffin had remained. Up-ended and neatly fitted with shelves, it served as a store cupboard, without a door, pending its proper use. But it was a terribly expensive store cupboard and it stood in Mr. Pinnock's parlour as a gloomy monument to the folly of rash and hazardous speculation.

VI

Penny Green, like Rome, had not been built in a day. The houses of the Penny Green Garden Home, on the other hand, were being run up in as near to a day as enthusiastic developers, feverish contractors (vying one with another) and impatient tenants could encompass. Nor was Penny Green built for a day. The houses and cottages of Penny Green had been built under the influence of many and different styles of architecture; and they had been built not only by people who intended to live in them, and proposed to be roomy and well cup boarded and stoutly beamed and floored in them, but who, not foreseeing restless and railwayed generations, built them to endure for the children of their children's children and for children yet beyond. Sabre's house was of grey stone and it presented over the doorway the date 1667.

"Nearly two hundred and fifty years," Mabel had once said.

"And I bet," Sabre had replied, "it's never been better kept or run than you run it now, Mabel."

The tribute was well deserved. Mabel, who was in many ways a model woman, was preëminently a model housewife. "Crawshaws" was spotlessly kept and perfectly administered. Four living rooms, apart from the domestic offices, were on the ground floor. One was the morning room, in which they principally lived; one the dining room and one the drawing-room. They were entered by enormously heavy doors of oak, fitted with latches, the drawing-room up two steps, the dining room down one step and the morning room and the fourth room on the level. All were low-beamed and many-windowed with lattice windows; all were stepped into as stepping into a very quiet place, and somehow into a room which one had not expected to be there, or not quite that shape if a room were there. Sabre never quite lost that feeling of pleasant surprise on entering them. They had moreover, whether due to the skill of the architect or the sagacity of Mabel, the admirable, but rare attribute of being cool in summer and warm in winter.

The only room in the house which Sabre did not like was the fourth sitting room on the ground floor; and it was his own room, furnished and decorated by Mabel for his own particular use and comfort. But she called it his "den", and Sabre loathed and detested the word den as applied to a room a man specially inhabits. It implied to him a masculine untidiness, and he was intensely orderly and hated untidiness. It implied customs and manners of what he called "boarding-house ideas",—the idea that a man must have an untidily comfortable apartment into which he can retire and envelop himself in tobacco smoke, and where he "can have his own things around him", and "have his pipes and his pictures about him", and where he can wear "an old shooting jacket and slippers",—and he loathed and detested all these phrases and the ideas they connoted. He had no "old shooting jacket" and he would have given it to the gardener if he had; and he detested wearing slippers and never did wear slippers; it was his habit to put on his boots after his bath and to keep them on till he put on shoes when changing for dinner. Above all, he loathed and detested the vision which the word "den" always conjured up to him. This was a vision of the door of a typical den being opened by a wife, and of the wife saying in a mincing voice, "This is George in his den," and of boarding-house females peering over the wife's shoulder and smiling fatuously at the denizen who, in an old shooting jacket and slippers, grinned vacuously back at them. To Mark this was a horrible and unspeakable vision.

Mabel could not in the least understand it, and common sense and common custom were entirely on her side; Mark admitted that. The ridiculous and trivial affair only took on a deeper significance—not apparent to Mark at the time, but apparent later in the fact that he could not make Mabel understand his attitude.

The matter of the den and another matter, touching the servants, came up between them in the very earliest days of their married life. From London, on their return from their honeymoon, Mark had been urgently summoned to the sick-bed of his father, in Chovensbury. Mabel proceeded to Crawshaws. He joined her a week later, his father happily recovered. Mabel had been busy "settling things", and she took him round the house with delicious pride and happiness. Mark, sharing both, had his arm linked in hers. When they came to the fourth sitting room Mabel announced gaily, "And this is your den!"

Mark gave a mock groan. "Oh, lord, not den!"

"Yes, of course, den. Why ever not?"

"I absolutely can't stick den." He glanced about "Who on earth's left those fearful old slippers there?"

"They're a pair of father's. I took them specially for you for this room. You haven't got any slippers like that."

He gazed upon the heels downtrodden by her heavy father. He did not much like her heavy father. "No, I haven't," he said, and thought grimly, "Thank God!"

"But, Mark, what do you mean, you can't stick 'den'?"

16

He explained laughingly. He ended, "It's just like lounge hall. Lounge hall makes me feel perfectly sick. You're not going to call the hall a lounge hall, are you?"

She was quite serious and the least little bit put out. "No—I'm not. But I can't see why. I've never heard such funny ideas."

He was vaguely, transiently surprised at her attitude towards his funny ideas. "Well, come on, let's see upstairs."

"Yes, let's, dear."

He stepped out, and she closed the door after them. "Well, that's your den."

As if he had never spoken! A vague and transient discomfort shot through him.

VII

It was when they came down again, completely happy and pleased, that the servant incident occurred. Mabel was down the stairs slightly before him and turned a smiling face up to him as he descended. "By Jove, it's jolly," he said. "We'll be happy here," and he kissed her.

"You'd better see the kitchen. It's awfully nice;" and they went along.

At the kitchen door she paused and began in a mysterious whisper a long account of the servants. "I think they'll turn out quite nice girls. They're sisters, you know, and they're glad to be in a place together. They've both got young men in the village. Fancy, the cook told me that at Mrs. Wellington's where she was, at Chovensbury, she wasn't allowed to use soda for washing up because Mrs. Wellington fussed so frightfully about the pattern on her china! Fancy, in their family they've got eleven brothers and sisters. Isn't it awful how those kind of people—"

Her voice got lower and lower. She seemed to Mark to be quivering with some sort of repressed excitement, as though the two maids were some rare exhibit which she had captured with a net and placed in the kitchen, and whom it was rather thrilling to open the door upon and peep at. He could hardly hear her voice and had to bend his head. It was dim in the lobby outside the kitchen door. The dimness, her intense whispers and her excitement made him feel that he was in some mysterious conspiracy with her. The whole atmosphere of the house and of this tour of inspection, which had been deliciously absorbing, became mysteriously conspiratorial, unpleasing.

"...She's been to a school of cookery at Tidborough. She attended the whole course!"

"Good. That's the stuff!"

"Hush!"

Why hush? What a funny business this was!

VIII

Mabel opened the kitchen door. "The master's come to see how nice the kitchen looks."

Two maids in black dresses and an extraordinary amount of stiffly starched aprons and caps and streamers rose awkwardly and bobbed awkward little bows. One was very tall, the other rather short. The tall one looked extraordinarily severe and the short one extraordinarily glum, Mark thought, to have young men. Mabel looked from the girls to Mark and from Mark to the girls, precisely as if she were exhibiting rare specimens to her husband and her husband to her rare specimens. And in the tone of one exhibiting pinned, dried, and completely impersonal specimens, she announced, "They're sisters. Their name is Jinks."

Mark, examining the exhibits, had been feeling like a fool. Their name humanized them and relieved his awkward feeling. "Ha! Jinks, eh? High Jinks and Low Jinks, what?" He laughed. It struck him as rather comic; and High Jinks and Low Jinks tittered broadly, losing in the most astonishing way the one her severity and the other her glumness.

Mabel seemed suddenly to have lost her interest in her exhibits and their cage. She rather hurried Mark through the kitchen premises and, moving into the garden, replied rather abstractedly to his plans for the garden's development.

Suddenly she said, "Mark, I do wish you hadn't said that in the kitchen."

He was mentally examining the possibilities of a makeshift racket court against a corner of the stable and barn. "Eh, what in the kitchen, dear?"

"That about High Jinks and Low Jinks."

"Mabel, I swear we could fix up a topping sort of squash rackets in that corner. Those cobbles are worn absolutely smooth—"

"I wish you'd listen to me, Mark."

He caught his arm around her and gave her a playful squeeze. "Sorry, old girl, what was it? About High Jinks and Low Jinks? Ha! Dashed funny that, don't you think?"

"No, I don't. I don't think it's a bit funny."

Her tone was such that, relaxing his arm, he turned and gazed at her. "Don't you? Don't you really?"

"No, I don't. Far from funny."

Some instinct told him he ought not to laugh, but he could not help it. The idea appealed to him as distinctly and clearly comic. "Well, but it is funny. Don't you see? High Jinks alone is such a funny expression—sort of—well, you know what I mean. Apart altogether from Low Jinks," and he laughed again.

Mabel compressed her lips. "I simply don't. Rebecca is not a bit like High Jinks."

He burst out laughing. "No, I'm dashed if she is. That's just it!"

"I really do not see it."

"Oh, go on, Mabel! Of course you do. You make it funnier. High Jinks and Low Jinks! I shall call them that."

"Mark." She spoke the word severely and paused severely. "Mark. I do most earnestly hope you'll do nothing of the kind."

He stared, puzzled. He had tried to explain the absurd thing, and she simply could not see it. "I simply don't."

And again that vague and transient discomfort shot through him.

IX

Sabre awoke in the course of that night and lay awake. The absurd incident came immediately into his mind and remained in his mind. High Jinks and Low Jinks was comic. No getting over it. Incontestably comic. Stupid, of course, but just the kind of stupid thing that tickled him irresistibly. And she couldn't see it. Absolutely could not see it. But if she were never going to see any of these stupid little things that appealed to him—? And then he wrinkled his brows. "You remember how he used to wrinkle up his old nut," as the garrulous Hapgood had said.

A night-light, her wish, dimly illumined the room. He raised himself and looked at her fondly, sleeping beside him. He thought, "Dash it, the thing's been just the same from her point of view. That den business. She likes den, and I can't stick den. Just the same for her as for me that High Jinks and Low Jinks tickles me and doesn't tickle her."

He very gently moved with his finger a tress of her hair that had fallen upon her face.... Mabel!... His wife!... How gently beneath her filmy bedgown her bosom rose and fell!... How utterly calm her face was. How at peace, how secure, she lay there. He thought, "Three weeks ago she was sleeping in the terrific privacy of her own room, and here she is come to me in mine. Cut off from everything and everybody and come here to me."

An inexpressible tenderness filled him. He had a sudden sense of the poignant and tremendous adventure on which they were embarked together. They had been two lives, and now they were one life, altering completely the lives they would have led singly: a new sea, a new ship on a new, strange sea. What lay before them?

She stirred.

His thoughts continued: One life! One life out of two lives; one nature out of two natures! Mysterious and extraordinary metamorphosis. She had brought her nature to his, and he his nature to hers, and they were to mingle and become one nature.... Absurdly and inappropriately his mind picked up and presented to him the grotesque words, "High Jinks and Low Jinks." A note of laughter was irresistibly tickled out of him.

She said very sleepily, "Mark, are you laughing? What are you laughing at?"

He patted her shoulder. "Oh, nothing."

One nature?

CHAPTER III

I

One nature? In the fifth year of their married life thoughts of her and of the poignant and tremendous adventure on which they were embarked together were no longer possible while she lay in bed beside him. They had come to occupy separate rooms.

In the fifth year of their married life measles visited Penny Green. Mabel caught it. Their bedroom was naturally the sick room. Sabre went to sleep in another room,—and the arrangement prevailed. Nothing was said between them on the matter, one way or the other. They naturally occupied different rooms during her illness. She recovered. They continued to occupy different rooms. It was the most natural business in the world.

The sole reference to recognition of permanency in this development of the relations between them was made when Sabre, on the first Saturday afternoon after Mabel's recovery—he did not go to his office at Tidborough on Saturdays—carried out his idea, conceived during her sickness, of making the bedroom into which he had moved serve as his study also. He had never got rid of his distaste for his "den." He had never felt quite comfortable there.

At lunch on this Saturday, "I tell you what I'm going to do this afternoon," he said. "I'm going to move my books up into my room."

He had been a little afraid the den business would be reopened by this intention, but Mabel's only reply was, "You'd better have the maids help you."

"Yes, I'll get them."

"No, I'll give the order, if you don't mind."

"Right!"

And in the afternoon the books were moved, the den raped of them, his bedroom awarded them. High Jinks and Low Jinks rather enjoyed it, passing up and down the stairs with continuous smirks at this new manifestation of the master's ways. The bookshelves proved rather a business. There were four of them, narrow and high. "We'll carry these longways," Sabre directed, when the first one was tackled. "I'll shove it over. You two take the top, and I'll carry the foot."

In this order they struggled up the stairs, High Jinks and Low Jinks backwards, and the smirks enlarged into panting giggles. Halfway up came a loud crack.

"What the devil's that?" said Sabre, sweating and gasping.

"I think it's the back of my dress, sir," said High Jinks.

"Good lord!" (Convulsive giggles.) "You know, Low, you're practically sitting on the dashed thing. You've twisted yourself round in some extraordinary way—"

Agonising giggles.

Mabel appeared in the hail beneath. "Raise it up, Rebecca. Raise it, Sarah. How can you expect to move, stooping like that?"

They raised it to the level of their waists, and progression became seemly.

"There you are!" said Sabre.

There was somehow a feeling at both ends of the bookcase of having been caught.

II

Sabre liked this room. Three latticed windows, in the same wall, looked on to the garden. In the spaces between them, and in the two spaces between the end windows and the end walls, he placed his bookshelves, a set of shelves in each space.

Mabel displayed no interest in the move nor made any reference to it at teatime. In the evening, hearing her pass the door on her way to dress for dinner, he called her in.

He was in his shirt sleeves, arranging the books. "There you are! Not bad?"

She regarded them and the room. "They look all right. All the same, I must say it seems rather funny using your bedroom for your things when you've got a room downstairs."

"Oh, well, I never liked that room, you know. I hardly ever go into it."

"I know you don't."

And she went off.

III

But the significance of the removal rested not in the definite relinquishment of the den, but in her words "using your bedroom": the definite recognition of separate rooms.

And neither commented upon it.

After all, landmarks, in the course of a journey, are more frequently observed and noted as landmarks, when looking back along the journey, than when actually passing them. They belong generically to the past tense; one rarely says, "This is a landmark"; usually "That was a landmark."

IV

The bookcases were of Sabre's own design. He was extraordinarily fond of his books and he had ideas about their arrangement. The lowest shelf was in each case three feet from the ground; he hated books being "down where you can't see them." Also the cases were open, without glass doors; he hated "having to fiddle to get out a book." He liked them to be just at the right height and straight to his hand. In a way he could not quite describe (he was a bad talker, framing his ideas with difficulty) he was attached to his books, not only for what was in them, but as entities. He had written once in a manuscript book in which he sometimes wrote things, "I like the feel of them and I know the feel of them in the same way as one likes and knows the feel of a friend's hand. And I can look at them and read them without opening them in the same way as, without his speaking, one looks at and can enjoy the face of a friend. I feel towards them when I look at them in the shelves,—well, as if they were feeling towards me just as I am feeling towards them." And he had added this touch, which is perhaps more illuminating. "The other day some one had had out one of my books and returned it upside down. I swear it was as grotesque and painful to me to see it upside down as if I had come into the room and found my brother standing on his head against the wall, fastened there. At least I couldn't have sprung to him to release him quicker than I did to the book to upright it."

The first book he had ever bought "specially"—that is to say not as one buys a bun but as one buys a dog—was at the age of seventeen when he had bought a Byron, the Complete Works in a popular edition of very great bulk and very small print. He bought it partly because of what he had heard during his last term at school of Don Juan, partly because he had picked up the idea that it was rather a fine thing to read poetry; and he kept it and read it in great secrecy because his mother (to whom he mentioned his intention) told him that Byron ought not to be read and that her father, in her girlhood, had picked up Byron with the tongs and burnt him in the garden. This finally determined him to buy Byron.

He began to read it precisely as he was accustomed to read books,—that is to say at the beginning and thence steadily onwards. "On the Death of a Young Lady" (Admiral Parker's daughter, explained a footnote); "To E——"; "To D——" and so on. There were seven hundred and eight pages of this kind of thing and Don Juan was at the end, in the five hundreds.

When he had laboriously read thirty-six pages he decided that it was not a fine thing to read poetry, and he moved on to Don Juan, page five hundred and thirty-three. The rhymes surprised him. He had no idea that poetry—poetry—rhymed "annuities" with "true it is" and "Jew it is." He turned on and numbered the cantos,—sixteen; and then the number of verses in each canto and the total,—two thousand one hundred and eighty.... Who-o-o!... It was as endless as the seven hundred and eight pages had appeared when he had staggered as far as page thirty-six. He began to hunt for the particular verses which had caused Don Juan to be recommended to him and presumably had caused his grandfather to carry out Byron with the tongs and burn him in the garden. He could not find them. He chucked the rotten thing.

But as he was putting the rotten thing away, his eye happened upon two lines that struck into him—it was like a physical blow—the most extraordinary sensation:

The isles of Greece, the isles of Greece

Where burning Sappho loved and sung.

He caught his breath. It was extraordinary. What the dickens was it? A vision of exquisite and unearthly and brilliantly coloured beauty seemed to be before his eyes. Islands, all white and green and in a sea

of terrific blue.... And music, the thin note of distant trumpets....
Amazing! He read on. "Where Delos rose and Phoebus sprung!
Eternal Summer gilds them yet." Terrific, but not quite so terrific. And
then again the terrific, the stunning, the heart-clutching thing. On a
different note, with a different picture, coloured in grays.

The mountains look on Marathon—

And Marathon looks on the sea.

Music! The trumpets thinned away, exquisitely thin, tiny, gone! And
high above the mountains and far upon the sea an organ shook.

He said, "Well, I'm dashed!" and put the book away.

V

It was years after the Byron episode—after he had come down from
Cambridge, after he had travelled fairly widely, and luckily, as tutor to
a delicate boy, and after he had settled down, from his father's house at
Chovensbury, to learn the Fortune, East and Sabre business that he
began to collect the books which now formed his collection. His
intense fondness for books had come to him late in life, as love of
literature goes. He was reading at twenty-eight and thirty literature
which, when it is read at all, is as a rule read ten years younger
because the taste is there and is voracious for satisfaction,—as a young
and vigorous animal for its meals. But at twenty-eight and thirty,
reading for the first time, he read sometimes with a sense of
revelation, always with an enormous satisfaction. Especially the poets.
And constantly in the poets he was coming across passages the sheer
beauty of which shook him precisely as the Byron lines had first
shaken him.

His books appeared to indicate a fair number and a fair diversity of
interests; but their diversity presented to him a common quality or
group of qualities. Some history, some sociology, some Spencer, some
Huxley, some Haeckel, a small textbook of geology, a considerable
proportion of pure literature, Morley's edition of lives of literary men,
the English essayists in a nice set, Shakespeare in many forms and so
much poetry that at a glance his library was all poetry. All the books
were picked up at second-hand dealers' in Tidborough, none had cost
more than a few shillings. The common quality that bound them was
that they stirred in him imaginative thought: they presented images,
they suggested causes, they revealed processes; the common group of

qualities to which they ministered were beauty and mystery, sensibility and wonder. They made him think about things, and he liked thinking about things; the poets filled his mind with beauty, and he was strangely stirred by beauty.

VI

Here, in the effect upon him of beauty and of ideas communicated to his mind by his reading—first manifested to him by the Byron revelation—was the mark and label of his individuality: here was the linking up of the boy who as Puzzlehead Sabre would wrinkle up his nut and say, "Well, I can't quite see that, sir," with the man in whom the same habit persisted; he saw much more clearly and infinitely more intensely with his mind than with his eye. Beauty of place imagined was to him infinitely more vivid than beauty seen. And so in all affairs: it was not what the eye saw or the ear heard that interested him; it was what his mind saw, questing behind the scene and behind the speech, that interested him, and often, by the intensity of its perception, shook him. And precisely as beauty touched in him the most exquisite and poignant depths, so evil surroundings, evil faces dismayed him to the point of mysterious fear, almost terror—

On a Sunday of his honeymoon in London he had conceived with Mabel the idea of a bus ride through the streets,—"anywhere, the first bus that comes." The first bus that came took them through South London, dodged between main roads and took them through miles of mean and sordid dwelling houses. At open windows high up sat solitary women, at others solitary, shirt-sleeved men; behind closed windows were the faces of children. All staring,—women and men and children, impassively prisoned, impassively staring. Each house door presented, one above the other, five or six iron bell-knobs, some hanging out and downwards, as if their necks were broken. On the pavements hardly a soul. Just street upon street of these awful houses with their imprisoned occupants and the doors with their string of crazy bells.

An appalling and abysmal depression settled upon Sabre. He imagined himself pulling the dislocated neck of one of those bells and stepping into what festered behind those sinister doors: the dark and malodorous stairways, the dark and malodorous rooms, their prisoned occupants opening their prisons and staring at him,—those women, those men, those children. He imagined himself in one of those rooms, saw it, felt it, smelt it. He imagined himself cutting his throat in one of those rooms.

At tea in their hotel on their return Mabel chattered animatedly on all they had seen. "I'm awfully glad we went. I think it's a very good thing to know for oneself just how that side of life lives. Those awful people at the windows!"—and she laughed. He noticed for the first time what a sudden laugh she had, rather loud.

Sabre agreed. "Yes, I think it's a good thing to have an idea of their lives. I can't say I'm glad I went, though. You've no idea how awfully depressed that kind of thing makes me feel."

She laughed again. "Depressed! How ever can it? How funny you must be!"

Then she said, "Yes, I'm glad I've seen for myself. You know, when those sort of people come into your service—the airs they give themselves and the way they demand the best of everything—and then when you see the kind of homes they come from—!"

"Yes, it makes you think, doesn't it?"

"It does!"

But what it made Sabre think was entirely different from what it made Mabel think.

VII

"Puzzlehead" they had called him at his preparatory school,—Old Puzzlehead Sabre, the chap who always wrinkled up his nut over things and came out with the most extraordinary ideas. He had remained, and increasingly become, the puzzler. And precisely as he ceased to share a room with Mabel and carried himself with satisfaction to his own apartment, so, by this fifth year of his married life, he had come to know well that he shared no thoughts with her: he carried them, with increasing absorption in their interest, to the processes of his own mind.

An incident of those early school days had always remained with him, in its exact words. The exact words of a selectly famous professor of philosophy who, living the few years of his retirement in the neighbourhood of the preparatory school, had given—for pure love of seeing young things and feeling the freshness of young minds—a weekly "talk on things" to the small schoolboys. And whatever the

28

subject of his talk, he almost invariably would work off his familiar counsel:

"And a very good thing (he used to say), an excellent thing, the very best of practices, is to write a little every day. Just a little scrap, but cultivate the habit of doing it every day. I don't mean what is called keeping a diary, you know. Don't write what you do. There's no benefit in that. We do things for all kinds of reasons and it's the reasons, not the things, that matter. Let your little daily scrap be something you've thought. What you've done belongs partly to some one else; often you're made to do it. But what you think is you yourself: you write it down and there it is, a tiny little bit of you that you can look at and say, 'Well, really!' You see, a little bit like that, written every day, is a mirror in which you can see your real self and correct your real self. A looking-glass shows you your face is dirty or your hair rumpled, and you go and polish up. But it's ever so much more important to have a mirror that shows you how your real self, your mind, your spirit, is looking. Just see if you can't do it. A little scrap. It's very steadying; very steadying...."

And his small hearers, desiring, like young colts in a field, nothing so little as anything steadying, paid as much attention to this "jaw" as to any precept not supported by cane or imposition. They made of it, indeed, a popular school joke, "Oh, go and write a little every day and boil yourself, you ass!" But it appealed, dimly, to the reflective quality in the child Sabre's mind. He contracted the habit of writing, in a "bagged" exercise book, sentences beginning laboriously with "I thought to-day—." It remained with him, as he grew up, in the practice of writing sometimes ideas that occurred to him, as in the case of his feelings about his books and—much more strongly—in deliberately thinking out ideas.

"You yourself. The real you."

In the increasing solitariness of his married life, it came to be something into which he could retire, as into a private chamber; which he could put on, as a garment: and in the privacy of the chamber, or within the sleeves of the garment, he received a sense of detachment from normal life in which, vaguely, he pondered things.

VIII
Vaguely,—without solution of most of the problems that puzzled him, and without even definite knowledge of the line along which solution

29

might lie. Here, in these cloisters of another world—his own world—he paced among his ideas as a man might pace around the dismantled and scattered intricacies of an intricate machine, knowing the parts could be put together and the thing worked usefully, not knowing how on earth it could be done.... "This goes in there, and that goes in there, but how on earth—?" Here, into these cloisters, he dragged the parts of all the puzzles that perplexed him; his relations with Mabel; his sense, in a hundred ways as they came up, of the odd business that life was; his strong interest in the social and industrial problems, and in the political questions from time to time before the public attention.

He could be imagined assembling the parts, dragging them in, checking them over, slamming the door, and—"How on earth? What on earth?" There was a key to all these problems. There was a definite way of coördinating the parts of each. But what?

He began to have the feeling that in all the puzzles, not only, though particularly, of his own life as he had come to live it, but of life in general as it is lived, some mysterious part was missing.

That was as far as he could get. He was like a man groping with his hand through a hole in a great door for a key lying on the other side. Nothing was to be seen through the hole, and only the arm to the elbow could get through it. Not the shape of the key nor its position was known.

But he was absolutely certain it was there.

One day he might put his hand on it.

CHAPTER IV

I

Mabel was two years younger than Sabre, twenty-five at the time of her marriage and just past her thirtieth birthday when the separate rooms were first occupied. Her habit of sudden laughter, rather loud, which Sabre first noticed in connection with their differing views on the mean streets visit, was rather characteristic of her. Her laugh came suddenly, and very heartily, at anything that amused her and without her first smiling or suggesting by any other sign that she was amused. And it came thus abruptly out of a face whose expression was normally rather severe. Probably of the same mentality was her habit of what Sabre called "flying up." She "flew up" without her speech first warming up; but of her flying up, unlike her sudden burst of laughter, Sabre came to know certain premonitory symptoms in her face. Her face what he called "tightened." In particular he used to notice a curious little constriction of the sides of her nose, rather as though invisible tweezers were pressing it.

She had rather a long nose and this pleased her, for she once read somewhere that long noses were aristocratic. She stroked her nose as she read.

Her complexion was pale, though this was perhaps exaggerated by her colouring, which was dark. Her features were noticeably regular and noticeably refined, though her eyes were the least little bit inclined to be prominent: when Sabre married the Dean of Tidborough's only daughter, it was said that he had married "a good-looking girl"; also that he had married "a very nice girl"; those were the expressions used. She liked the company of men and she was much liked by men (the opinion of the garrulous Hapgood may be recalled in this connection). She very much liked the society of women of her own age or older than herself, and she was very popular with such. She did not like girls, married or unmarried.

II

Mabel belonged to that considerable class of persons who, in conversation, begin half their sentences with "And just imagine—"; or "And only fancy—"; or "And do you know—." These exclamations, delivered with much excitement, are introductory to matters considered extraordinary. Their users might therefore be imagined somewhat easily astonished. But they have a compensatory steadiness of mind in regard to much that mystifies other people. To Mabel there was nothing mysterious in birth, or in living, or in death. She simply

31

would not have understood had she been told there was any mystery in these things. One was born, one lived, one died. What was there odd about it? Nor did she see anything mysterious in the intense preoccupation of an insect, or the astounding placidity of a primrose growing at the foot of a tree. An insect—you killed it. A flower—you plucked it. What's the mystery?

Her life was living among people of her own class. Her measure of a man or of a woman was, Were they of her class? If they were, she gladly accepted them and appeared to find considerable pleasure in their society. Whether they had attractive qualities or unattractive qualities or no qualities at all did not affect her. The only quality that mattered was the quality of being well-bred. She called the classes beneath her own standard of breeding "the lower classes", and so long as they left her alone she was perfectly content to leave them alone. In certain aspects the liked them. She liked "a civil tradesman" immensely; she liked a civil charwoman immensely; and she liked a civil workman immensely. It gave her as much pleasure, real pleasure that she felt in all her emotions, to receive civility from the classes that ministered to her class—servants, tradespeople, gardeners, carpenters, plumbers, postmen, policemen—as to meet any one in her own class. It never occurred to her to reckon up how enormously varied was the class whose happy fortune it was to minister to her class and she would not have been in the remotest degree interested if any one had told her how numerous the class was. It never occurred to her that any of these people had homes and it never occurred to her that the whole of the lower classes lived without any margin at all beyond keeping their homes together, or that if they stopped working they lost their homes, or that they looked forward to nothing beyond their working years because there was nothing beyond their working years for them to look forward to. Nor would it have interested her in the remotest degree to hear this. The only fact she knew about the lower classes was that they were disgustingly extravagant and spent every penny they earned. The woman across the Green who did her washing had six children and a husband who was an agricultural labourer and earned eighteen and sixpence a week. These eight lived in three rooms and "if you please" they actually bought a gramophone! Mabel instanced it for years after she first heard it. The idea of that class of person spending money on anything to make their three rooms lively of an evening was scandalous to Mabel. She heard of the gramophone outrage in 1908 and she was still instancing it in 1912. "And those are the people, mind you," she said in 1912, "that we have to buy these National Insurance stamps for!"

III

Mabel was not demonstrative. She had no enthusiasms and no sympathies. Enthusiasms and sympathies in other people made her laugh with her characteristic burst of sudden laughter. It was not, as with some persons, that matters calling for sympathy made her impatient,—as very robust people are often intensely impatient with sickness and infirmity. She never would say, "I have no patience with such and such or so and so." She had plenty of patience. It was simply that she had no imagination whatsoever. Whatever she saw or heard or read, she saw or heard or read exactly as the thing presented itself. If she saw a door she saw merely a piece of wood with a handle and a keyhole. It may be argued that a door is merely a piece of wood with a handle and a keyhole, and that is what Mabel would have argued. But a door is in fact the most intriguing mystery in the world because of what may be the other side of it and of what goes on behind it. To Mabel nothing was on the other side of anything she saw and nothing went on behind it.

A person or a creature in pain was to Mabel a person or a creature "laid up." Laid up—out of action—not working properly: like a pencil without a point. A picture was a decoration in paint and was either a pretty decoration in paint or a not pretty decoration in paint. Music was a tune, and was either a tune or merely music. A book was a story, and if it was not a story it was simply a book. A flower was a decoration. Poetry, such as

"While the still morn went out with sandals grey,"

was simply writing which, obviously, had no real meaning whatsoever, and obviously—well, read the thing—was not intended to have any meaning. A fine deed was fine precisely in proportion to the social position of the person who performed it. Scott's death at the South Pole, when that was announced in 1913, was fine because he was a gentleman. The disaster of the colliers entombed in the Welsh Senghenydd mine which happened in the same year was sad. "How sad!" She read the account, on the first day, with the paper held up wide open and said "How sad!" and turned on to something for which the paper might be folded back at the place and read comfortably. Scott's death she read with the paper folded back at the account. She liked seeing the pictures of Lady Scott and of Scott's little boy. She read the caption under one of the pictures of the wives and families of the four hundred and twenty-nine colliers killed in the Senghenydd

33

mine, but not under any of the others. The point she noted was that all the women "of that class" wore "those awful cloth caps",—the colliers' women just the same as the women in the mean streets of Tidborough Old Town.

She was never particularly grateful for anything given to her or done for her; not because she was not pleased and glad but because she could invest a gift with no imagination of the feelings of the giver. The thing was a present just as a pound of bacon was a pound of bacon. You said thank you for the present just as you ate the bacon. What more was to be said?

She revelled in gossip, that is to say in discussion with her own class of the manners and doings of other people. She thought charity meant giving jelly and red flannel to the poor; she thought generosity meant giving money to some one; she thought selfishness meant not giving money to some one. She had no idea that the only real charity is charity of mind, and the only real generosity generosity of mind, and the only real selfishness selfishness of mind. And she simply would not have understood it if it had been explained to her. As people are judged, she was entirely nice, entirely worthy, entirely estimable. And with that, for it does not enter into such estimates, she had neither feelings of the mind nor of the heart but only of the senses. All that her senses set before her she either overvalued or undervalued: she was the complete and perfect snob in the most refined and purest meaning of the word. She was much liked, and she liked many.

CHAPTER V

I

The Penny Green Garden House Development Scheme was begun in 1910. In 1908, the year of the measles and the separated bedrooms, no shadow of it had yet been thrown. It never occurred to any one that a railway would one day link Penny Green with Tidborough and all the rest of the surrounding world, or that a railway to Tidborough was desirable. Sabre bicycled in daily to Fortune, East and Sabre's, and the daily ride to and fro had become a curious pleasure to him.

There had once occurred to him as he rode, and thereafter had persisted and accumulated, the feeling that, on the daily, solitary passage between Tidborough and Penny Green, he was mysteriously detached from, mysteriously suspended between, the two centres that were his two worlds,—his business world and his home world.

With its daily recurrence the thought developed: it enlarged to the whimsical notion that here, on his bicycle on the road, he was magically escaped out of his two worlds, not belonging to or responsible to either of his two worlds, which amounted to delicious detachment from all the universe. A mysteriously aloof, free, irresponsible attitude of mind was thus obtained: it was a condition in which—as one looking down from a high tower on scurrying, antlike human beings—their oddness, their futility, the apparent aimlessness of their excited scurrying became apparent; hence frequent thought, on these rides, on the rather odd thing that life was.

He was not in the least aware that so simple, so practical and so obviously essential a thing as his daily ride—as simple, practical and obviously essential as getting out of bed in the morning and returning to bed at night—was moulding a mind always prone to develop meditative grooves. But it did develop his mind in the extraordinary way in which minds are moulded by the most simple habits. In this mere matter of conveyance a philosopher might trace back a singularly brutal and callous murder to the moulding into callous and brutal regard of other people's sufferings rendered into a perfectly gentle mind by the habit of daily travelling to business in London on the top of a motor omnibus. It would only need to be shown that the gentle mind secured his seat with dignity and comfort at the bus's starting point and daily for years watched with amusement, and then with callousness and so with brutality the struggles of the unhappy fellow creatures who fought to assail it at its stopping places on the way to the City.

Mark Sabre was not in the least aware of any steadily permeating influence from his sense of detachment on this daily habit of years. But he was influenced. On entering his Penny Green world on the return home, or on entering his Tidborough office world, on the way out, he had sometimes a curious feeling of descending into this odd affair of life to which he did not really belong. And for the few moments while the feeling persisted he sometimes, more or less unconsciously, took towards affairs a rather whimsical attitude, as though they did not really matter: an irritating attitude, unpractical, it was sometimes hinted by his partners; an irritating attitude—"You really are very difficult to understand sometimes"—it was often told him by Mabel.

II

This very matter of the bicycle ride, indeed, apart altogether from its effect upon his mood, supplied an instance of the kind of thing Mabel found it so difficult to understand in her husband.

He made what she called a childish game of it. Every day on the ride home, Sabre ceased pedalling at precisely the same point on the slope down into Penny Green and coasted until the machine came to a standstill within a few yards of his own gate. This point of cessation was never twice in a week at the same spot; and Sabre found great interest in seeing every day exactly where it would be, and by intense wriggling of his front wheel and prodigious feats of balancing, squeezing out of the machine's momentum the last possible fraction of an inch. There was a magnificent distance record when, on one single occasion only, he had been deposited plumb in line with his own gate; and there was a divertingly lamentable shortage record, touched on more than one occasion, when he had come to ground plumb in line with the gate of Mr. Fargus, his neighbour on that side.

Each of these records, though marked by the gates, was also and more exactly marked by a peg hammered into the edge of the Green.

This was childish; and Mabel said it was childish when her attention was drawn to the diversion. On the day the great distance record was created he came rather animatedly into the kitchen where she happened to be. "I say, what's happened to that small wood axe? Is it in here?"

Mabel followed the direction of the convulsive start made by Low Jinks and produced the small wood axe from under the dresser, also directing at Low Jinks a glance which told Low Jinks what she perfectly well knew: namely that under the dresser was not the place for the small wood axe. "Whatever do you want it for all of a sudden?" Mabel asked.

He felt the edge with his thumb. "Low"—Mabel's face twitched. He had persisted in the idiotic and indecorous names, and her face always twitched when he used them—"Low, do you keep my axe for chopping coal or what?" And he addressed Mabel. "I'm getting fat, I think. I don't want the axe to cut lumps off myself, though. I'm going to chop a marking peg. I've done a heavyweight world's record on that run in on my bike—"

"Oh, that!" said Mabel.

And when he had gone out into the wood yard, Low Jinks staring after him with the uplifted eyebrows with which both sisters, the glum and the grim, commonly received the master's "ways", Mabel said in the gently pained way which was her admirable method of administering rebukes in the kitchen: "The woodshed is the place for the small wood axe, Rebecca."

Rebecca promptly unsmirked her smirk. "Yes, m'm."

A little later the sound of loud hammering took Mabel to the gate. Across the road, at the edge of the Green, Sabre was energetically driving in the peg with the back of the axe. He was squatting and he looked up highly pleased with himself and, his words implied, with her. "Come to see it? Good! How's that for an effort, eh? Look here now. Yesterday I only got as far as here," and he walked some paces towards Mr. Fargus's gate and struck his heel in the ground and looked at her, smiling. "Absolutely the same conditions, mind you. No wind. And I always start from the top practically at rest; and yet always finish up different. Jolly funny, eh?"

She opened the gate for him. "What you can see in it!" she murmured.

He said, "Oh, well!"

III

But on the following day he was surprised and intensely pleased to see his champion peg gleaming white in the sunshine. Mabel was in the morning room, sewing.

"Hullo, sewing? I say, did you paint my peg? How jolly nice of you!"

She looked up. "Your peg? Whatever do you mean?"

"That record distance peg of mine. Painted it white, haven't you?"

"No, I didn't paint it!"

"Who the dickens—? Well, I'll just wash my hands. Not had tea, have you? Good."

When Low Jinks came to his room with hot water—a detail of the perfect appointment of the house under Mabel's management was her rule that Rebecca always came to the door for the master's bicycle, handed him the brush for his shoes and trousers, and then took hot water to his room—he asked her, "I say, Low Jinks, did you paint that peg of mine?"

Low Jinks coloured and spoke apologetically: "Well, I thought it would show up better, sir. There was a drop of whitewash in—"

"By Jove, it does. It looks like a regular winning-post. Jolly nice of you, Low."

Two months afterwards the bicycle did the worst on record. This was a surprising affair; the runs had recently been excitingly good; and when Low Jinks came out to take the bicycle he greeted her: "I say, Low Jinks, I only got just up to Mr. Fargus's gate just now. Worst I've ever done."

Low Jinks was enormously concerned. "Well! I never did!" exclaimed Low Jinks. "If those bicycles aren't just things! You'll want a peg for that, sir. Like you had one for the best."

"That's an idea, Low. What about painting it?"

"Oh, I will, sir!"

But he did not mention the new record to Mabel.

CHAPTER VI

I

The other end of the daily bicycle ride, the Tidborough end, provided no feats of cycling interest. The extremely narrow, cobbled thoroughfare in which the offices of Fortune, East and Sabre were situated usually caused Sabre's approach to them to be made on foot, wheeling his machine.

Fortune, East and Sabre, Ecclesiastical and Scholastic Furnishers and Designers, had in Tidborough what is called, in business and professional circles, a good address. A good address for a metropolitan money lender is the West End in the neighbourhood of Bond Street; a good address for a solicitor is Bloomsbury in the neighbourhood of Bedford Square: for an architect Westminster in the neighbourhood of Victoria Street, for commerce the City in the neighbourhood of the Bank. The idea is that, though clothes do not make the man, a good address makes, or rather bestows the reputation, and conveys the impression that the owner of the good address, being in that neighbourhood, is not within many thousands of miles (or pounds) of the neighbourhood of Bankruptcy.

The address of Fortune, East and Sabre was emphatically a good address because its business was with the Church and for the Church; with colleges, universities and schools and for colleges, universities and schools; with bishops, priests and clergy, churchwardens, headmasters, headmistresses, governors and bursars, and for bishops, priests and clergy, churchwardens, headmasters, headmistresses, governors and bursars.

Its address was The Precincts,—Fortune, East and Sabre, The Precincts, Tidborough.

The Precincts has a discreet and beautiful sound, a discreet and beautiful suggestiveness. High Street, Tidborough, or Cheapside, Tidborough, or Commercial Street, Tidborough, have only to be compared with The Precincts, Tidborough, to establish the discretion and beauty of the situation of the firm. And the names of the firm were equally euphonious and equally suggestive of high decorum and cultured efficiency. Fortune, East and Sabre had a discreet and beautiful sound. Finally Tidborough, the last line of the poem, though not in itself either discreet or beautiful, being intensely busy, suggested to all the cultured persons from bishops to bursars, with

39

whom business was done, the discreet and beautiful lines of Tidborough Cathedral and of Tidborough School, together with all that these venerable and famous institutions connoted. Not Winchester itself conveys to the cultured mind thoughts more discreet and beautiful than are conveyed by Tidborough. The care of the cathedral, for many years in a highly delicate state of health, and the care of the school, yearly ravaged by successive generations of the sons of those who could afford to educate their sons there were, it may be mentioned, established sources of income to the firm.

Thus the whole style and title of the firm had a discreet and beautiful sound, in admirable keeping with its business. Fortune, East and Sabre, The Precincts, Tidborough. Was any one so utterly removed from affairs as not to know them as ecclesiastical furnishers? "They're at Tidborough. They do Tidborough" (meaning the world-famous cathedral). Or as scholastic providers? "They're at Tidborough. They do Tidborough" (meaning the empire-famous school).

The frontage of Fortune, East and Sabre on The Precincts consisted of a range of three double-fronted shops. The central shop gave one window to a superb lectern in the style of a brass eagle whose outstretched wings supported a magnificent Bible; to a richly embroidered altar cloth on which stood a strikingly handsome set of communion plate; to a font chastely carried out in marble; to an altar chair in oak and velvet that few less than a suffragan bishop would have dared take seat in; and to an example or two of highest art in needlework and embroidery in the form of offertory bags and testament markers. The other window of the central shop was a lesson to the profane in the beauty, the dignity and the variety of vestments. It also informed rural choirboys, haply in Tidborough on a treat, what surplices can be like if the funds and the faith are sufficiently high to support them.

The windows of the shop to the left (as you faced the lectern and the vestments) displayed school furniture and school fittings bearing the characteristic "F.E. & S." stamp. Here were adjustable desks for boys at which no boy could possibly sit round-shouldered, which could be adjusted upwards for tall boys and downwards for short boys, and the seats of which could be advanced for boys afflicted with short legs and retired for boys in the possession of long legs. It was believed by those who had seen the full range of "F.E. & S." desk models that, if a headmaster or bursar had telegraphed to Fortune, East and Sabre the arrival of a Siamese twin boy at his school, a desk specially contrived for the nice accommodation of a Siamese twin boy would have been put on the railway before the telegraph messenger had loitered his way out of the shadow of The Precincts.

By an ingenious contrivance ink could not be spilt from the inkwells of the "F.E. & S." models; rubber beading most properly nullified the boyish idea that desk lids were made for the purpose of slamming to blazes the nerves of masters and the calm in which alone high education can be served.

Equal skill, science, art, and the experience of generations had produced the model of a master's desk which partnered the desks of the pupil. Maps of as many countries as might be desired showed in frames up and down which they followed one another by the silent turning of a handle. A blackboard on an easel looked across the desks at a wall into which was let a solid slab of blackboard. The window adjoining this display exhibited a miniature classroom in which the "F.E. & S." system of classroom ventilation maintained air so pure and fresh that the most comatose pupil could not but keep alert and receptive in it.

The shop front to the right paid testimony to the standing of Fortune, East and Sabre in their capacity as educational and ecclesiastical book publishers and binders. One window gave chastely, on purple velvet, not more than two or at most three exquisitely wrought Bibles and prayer books for lectern and altar; the other showed severely, on green baize, school textbooks of every subject and degree grouped about superbly handsome prize volumes in blue calf displaying the classic arms of Tidborough School.

Public entrance to these premises was gained by doors of the central shop only. It was considered proper and in keeping with the times to have window displays, but it was considered improper and out of keeping with the traditions of Fortune, East and Sabre to present more than the extreme minimum of shoppish appearance. You entered therefore by but one door, which was, moreover, not a shop door but a church door and one of the several models which Fortune, East and Sabre had designed and executed; you entered, between the vestments and the lecterns, not a shop but a vestry; and you passed, on the left, not into a shop but into a classroom, and on the right not into a shop but into a book-lined study.

It is said that if you loitered long enough in Fortune, East and Sabre's you would meet every dignitary of the Church and of education in the United Kingdom; and it was added that you would not have to wait long.

Fortune, East and Sabre, The Precincts, Tidborough.

II

Maintaining the unshoplike character of the ground-floor rooms upon which the plate-glass windows looked, virtually no business, in the vulgar form of buying and selling, was carried on in the vestry, in the classroom or in the book-lined study. Many modern and entirely worthy businesses are conducted under the strident banner of "Cash Only." Fortune, East and Sabre's did not know the word cash. One would as soon look for or expect a till, to say nothing of one of those terrific machines known as cash registers, in the vestry, the classroom or the study as one would look for a lectern or an adjustable school desk in a beer-house. "Credit only" was here the principle, and accounts were rendered, never on delivery, but quarterly. One does not, after all, pay for a font out of one's trouser pocket and carry it off under one's arm; nor for a school desk out of a purse and bear it away on one's head. Only in the book-lined study were trifling transactions occasionally carried out and these very rarely, constituting something of an event (and an event greatly deprecated by the Reverend Sebastian Fortune), the tactless misadventure of some pedagogue or student on excursion to the sights of Tidborough.

No one, in any case, committed twice the indiscretion of purchasing a single volume for cash. The book-lined study was in the care of a Mr. Tombs, a gentleman who combined the appearance of a mute at a funeral with the aloof and mysterious manner of a man waiting for his wife in a ladies' underwear department, and the peculiar faculty of making the haphazard visitor feel that he had strayed into a ladies' underwear shop also. "Have you an account with us, sir?" Mr. Tombs would inquire; and on being told "No" would look guiltily all around (as it were at partially undressed ladies) and whisper, "Except to the masters at the School, sir, who all have accounts, we are not supposed to sell single volumes. It is against our rule, sir."

And no one, once escaped, made Mr. Tombs break the rule on a second occasion.

III

Business—on credit only—was conducted on the first floor whereon were apartmented the three principals—the Reverend Sebastian Fortune, Mr. Twyning and Sabre. There was no longer an East in the firm. From the central, vestry-like showroom a broad and shallow stairway led to a half-landing, containing the clerks' office, and thence to the spacious apartment of Mr. Fortune with which, by doors at either end, communicated the offices of Sabre and of Mr. Twyning. Many stately and eminent persons—and no ill-to-do or doubtful persons—passed up and down this stairway on visits to the principals. It was not used by the clerks, the half-landing communicating with the outer world by the clerks' stairs leading to the clerks' entrance at the back of the building, and with the showrooms by the clerks' stairs leading at one end to the book-lined study and at the other to the model classroom. The clerks' office, by the taking down of original walls, ran the whole length of the building, and accommodated not only the clerks, but the designing room, the checking room and the dispatch room. This arrangement was highly inconvenient to the performers of the various duties thus carried on, but was essential to the more rapid execution of Mr. Fortune's habit of "keeping an eye" on everything. This habit of the Reverend Sebastian Fortune was roundly detested by all on whom his eye fell. He was called Jonah by his employees; and he was called Jonah partly because his visits to the places of their industry invariably presaged disaster, but principally for the gross-minded and wrongly-adduced reason that he had (in their opinion) a whale's belly.

IV

He bore a certain resemblance to a stunted whale. He was chiefly abdominal. His legs appeared to begin, without thighs, at his knees, and his face, without neck, at his chest. His face was large, both wide and long, and covered as to its lower part with a tough scrub of grey beard. The line of his mouth showed through the scrub and turned extravagantly downwards at the corners. He had a commanding, heavily knobbed brow, and small grey eyes of intense severity. His voice was cold, and his manner, though intensely polished and suave, singularly stern and decisive. He had an expression of "I have decided" and Sabre said that he kept this expression on ice. It had an icy sound and it certainly had the rigidity and imperviousness of an iceberg. Hearing it, one might believe that it could have a cruel sound.

The Reverend Sebastian Fortune had come into the business at the age of twenty-eight. He was now sixty-two. He had come in to find the controlling interest almost entirely in the hands of the Fortune branch of the firm, and in his thirty-four years of association, indeed in the first twenty, he had, by fortuitous circumstances, and by force of his decisive personality, achieved what amounted to sole and single control. Coming in as a young man of force and character, he had added to these qualities, by marriage, a useful sum of money (to which was attached a widow) and proceeded to deal decisively with the East and the Sabre (Mark Sabre's grandfather) of that day. Both were old men. The East, young Mr. Fortune bought out neck and crop. The Sabre, who owned then a fifth instead of a third interest in the business, and had developed, as an obsession, an unreasonable fear of bankruptcy, he relieved of all liability for the firm at the negligible cost of giving himself a free hand in the conduct of the business. The deed of partnership was altered accordingly. It was to this fifth share, without control, that Sabre's father and, in his turn, Sabre succeeded.

V

Sabre had been promised full partnership by Mr. Fortune. He desired it very greatly. The apportionment of duties in the establishment was that Sabre managed the publishing department. Twyning supervised the factory and workshops wherein the ecclesiastical and scholastic furniture was produced, and Fortune supervised his two principals and every least employee and smallest detail of all the business. Particularly orders. He very strongly objected to clients dealing directly with either Sabre or Twyning. His view was that it was the business of Sabre and of Twyning to produce the firm's commodities. It was his place to sell them. It was his place, to deal with clients who came to buy them, and it was his place to sign all letters that went out concerning them.

Sabre, in so far as his publications were concerned, resented this.

"If I bring out a new textbook," he had said on the occasion of a formal protest, "it stands to reason that I am the person to interest clients in it; to discuss it with them if they call and to correspond with those who take up our notices of it."

Mr. Fortune wheeled about his revolving chair by a familiar trick of his right leg against his desk. It presented his whale-like front to impressive advantage. "You do correspond with them."

"But you sign the letters. You frequently make alterations."

"That is what I am here for. They are my letters. It will be time to bring up this matter again when you are admitted to partnership."

Sabre gave the short laugh of one who has heard a good thing before. "When will that be?"

"Not to-day."

"Well, all I can say is—"

Mr. Fortune raised a whale-like but elegantly white fin. "Enough, I have decided."

With the same clever motion of his feet he spun his chair and his whale-like front to the table. A worn patch on the carpet and an abraised patch on the side of the desk marked the frequent daily use of these thrusting points.

Sabre kicked out of the room, using a foot to open the door, which stood ajar, and hooking back a foot to shut it, because he knew that this slovenly method of dealing with a door much annoyed Mr. Fortune.

He was not in the least in awe of Mr. Fortune, though Mr. Fortune had power to sever him from the firm. Mr. Fortune was aware that he struck no awe into Sabre, and this caused him on the one hand to dislike Sabre, and on the other (subconsciously, for he would emphatically have denied it) to respect him.

Twyning, Sabre's fellow sub-principal, did stand in awe of Mr. Fortune and did not resent having his letters signed for him and his callers interviewed for him. Indeed he frequently took opportunity to thank Mr. Fortune for alterations made in his letters and for dealings carried out with his clients, also for direct interference in his workshops. Mr. Fortune liked Twyning, but he did not respect Twyning, consciously or subconsciously.

VI

Sabre greatly desired the promised admission to partnership. He desired it largely for what he knew he would make it bring in the form of greater freedom from Mr. Fortune's surveillance, but much more for the solid personal satisfaction its winning would give him. It would be a tribute to his work, of all the greater value because he knew it would be bestowed grudgingly and unwillingly, and he was keenly interested in and proud of his work. The publishing of educational textbooks "for the use of schools" had been no part of the firm's business until he came into it. The idea had been his own, and Mr. Fortune, because the idea was not his own, had very half-heartedly assented to it and very disencouragingly looked upon it in the fiddlingly small way in which he permitted it to be begun.

From the outset it had been a very considerable success. Sabre was interested in books and interested in education. He had many friends among the large staff of Tidborough School masters and had developed many acquaintances among the large body of members of the teaching profession with whom the firm was in touch. He was fond of discussing methods and difficulties of encouraging stubborn youth in the arid paths of assimilating knowledge, and he had a peculiarly fresh and sympathetic recollection of his own boyish flounderings in those paths. To these tastes and qualities, and perhaps because of them, he found he was able to bring what was incontestably a flair for discovering the sort of book that needed to be compiled and, what was equally important, the sort of man to compile it. Also, in his capacity of general editor of the volumes, to give much stimulating suggestion and advice to the authors.

He had never been so pleased as on the day when the Spectator, in an extended notice of four new textbooks, had written, "It is always a pleasure to open one of the school textbooks bearing the imprint of Fortune, East and Sabre and issued in the pleasing format which this firm have made their own. Their publications give the impression of a directing mind inspired with the happy thought of presenting textbooks, not for the master, but for the pupil, and of carrying out this design with singular freshness and originality."

On the day when that notice appeared, Mr. Fortune, who considered that his mind was—or would be supposed to be—the directing mind referred to, had repeated his promise of partnership, first made when the enterprise began to show unexpected signs of responding to Sabre's enthusiasm. "Very good, Sabre, very good indeed. I am bound to say capital. I may tell you, as your father probably told you, that it was always understood between him and me that you should be taken into partnership if you showed signs of promise. Unquestionably you do. When you have brought the publishing into line with our established departments we will go into the matter and—" he made one of his nearest approaches to pleasantry—"take steps to restore the house of Sabre in some part to its ancient glories in the firm—in some part."

And when Sabre expressed his gratification, "Enough, I have decided."

In 1912 Sabre felt that he had now brought the publishing into line with the established departments. He had emphasized the firm's reputation in this activity by the considerable success that attended two textbooks bearing (one in collaboration) his own name. "Sabre and Owen's Elementary Mathematics" had been notably taken up by the schools. "Sabre's Modern History", shunned by the public schools in accordance with their principle of ignoring all history mellowed by fewer than three thousand years, had been received enthusiastically by the lesser schools wherein was then dawning the daring idea of presenting to the rising generation some glimmering conception of the constitutional and sociological facts into which it was arising.

The tributes with which this slim primer of one hundred and fifty pages for eighteen pence had been greeted inspired Sabre towards a much bolder work, on which the early summer of 1912 saw him beginning and into which he found himself able to pour in surprising volume thoughts and feelings which he had scarcely known to be his until the pen and the paper began to attract them. The title he had conceived alone stirred them in his mind and drew them from it as a magnet stirs and draws iron filings. "England." Just "England." He could see it printed and published and renowned as "Sabre's England." Kings were to enter this history but incidentally, as kings have in fact ever been but incidental to England's history. It was to be just "England"; the England of the English people and how and why. And the first sentence said so.

"This England" (it said) "is yours. It belongs to you. Many enemies have desired to take it because it is the most glorious and splendid country in the world. But they have never taken it, because it is yours and has been kept for you. This book is to tell you how it has come to be yours and how it has been kept for you,—not by kings or by statesmen, or by great men alone, but by the English people. Down the long years they have handed it on to you, as a torch is sent from hand to hand, and you in your turn will hand it on down the long years before you. They made the flame of England bright and ever brighter for you; and you, stepping into all that they have made for you, will make it bright and brighter yet. They passed and are gone; and you will pass and go. But England will continue. Your England. Yours."

CHAPTER VII

I

Mabel called Sabre's school textbooks "those lesson books." After she had thus referred to them two or three times he gave up trying to interest her in them. The expression hurt him, but when he thought upon it he reasoned with himself that he had no cause to be hurt. He thought, "Dash it, that's what they are, lesson books. What on earth have I got to grouse about?" But they meant to him a good deal more than what was implied in the tone and the expression "those lesson books."

However, "England" was going to be something very different. No one would call "England" a lesson book. Even Mabel would see that: and in his enthusiasm he spoke of it to her a good deal, until the day when it came up—of all unlikely connections in the world—in a discussion with her on the National Insurance Act, then first outraging the country.

One day when English society was first shaken to its depths by the disgusting indignity of what Mabel, in common with all nice people, called "licking stamps for that Lloyd George", she mentioned to Sabre that, "Well, thank goodness some of us know better than to steal the money out of the poor creatures' wages."

She knew that this would please her husband because he was always doing what she called "sticking up for the servants and all that class."

That it did not please him was precisely an example of his "absolutely un-understandable" ways of looking at things that so desperately annoyed her.

Sabre asked, "How do you mean—knowing better than to steal the money out of their wages?"

"Why, making them pay their thruppence for those wretched stamps. I believe Mrs. Castor does. How she's got the face to I can't imagine."

"Why, aren't you going to make them pay, Mabel?"

Mabel was quite indignant. "Is it likely? I should hope not!"

"Really? Haven't you been making High and Low pay their share of the stamps all this time?"

"Of course I've not."

"You've been paying their contribution?"

"Of course I have."

"Well, but Mabel, that's wrong, awfully wrong."

She simply stared at him. "You really are beyond me, Mark. What do you mean 'wrong'?"

"Well, it's not fair—not fair on the girls—"

"Not fair to pay them more than their wages!"

"No, of course it's not. Don't you see half the idea of the Act is to help these people to learn thrift and forethought—to learn the wisdom of putting by for a rainy day. And to encourage their independence. When you go and pay what they ought to pay, you're simply taking away their independence."

She gave her sudden burst of laughter. "You're the first person I've ever heard say that the lower classes want their independence encouraged. It's just what's wrong with them—independence."

He began to talk with animation. This was one of the things that much interested him. He seemed to have quite forgotten the origin of the conversation. "No, it isn't, Mabel—it isn't. That's jolly interesting, that point. It's their dependence that's wrong with them. They're nearly all of them absolutely dependent on an employer, and that's bad, fatal, for anybody. It's the root of the whole trouble with the less-educated classes, if people would only see it. What they want is pride in themselves. They just slop along taking what they can get, and getting so much for nothing—votes and free this, that and the other—that they don't value it in the least. They're dependent all the time. What you want to help them to is independence, pride in themselves and confidence in themselves—that sort of independence. You know, all this talk that they put up, or that's put up for them, about their right to this and their right to that—of course you can't have a right to anything without earning it. That's what they want to be shown, see? And that's what they want to be given—the chance to earn the right to things, see? Well, this Insurance Act business—"

She laughed again. "I was beginning to wonder if you were ever coming back to that."

He noticed nothing deprecatory in her remark. "Yes, rather. Well, this Insurance Act business—that's really a jolly good example of the way to do things. You see, it's not giving them the right to free treatment when they're ill; it's giving them the chance to earn the right. That's what you want to explain to High and Low. See—you want to say to them, 'This is your show. Your very own. Fine. You're building this up, I'm helping. You're helping all sorts of poor devils and you're helping yourself at the same time. You're stacking up a great chunk of the State and it belongs to you. England's yours and you want to pile it up all you know'—"

He was quite flushed.

"That's the sort of thing I'm putting into that book of mine. 'England's yours', you know. Precious beyond price; and therefore grand to be making more precious and more your own. I wish you'd like to see how the book's getting on; would you?"

"What book?"

"Why 'England.' I told you, you know. That history."

"Oh, that lesson book! I wish you'd write a novel."

He looked at her. "Oh, well!" he said.

II

After that he never mentioned "England" again to her. But he most desperately wanted to talk about it to some one. There was no one in Penny Green from whom he could expect helpful suggestions; but it was not helpful suggestions he wanted. He wanted merely to talk about it to a sympathetic listener. And not only about the book,—about all sorts of things that interested him. And indirectly they all helped the book. To talk with one who responded sympathetically was in some curious way a source of enormous inspiration to him. Not always precisely inspiration,—comfort. All sorts of warming feelings stirred pleasurably within him when he could, in some sympathetic company, open out his mind.

He was not actively aware of it, but what, in those years, he came to crave for as a starved child craves for food was sympathy of mind.

He found it, in Penny Green, with what Mabel called "the most extraordinary people." "What you can find in that Mr. Fargus and that young Perch and his everlasting mother," she used to say, "I simply cannot imagine."

He found a great deal.

III

Mr. Fargus, who lived next door down the Green, and outside whose gate the bicycle had made its celebrated shortage record, was a grey little man with grey whiskers and always in a grey suit. He had a large and very red wife and six thin and rather yellowish daughters. Once a day, at four in summer and at two in winter, the complete regiment of Farguses moved out in an immense mass and proceeded in a dense crowd for a walk. The female Farguses, having very long legs, walked very fast, and the solitary male Fargus, having very short legs, walked very slowly, and was usually, therefore, trotting to keep up with the pack. He had, moreover, not only to keep pace but also to keep place. He was forever getting squeezed out from between two tall Farguses and trotting agitatedly around the heels of the battalion to recover a position in it. He always reminded Sabre of a grey old Scotch terrier toddling along behind and around the flanks of a company of gaunt, striding mastiffs. He returned from those walks panting slightly and a little perspiring, and at the door gave the appearance of being dismissed, and trotted away rather like a little grey old Scotch terrier toddling off to the stables. The lady Farguses called this daily walk "exercise"; and it certainly was exercise for Mr. Fargus.

The eldest Miss Fargus was a grim thirty-nine and the youngest Miss Fargus a determined twenty-eight. They called their father "Papa" and used the name a good deal. When Sabre occasionally had tea at the Farguses' on a Sunday afternoon Mr. Fargus always appeared to be sitting at the end of an immense line of female Farguses. Mrs. Fargus would pour out a cup and hand it to the Miss Fargus at her end of the line with the loud word "Papa!" and it would whiz down the chain from daughter to daughter to the clamorous direction, each to each, "Papa!—Papa!—Papa!—Papa!" The cup would reach Mr. Fargus at the speed of a thunderbolt; and Mr. Fargus, waiting for it with agitated hands as a nervous fielder awaits a rushing cricket ball, would stop it convulsively and usually drop and catch at and miss the spoon, whereupon the entire chain of Farguses would give together a very loud "Tchk!" and immediately shoot at their parent a plate of buns with "Buns—Buns—Buns—Buns" all down the line. Similarly when Mr. Fargus's grey little face would sometimes appear above the dividing wall to Sabre in the garden there would come a loud cry of "Papa, the plums!" and from several quarters of the garden this would he echoed "Papa, the plums!" "Papa, the plums!" and the grey little head, in the middle of a sentence, would disappear with great swiftness.

The Farguses kept but one servant, a diminutive and startled child with one hand permanently up her back in search of an apron shoulder string, and permanently occupied in frantically pursuing loud cracks, like pistol shots, of "Kate!—Kate!—Kate!" Each Miss Fargus "did" something in the house. One "did" the lamps, another "did" the silver, another "did" the fowls. And whatever it was they "did" they were always doing it. Each Miss Fargus, in addition, "did" her own room, and unitedly they all "did" the garden. Every doing was done by the clock; and at any hour of the day any one Miss Fargus could tell a visitor precisely what, and at what point of what, every other Miss Fargus was doing.

In this well-ordered scheme of things what Mr. Fargus principally "did" was to keep out of the way of his wife and daughters, and this duty took him all his time and ingenuity. From the back windows of Sabre's house the grey little figure was frequently to be seen fleeting up and down the garden paths in wary evasion of daughters "doing" the garden, and there was every reason to suppose that, within the house, the grey figure similarly fleeted up and down the stairs and passages. "Where is Papa?" was a constant cry from mouth to mouth of the female Farguses; and fatigue parties were constantly being detached from their duties to skirmish in pursuit of him.

In his leisure from these flights Mr. Fargus was intensely absorbed in chess, in the game of Patience, and in the solution of acrostics. Sabre was also fond of chess and attracted by acrostics; and regular evenings of every week were spent by the two in unriddling the problems set in the chess and acrostic columns of journals taken in for the purpose. They would sit for hours solemnly staring at one another, puffing at pipes, in quest of a hidden word beginning with one letter and ending with another, or in search of the two master moves that alone would produce Mate. (It was a point of honour not to work out chess problems on a board but to do them in your head.) Likewise for hours the two in games of chess and in competitive Patience, one against the other, to see who would come out first. And to all these mental exercises—chess, acrostics and Patience—an added interest was given by Mr. Fargus's presentation of them as illustrative of his theory of life.

Mr. Fargus's theory of life was that everybody was placed in life to fulfil a divine purpose and invested with the power to fulfil it. "No, no, it's not fatalism," Mr. Fargus used to say. "Not predestination. It's just exactly like a chess problem or an acrostic. The Creator sets it. He knows the solution, the answer. You've got to work it out. It's all keyed for you just as the final move in chess or the final discovery in an acrostic is keyed up to right from the start." And on this argument Mr. Fargus introduced Sabre to the great entertainment in "working back" when a game of Patience failed to come out or after a defeat in chess. You worked back to the immense satisfaction of finding the precise point at which you went wrong. Up to that point you had followed the keyed path; precisely there you missed it.

"Tremendous, eh?" Mr. Fargus used to say. "Terrific. If you hadn't done that you'd have got it. That one move, all that way back, was calamity. Calamity! What a word!"

And they would stare bemused eyes upon one another.

"You put that into life," Mr. Fargus used to say. "Imagine if every life, at death, was worked back, and where it went wrong, where it made its calamity, and the date, put on the tombstone. Eh? What a record! Who'd dare walk through a churchyard?"

Sabre's objection was, "Of course no one would ever know. Suppose your idea's correct, who's to say what a man's purpose in life was, let alone whether he'd fulfilled it? How can you work towards a purpose if you don't know what it is?"

Then little old Mr. Fargus would grow intense. "Why, Sabre, that's just where you are with an acrostic or in chess. How can you work out the solution when you don't know what the solution is?"

"Yes, but you know there is a solution."

Mr. Fargus's eyes would shine. "Well, there you are! And you know that in life there is a purpose."

And what attracted and interested Sabre was that the little man, living here his hunted life among the terrific "doings" of the seven female Farguses, firmly believed that he was working out and working towards his designed purpose. He had "worked back" his every event in life, he said, and it had brought him so inevitably to Penny Green and to skipping about among the seven that he was assured it was the keyed path to his purpose. He amazed Sabre by telling him, without trace of self-consciousness and equally without trace of religious mania, that he was waiting, daily, for God to call upon him to fulfil the purpose for which he was placed there. He expected it as one expects a letter by the post. When he talked about it to Sabre he positively trembled and shone with eagerness as a child trembling and shining with excitement before an unopened parcel.

One day Sabre protested. "But look here, Fargus. Look here, how are you going to know when it comes? It might be anything. You don't know what it is and—well, you won't know, will you?"

The little man said, "I believe I shall, Sabre. I've 'worked back' for years, as far as ever my memory will carry, and everything has been so exactly keyed that I'm convinced I'm in the way of my purpose. I believe you can feel it if you've waited for it like that. I believe you're asked 'Ready?' and I want to say, whatever it is, 'Aye, Ready!'"

Mysterious and awful suggestion, Sabre thought. To believe yourself at any moment to be touched as by a finger and asked "Ready?" "Aye, Ready!"

Mysterious and awful intimacy with God!

IV

And then there were the Perches—"Young Perch and that everlasting old mother of his", as Mabel called them.

Sabre always spoke of them as "Young Rod, Pole or Perch" and "Old Mrs. Rod, Pole or Perth." This was out of what Mabel called his childish and incomprehensible habit of giving nicknames,—High Jinks and Low Jinks the outstanding and never-forgiven example of it. "Whatever's the joke of it?" she demanded, when one day she found Sabre speaking of Major Millet, another neighbour and a great friend of hers, as "Old Hopscotch Millet."

"Whatever's the joke of it? He doesn't play hopscotch."

"No, but he bounds about," Sabre explained. "You know the way he bounds about, Mabel. He's about ninety—"

"I'm sure he isn't, nor fifty."

"Well, anyway, he's past his first youth, but he's always bounding about to show how agile he is. He's always calling out 'Ri—te O!' and jumping to do a thing when there's no need to jump. Hopscotch. What can you call him but Hopscotch?"

"But why call him anything?" Mabel said. "His name's Millet."

Her annoyance caused her voice to squeak. "Why call him anything?"

Sabre laughed. "Well, you know how a ridiculous thing like that comes into your head and you can't get rid of it. You know the way."

Mabel declared she was sure she did not know the way. "They don't come into my head. Look at the Perches—not that I care what name you call them. Rod, Pole or Perch! What's the sense of it? What does it mean?"

Sabre said it didn't mean anything. "You just get some one called Perch and then you can't help thinking of that absurd thing rod, pole or perch. It just comes."

"I call it childish and rude," Mabel said.

V

Mrs. Perch was a fragile little body whose life should have been and could have been divided between her bed and a bath chair. She was, however, as she said, "always on her legs." And she was always on her legs and always doing what she had not the strength to do, because, as she said, she "had always done it." She conducted her existence in the narrow space between the adamant wall of the things she had always done, always eaten, and always worn, and the adamant wall of the things she had never done, never eaten, and never worn. There was not much room between the two.

She was intensely weak-sighted, but she never could find her glasses; and she kept locked everything that would lock, but she never could find her keys. She held off all acquaintances by the rigid handle of "that" before their names, but she was very fond of "that Mr. Sabre", and Sabre returned a great affection for her. With his trick of seeing things with his mental vision he always saw old Mrs. Perch toddling with moving lips and fumbling fingers between the iron walls of her prejudices, and this was a pathetic picture to him, for ease or pleasure were not discernible between the walls. Nevertheless Mrs. Perch found pleasures therein, and the way in which her face then lit up added, to Sabre, an indescribable poignancy to the pathos of the picture. She never could pass a baby without stopping to adore it, and an astounding tide of rejuvenation would then flood up from mysterious mains, welling upon her silvered cheeks and through her dim eyes, stilling the movement of her lips and the fumbling motions of her fingers.

Also amazing tides of glory when she was watching for her son, and saw him.

Young Perch was a tall and slight young man with a happy laugh and an air which suggested to Sabre, after puzzlement, that his spirit was only alighted in his body as a bird alights and swings upon a twig, not engrossed in his body. He did not look very strong. His mother said he had a weak heart. He said he had a particularly strong heart and used to protest, "Oh, Mother, I do wish you wouldn't talk that bosh about me." To which Mrs. Perch would say, "It's no good saying you haven't got a weak heart because you have got a weak heart and you've always had a weak heart. Surely I ought to know."

Young Perch would reply, "You ought to know, but you don't know. You get an idea in your head and nothing will ever get it out. Some day you'll probably get the idea that I've got two hearts and if Sir Frederick Treves swore before the Lord Chief Justice that I only had one heart you'd just say, 'The man's a perfect fool.' You're awful, you know, Mother."

He used to reprove his mother like that.

Mrs. Perch would give a grim little laugh, relishing her strength, and then Young Perch would give an involuntary little laugh, accepting his weakness.

That was how they lived.

Young Perch always carried about in one pocket a private pair of spectacles for his mother and in another a private set of keys for her most used receptacles. When the search for her spectacles had exhausted even her own energy, Young Perch would say, "Well, you'd better use these, Mother." It was of no use to offer them till she was weakening in the search, and she would take them grudgingly with, "They don't suit me." Similarly with the keys, accepted only after prolonged and maddening search. "Well, you'd better try these, Mother."—"They injure the lock."

Sabre often witnessed and took part in these devastating searches. Young Perch would always say, "Now just sit down, Mother, instead of rushing about, and try to think quite calmly when you last used them."

Mrs. Perch, intensely fatigued, intensely worried:

"How very silly you are, Freddie! I don't know when I last used them. If I knew when I used them, I should know where they are now."

"Well, you'd better use these now, Mother."

"They don't suit me. They ruin my eyes."

Yet Mrs. Rod, Pole or Perch, who confided much in Sabre, and who had no confidences of any kind apart from her son, would often say to Sabre: "Freddie always finds my keys for me, you know. He finds everything for me, Mr. Sabre."

And the tide of glory would flood amazingly upon her face, transfiguring it, and Sabre would feel an immensely poignant clutch at the heart.

VI

The Perchs' house was called Puncher's—Puncher's Farm, a few hundred yards along the lane leading to the great highroad—and it was the largest and by far the most untidy house in Penny Green. Successive Punchers of old time, when it had been the most considerable farm in all the country between Chovensbury and Tidborough, had added to it in stubborn defiance of all laws of comfort and principles of domestic architecture, and now, shorn alike of its Punchers and of its pastures, the homestead that might easily have housed twenty, was mysteriously filled to overflowing by two.

Mrs. Perch was fond of saying she had lived in nineteen houses "in her time", and Sabre had the belief that the previous eighteen had all been separately furnished and the entire accumulation, together with every newspaper taken in during their occupation, brought to Puncher's. Half the rooms of Puncher's were so filled with furniture that no more furniture, and scarcely a living person, could be got in; and half the rooms were so filled with boxes, packages, bundles, trunks, crates, and stacks of newspapers that no furniture at all could be got in. Every room was known to Mrs. Perch and to Young Perch by the name of some article it contained and Mrs. Perch was forever "going to sort the room with your Uncle Henry's couch in it", or "the room with the big blue box with the funny top in it", or some other room similarly described.

Mrs. Perch was always "going to", but as the task was always contingent upon either "when I have got a servant into the house", or "when I have turned the servant out of the house"—these two states representing Mrs. Perch's occupation with the servant problem—the couch of Uncle Henry, the big blue box with the funny top, and all the other denizens of the choked rooms remained, like threatened men, precariously but securely.

But not unvisited!

Sabre once spent a week in the house, terminating a summer holiday a little earlier than Mabel, and he had formed the opinion that mother and son never went to bed at night and never got up in the morning. In remote hours and in remote quarters of the house mysterious sounds disturbed his sleep. Eerily peering over the banisters, he discerned the pair moving, like lost souls, about the passages, Mrs. Perch with the skirts of a red dressing-gown in one hand and a candle in the other, Young Perch disconsolately in her wake, yawning, with another candle. Young Perch called this "Prowling about the infernal house all night"; and one office of the prowl appeared to Sabre to be the attendance of pans of milk warming in a row on oil stoves and suggesting, with the glimmer of the stoves and the steam of the pans, mysterious oblations to midnight gods.

VII

Mrs. Perch believed her son could do anything and, in the matter of his capabilities, had the strange conviction that he had only to write and ask anybody, from Mr. Asquith downwards, for employment in the highest offices in order to obtain it. Young Perch—who used to protest, "Well, but I've got my work, Mother"—was in fact a horticulturist of very fair reputation. He specialised in sweet peas and roses; and Sabre, in the early days of his intimacy with the Rod, Pole or Perch household, was surprised at the livelihood that could apparently be made by the disposal of seeds, blooms and cuttings.

"Fred's getting quite famous with his sweet peas," Sabre once said to Mrs. Perch. "I've been reading an illustrated interview with him in The Country House."

Tides of glory into Mrs. Perch's face. "Ah, if only he hadn't worn that dreadful floppy hat of his, Mr. Sabre. It couldn't have happened on a more unfortunate day. I fully intended to see how he looked before the photographs were taken and of course it so happened I was turning a servant out of the house and couldn't attend to it. That dreadful floppy hat doesn't suit him. It never did suit him. But he will wear it. It's no good my saying anything to him."

This was an opinion that old Mrs. Perch was constantly reiterating. Young Perch was equally given to declaring, "I can't do anything with my Mother, you know." And yet it was Sabre's observation that each life was entirely guided and administered by the other. Young Perch once told Sabre he had never slept a night away from his mother since he was seventeen, and he was never absent from her half a day but she was at the window watching for his return.

Sabre was extraordinarily attracted by the devotion between the pair. Their interests, their habits, their thoughts were as widely sundered as their years, yet each was wholly and completely bound up in the other. When Sabre sat and talked with Young Perch of an evening, old Mrs. Perch would sit with them, next her son, in an armchair asleep. At intervals she would start awake and say querulously, "Now I suppose I must be driven off to bed."

Young Perch, not pausing in what he might be saying, would stretch a hand and lay it on his mother's. Mrs. Perch, as though Freddie's hand touched away enormous weariness and care, would sigh restfully and sleep again. It gave Sabre extraordinary sensations.

If he had been asked to name his particular friends these were the friends he would have named. He saw them constantly. Infrequently he saw another. Quite suddenly she came back into his life.

Nona returned into his life.

PART TWO

NONA

CHAPTER I

I

Sabre, ambling his bicycle along the pleasant lanes towards Tidborough one fine morning in the early summer of 1912, was met in his thoughts by observation, as he topped a rise, of the galloping progress of the light railway that was to link up the Penny Green Garden Home with Tidborough and Chovensbury. In the two years since Lord Tybar had, as he had said, beneficially exercised his ancestors in their graves by selling the land on which the Garden Home Development was to develop, Penny Green Garden Home had sprung into being at an astonishing pace.

The great thing now was the railway.

And the railway's unsightly indications strewn across the countryside—ballast heaps, excavations, noisy stationary engines, hand-propelled barrows bumping along toy lines, gangs of men at labour with pick and shovel—met Sabre's thoughts on this June morning because he was thinking of the Penny Green Garden Home and of Mabel, and of Mabel and of himself in connection with the Penny Green Garden Home. Puzzling thoughts.

Here was a subject, this ambitiously projected and astonishingly popular Garden Home springing up at their very doors, that interested him and that intensely interested Mabel, and yet it could never be mentioned between them without.... Only that very morning at breakfast.... And June—he always remembered it—was the anniversary month of their wedding.... Eight years ago.... Eight years....

II

What interested Sabre in the Garden Home was not the settlement itself—he rather hated the idea of Penny Green being neighboured and overrun by crowds of all sorts of people—but the causes that gave rise to the modern movement of which it was a shining example. The causes had their place in one of the sections he had planned for

"England" and it encouraged his ideas for that section to see the results here at his doors. Overcrowding in the towns; the desire of men to get away from their place of business; the increasing pressure of business and the increasing recreational variety of life that, deepening and widening through the years, actuated the desire; the extension of traffic facilities that permitted the desire; all the modern tendencies that made work less of a pleasure and more of a toil,—and out of that the whole absorbing question of the decay of joy in craftsmanship, and why.—Jolly interesting!

These were the pictures and the stories that Sabre saw in the roads and avenues and residences and public buildings leaping from mud and chaos into order and activity in the Garden Home; these were the reasons the thing interested him and why he rather enjoyed seeing it springing up about him. But these, he thought as he rode along, were not the reasons the thing interested Mabel. And when he mentioned them to her.... And when she, for her part, spoke of it to him—and she was always speaking of it—the reasons for her enthusiasm retired him at once into a shell. Funny state of affairs!

Mabel was convinced he loathed and detested the Penny Green Garden Home Development; and actually he rather liked the Penny Green Garden Home Development; and yet he couldn't tell her so; and she did not understand in the least when he tried to tell her so. Funny—eight years ago this month....

His thoughts went on. And, come to think of it, the relations between them were precisely similar in regard to nearly everything they ever discussed. And yet they would be called, and were, a perfectly happy couple. Perfectly? Was every happy married couple just what they were? Was married happiness, then, merely the negation of violent unhappiness? Merely not beating your wife, and your wife not drinking or running up debts? He thought: "No, no, there's something more in it than that." And then his forehead wrinkled up in his characteristic habit and he thought: "Of course, it's my fault. It isn't only this dashed Garden Home. It's everything. It isn't only once. It's always. It can't possibly be her fault always. It's mine. I can see that.

"Take this morning at breakfast. Perfectly good temper both of us. Then she said, 'Those houses in King's Close are going to be eighty pounds a year; and, what do you think, Mrs. Toller is going to take one!' Immediately I was riled. Why should I get riled because she says that Mrs. Toller is going to take a house for eighty pounds a year? I just rustled the newspaper. Why on earth couldn't I say, 'Good lord, is she?' or something like that? Why on earth couldn't I even not rustle the newspaper? She knows what it means when I rustle the paper. I meant her to know. Why should I? It's the easiest thing on earth for me to respond to what she says. I know perfectly well what she's getting at. I could easily have said that Mrs. Toller would have old Toller in the workhouse one of these days if he didn't watch it. I could have said, 'She'll be keeping three servants next, and she can't keep one as it is.' Mabel would have loved that. She'd have laughed."

He thought, "Why should she love that sort of tripe—gossip?"

He thought, "Damn it, why shouldn't she? Why should I mind? Why should I rustle the newspaper? She can't enter into things that interest me; but I can, I could enter into things that interest her. Why don't I? Of course I can see perfectly clearly how she looks at things. It's just as rotten for her that I can't talk with her about her ideas as it is rotten for me that she doesn't see my ideas. And it isn't rotten for me. I don't mind it. I don't expect it. I don't expect it...."

And at that precise moment of his thoughts, the garrulous Hapgood, seeing his face, could have said to another, as he said before, "There! See what I mean? Looks as though he'd lost something and was wondering where it was. Ha!"

III

A genial shouting and the clatter of agitated hoofs jerked Sabre from his thoughts.

"Hullo! Hi! Help! Out collision-mats! Stop the cab! Look out, Sabre! Sabre!"

He suddenly became aware—and he jammed on his brakes and dismounted by straddling a leg to the ground—that in the narrow lane he was between two plunging horses. Their riders had divided to make way for his bemused approach. They had violently sundered, expecting him to stop, until he was almost on top of them, and one of the pair was now engaged in placating his horse, which resented this sudden snatching at bit and prick of spur, and persuading it to return to the level road.

On one side the lane was banked steeply up in a cutting. The horse of the rider on this side stood on its hind legs and appeared to be performing a series of postman's double knocks on the bank with its forelegs. Lord Tybar, who bestrode it, and who did not seem to be at all concerned by his horse copying a postman, looked over his shoulder at Sabre, showing an amused grin, and said, "Thanks, Sabre. This is jolly. I like this. Come on, old girl. This way down. Keep passing on, please."

The old girl, an extraordinarily big and handsome chestnut mare, dropped her forelegs to the level of the road, where she exchanged the postman's knocking for a complicated and exceedingly nimble dance, largely on two legs.

Lord Tybar, against her evident intentions, skilfully directed the steps of this dance into a turning movement so that she and her rider now faced Sabre; and while she bounded through the concluding movements of the pas seul he continued in the same whimsical tone and with the same engaging smile, "Thanks still more, Sabre. This is extraordinarily good for the liver. Devilish graceful, aren't I? See, I'm only holding on with one hand! Marvellous. No charge for this." And as the mare came to rest and quivered at Sabre with her beautiful nostrils, "Ah, the music's stopped. Delicious. How well your step suits mine!"

"Ass!" laughed a voice above them; and Sabre, who had almost forgotten there was another horse when he had abruptly wakened and dismounted, looked up at it.

The other horse was standing with complete and entirely unconcerned statuesqueness on the low bank which bounded the lane on his other side. Lady Tybar had taken it—or it had taken Lady Tybar—out of danger in a sideways bound, and horse and rider remained precisely where the sideways bound had taken them as if it were exactly where they had intended to go all that morning, and as if they were now settled there for all time as a living equestrian statue,—a singularly striking and beautiful statue.

"We are up here," said Lady Tybar. Her voice had a very clear, fine note. "We are rather beautiful up here, don't you think? Rather darlings? No one takes the faintest notice of us; we might be off the earth. But we don't mind a bit. Hullo, Derry and Toms, Marko is actually taking off his hat to us. Bow, Derry."

Her horse, as if he perfectly understood, tossed his head, and she drew attention to it with a deprecatory little gesture of her hand and then said, "Shall we come down now? Is your dance quite finished, Tony? Are you content, Marko? All right. We'll descend. This is us descending. Lady Tybar, who is a superb horsewoman, descending a precipice on her beautiful half-bred Derry and Toms, a winner at several shows."

Derry and Toms stepped down off the bank with complete assurance and superb dignity. With equal precision, moving his feet as though there were marked for them certain exact spots which he covered with infinite lightness and exactitude, he turned about and stood beside his partner in exquisite and immobile pose.

IV

Thus the two riders faced Sabre, smiling upon him. He stood holding his bicycle immediately in front of them. The mare continued to quiver her beautiful nostrils at him; every now and then she blew a little agitated puff through them, causing them to expand and reveal yet more exquisitely their glorious softness and delicacy.

Sabre thought that the riders, with their horses, made the most striking, and somehow affecting picture of virile and graceful beauty he could ever have imagined.

Lord Tybar, who was thirty-two, was debonair and attractive of countenance to a degree. His eyes, which were grey, were extraordinarily mirthful, mischievous. A supremely airy and careless and bold spirit looked through those eyes and shone through their flashes and glints and sparkles of diamond light. His face was thin and of tanned olive. His face seemed to say to the world, challengingly, "I am here! I have arrived! Bring out your best and watch me!" There were people—women—who said he had a cruel mouth. They said this, not with censure or regret, but with a deliciously fearful rapture as though the cruel mouth (if it were cruel) were not the least part of his attraction.

Lord Tybar's lady, who was twenty-eight, carried in her countenance and in her hair the pleasing complement of her lord's tan and olive hue and of his cropped black poll. She was extraordinarily fair. Her skin was of the hue and of the sheen of creamy silk, and glowed beneath its hue. It presented amazing delicacy and yet an exquisite firmness. Children, playing with her, and she delighted in playing with children (but she was childless), often asked to stroke her face. They would stare at her face in that immensely absorbed way in which children stare, and then ask to touch her face and just stroke it; their baby fingers were not more softly silken. Of her hair Lady Tybar had said frequently, from her girlhood upwards, that it was "a most sickening nuisance." She bound it tightly as if to punish and be firm with the sickening nuisance that it was to her. And these close, gleaming plaits and coils children also liked to touch with their soft fingers.

Her name was Nona.

Out of a hundred people who passed her by quite a considerable number would have denied that she was beautiful. Her face was round and saucy rather than oval and classical. Incontestable the striking attraction of her complexion and of her hair; but not beautiful,—quite a number would have said, and did say. Oh, no; pretty, perhaps, in a way, but that's all.

But her face was much more than beautiful to Sabre.

V

Until this moment, standing there with his bicycle, she on her beautiful horse, he had not seen her, nor Lord Tybar, for two years. They had been travelling. Now seeing her, thus unexpectedly and thus gallantly environed, his mind, with that astonishing precision of detail and capriciousness of selection with which the mind retains pictures, reproduced certain masculine discussion of her looks at a time when, as Nona Holiday of Chovensbury Court, daughter of Sir Hadden Holiday, M.P. for Tidborough, she had contributed to local gossip by becoming engaged to Lord Tybar.

"Pretty girl, you know," masculine discussion had said; and Sabre had thought, "Fools!"

"Oh, hardly pretty," others had maintained; and again "Fools!" he had thought. "Pretty—pretty! Hardly pretty—hardly—!" Furious, he had flung away from them.

The time and the place of the discussion had been when the news of her engagement had just been brought into the clubhouse of the Penny Green Golf Club. He had flung out into the rain which had caused the pavilion to be crowded. Fools! Was she pretty! Did they mean to say they couldn't see in her face what he saw in her face? And then he thought, "But of course they haven't loved her. It's nothing to them what they've only just heard, but what she told me herself this morning.... And she knew what it meant to me when she told me.... Although we said nothing. Of course I see her differently."

He saw her "differently" now after two years of not seeing her, and ten years since that day of gossip at the golf club. Pretty!... Strange how he could always remember that smell of the rain as he had come out of the clubhouse ... and a strange fragrance in the air as now he looked upon her.

Upon the warm and trembling air, as he stood with his bicycle before the horses, were borne to him savour of hay newly turned in the fields about, and of high spring-tide blowing in the hedgerows; and with them delicious essence from the warm, gleaming bodies of the horses, and pungent flavour of the saddlery, and the mare's sweet breath puffed close to his face in little gusty agitations.

The shining, tingling picture of strength and beauty superbly modelled that the riders and their horses made, seemed, as it were, to arise out of and be suspended shimmering in the heart of the warm incense that he savoured. So when a sorcerer casts spiced herbs upon the flame, and scented vapour uprises, and in the vapour images appear.

Exquisite picture of strength and beauty superbly modelled: the horses' glossy coats glinting all a polished chestnut's hues; the perfect artistry and symmetry of slender limbs, and glorious, arching necks, and noble heads, and velvet muzzles; the dazzling bits and chains and buckles; the glinting bridles, reins and saddles; Lord Tybar's exquisitely poised figure, so perfectly maintaining and carrying up the symmetry of his horse as to suggest the horse would be disfigured, truncated, were he to dismount; his taking swagger, his gay, fine face; and she....

An incantation: jingle of bits mouthed in those velvet muzzles; a hoof pawed sharply on the road; swish of long, restless tails; creaking of saddlery; and sudden bursts of all the instruments in unison when heads were tossed and shaken. Remotely the whirr of a reaping machine. And somewhere birds....

Pretty!

VI

Greetings had been exchanged; his apologies for his blundering descent upon them laughed at. Lord Tybar was saying, "Well, it's a tiger of a place, this Garden Home of yours, Sabre—"

"It's not mine," said Sabre. "God forbid."

"Ah, you've not got the same beautiful local patriotism that I have. It's one of my most elegant qualities, my passionate devotion to my countryside. That was what that corker of a vicar of yours, Boom Bagshaw, told me I was when I wept with joy while he was showing me round. Yes, and now I'm a patron of the Garden Home Trust or a governor or a vice-priest or something. I am really. What is it I am, Nona?"

"You're a bloated aristocrat and a bloodsucker," Nona told him in her clear, fine voice. "And you're living on estates which your brutal ancestors ravaged from the people. That's what you are, Tony. I showed it you in the Searchlight yesterday. And, I say, don't use 'elegant'; that's mine."

"Oh, by gad, yes, so I am," said Lord Tybar. "Bloodsucker! Good lord, fancy being a bloodsucker!"

He looked so genuinely rueful and abashed that Sabre laughed; and then said to Nona, "Why is elegant 'yours', Lady Tybar?"

She made a little pouting motion at him with her lips. "Marko, I wish to goodness you wouldn't call me Lady Tybar. Dash it, we've called one another Nona and Marko for about a thousand years, long before I ever knew Tony. And just because I'm married—"

"And to a mere loathsome bloodsucker, too," Lord Tybar interposed.

"Yes, especially to a bloodsucker. Just remember to say Nona, will you, otherwise there'll be a cruel scene between us. I told you about it before I went away. You don't suppose Tony minds, do you?"

"And Sabre," said Lord Tybar, "what the devil does it matter what a bloated robber minds, anyway? That's the way to look at me, Sabre. Trample me underfoot, my boy. I'm a pestilent survivor of the feudal system, aren't I, Nona?"

"Absolutely. So, Marko, don't be a completer noodle than you already are."

"Ah, you're getting it now." Lord Tybar murmured. "I'm a noodle, too, the Searchlight says."

He somehow gave Sabre the impression of taking an even deeper enjoyment in the incident between his wife and Sabre than the enjoyment he clearly had in his own facetiousness. He was slightly turned in his saddle so as to look directly at Nona, and he listened and interposed, and turned his eyes from her face to Sabre's, and from Sabre's back to hers, with his handsome head slightly cocked to one side and with much gleaming in his eyes; rather as if he had on some private mock.

Fantastical notion! What mock could he have?

"Well, about my word 'elegant'," Nona was going on, "and why it is mine—weren't you asking?"

Sabre said he had. "Yes, why yours?"

"Why, you see, Derry and Toms is a case of it." She tickled her horse's ears with her riding switch, and he stamped a hoof on the ground and arched his neck as though he knew he was a case of it and was proud of being a case of it. "I wanted an elegant name for him and I always think two names are so elegant for a firm—"

"Bloodsucker and Noodle are mine," said Lord Tybar in a very gloomy voice; and they laughed.

"—So I called him Derry and Toms."

Sabre pointed out that this still left her own possession of the word unexplained.

"Oh, Marko, you're dreadfully matter-of-fact. You always were. Why, Tony and I get fond of a word and then we have it for our own, whichever of us it is, and use it for everything. And elegant's mine just now. I'm dreadfully fond of it. It's so—well, elegant: there you are, you see!"

Lord Tybar announced that he had just become attached to a new word and desired to possess it. He was going to have blood. "You see, if I live by sucking blood—"

"Tony, you're disgusting!"

"I know. I'm the most frightful things. I'm just beginning to realise it. Yes, blood's mine, Nona. Copyright. All rights reserved. Blood."

"Well, so long as you stick to the noun and don't use the adjective," she said; and they all laughed again.

Lord Tybar gathered up his reins and stroked his left hand along them. "Well, kindness to animals!" he said. "That's another of my beautiful qualities. The perfect understanding between me and my horses tells me the mare has seen enough of you, Sabre. She tells me all her thoughts in her flanks and they Marconi up my nervous and receptive legs. I must write and tell the Searchlight that. Perhaps they'll think better of me."—The mare, feeling his hand, began to dance coquettishly. "You'll come up and see us often, now you know we're back, won't you? Nona likes seeing you, don't you, Nona?" And again he looked from Nona to Sabre and back at Nona again with that look of mocking drollery.

"Oh, you're all right, Marko," Nona agreed, "when you're not too matter-of-fact. Yes, do come up. There's always a harsh word and a blow for you at Northrepps."

The mare steadied again. She stretched out her neck towards Sabre and quivered her nostrils at him, sensing him. He put up a hand to stroke her beautiful muzzle and she threw up her head violently and swerved sharply around.

Not in the least discomposed, Lord Tybar, his body in perfect rhythm with her curvettings, laughed at Sabre over his shoulder. "She thinks you're up to something, Sabre. She thinks you've got designs on us. Marvellous how I know! Whisper and I shall hear, loved one. You'll hurt yourself in a minute."

The light in his smiling eyes was surely a mocking light. "Thinks you're up to something! Thinks you've got designs on us!"

71

The mare was wheedled round again to her former position; against her will, but somehow as the natural result of her dancing. Marvellous how he directed her caprices into his own intentions and against her own. But Lord Tybar was now looking away behind him to where the adjoining meadow sloped far away and steeply to a copse. In the hollow only the tops of the trees could be seen. His eyes were screwed up in distant vision. He said, "Dash it, there's that old blighter Sooper. He's been avoiding me. Now I've got him. Nona, you won't mind getting back alone? I must speak to Sooper. I'm going to have his blood over that fodder business. Blood! My word! Good!"

He twisted the mare in a wonderfully quick and dexterous movement. "Good-by, Sabre. You don't mind, Nona?" And he flashed back a glance. He lifted the mare over the low bank with a superbly easy motion. He turned to wave his hand as she landed nimbly in the meadow, and he cantered away, image of grace, poetry of movement. Fortune's favourite!

The two left watched him. At the brow of the meadow he turned again in his saddle and waved again jauntily. They waved reply. He was over the brow. Out of sight.

VII

The features of the level valley beyond the brow where only he could have seen the individual he sought, were, at that distance, of Noah's Ark dimensions. "How he could have recognised any one!" said Nona, her gaze towards the valley. "I can't even see any one. He's got eyes like about four hawks!"

Sabre said, "And rides like a—what do they call those things?—like a centaur."

She turned her head towards him. "He does everything better than any one else," she said. "That's Tony's characteristic. Everything. He's perfectly wonderful."

These were enthusiastic words; but she spoke them without enthusiasm; she merely pronounced them. "Well, I'm off too," she said. "And what about you, Marko? You're going to work, aren't you? I don't think you ought to be able to stop and gossip like this. You're not getting an idler, are you? You used to be such a devoted hard-worker. My word!" and she laughed as though at some amused memory of his devotion to work.

He laughed too. They certainly had many recollections in common, though not all laughable. "I don't think I'm quite so—so earnest as I used to be," he smiled.

"Ah, but I like you earnest, Marko."

There was the tiniest silence between them. Yet it seemed to Sabre a very long silence.

She was again the one to speak, and her tone was rather abrupt and high-pitched as if she, too, were conscious of a long silence and broke it deliberately, as one breaks, with an effort, constraint.

"And how's Mabel?"

"She's all right. She's ever so keen on this Garden Home business."

"She would be," said Nona.

"And so am I!" said Sabre. Something in her tone made him say it defiantly.

She laughed. "I'm sure you are, Marko. Well, good-by"; and as Derry and Toms began to turn with his customary sedateness of motion she made the remark, "I'm so glad you don't wear trouser clips, Marko. I do loathe trouser clips."

He told her that he rode "one of those chainless bikes."

He said it rather mumblingly. Exactly in that tone she used to say things like, "I do like you in that brown suit, Marko."

VIII

He resumed his ride. A mile farther on he overtook, on a slight rise, an immense tree trunk slung between three pairs of wheels and dragged by two tremendous horses, harnessed tandemwise. As he passed them came the smell of warm horseflesh and his thought was "Pretty!"

He shot ahead and a line came into his mind:

"Was this the face that launched a thousand ships?"

73

Well, he had had certain aspirations, dreams, visions....

He was upon the crest whence the road ran down into Tidborough. Beneath him the spires of the Cathedral lifted exquisitely above the surrounding city.

"Those houses in King's Close are going to be eighty pounds a year, and what do you think, Mrs. Toller is going to take one!"...

CHAPTER II

I

Sabre found but little business awaiting him when he got to his office. When he had disposed of it he sat some little time staring absentmindedly at the cases whereon were ranged the books of his publication. Then he took out the manuscript of "England" and turned over the pages. He wondered what Nona would think of it. He would like to tell her about it.

Twyning came in.

Twyning rarely entered Sabre's room. Sabre did not enter Twyning's twice in a year. Their work ran on separate lines and there was something, unexpressed, the reverse of much sympathy between them. Twyning was an older man than Sabre. He was only two years older in computation by age but he was very much more in appearance, in manner and in business experience. He had been in the firm as a boy checker when Sabre was entering Tidborough School. He had attracted Mr. Fortune's special attention by disclosing a serious scamping of finish in a set of desks and he had risen to head clerk when Sabre was at Oxford. On the day that Sabre entered the firm he had been put "on probation" in the position he now held, and on the day that Sabre's father retired he had been confirmed in the position. He regarded Sabre as an amateur and he was privately disturbed by the fact that a man who "did not know the ropes" and had not "been through the mill" should come to a position equal in standing to his own. Nevertheless he accepted the fact, showing not the smallest animosity. He was always very ready to be cordial towards Sabre; but his cordiality took a form in which Sabre had never seen eye to eye with him. The attitude he extended to Sabre was that he and Sabre were two young fellows under a rather pig-headed old employer and that they could have many jokes and grievances and go-ahead schemes in companionship together. Sabre did not accept this view. He gave Twyning, from the first, the impression of considering himself as working alongside Mr. Fortune instead of beneath him; and he was cold to and refused to participate in the truant schoolboy air which Twyning adopted when they were together. Twyning called this "sidey." He was anxious to show Sabre, when Sabre first came to the firm, the best places to lunch in Tidborough, but Sabre was frequently lunching with one of the School housemasters or at the Masters' common room. Twyning thought this stand-offish.

II

Twyning was of middle height, very thin, black-haired. His clean-shaven face was deeply furrowed in rigid-looking furrows which looked as though shaving would be an intricate operation. He held himself very stiffly and spoke stiffly as though the cords of his larynx were also rigidly inclined. When not speaking he had a habit of breathing rather noisily through his nose as if he were doing deep breathing exercises. He was married and had a son of whom he was immensely proud, aged eighteen and doing well in a lawyer's office.

He came in and closed the door. He had a sheet of paper in his hand.

Sabre, engrossed, glanced up. "Hullo, Twyning." He wrote a word and then put down his pen. "Anything you want me about?" He lay back in his chair and stared, frowning, at the manuscript before him.

"Nothing particular, if you're busy," Twyning said. "I just looked in." He advanced the paper in his hand and looked at it as if about to add something else. But he said nothing and stood by Sabre's chair, also looking at the manuscript. "That that book?"

"M'm." Sabre was trying to retain his thoughts. He felt them slipping away before Twyning's presence. He could hear Twyning breathing through his nose and felt incensed that Twyning should come and breathe through his nose by his chair when he wanted to write.

But Twyning continued to stand by the chair and to breathe through his nose. He was reading over Sabre's shoulder.

The few pages of "England" already written lay in front of Sabre's pad, the first page uppermost. Twyning read and interjected a snort into his nasal rhythm.

"Well, that book's not written for me, anyway," he remarked.

Sabre agreed shortly. "It isn't. But why not?"

Twyning read aloud the first words. "'This England you live in is yours.' Well, I take my oath it isn't mine. Not a blooming inch of it. D'you know what's happening to me? I'm being turned out of my house. The lease is out and the whole damned house and everything I've put on to it goes to one of these lordlings—this Lord Tybar—just because one of his ancestors, who'd never even dreamt of the house, pinched the land it stands on from the public common and started to pocket ground rent. Now I'm being pitched into the street to let Lord Tybar have a house that's no more his than the man in the moon's. D'you call that right?"

"No, I don't," said Sabre, but with a tinge of impatience. "I call it rotten."

Twyning seemed surprised. "Do you, though? Well, how about that book? I mean to say—"

"I shall say so in the book. Or as good as say so."

Twyning pondered. "Shall you, by Jove? Well, but I say, that's liberalism, radicalism, you know. That's not the sort of pap for kids."

"Well, the book isn't going to be pap for kids."

Twyning snorted a note of laughter through his nose. "Sorry, old man. Don't get shirty. But I say though, seriously, we can't put out that sort of stuff, you know. Radicalism. Not with our connection. I mean to say—"

Sabre gathered up the papers and dropped them into a drawer. "Look here, Twyning, suppose you wait till the book's written before you criticise it. How about that for an idea?"

"All right, all right, old man. I'm not criticising. What's it going to be called?"

"England."

Silence.

Sabre, appreciating, with the author's intense suspicion for his child, something in the silence, looked up at Twyning. "Anything wrong about that? 'England.' You read the first sentence?"

Twyning said slowly, "Yes, I know I did. I thought of it then."

"Thought of what?"

"Well—'England'—'this England.' I mean to say—What about Scotland?"

"Well, what about Scotland?"

Twyning seemed really concerned. The puckers on his face had visibly deepened. He used a stubborn tone. "Well, you know what people are. You know how damned touchy those Scotchmen are. I mean to say, if we put out a book like that, the Scotch—"

Sabre smote the desk. This kind of thing from Twyning made him furious, and he particularly was not in the mood for it this morning. He struck his hand down on the desk: "Well, damn the Scotch. What's it got to do with the Scotch? This book isn't about Scotland. It's about England. England. I'll tell you another thing. You say if 'we' put out a book like that. It isn't 'we.' Excuse me saying so, but it certainly isn't you. It's I." He stopped, and then laughed. "Sorry, Twyning."

III

Twyning's face had gone very dark. His jaw had set. "Oh, all right." He turned away, but immediately returned again, his face relaxed. "That's all right. Only my chipping, you know. I say though," and he laughed nervously. "That 'not we.' You've said it! I'd come in to tell you. It's going to be 'we.'" He advanced the paper he had been holding in his hand, his thumb indicating the top left-hand corner. "What do you think of me above the line, my boy?"

The paper was a sheet of the firm's notepaper. In the upper left-hand corner was printed in small type, "The Rev. Sebastian Fortune." Beneath the name was a short line and beneath the line, "Mr. Shearman Twyning. Mr. Mark Sabre":

The Rev. Sebastian Fortune.

─────────

Mr. Shearman Twyning.
Mr. Mark Sabre.

Sabre said slowly, "What do you mean—you 'above the line'?"

Twyning indicated the short line with a forefinger. "That line, my boy. Jonah's going to take me into partnership. Just told me."

He had released the paper into Sabre's hand. Sabre handed it back with a single word, "Good."

Twyning's face darkened again and darkened worse. He crumpled the paper violently in his hand and spoke also but a single word, "Thanks!" He turned sharply on his heel and went to the door.

"I say, Twyning!" Sabre jumped to his feet and went to Twyning with outstretched hand. "I didn't mean to take it like that. Don't think I'm not—I congratulate you. Jolly good. Splendid. I tell you what—I don't mind telling you—it was a bit of a smack in the eye for me for a moment. You know, I've rather sweated over this business,"—his glance indicated the stacked bookshelves, the firm's publications, his publications.... "See what I mean?"

A certain movement in his throat and about his mouth indicated, more than his words, what he meant. A slight.

Twyning took the hand and gripped it with a firmness characteristic of his handshake.

"Thanks, old man. Thanks awfully. Of course I know what you mean. But after all, look at the thing, eh? I mean to say, you've been here—what—ten or twelve years. Well, I've been over twenty-five. Natural, eh? And you're doing splendidly. Every one knows that. It's only a question of time. Thanks awfully." He reached for Sabre's hand again and again gripped it hard.

Sabre went back and sat against his desk. "What rather got me, you know, coming all of a sudden like that, was that Fortune promised me partnership, twice, quite a bit ago."

Twyning, who had been speaking with an emotion in consonance with the grip of his hand, said a little blankly, "Did he? That so?"

"Yes, twice. And this looked like, when you told me—well, like dissatisfaction since, see? Eh?"

Twyning did not take up the point. "I say, you never told me."

"I'm telling you now," Sabre said. And he laughed ruefully. "It comes to much the same thing—as it turns out."

"Yes, but still.... I wish we worked in a bit more together, Sabre. I'm always ready to, you know. Let's, shall we?"

Sabre made no reply. Twyning repeated "Let's" and nodded and left the room. Immediately he opened the door again and reappeared. "I say, you won't say anything to Jonah, of course?"

Sabre smiled grimly. "I'm going to."

Again the darkening. "Dash it, that's not quite playing the game, is it?"

"Rot, Twyning. Fortune's made me a promise, and I'm going to ask if he has any reason for withdrawing it, that's all. It's nothing to do with your show."

"You're bound to tell him I've told you."

"Well, man alive, I'm bound to know, aren't I?"

"Yes—in a way. Oh, well, all right. Remember about working in more together." He withdrew and closed the door.

Outside the door he clenched his hands. He thought, "Smack in the eye for you, was it? You'll get a damn sight worse smack in the eye one of these days. Dirty dog!"

IV

Immediately the door was closed Sabre went what he would have called "plug in" to Mr. Fortune; that is to say, without hesitation and without reflection. He went in by the communicating door, first giving a single tap but without waiting for a reply to the tap. Mr. Fortune, presenting a whale-like flank, was at his table going through invoices and making notes in a small black book which he carried always in a tail pocket of his jacket.

"Can I speak to you a minute, Mr. Fortune?"

Mr. Fortune entered a note in the small black book: "Twenty-eight, sixteen, four." He placed a broad elastic band round the book and with the dexterity of practice passed the book round his bulk and into the tail pocket. He flicked his hands away and extended them for an instant, palms upward, much as a conjurer might to show there was nothing in them. "Certainly you may speak to me, Sabre." He performed his neat revolving trick. "As a matter of fact, I rather wanted to speak to you." He pointed across the whale-like front to the massive leathern armchair beside his desk.

The seat of the armchair marked in a vast hollow the cumulative ponderosity of the pillars of Church and School who were wont to sit in it. Sabre seated himself on the arm. "Was it about this partnership business?"

Mr. Fortune had already frowned to see Sabre upon the arm of the chair, a position for which the arm was not intended. His frown deepened. "What partnership business?"

"Well, you recollect promising me—being good enough to promise me—twice—that I was going to come into partnership—"

Mr. Fortune folded his hands upon the whale-like front. "I certainly do not recollect that, Sabre." He raised a hand responsive to a gesture. "Allow me. I recollect no promise. Either twice or any other number of times, greater or fewer. I do recollect mentioning to you the possibility of my making you such a proposal in my good time. Is that what you refer to as 'this partnership business'?"

"Yes—partly. Well, look here, sir, it's been a pretty good time, hasn't it? I mean since you spoke of it."

Mr. Fortune tugged strongly at his watch by its gold chain and looked at the watch rather as though he expected to see the extent of the good time there recorded. He forced it back with both hands rather as though it had failed of this duty and was being crammed away in disgrace. "I am expecting Canon Toomuch." He hit the watch, cowering (as one might suppose) in his pocket. "You know, my dear Sabre, I do think this is a little odd. A little unusual. You cannot bounce into a partnership, Sabre. I know your manner. I know your manner well. Oblige me by not fiddling with that paper knife. Thank you. And I make allowances for your manner. But believe me a partnership is not to be bounced into. You give me the impression—I do not say you mean it, I say you give it—of suddenly and without due cause or just im—just opportunity, trying to bounce me into taking you into partnership. I most emphatically am not to be bounced, Sabre. I never have been bounced and you may quite safely take it from me that I never propose or intend to be bounced."

Sabre thought, "Well, it would take a steam crane to bounce you, anyway." He said. "I hadn't the faintest intention of doing any such thing. If I made you think so, I'm sorry. I simply wanted to ask if you have changed your mind, and if so why. I mean, whether I have given you any cause for dissatisfaction since you prom—since you first mentioned it to me."

Mr. Fortune's whale-like front had laboured with some agitation during his repudiation of liability to being bounced. It now resumed its normal dignity. "You certainly have not, Sabre. No cause for dissatisfaction. On the contrary. You know quite well that there are certain characteristics of yours of which, constituted as I am, I do not approve. I really must beg of you not to fiddle with those scissors. Thank you. But they are, happily, quite apart from your work. I do not permit them to influence my opinion of you by one jot or tittle. You may entirely reassure yourself. May I inquire why you should have supposed I had changed my mind?"

"Because I've just heard that you've told Twyning you're going to take him into partnership."

The whale-like front gave a sudden leap and quiver precisely as if it had been struck by a cricket ball. Mr. Fortune's voice hardened very remarkably. "As to that, I will permit myself two remarks. In the first place, I consider it highly reprehensible of Twyning to have communicated this to you—"

Sabre broke in. "Well, he didn't. I'd like you to be quite clear on that point, if you don't mind. Twyning didn't tell me. It came out quite indirectly in the course of something I was saying to him. I doubt if he knows that I know even. I inferred it. It seems I inferred correctly."

There flashed through Mr. Fortune's mind a poignant regret that, this being the case, he had not denied it. He said, "I am exceedingly glad to hear it. I might have known Twyning would not be capable of such a breach of discretion. Resuming what I had to say—and, Sabre, I shall indeed be most intensely obliged if you will refrain from fiddling with the things on my table—resuming what I had to say, I will observe in the second and last place that I entirely deprecate, I will go further, I most strongly resent any questioning by any one member of my staff based on any intentions of mine relative to another member of my staff. This business is my business. I think you are sometimes a little prone to forget that. If it seems good to me to strengthen your hand in your department that has nothing whatever to do with Twyning. And if it seems good to me to strengthen Twyning's hand in Twyning's department that has nothing whatever to do with you."

Sabre, despite his private feelings in the matter, characteristically followed this reasoning completely, and said so. "Yes, that's your way of looking at it, sir, and I don't say it isn't perfectly sound—from your point of view—"

Mr. Fortune inclined his head solemnly: "I am obliged to you."

"—Only other people look at things on the face of them, just as they appear. You know—it's difficult to express it—I've put my heart into those books." He made a gesture towards his room. "I can't quite explain it, but I felt that the slight, or what looks like a slight, is on them, not on me." He put his hand to the back of his head, a habit characteristic when he was embarrassed or perplexed. "I'm afraid I can't quite express it, but it's the books. Not myself. I'm—fond of them. They're not just paper and print to me. I feel that they feel it. You won't quite understand, I'm afraid—"

"No, I confess that is a little beyond me," said Mr. Fortune, smoothing his front; and they remained looking at one another.

A sudden and unearthly moan sounded through the room. Mr. Fortune spun himself with relief to his desk and applied his lips to a flexible speaking tube. "Yes?" He dodged the tube to his ear, then to his lips again.

"Beg Canon Toomuch to step up to my room." He laid down the tube.

Sabre roused himself and stood up abruptly. "Ah, well! All right, sir." He moved towards his door.

"Sabre," inquired Mr. Fortune, "you get on well with Twyning, I trust?"

"Get on? Oh yes. We don't have much to do with each other."

"Do you dislike Twyning?"

"I don't dislike him. I'm indifferent to him."

"I regret to hear that," said Mr. Fortune.

From the door Sabre put a question in his turn: "When are you going to make this change with Twyning?"

"Not to-day."

"Am I still to remember that you held out partnership to me?"

"Certainly you may."

"When is it likely to be?"

"Not to-day."

Maddening expression!

Sabre, in his room, went towards his chair. He was about to drop into it when he recollected something. He went out into the corridor and along the corridor, past Mr. Fortune's door (Canon Toomuch coming heavily up the stairs) to Twyning's room. He put in his head. "Oh, I say, Twyning, if Fortune should ever ask you if you told me about that business, you can tell him you didn't."

"Oh—oh, right-o," said Twyning; and to himself when the door closed, "Funked speaking to him!"

V

Arrived again in his room, Sabre dropped into his chair. In his eyes was the look that had been in them when he had tried to explain to Mr. Fortune about the books, what Mr. Fortune had confessed he found a little beyond him. He thought: "The books.... Of course Fortune hasn't imagined them ... seen them grow helped them to grow.... But it hurts. Like hell it hurts.... And I can't explain to him how I feel about them.... I can't explain to any one."

His thoughts moved on: "I've been twelve years with him. Twelve years we've been daily together, and when I said that about the books I sat there and he sat there—and just looked. Stared at each other like masks. Masks! Nothing but a mask to be seen for either of us. I sit behind my mask and he sits behind his and that's all we see. Twelve mortal years! And there're thousands of people in thousands of offices ... thousands of homes ... just the same. All behind masks. Mysterious business. Extraordinary. How do we keep behind? Why do we keep behind? We're all going through the same life. Come the same way. Go the same way. You look at insects, ants, scurrying about, and not two of them seem to have a thing in common, not two of them seem to know one another; and you think it's odd, you think it's because they don't know they're all in the same boat. But we're just the same. They might think it of us. And we do know. And yet you get two lives and put them together twelve years in an office ... in a house.... Mabel and I ... practically we just sit and look at each other. Her mask. My mask...."

He thought: "One knows what it is, what it looks like, with ants. They're all plugging about like mad like that, not knowing one another, nor caring, because they all seem to be looking for something. I wonder.... I wonder—are we? Is that the trouble? All looking for something.... You can see it in half the faces you see. Some wanting, and knowing they are wanting something. Others wanting something but just putting up with it, just content to be discontented. You can see it. Yes, you can. Looking for what? Love? But lots have love. Happiness? But aren't lots happy? But are they?"

He knitted his brows: "It goes deeper than that. It's some universal thing that's wanting. Is it something that religion ought to give, but doesn't? Light? Some new light to give every one certainty in religion, in belief. Light?"

His thoughts went to Mabel. "Those houses in King's Close are going to be eighty pounds a year, and what do you think, Mrs. Toller is going to take one." And he had not answered her but had rustled the newspaper and had intended her to know why he had rustled the paper: to show he couldn't stick it! Unkind. His heart smote him for Mabel. Such a pathetically simple thing for Mabel to find enjoyment in! Why, he might just as reasonably rustle the newspaper at a baby because it had enjoyment in a rattle. A rattle would not amuse him, and Mrs. Toller taking a house beyond her means did not amuse him; but why on earth should he—?

He put the thing to himself in his reasoning way, his brow wrinkled up: She was his wife. She had left her home for his home. She had a right to his interest in her ideas. He had a duty towards her ideas. Unkind. Rotten.

Upon a sudden impulse he looked at his watch. Only just after twelve. He could get back in time for lunch. Lonely for her, day after day, and left as he had left her that morning. They could have a jolly afternoon together. He could make it a jolly afternoon. Nona kept coming into his thoughts—and more so after this Twyning business. He would have Mabel in his thoughts.

He went in and told Mr. Fortune he rather thought of taking the afternoon off if he was not wanted. He mounted his bicycle and rode purposefully back to Mabel.

CHAPTER III

I

The free-wheel run down into Perry Green landed him a little short of his gate,—not bad! Pirrip, the postman, whom he had passed in the bicycle's penultimate struggles, overtook him in its death throes and watched with interest the miracles of balancing with which, despite his preoccupation of mind, habit made him prolong them to the uttermost inch.

He dismounted. "Anything for me, Pirrip?"

"One for you, Mr. Sabre."

Sabre took the letter and glanced at the handwriting.

It was from Nona.

Her small, neat, masculine script had once been as familiar to him as his own. It was curiously like his own. She had the same trick of not linking all the letters in a word. Her longer words, like his own, looked as if they were two or three short words close together. To this day, when he did not get a letter from her once in a year—or in five years—his address on an envelope in her handwriting was a thing he could bring, and sometimes did bring with perfect clearness before his mental vision.

He glanced at it, regarded it for slightly longer than a glance, and with a little pucker of brows and lips, then made the action of putting it, unopened, in his pocket. Then he rested the bicycle against his hip and opened her letter.

"Northrepps. Tuesday." She never dated her letters. He used to be always telling her about that. Tuesday was yesterday.

Dear Marko—We're back. We've been from China to Peru—almost. Come up one day and be bored about it. How are you?

Nona.

He thought: "Funny she didn't mention she'd written just now. Perhaps she thought it was funny I didn't say I'd had it. I must tell her."

He returned her letter to its envelope and put the envelope in his pocket. Then wheeled his bicycle into his gate. He smiled. "Mabel will be surprised at me back like this."

Mabel was descending the stairs as he entered the hall. In the white dress she wore she made a pleasant picture against the broad, shallow stairway and the dark panelling. But she did not appear particularly pleased to see him. But he thought, "Why should she be? That's just it. That's why I've come back."

"Hullo?" she greeted him. "Have you forgotten something?"

He smiled invitingly. "No, I've just come back. I suddenly thought we'd have a holiday."

She showed puzzlement. "A holiday? What, the office? All of you?"

She had paused three steps from the foot of the stairs, her right hand on the banisters.

His wife!...

He slid his hand up the rail and rested it on hers. "Good lord, no. Not the office. No, I suddenly thought we'd have a holiday. You and I."

He half hoped she would respond to the touch of his hand by turning the palm of her own to it. But he thought, "Why should she?" and she did not. She said, "But how extraordinary! Whatever for?"

"Well, why not?"

"But what did you say at the office? What reason did you give?"

"Didn't give any. I just said I thought I wouldn't be back."

"But whatever will Mr. Fortune think?"

"Oh, what does it matter what he thinks? He won't think anything about it."

"But he'll think it's funny."

He thought, "Dash these buts!" This was what he called "niggling." It was on the tip of his tongue to say, "Why niggle about the thing?" but he recollected his purpose; that was him all over and that was just it! He said brightly, "Let him. Do him good. The idea suddenly came to me as a bit of a lark to have an unexpected holiday with you, and I just cleared off and came!"

She had descended and he moved along the hall with her towards the morning room.

"It's rather extraordinary," she said.

She certainly was not enthusiastic over it. She asked, "Well, what are you going to do?"

He wished he had thought of some plan as he came along. "What time's lunch? Half-past one? What about getting your bike and going for a bit of a run first?"

She was at a drawer of her table where she kept, with beautiful neatness, implements for various household duties. A pair of long scissors came out. "I can't possibly. I've things to do. Besides some one's coming to lunch."

He began to feel he had been a fool. The feeling nettled him and he thought, "Why 'some one'? Dash it, I might be a stranger in the house. Why doesn't she say who?" And then he thought, "Why should she? This is just it. I'd have heard all about it at breakfast if I'd been decently communicative."

He said, "Good. Who?"

She took a shallow basket from the shelf. He knew this and the long scissors for her flower-cutting implements. "Mr. Bagshaw."

And before he could stop himself he had groaned, "Oh, lord!"

She "flew up" and he rushed in tumultuously to make amends for his blunder and prevent her flying up.

"Mark, I do wish—"

"I'm sorry. I'm sorry. I really am most awfully sorry, Mabel. 'Oh, lord''s not really profanity. You know it's not. It's just my way—"

"I know that."

But he persevered. "As a matter of fact, it's clear connection of thought in this case. Bagshaw's a clergyman, and my mind flew instantly to celestial things."

She did not respond to this. "In any case, I really cannot see why you should object to Mr. Boom Bagshaw."

"I don't. I don't in the least."

"I've heard you say—often—that he's far and away the best preacher you've ever heard."

"He is. Absolutely."

"Well, then?"

"It's just his coming to lunch. He's such a terrific talker and you know I can't stick talkers."

"Yes, that's just why I invite them when you're not here."

He laughed and came across the room towards her impulsively. He was going to carry this through. "You've got me there. Properly." He took the basket from her hand. "Come on, we'll cut the flowers. I'll be absolutely chatty with old Bagshaw."

She smiled and her smile encouraged him tremendously. This was the way to do it! They went through the glass doors into the garden and he continued, "Really chatty. I'm going to turn over a new leaf. As a matter of fact, that's why I came back. I got out of bed the wrong side this morning, didn't I?"

He felt as he always remembered once feeling as a boy when, after going to bed, he had come downstairs in his nightshirt and said to his father, "I say, father, I didn't tell the truth this morning. I had been smoking." He had never forgotten the enormous relief of that confession, nor the bliss of his father's, "That's all right, old man.

That's fine. Don't cry, old chap." And he felt precisely that same enormous relief now.

She said, "Was that the reason? How awfully funny of you!" and she gave one of her sudden bursts of laughter.

He had a swift feeling that this was not quite the same as the reception of his confession by his father in that long-ago; but he thought immediately, "The thing's quite different." Anyway, he had confessed. She knew why he had come back so suddenly. He felt immensely happy. And when she said, "I think we'll have some of the roses," he gaily replied, "Yes, rather. These roses!"

Fine! How easy to be on jolly terms!

And immediately it proved not so easy. He had got over the rocks of "niggling"; he found himself in the shoals of exasperation.

II

She cut the first rose and held it to her lips, smelling it. "Lovely. Who was your letter from, Mark?"

He thought, "How on earth did she know?" He had forgotten it himself. "How ever did you know? From Lady Tybar. They're back."

"I saw you from the window with the postman. Lady Tybar! Whatever was she writing to you about?"

He somehow did not like this. Why "whatever"? And being watched was rather beastly; he remembered he had fiddled about with the letter,—half put it in his pocket and then taken it out again. And why not? What did it matter? But he had a prevision that it was going to matter. Mabel did not particularly like Nona. He said, "Just to say they're back. She wants us to go up there."

"An invitation? Whyever didn't she write to me?"

"Whyever" again!—"May I see it?"

He took the letter from his pocket and handed it to her. "It's not exactly an invitation—not formal."

She did what he called "flicked" the letter out of its envelope. He watched her reading it and in his mind he could see as perfectly as she with her eyes, the odd, neat script; in his mind he read it with her, word by word.

Dear Marko—We're back. We've been from China to Peru almost. Come up one day and be bored about it. How are you?

Nona.

His thought was, "Damn the letter!"

Mabel handed it back, without returning it to its envelope. She said, "No, it's not formal."

She snipped three roses with astonishing swiftness,—snip, snip, snip!

Sabre sought about in his mind for something to say. There was nothing in his mind to say. He had an absurd vision of his two hands feeling about in the polished interior of a skull, as one might fumble for something in a large jar.

At the end of an enormous cavity of time he found some slight remark about blight on the rose trees—the absence of it this year—and ventured it. He had again an absurd vision of dropping it into an enormous cavern, as a pea into an immense bowl, and it seemed to tinkle feebly and forlornly, as a pea would. "No blight this year, eh?"

"No; is there?" agreed Mabel,—snip!

Nevertheless conversation arose from the forlorn pea and was maintained. They moved about the garden from flower bed to flower bed. In half an hour the shallow basket was beautified with fragrant blooms and Mabel thought she had enough.

"Well, that's that," said Sabre as they reëntered the morning room.

III

Low Jinks, her matchless training at the level of mysteriously performed duties pat to the moment and without command, appeared with a tray of vases. Each vase was filled to precisely half its capacity with water. There were also a folded newspaper, a pair of small gilt scissors and a saucer. Low Jinks spread the newspaper at one end of the table, arranged the vases in a semicircle upon it, and placed the gilt scissors precisely in alignment with the right-hand vase of the semicircle, and the saucer (for the stalk ends) precisely in alignment with the left-hand vase. She then withdrew, closing the door with exquisite softness. Sabre had never seen this rite before. The perfection of its performance was impressive. He thought, "Mabel is marvellous." He said, "Shall I take them out of the basket?"

"No, leave them. I take them up just as I want them."

She took up a creamy rose and snipped off a fragment of stalk over the saucer. "Why does she call you 'Marko'?"

He was utterly taken aback. If the question had come from any one but Mabel, he would have quite failed to connect it with the letter. But there had distinctly been an "incident" over the letter, though so far closed, as he had imagined, that he was completely surprised.

He said "Who? Nona?"

"Yes, Nona, if you like. Lady Tybar."

"Why, she always has. You know that."

Mabel put the rose into a specimen vase with immense care and touched a speck off its petals with her fingers. "I really didn't."

"Mabel, you know you do. You must have heard her."

"Well, I may have. But long ago. I certainly didn't know she used it in letters."

He felt he was growing angry.

"What on earth's the difference?"

"It seems to me there's a great deal of difference. I didn't know she wrote you letters."

He was angry. "Damn it, she doesn't write me letters."

She shrugged her shoulders. "You seem to get them anyway."

Maddening!

And then he thought, "I'm not going to let it be maddening. This is just what happens." He said, "Well, this is silly. I've known her—we've known one another—for years, since we were children, pretty well. She's called me by my Christian name since I can remember. You must have heard her. We don't see much of her—perhaps you haven't. I thought you had. Anyway, dash the thing. What does it matter?"

"It doesn't matter"—she launched a flower into a vase—"a bit. I only think it's funny, that's all."

"Well, it's just her way."

Mabel gave a little sniff. He thought it was over. But it wasn't over. "If you ask me, I call it a funny letter. You say your Christian name, but it isn't your Christian name—Marko! And then saying, 'How are you?' like that—"

"Like what? She just said it, didn't she?"

"Yes I know. And then 'Nona.' Don't you call that funny?"

"Well, I always used to call her 'Nona.' She'd have thought it funny, as you call it, to put anything else. I tell you it's just her way."

"Well, I think it's a very funny way and I think anybody else would think so. I don't like her. I never did like her."

There seemed no more to say.

IV

He walked up to his room. He closed the door behind him and sat on a straight-backed chair, his legs outthrust. Failure? He had come back home thus suddenly with immensely good intentions. Failure? On the whole, no. There was a great deal more he could have said downstairs, and a great deal more he had felt uncommonly inclined to say. But he had left the morning room without saying it, and that was good; that redeemed his sudden return from absolute failure.

Why had he returned? He "worked back" through the morning on the Fargus principle. Not because of his thoughts after the Twyning business; not because of the disturbance of the Twyning business. No.

He had returned because he had seen Nona. Thoughts—feelings—had been stirred within him by meeting her. And it had suddenly been rather hateful to have those thoughts and to feel that—that Mabel had no place in them.

Well, why had he come up here? What was he doing up here? Well, it hadn't been altogether successful. Mabel hadn't been particularly excited to see him. No, but that didn't count. Why should she be? He had gone off after breakfast, glum as a bear. Well, then there was that niggling business over why he had returned. Always like that. Never plump out over a thing he put up. Niggling. And then this infernal business about the letter. That word "funny." She must have used it a hundred times. Still.... The niggling had been carried off, they had gone into the garden together; and this infernal letter business—at least he had come away without boiling over about it. Much better to have come away as he did.... Still....

V

A gong boomed enormously through the house. It had been one of her father's wedding presents to Mabel and it always reminded Sabre of the Dean's, her father's voice. The Dean's voice boomed, swelling into a loud boom when he was in mid-speech and reverberating into a distant boom as his periods terminated. This was the warning gong for lunch. In ten minutes, in this perfectly ordered house, a different gong, a set of chimes, would announce that lunch was ready. The reverberations had scarcely ceased when Low Jinks, although she had caused the reverberations, appeared in his room with a brass can of hot water.

"Mr. Boom Bagshaw has not arrived yet, sir," said Low Jinks; "but the mistress thought we wouldn't wait any longer."

She displaced the ewer from the basin and substituted the brass can. She covered the can with a white towel, uncovered the soap dish, and disappeared, closing the door as softly as if it and the doorpost were padded with velvet. Perfect establishment!

Sabre washed his hands and went down. Mabel was in the morning room, seated at the centre table where the flowers had been and where now was her embroidery basket. She was embroidering, an art which, in common with all the domestic arts, she performed to perfection. "Bagshaw's late?" said Sabre.

Mabel glanced at the clock. Her gesture above her busy needle was pretty.

"Well, he wasn't absolutely sure about coming. I thought we wouldn't wait. Ah, there he is."

Sabre thought, "Good. That business is over. Nothing in it. Only Mabel's way."

Sounds in the hall. "In the morning room," came Low Jinks's voice. "Lunch ... wash your hands, sir?"

There was only one person in all England who, arriving at Crawshaws, would not have been gently but firmly enfolded by the machine-like order of its perfect administration and been led in and introduced with rites proper to the occasion. But that one person was the Reverend Cyril Boom Bagshaw, and he now strolled across the threshold and into the room.

VI

He strolled in. He wore a well-made suit of dark grey flannel, brown brogue shoes and a soft collar with a black tie tied in a sailor's knot. He disliked clerical dress and he rarely wore it. He was dark. His good-looking face bore habitually a rather sulky expression as though he were a little bored or dissatisfied. You would never have thought, to look at him, that he was a clergyman, or, as he would have said, a priest, and in not thinking that you would have paid him the compliment that pleased him most. This was not because Mr. Boom Bagshaw lacked earnestness in his calling, for he was enormously in earnest, but because he disliked and despised the conventional habits and manners and appearance of the clergy and, in any case, intensely disliked being one of a class. For the same reasons he wore a monocle; not because the vision of his right eye was defective but because no clergyman wears a monocle. It is not done by the priesthood and that is why the Reverend Cyril Boom Bagshaw did it.

He strolled negligently into the morning room, his hands in his trouser pockets, the skirt of his jacket rumpled on his wrists. He gave the impression of having been strolling about the house all day and of now strolling in here for want of a better room to stroll into. He nodded negligently to Sabre, "Hullo, Sabre." He smiled negligently at Mabel and seated himself negligently on the edge of the table, still with his hands in his pockets. He swung one leg negligently and negligently remarked, "Good morning, Mrs. Sabre. Embroidery?"

Sabre had the immediate and convinced feeling that the negligent and reverend gentleman was not in his house but that he was permitted to be in the house of the negligent and reverend gentleman. And this was the feeling that the negligent and reverend gentleman invariably gave to his hosts, whoever they might be; likewise to his congregations. Indeed it was said by a profane person (who fortunately does not enter this history) that the Deity entered Mr. Boom Bagshaw's church on the same terms, and accepted them.

As he sat negligently swinging his leg he frequently strained his chin upwards and outwards, rather as if his collar were tight (but it was neatly loose), or as if he were performing an exercise for stretching the muscles of his neck. This was a habit of his.

VII

A silver entrée dish was placed before Mabel, another before Sabre. Low Jinks removed her mistress's cover and Mr. Boom Bagshaw pushed aside a flower vase to obtain a view.

"I don't eat salmon," he remarked. The vase was now between himself and Sabre. He again moved it, "Or cutlets."

Mabel exclaimed, "Oh, dear! Now I got this salmon in specially from Tidborough."

"I'll have some of that ham," said Mr. Boom Bagshaw; and he arose sulkily and strolled to the sideboard where he rather sulkily cut from a ham in thick wedges. The house was clearly his house.

He addressed himself to Mabel. "Now in a very few weeks you'll no longer have to get things from Tidborough, Mrs. Sabre—salmon or anything else. The shops in Market Square are going the minute they're complete. I got a couple of fishmongers only yesterday."

He spoke as if he had shot a brace of fishmongers and slung them over his shoulder and flung them into Market Square. Market Square was that portion of the Garden Home designed for the shopping centre.

"Two!" said Mabel.

"Two. I encourage competition. No one is going to sleep in the Garden Home."

"What will all the bedrooms be used for then?" Sabre inquired.

Mr. Boom Bagshaw, who was eating his ham with a fork only, holding it at its extremity in the tips of his fingers and occasionally flipping a piece of ham into his mouth and swallowing it without visible mastication, flipped in another morsel and with his right hand moved three more vases which stood between himself and Sabre. He moved each deliberately and set it down with a slight thump, rather as if it were a chessman.

He directed the fork at Sabre and after an impressive moment spoke:

"You know, Sabre, I don't think you're quite alive to what it is that is growing up about you. Flippancy is out of place. I abominate flippancy." ("Well, dash it, it's my house!" Sabre thought.) "This Garden Home is not a speculation. It's not a fad. It's not a joke. What is it? You're thinking it's a damned nuisance. You're right. It is a damned nuisance—"

Sabre began, "Well—"

"Now, listen, Sabre. It is a damned nuisance; and I put it to you that, when a toad is discovered embedded in a solid mass of coal or stone, that coal or stone, when it was slowly forming about that toad, was a damned nuisance to the toad."

Sabre asked, "Well, am I going to be discovered embedded—"

"Now, listen, Sabre. Another man in my place would say he did not intend to be personal. I do intend to be personal. I always am personal. I say that this Garden Home is springing up about you and that you are not realising what is happening. This Garden Home is going to enshrine life as it should be lived. More. It is going to make life be lived as it should he lived. Some one said to me the other day—the Duchess of Wearmouth; I was staying at Wearmouth Castle—that the Garden Home is going to be a sanctuary. I said 'Bah!' like that—'Bah!' I said, 'Every town, every city, every village is a sanctuary; and asleep in its sanctuary; and dead to life in its sanctuary; and dead to Christ in its sanctuary.' I said, 'The Garden Home is not going to be a sanctuary, nor yet a sepulchre, nor yet a tomb. It is going to be a symbol, a signal, a shout.' More ham."

He paused, pushed his plate to one side more as if it had bitten him than as if he desired more ham to be placed upon it, and looked around the room before him, sulkily, and exercising his chin.

Sabre had a vision of dense crowds of bishops in lawn sleeves, duchesses in Gainsborough hats, and herds of intensely fashionable rank and file applauding vigorously. He could almost hear the applause. But how to deal with this man he never knew. He always felt he was about fourteen when Mr. Boom Bagshaw thus addressed him. He therefore said, "Great!" and Mabel murmured, "How splendid!"

VIII

But Sabre's thought was—and it remained with him throughout the meal, acutely illustrated by the impressive monologues which Mr. Boom Bagshaw addressed to Mabel, and by her radiant responses— his thought was, "I simply can't get on with this chap—or with any of Mabel's crowd. They all make me feel like a kid. I can't answer them when they talk. They say things I've got ideas about but I never can explain my ideas to them. I never can argue my ideas with them. They've all got convictions and I believe I haven't any convictions. I've only got instincts and these convictions come down on instincts like a hammer on an egg."

Mr. Boom Bagshaw was saying, "And we shall have no poor in the Garden Home. No ugly streets. No mean surroundings. Uplift. Everywhere uplift."

There slipped out of Sabre aloud, "There you are. That's the kind of thing."

Mr. Boom Bagshaw, as if to disclose without fear precisely where he was, dismantled from between them the hedge of flowers which he had replaced and looked sulkily across. "What kind of thing?"

Sabre had a vision of himself advancing an egg for Mr. Bagshaw's hammer. "About having no poor in the Garden Home. Isn't there something about the poor being always with us?"

"Certainly there is."

"In the Bible?"

"In the Bible. Do you know to whom it was addressed?"

Sabre admitted that he didn't.

"To Judas Iscariot." (Smash went the egg!)

Sabre said feebly—he could not handle his arguments—"Well, anyway, 'always with us'—there you are. If you're going to create a place where life is going to be lived as it should be lived, I don't see how you're going to shut the poor out of it. Aren't they a part of life? They've got as much right to get away from mean streets and ugly surroundings as we have—and a jolly sight more need. Always with us. It doesn't matter tuppence whom it was said to."

"It happens," pronounced Mr. Boom Bagshaw, "to matter a great deal more than tuppence. It happens to knock the bottom clean out of your argument. It was addressed to the Iscariot because the Iscariot was trying to do just what you are trying to do. He was trying to make duty to the poor an excuse for grudging service to Christ. Now, listen, Sabre. If people thought a little less about their duty towards the poor and a little more about their duty towards themselves, they would be in a great deal fitter state to help their fellow creatures, poor or rich. That is what the Garden Home is to do for those who live in it, and that is what the Garden Home is going to do."

He stabbed sharply with the butt of a dessert knife on the dessert plate which had just been placed before him. The plate split neatly into two exact halves. He gazed at them sulkily, put them aside, drew another plate before him, and remarked to Mabel:

"You know we are moving into the vicarage to-morrow? We are giving an At Home to-morrow week. You will come."

The plural pronoun included his mother. He was intensely celibate.

IX
The day ended in a blazing row.

In the afternoon Mr. Boom Bagshaw carried off Mabel to view the progress of the Garden Home. While they dallied over coffee at the luncheon table, Sabre was fidgeting for Bagshaw to be gone. Mabel, operating dexterously behind the blue flame of a spirit lamp, Low Jinks hovering around in well-trained acolyte performances, said, "Now I rather pride myself on my Turkish coffee, Mr. Boom Bagshaw."

Mr. Bagshaw, who appeared to pride himself at least as much on his characteristics, replied by sulkily looking at his watch; and a moment later by sulkily taking a cup, rather as if he were a schoolboy bidden to take lemonade when mannishly desirous of shandygaff, and sulkily remarking, "I must go."

Sabre fidgeted to see the words put into action. He wanted Bagshaw to be off. He wanted to resume his sudden intention of remedying his normal relations with Mabel and the afternoon promised better than the intention had thus far seen. That niggling over the unexpectedness of his return,—well, of course it was unexpected and upsetting of her household routine; but the unexpectedness was over and the letter incident over, and Mabel, thanks to her guest, delightfully mooded. Good, therefore, for the afternoon. When the dickens was this chap going?

Then Bagshaw, rising sulkily, "Well, you'd better come up and have a look round."

And Mabel, animatedly, "I'd like to"; and to Sabre, "You won't care to come, Mark."

Sabre said, "No, I won't."

X

Throughout dinner—Mabel returned only just in time to get ready for dinner—Sabre examined with dispassionate interest the exercise of trying to say certain words and being unable to say them. They conversed desultorily; in their usual habit. He told himself that he was speaking several hundred "other" words; but the intractable words that he desired to utter would not be framed. He counted them on his fingers under the table. Only seven: "Well, how was the Garden Home looking?" Only seven. He could not say them. The incident they brought up rankled. He had come home to take a day off with her. She knew he was there at the luncheon table to take a day off with her. It had interested her so little, she had been so entirely indifferent to it, that she had not even expressed a wish he should so much as attend her on the inspection with Bagshaw. The more he thought of it the worse it rankled. She knew he was at home to be with her and she had deliberately walked off and left him.... "Well, how was the Garden Home looking?" No. Not much. He couldn't. He visualised the impossible seven written on the tablecloth. He saw them in script; he saw them in print; he imagined them written by a finger on the wall. Say them—no.

Mabel left him sitting at the table with a cigarette. There came suddenly to his assistance in the fight with the stubborn seven, abreast of the thoughts in the office that had brought him home, a realisation of her situation such as he had had that first night together in the house, eight years before; there she was in the morning room, alone. She had given up her father's home for his home—and there she was: a happy afternoon behind her and no one to discuss it with. Just because he could not say, "Well, how was the Garden Home looking?"

He thought, "I'm hateful." He got up vigorously and strode into the morning room: "Well, how was the Garden Home looking?" His voice was bright and interested.

She was reading a magazine. She did not raise her eyes front the page. "Eh? Oh, very nice. Delightful."

"Tell us about it."

"What? Oh ... yes." Her mind was in the magazine. She read on a moment. Then she laid the magazine on her lap and looked up. "The Garden Home? Yes—oh, yes. It was charming. It's simply springing up. You ought to have come."

He stretched himself in a big chair opposite her. He laughed. "Well, dash it, I like that. You didn't exactly implore me to."

She yawned. "Oh, well. I knew you wouldn't care about it." She yawned again, "Oh dear. I'm tired. We must have walked miles, to and fro." She put down her hands to take up her magazine again. She clearly was not interested by his interest. But he thought, "Well, of course she's not. For her it's like eating something after it's got cold. Dinner was the time."

He said, "I expect you did—walk miles. Bagshaw all over it, I bet."

She did what he called "tighten herself." "Well, naturally, he's pleased—enthusiastic. He's done more than any one else to keep the idea going."

Sabre laughed. "I should say so! Marvellous person! What's he going to do about not wearing clerical dress when he has to wear gaiters?"

"What do you mean—gaiters?"

Signs of flying up. What on earth for? "Why, when he's a bishop. Don't you—"

She flew up. "I suppose that's some sneer!"

"Sneer! Rot. I mean it. A chap like Bagshaw's not going to be a parish priest all his life. He's out to be a bishop and he'll be a bishop. If he changed his mind and wanted to be a Judge or a Cabinet Minister, he'd be a Judge or a Cabinet Minister. He's that sort."

"I knew you were sneering."

"Mabel, don't be silly. I'm not sneering. Bagshaw's a clever—"

"You say he's 'that sort.' That's a sneer." She put her hands on the arms of her chair and raised herself to sit upright. She spoke with extraordinary intensity. "Nearly everything you say to me or to my friends is a sneer. There's always something behind what you say. Other people notice it—"

"Other people."

"Yes. Other people. They say you're sarcastic. That's just a polite way—"

He said, "Oh, come now, Mabel. Not sarcastic. I swear no one thinks I'm sarcastic. I promise you Bagshaw doesn't. Bagshaw thinks I'm a fool. A complete fool. Look at lunch!"

She caught him up. She was really angry. "Yes. Look at lunch. That's just what I mean. Any one that comes to the house, any of my friends, anything they say you must always take differently, always argue about. That's what I call sneering—"

He, flatly, "Well, that isn't sneering. Let's drop it."

She had no intention of dropping it. "It is sneering. They don't know it is. But I know it is."

XI

He had the feeling that his anger would arise responsive to hers, as one beast calling defiance to another, if this continued. And he did not want it to arise. He had sometimes thought of anger as a savage beast chained within a man. It had helped him to control rising ill-temper. He thought of it now: of her anger. He had a vision of it prowling, as a dark beast among caves, challenging into the night. He wished to retain the vision. His own anger, prowling also, would not respond while he retained the picture. It was prowling. It was suspicious. It would be mute while he watched it. While he watched it....

He pulled himself sharply to his feet.

"Well, well,", he said. "It's not meant to be sneering. Let's call it my unfortunate manner."

He stood before her, half-smiling, his hands in his pockets, looking down at her.

She said, "Perhaps you're different with your friends. I hope you are. With your friends."

He caught a glint in her eye as she repeated the words. Its meaning did not occur to him.

He bantered, "Oh, I'm not as bad as all that. And anyway, the friends are all the same friends. This place isn't so big."

Then that quick glint of her eye was explained—the flash before the discharge.

"Perhaps your friends are just coming back," she said. "Lady Tybar."

The vision of his dark anger broke away. Mute while he watched it, immediately it lifted its head and answered her own. "Look here—" he began; and stopped. "Look here," he said more quietly, "don't begin that absurd business again."

"I don't think it is absurd."

"No, you called it 'funny.'"

She drew in her feet as if to arise. "Yes, and I think it's funny. All of it. I think you've been funny all day to-day. Coming back like that!"

"I told you why I came back. To have a day off with you. Funny day off it's been! You're right there!"

"Yes, it has been a funny day off."

He thought, "My God, this bickering! Why don't I get out of the room?"

"Come back for a day off with me! It's a funny thing you came back just in time to get that letter! Before it was delivered! There! Now you know!"

He was purely amazed. He thought, and his amazement was such that, characteristically, his anger left him; he thought, "Well, of all the—!"

But she otherwise interpreted his astonishment. She thought she had made an advantage and she pressed it. "Perhaps you knew it was coming?"

"How on earth could I have known it was coming?"

She seemed to pause, to be considering. "She might have told you. You might have seen her."

He said, "As it happens, I did see her. Not three hours before I came back."

She seemed disappointed. She said, "I know you did. We met Lord Tybar."

And he thought, "Good lord! She was trying to catch me."

She went on, "You never told me you'd met them. Wasn't that funny?"

"If you'd just think a little you'd see there was nothing funny about it. You found the letter so amazingly funny that, to tell you the truth, I'd had about enough of the Tybars. And I've had about enough of them."

"I daresay you have—with me. Perhaps you'll tell me this—would you have told me about the letter if I hadn't seen you get it?"

He thought before he answered and he answered out of his thoughts. He said slowly, "I—don't—believe—I—would. I wouldn't. I wouldn't because I'd have known perfectly well that you'd have thought it—funny."

XII

No answer he could have made could have more exasperated her. "I—don't—believe—I—would."   Deliberation!   Something incomprehensible to her going on in his mind, and as a result of it a statement that no one on earth (she felt) but he would have made. Any one else would have said boldly, blusteringly, "Of course I would have told you about the letter." She would have liked that. She would have disbelieved it and she could have said, and enjoyed saying, she disbelieved it. Or any one else would have said furiously, "No, I'm damned if I'd have shown you the letter." She would have liked that. It would have affirmed her suspicions that there was "something in it"; and she wished her suspicions to be affirmed. It would have been something definite. Something justifiably incentive of anger, of resentment, of jealousy. Something she could understand.

For she did not understand her husband. That was her grievance against him. She never had understood him. That den incident in the very earliest days of their marriage had been an intimation of a way of looking at things that to her was entirely and exasperatingly inexplicable; and since then, increasingly year by year, her understanding had failed to follow him. He had retired farther and farther into himself. He lived in his mind, and she could by no means penetrate into his mind. His ideas about things, his attitude towards things, were wholly and exasperatingly incomprehensible to her.

"It's like," she had once complained to her father, "it's like having a foreigner in the house."

Things, in her expression, "went on" in his mind, and she could not understand what went on in his mind, and it exasperated her to know they were going on and that she could not understand them.

106

"I—don't—believe—I—would." Characteristic, typical expression of those processes of his mind that she could not understand! And then the reason: "I wouldn't because I'd have known perfectly well that you'd have thought it—funny."

And, exasperation on exasperation's head, he was right. She did think it funny; and by his very reply—for she knew him well enough, so exasperatingly well, to know that this was complete sincerity, complete truth—he proved to her that it was not really funny but merely something she could not understand. Robbery of her fancy, her hope that it was something definite against him, something justifiably incentive of resentment, of jealousy!

It was as if he had said, "You can't understand a letter like this. There's nothing in it to understand. And that's just what you can't understand. Look here, you see my head. I'm in there. You can't come in. You don't know how to. I can't tell you how to. Nobody could tell you. And you wouldn't know what to make of it if you did get in."

Exasperating. Insufferable. Insupportable!

She could not express her feelings in words. She expressed them in action. She arose violently and left the room. The whole of her emotions she put into the slam of the door behind her. The ornaments shivered. A cup sprang off a bracket and dashed itself to pieces on the floor.

XIII

Sabre regarded the broken cup much as Sir Isaac Newton presumably regarded the fallen apple. He "worked back" from the cup through the events of the day, and through the events of the day returned to the cup. It interested him to find that the fragments on the floor were as logical a result of the movements of the day as they would have been of getting the small hand axe out of the woodshed, aiming a blow at the cup, and hitting the cup.

He thought, "I started to break that cup when I rustled the newspaper at breakfast. I went on when I suddenly came back and got into that niggling business over why I had come back. Went on when I walked off to my room after that letter business. Practically took up the axe when I couldn't say, 'Well, how's the Garden Home going on?' at dinner. And smashed it when I chaffed about Bagshaw an hour ago. Rum business! Rotten business."

That was the day's epitaph. But for the murder of the cup he found— gone to bed and lying awake—a culprit other than himself. He thought, "It was meeting Nona made me come home like that. But if that had been the first time I'd ever met Nona I shouldn't have returned. So it goes back further than that. Nine—ten years. The day she married Tybar. If she hadn't married Tybar she'd have married me. The cup wouldn't have been broken. Nona broke that cup."

CHAPTER IV

I

These events were on a Monday. On the following Thursday Nona came to see him at his office.

She was announced through the speaking-tube on his desk:

"Lady Tybar to see you, sir."

Nona! But he was not really surprised. He had taken no notice of her letter. He had wanted to go up to Northrepps to see her, but he had not been. When two days passed and still he prevented himself from going, he began to have the feeling—somehow—that she would come to see him. It was the third day and she was here, downstairs.

"Ask her to come up," he said.

She came in. She wore (as Sabre saw it) "a pale-blue sort of thing" and "a sort of black hat." He had considered it as an odd thing, in his thoughts of her since their meeting, that, though he could always have some kind of notion what other women were wearing, he never could remember any detail of Nona's dress.

But it was her face he always looked at.

She stood still immediately she was across the threshold and the door closed behind her. She was smiling as though she felt herself to be up to some lark. "Hullo, Marko. Don't you hate me for coming in here like this?"

"It's jolly surprising."

"That's another way of saying it. Now if you'd said it was surprisingly jolly! Well, shake hands, Marko, and pretend you're glad."

He laughed and put out his hand. But she delayed response; she first slipped off the gauntlets she was wearing and then gave him her hand. "There!" she said.

"There!" It was as though she had now done something she much wanted to do; as one says "There!" on at last sitting down after much fatigue.

109

She tossed her gauntlets on to a chair. She walked past him towards the window. "You got my letter?"

"Yes."

Her face was averted. Her voice had not the bantering note with which she had spoken at her entry.

"You never answered it."

"Well, I'd just seen you—just before I got it."

She was looking out of the window. "Why haven't you been up?"

"Oh—I don't know. I was coming."

"Well, I had to come," she said.

He made no reply. He could think of none to make.

II

She turned sharply away from the window and came towards him, radiant again, as at her entry. And in her first bantering tone, "I know you hate it," she smiled, resuming her first suggestion, "me coming here, like this. It makes you feel uncomfortable. You always feel uncomfortable when you see me, Marko. I'd like to know what you thought when they told you I was here—"

He started to speak.

She went on, "No, I wouldn't. I'd like to know just what you were doing before they told you. Tell me that, Marko."

"I believe I wasn't doing anything. Just thinking."

"Well, I like you best when you're thinking. You puzzle, don't you, Marko? You've got a funny old head. I believe you live in your old head, you know. Puzzling things. Clever beast! I wish I could live in mine." And she gave a note of laughter.

"Where do you live, Nona?"

"I don't live. I just go on"—she paused—"flotsam."

Strange word to use, strangely spoken!

It seemed to Sabre to drop with a strange, detached effect into the conversation between them. His habit of visualising inanimate things caused him to see as it were a pool between them at their feet, and from the word dropped into it ripples that came to his feet upon his margin of the pool and to her feet upon hers.

III

He took the word away from its personal application. "I believe that's rather what I was thinking about when you came, Nona. About how we just go on—flotsam. Don't you know on a river where it's tidal, or on the seashore at the turn, the mass of stuff you see there, driftwood and spent foam and stuff, just floating there, uneasily, brought in and left there—from somewhere; and then presently the tide begins to take it and it's drawn off and moves away and goes—somewhere. Arrives and floats and goes. That's mysterious, Nona?"

She said swiftly, as though she were stirred, "Oh, Marko, yes, that's mysterious. Do you know sometimes I've seen drift like that, and I've felt—oh, I don't know. But I've put out a stick and drawn in a piece of wood just as the stuff was moving off, just to save it being carried away into—well, into that, you know."

"Have you, Nona?"

She answered, "Do you think that's what life is, Marko?"

"It's not unlike," he said. And he added, "Except about some one coming along with a stick and drawing a bit into safety. I'm not so sure about that. Perhaps that's what we're all looking for—"

He suddenly realised that he was back precisely at the thoughts his mind had taken up on the morning he had met her. But with a degree more of illumination. Two feelings came into his mind, the second hard upon the other and overriding it, as a fierce horseman might catch and override one pursued. He said, "It's rather jolly to have some one that can see ideas like that." And then the overriding, and he said with astonishing roughness, "But you—you aren't flotsam! How can you be flotsam—the life you've—taken?"

And, lo, if he had struck her, and she been bound, defenceless, and with her eyes entreating not to be struck again, she could not deeper have entreated him than in the glance she fleeted from her eyes, the quiver of her lids that first released, then veiled it.

It stopped his words. It caught his throat.

IV

He got up quickly. "I say, Nona, never mind about thinking. I'll tell you what's been doing. Rotten. Happened just after I met you the other day."

"The dust on these roads!" she said. She touched her eyes with her handkerchief. "What, Marko?"

"Well, old Fortune promised to take me into partnership about an age ago."

"Marko, he ought to have done it an age ago. What's there rotten about that?" Her voice and her air were as gay as when she had entered.

"The rotten thing is that he's turned it down. At least practically has. He—" He told her of the Twyning and Fortune incident. "Pretty rotten of old Fortune, don't you think?"

"Old fiend!" said Nona. "Old trout!"

Sabre laughed. "Good word, trout. The men here all say he's like a whale. They call him Jonah," and he told her why.

She laughed gaily. "Marko! How disgusting you are! But I'm sorry. I am. Poor old Marko.... Of course it doesn't matter a horse-radish what an old trout like that thinks about your work, but it does matter, doesn't it? I know how you feel. They had an author man at a place we were staying at the other day—Maurice Ash—and he told me that although he says it doesn't matter, and knows it doesn't matter, when an absolutely trivial person says something riling about any of his stuff, still it does matter. He said a thing you've produced out of yourself you can't bear to have slighted—not by the butcher. Gladys Occleve made us laugh. Maurice Ash said to her, 'It's like a mother's child. Look here, you're a countess,' he said to her. 'You oughtn't to mind what a butcher thinks of your children; but supposing the butcher said your infant Henry was a stupid little brat; what would you do?' Gladys said she'd dash a best end of the neck straight into his face."

Sabre laughed. "Yes, that's the feeling. But of course, all these books"—he indicated the shelves—"aren't mine, not my children, more like my adopted children."

She declared it was the same thing. "More so, in a way. You've invented them, haven't you, called them out of the vasty deep sort of thing and brought them up in the way they should go. I do think it's rather fine, Marko."

She was at the shelves, scanning the books. Her fond, her almost tender sympathy made him, too, feel that it was rather fine. Her light words in her high, clear tone voiced exactly his feelings towards the books. Talking with her was, in the reception and return of his thoughts, nearer to reading a book that delighted him than to anything else with which he could compare it. There was the same interchange of ideas, not necessarily expressed; the same creation and play of fancy, imagined, not stated.

Her hands were moving about the volumes, pulling out a book here and there; she mused the titles. "'Greek Unseens—Prose'; 'Greek Unseens—Verse'; 'Latin Unseens—Verse.' Marvellous person, Marko! 'The Shell Algebra'; 'The Shell Latin Grammar'; 'The Shell English Literature': 'The Shell Modern Geography.' That's a series 'The Shell,' eh? I do call that a good idea. 'The Six Terms Chemistry'; 'The Six Terms Geology.'"

"Yes, that's another series," he said. He was standing beside her. Delightful this! His pride in his work thrilled anew. "You see the idea of the thing. Gives the boy the feeling of something definite to get through in a definite time."

She was reading one of the prefaces, signed with his initials. "Yes, that's ever so good. I see what you've written here, '...avoiding the formidable and unattractive wilderness that a new textbook commonly presents to the pupil's mind.' I call that jolly good, Marko. I call it all awfully good. Fancy you sitting in here and thinking out all those ideas. Or do you think them out at home? Do you talk them out with Mabel?"

113

He thought of Mabel's expression. "Those lesson books." He lied. "Oh, yes. Pretty often."

"Show me which was the first one of all—the one you began with."

He showed her. "Fancy!" She handled it. "How fearfully proud of it you must have been, Marko. And Mabel; wasn't she proud? The very first!" She called it "Dear thing" and returned it to its place with a little pat, as of affection.

He turned away. "Oh, well, that's enough," he said.

V

She moved about the room, touching things, looking at things.

"Show me something else. Is that where the old trout basks? Can he hear us? I'm glad I've seen your room, Marko. I shall imagine you puzzling in here."

Touching things, looking at things.... He thought the room would always look different—after this. He felt strangely disturbed. He could with difficulty reply to her. His mind threw back, in its habit, to some dim occasion when he had felt in some degree as he was feeling now. When? Certainly he had felt it before. When?

He remembered. It was a Saturday in the first month of his first term at Tidborough School when his father had come over to see him. The loneliness of newness was still upon him. He had been affected almost to tears by being with some one whose mind was open, as it were, for him to jump into: some one to whom he could open his mind, unseal the home thoughts, unlock the timid tongue. He had talked how he had talked! He had felt bursting to talk; and only talking could ease the feeling; and how it had eased! Yes, this was the same again. He did not want her to go. He wanted to talk—how he wanted to talk!—to tell, unseal, unlock, expose.

He said, "I tell you what, Nona. I'll tell you something. I've an idea sometimes of cutting out from all this place and starting an educational publishing business on my own."

She was enormously interested. "Oh, Marko, if only you would!"

"Well, I think about it. I do. I can see a biggish thing in it. The Tidborough Press, I'd call it. Like the University Press, you know, Oxford and Cambridge. By Jove, it might go any distance, you know!"

"Oh, you must! You must!"

He began to pour out the tremendous and daring scheme.

VI

He talked animatedly,—these long pent up enthusiasms. She attended, rapt and gleaming-eyed, following him with most delicious "Yes— yes" and with little nods; and he suddenly became aware of how poignant to him was the sympathy of her interest,—and stopped. Thus to pour out, thus to be heard, was to experience the exquisite pain that comes with sudden relief of intolerable pain, as when an anodyne steals through the veins of torture. He stopped. He could not bear it.

"Well, that's all," he said.

She declared, "It's splendid. How well you're doing, Marko. I knew you would." She paused. "Not that that matters," she said.

He asked her, "What do you mean—'not that that matters'?"

She made a little face at him. "Marko, you're not to snap me up like that. I've noticed it two or three times. I mean it doesn't matter what a man does. It's what he is that matters."

He laughed. "Well, that lets me down pretty badly if that's the estimate. I'm awful, you know."

She shook her head. "Oh, you're not so bad."

"You don't know me. I've been growing awful these years."

"Tell me how awful you are. Does Mabel think you're awful?"

"You ask her! I'm the most unsatisfactory sort of person it's possible to meet. Really."

"Go on; tell me, Marko. I like this."

"What, like hearing how unsatisfactory I am?"

"I like hearing you talk. You've got rather a nice voice—I used to tell you that, didn't I?—and I like hearing you stumbling about trying to explain your ideas. You've got ideas. You're rather an ideary person. Go on. Why are you unsatisfactory?"

How familiar her voice was on that note,—caressing, drawing him on.

He said, "I'll tell you, Nona. I'm unsatisfactory because I've got the most infernal habit of seeing things from about twenty points of view instead of one. For other people, that's the most irritating thing you can possibly imagine. I've no convictions; that's the trouble. I swing about from side to side. I always can see the other side of a case, and you know, that's absolutely fatal—"

She said gently, "Fatal to what, Marko?"

He was going to say, "To happiness"; but he looked at her and then looked away. "Well, to everything; to success. You can't possibly be successful if you haven't got convictions—what I call bald-headed convictions. That's what success is, Nona, the success of politicians and big men whose names are always in the papers. It's that: seeing a thing from only one point of view and going all out for it from that point of view. Convictions. Not mucking about all round a thing and seeing it from about twenty different sides like I do. You know, you can't possibly pull out this big, booming sort of stuff they call success if you're going to see anybody's point of view but your own. You must have convictions. Yes, and narrower than that, not convictions but conviction. Only one conviction—that you're right and that every one who thinks differently from you is wrong to blazes." He laughed. "And I'm dashed if I ever think I'm right, let alone conviction of it. I can always see the bits of right on the other side of the argument. That's me. Dash me!"

She said, "Go on, Marko. I like this."

"Well, that's all there is to it, Nona. These conviction chaps, these booming politicians and honours-list chaps, these Bagshaw chaps— you know Bagshaw?—they go like a cannon ball. They go like hell and smash through and stick when they get there. My sort's like the footballs you see down at the school punt-about. Wherever there's a punt I feel it and respond to it. My sort's out to be kicked—" He laughed again. "But I couldn't be any other sort."

She said, "I'm glad you couldn't be, Marko. You're just the same as you used to be. I'm glad you're the same."

He did not reply.

VII

She sat briskly forward in the big armchair in which she faced him, making of the motion a movement as though throwing aside a turn the conversation had taken. "Well, go on, Marko. Go on talking. I'm not going to let you stop talking yet. I love that about how people get success nowadays. It's jolly true. I never thought of it before. Yes, you're still a terribly thinky person, Marko. Go on. Think some more. Out loud."

Caressing—drawing him on—just as of old.

He said thoughtfully, "I tell you a thing I often think a lot about, Nona. You being here like this puts it in my mind. Conventions."

She smiled teasingly. "Ah, poor Marko. I knew you'd simply hate it, my coming in like this. Does it seem terribly unconventional, improper, to you, shut up with me in your office?"

He shook his head. "It seems very nice. That's all it seems. But it does bring into my mind that you're the sort of person that doesn't think tuppence about what's usually done or what's not usually done; and that reminded me of things I've thought about conventions. Look here, Nona, this really is rather interesting—"

"Yes," she said. "Yes."

Just so he used to bring ideas to her; just so, with "Yes—yes," she used to receive them.

But he went on. "Why, convention, you know, it's the most mysterious, extraordinary thing. It's a code society has built up to protect itself and to govern itself, and when you go into it it's the most marvellous code that ever was invented. All sorts of things that the law doesn't give, and couldn't give, our conventions shove in on us in the most amazing way. And all probably originated by a lot of Mother Grundy-ish old women, that's what's so extraordinary. You know, if all the greatest legal minds of all the ages had laid themselves out to

117

make a social code they could never have got anywhere near the rules the people have built up for themselves. And that's what I like, Nona—that's what I think so interesting and the best thing in life: the things the people do for themselves without any State interference. That's what I'd encourage all I knew how if I were a politician—"

He broke off. "I say, aren't I the limit, gassing away like this? I hardly ever get off nowadays and when I do!—Why don't you stop me?"

She made a little gesture deprecatory of his suggestion. "Because I like to hear you. I like to watch your funny old face when you're on one of your ideas. It gets red underneath, Marko, and the red slowly comes up. Funny old face! Go on. I want to hear this because I'm going to disagree with you, I think. I think conventions, most of them, are odious, hateful, Marko. I hate them."

VIII

He had been strangely affected by the words of her interruptions: a contraction in the throat,—a twitching about the eyes.... But he was able, and glad that he was able to catch eagerly at her opinion. "Yes, yes, I know, odious, hateful, and much more than that, cruel— conventions can be as cruel, as cruel as hell. I was just coming to that. But they're all absolutely rightly based, Nona. That's the baffling and the maddening part of them. That's what interests me in them. In their application they're often unutterably wrong, cruel, hideously cruel and unjust, but when you examine them, even at their cruellest, you can't help seeing that fundamentally they're absolutely right and reasonable and necessary. Look, take quite a silly example. There's a convention against going to church in any but your best clothes. It's easy to conceive wrongness in the application of it. It's easy to conceive a person wanting to go to church and likely to benefit by going to church, but staying away because of feeling too shabby. But you can't help seeing the rightness at the bottom of it—the idea of presenting yourself decently at worship, as before princes. That makes you laugh—"

"It doesn't, Marko. I can see much worse things just on the same principle."

He said pleasedly, "Of course you can, can't you? Look at all this stuff there's been in the papers lately about what they call the problem of the unmarried mother. Now there's a brute of a case for you: a girl gets into trouble and while she sticks to her baby she's made an outcast;

every door is shut to her; her own people will have nothing to do with her; no one will take her in—so long as she's got the baby with her. That's convention and you can imagine cases where it's cruel beyond words. But it's no good cursing society about it. You can't help seeing that the convention is fundamentally right and essential. Where on earth would you be if girls with babies could find homes as easily as girls without babies?" He smiled. "You'd have babies pouring out all over the place. See it?"

She nodded. "I do think that's interesting, Marko. I think that's most awfully interesting. Yes, cruel and hateful and preposterous, many of them, but all fundamentally right. I think that's absorbing. I shall look out for conventions now, and when they annoy me most I'll think out what they're based on. I will!"

"Well, it's not a bad idea," he said. "It helps in all sorts of ways to think things out as they happen to you. You don't realise what a mysterious business life is till you begin to do that; and once you begin to feel the mysteriousness of it there's not much can upset you. You get the feeling that you're part of an enormous, mysterious game, and you just wonder what the last move means. Eh?"

She did not answer.

Presently she said, "Yes, you do still think things, Marko. You haven't changed a bit, you know. You're just the same."

He smiled. "Oh, well, it's only two years, you know—less than two years since you went away."

"I wasn't thinking of two years."

"How many years were you thinking of?"

"Ten."

They just sat there.

IX

The insistent shrieking of a motor siren in the street below began to penetrate their silence. When it came to Sabre's consciousness he had somehow the feeling that it had been going on a very long time. He

119

jumped to his feet. The siren had the obscene and terrific note of a gigantic hen in delirium. "What the devil's that?"

She received his question with the blank look of one whose mind had no idea of the question's reason. The strangled gurgle and shriek from without informed her in paroxysms of hideous sound. With a motion of her body, as of one shaking off dreams, she threw away the bemusement in which she had sat. She screwed up her face in torture. "Oh, wow! Isn't it too awful! That's Tony. In the car. I told him I'd look in here." She glanced at the clock. "Marko; it's one o'clock. I've been here two mortal hours!"

The gigantic hen screamed in delirious death agony.

"Oh, good heavens, that noise!" She stepped to the window and opened the casement. "Tony! That noise! Tony, for goodness' sake!"

An extravagantly long motor car was drawn against the curb. Lord Tybar, in a dust coat and a sleek bowler hat of silver grey, sat in the driver's seat. He was industriously and without cessation winding the handle of the siren. An uncommonly pretty woman sat beside him. She was massed in furs. In her ears she held the index finger of each hand, her elbows sticking out on each side of her head. Thus severally occupied, she and Lord Tybar made an unusual picture, and a not inconsiderable proportion of the youth and citizens of Tidborough stood round the front of the car and enjoyed the unusual picture that they made.

The spectators looked up at Nona's call; Lord Tybar ceased the handle and looked up with his engaging smile; the uncommonly pretty woman removed her fingers from her ears and also turned upwards her uncommonly pretty face.

"Hullo!" called Lord Tybar. "Did you happen to hear my sighs?"

"That appalling noise!" said Nona. "You ought to be prosecuted!"

"If you'd had it next to you!" piped the uncommonly pretty lady in an uncommonly pretty voice. "It's like a whole ship being seasick together."

"It's nothing of the kind," protested Lord Tybar. "It's the plaintive lament of a husband entreating his wife." He directed his eyes further backward. "Good morning, Mr. Fortune. Did you recognize my voice calling my wife? There were tears in it. Perhaps you didn't."

"Good lord," said Sabre, "there's old Fortune at his window. I'll come down with you, Nona."

As they went down he asked her, "Who's that with him in the car?"

"One of his friends. Staying with us."

Something in her voice made it—afterwards—occur to him as odd that she spoke of one of "his", not one of "our" friends, and did not mention her name.

"Well, the whole of Tidborough knows where you've been, Nona," Lord Tybar greeted them. "And a good place too." He addressed the lady by his side. "Puggo, look at those pulpits and things in the window. You never go to church. It'll do you good. That's a pulpit, that tall thing. They preach from that."

The lady remarked, "Thanks. I can remember it. At least I was married in a church, you know."

"And, of course," said Nona, "you always remember you're married, don't you?"

Sabre glanced quickly at her. Her tone cut across the frivolous exchanges with an acid note. So utterly unlike Nona!

And the thing was real, not imagined; and went further. The uncommonly pretty woman addressed as Puggo replied, "Oh, always. And so do you, don't you, dear?" and her uncommonly pretty eyes went in a quick glance from Nona's face to Sabre's, where they hovered the fraction of a moment, and thence to Lord Tybar's where also they hovered, and smiled.

And Lord Tybar, his small, handsome head slightly on one side, looked from one to another with precisely that mock in his glance that Sabre had noticed, and transiently wondered at, on the day he had met them riding.

Funny!

"But, Puggo, you don't know Sabre, do you?" Lord Tybar said. "Sabre, this is Mrs. Winfred. A woman of mystery. One mystery is how she ever won Fred and the other why she is called Puggo. There must be something pretty dark in her past to have got her a name like Puggo."

The woman of mystery shrugged her shoulders. "Of course Tony's simply a fool," she observed. "You know that, don't you, Mr. Sabre?"

"It's not her face," Lord Tybar continued. "You might think it's her figure the way she hides it up under all those furs on a day like this. But a pug's figure—"

Nona broke in. "I suppose we're going to start some time?"

"Will you come and sit here?" Puggo inquired, but without making any movement.

"No, I'll sit behind."

She got in. "Good-by, Marko." Her voice sounded tired. She gave Sabre her hand. "Jolly, the books," she said. "And our talk."

"Now throw yourself in front, any boy who wants to be killed," Lord Tybar called to the idlers. "No corpses to-day?" He let in the clutch. "Good-by, Sabre. Good-by, good-by." He waved his hand airily. The big car slid importantly up the street.

Sabre watched them pass out of sight. As the car turned out of The Precincts into High Street—a nasty corner—Lord Tybar, alone of the three, one hand on the steering wheel, half turned in his seat and twirled the silver-grey bowler in gay farewell.

Or mockery?

X

Through the day Sabre's thoughts, as a man sorting through many documents and coming upon and retaining one, fined down towards a picture of himself alone with Nona—alone with her, watching her beautiful face—and saying to her: "Look here, there were three things you said, three expressions you used. Explain them, Nona."

Fined down towards this picture, sifting the documents.

He thought, "Tybar—Tybar.—They're just alike in their way of saying things, Nona and Tybar. That bantering way they talk when they're together—when they're together. Tybar does, whoever he's with. Not Nona. Not with me. But with Tybar. She plays up to him when they're together. And he plays up to her. Everybody says how amusing they are. They're perfectly suited. They look so dashed handsome, the pair of them. And always that bantering talk. Nona chose deliberately between Tybar and me. I know she did. She loved me, till he came along. It's old. Ten years old. I can look at it. She chose deliberately. I can see her choosing: 'Tybar or Marko?—oh, dash it, Tybar.' And she chose right. She's just his mate. He's just her mate. They're a pair. That bantering, airy way of theirs together. That's just characteristic of the oneness of their characters. I couldn't put up that bantering sort of stuff. I never could. I'm a jolly sight too serious. And Nona knew it. She used to laugh at me about it. She still does. 'You puzzle, don't you, Marko?' she said this very morning."

He thought, "No, that wasn't laughing at me. Not that. No, it wasn't. Not that—nor any of it. What did she mean when she said 'There!' like that when she gave me her hand when she first came in? And took off her glove first. What did she mean when she said she had to come? 'Well, I had to come,' she said.—What did she mean when she said she was flotsam?—Flotsam! Why? Made me angry in my voice when I asked her. I said, 'How can you be flotsam?' And how the devil can she?—Nona, with Tybar, flotsam? But she said it. I said, 'How can you be flotsam, the life you've—taken?' I didn't mean to say 'taken' like that. I meant to have said 'the life you've got, you live.' But I meant taken, chosen. She did take it, deliberately. She chose between us. I might almost have heard her choose 'Marko or Tybar? Oh, dash it—Tybar.' I never reproached her, not by a look. I saw her point of view. My infernal failing, even then. Not by a look I ever reproached her. I thought I'd forgotten it, absolutely. But I haven't. It came out in that moment that I haven't. 'The life you've—taken!' I meant it to sting. Damn me, it did sting. That look she gave! As if I had struck her.— What rot! How could it sting her? How could she mind? Only if she regretted.—Is it likely?"

He thought, "But is she happy? Is it all what it appears between them? That remark she made to that woman and the extraordinary way she said it. 'You never forget you're married, do you?' Amazing thing to say, the way she said it. What did she mean? And that woman. She said something like, 'Nor you, do you?' and looked at me and then at

Tybar. And Tybar looked—at Nona, at me, as if he'd got some joke, some mock...."

He thought, "What rot! She chose. She knew he was her sort. She knew I wasn't. She chose deliberately...."

Clearly, as it were yesterday, he remembered the day she had declared to him her choice. In the Cathedral cloisters. Walking together. And suddenly, in the midst of indifferent things, she told him, "I say, Marko, I'm going to marry Lord Tybar."

And his reply, the model of indifference. "Are you, Nona?"

Nothing else said of it between them. There would certainly have been more discussion if she had said she was going to buy a packet of hairpins. And his thought had immediately been, not this nor that nor the other of a hundred thoughts proper to a blow so stunning, but merely and immediately and precisely that he would tell his father Yes to what that very morning he had told him No,—that he would go into the Fortune, East and Sabre business. Extraordinary effect from such a cause! Grotesque. Paradoxical. Going into Fortune, East and Sabre meant "settling down"; marriage conventionally involved settling down; yet, while he had visioned marriage with Nona, settling down had been the last thing in the world to think of,—because he projected marriage with Nona, he had that very morning rejected settling down. He was not to marry her; therefore, yes, he would settle down. Amazing. He had not realised how amazing till now.

And catastrophic. Not till now had he realised to what catastrophe he then had plunged. He thought, "The fact was Nona touched things in me that helped me. Without her I just shut down—I just go about— longing, longing, and all shut up, day after day, year after year—all shut up. And now there's this—she's come back like this—"

He came upon the picture of himself alone with Nona—alone with her watching her beautiful face—and saying to her, "Look here, there were three things you said, three expressions you used. Explain them, Nona. Explain 'There!' with your glove off. Explain 'Flotsam.' Explain 'Well, I had to come.' Explain them, Nona—for God's sake."

CHAPTER V

I

But it was October before he asked her to explain them. The Tybars, as he learnt when next he met her, a week after her visit to the office, were only at Northrepps for a breathing space after their foreign tour. Through the summer they were going the usual social round, ending in Scotland. Back in October for the shooting, and wintering there through the hunting season.

So she told him; and he thought while she was speaking, "All right. I'll accept that. That helps to stop me asking her. If an opportunity occurs before she goes I'll ask her. I must. But if it doesn't occur I'll accept that. I won't make an opportunity."

It did not occur, and he abode by his resolution. He met her once or twice, always in other company. And she was always then particularly gay, particularly airy, particularly bantering. But answering her banter he once caught an expression behind her airiness. He thought, "It is a shield"; and he turned away abruptly from her. He could not bear it.

This was on the occasion of a little dinner party at Northrepps to which he had come with Mabel; Major Hopscotch Millet and one or two others were among the guests. Major Millet, who had been in particularly hopscotch, Ri—te O! form throughout the evening, was walking back, but Mabel invited him to accompany them in the ancient village fly. "Ri—te O!" said Major Millet with enormous enthusiasm.

Nona came with them to the door on their departure. Sabre was last down the steps. "Well, I shan't see you again till October," she said.

"No, till October." He no more than touched her hand and turned away. He had kept his resolution.

She was close behind him. He heard her give the tiniest little catch at her breath. She said, "Shall I write to you, Marko?"

He turned towards her. She was smiling as though it was a chaffing remark she had made. Her shield!

And he answered her from behind his own shield, "Oh, well, I'm bad at letters, you know."

But their eyes met with no shields before them; and she was wounded, for he just caught her voice as he went down the steps, "Oh, Marko, do write to me!"

The Ri—te O voice of the Hopscotch. "Come on, Sabre, my boy! Come on! Come on!"

He got into the cab. Major Millet had taken the seat next Mabel. "Ri—te O, Cabby!" the Hopscotch hailed.

As the horse turned with the staggering motions proper to its burden of years and infirmity, Mabel inquired, "What was Lady Tybar talking to you about all that time?"

He said, "Oh, just saying good-by."

But he was thinking, "That's a fourth question: Why did you say, 'Oh, Marko, do write to me'? Or was that the answer to the other questions, although I never asked them?"

II

He did not write to her. But in October a ridiculous incident impelled afresh the urgent desire to ask her the questions: an incident no less absurd than the fact that in October Low Jinks knocked her knee.

Mabel spent two months of the summer on visits to friends. In August she was with her own people on their annual holiday at Buxton. There Sabre, who had a fortnight, joined her. It happened to be the fortnight of the croquet tournament, and it happened that Major Millet was also in Buxton. Curiously enough he had also been at Bournemouth, whence Mabel had just come from cousins, and they had played much croquet there together. It was projected as great fun to enter the Buxton tournament in partnership, and Sabre did not see a great deal of Mabel.

It was late September when they resumed life together at Penny Green. In their absence the light railway linking up the Garden Home with Tidborough and Chovensbury had been opened with enormous excitement and celebration; and Mabel became at once immersed in paying calls and joining the activities of the new and intensely active community.

Then Low Jinks knocked her knee.

The knee swelled and for two days Low Jinks had to keep her leg on a chair. It greatly annoyed Mabel to see Low Jinks sitting in the kitchen with her leg "stuck out on a chair." She told Sabre it was extraordinary how "that class of person" always got in such a horrible state from the most ridiculous trifles. "I suppose I knock my knee a dozen times a week, but my knee doesn't swell up and get disgusting. You're always reading in the paper about common people getting stung by wasps, or getting a scratch from a nail, and dying the next day. They must be in a horrible state. It always makes me feel quite sick."

Sabre laughed. "Well, I expect poor old Low Jinks feels pretty sick too."

"She enjoys it."

"What, sitting there with a knee like a muffin? I had a look at her just now. Don't you think she might have one of those magazines to read? She looks pretty sorry for herself."

Signs of "flying up." "You haven't given her a magazine, have you?"

"No—I haven't. But I told her I would after dinner."

"If you don't mind you won't. Rebecca has plenty to occupy her time. She can perfectly well clean the silver and things like that, and she has her sewing. She has upset the house quite enough with her leg stuck out on a chair all day without reading magazines."

And then in the extraordinary way in which discussions between them were suddenly lifted by Mabel on to unsuspected grievances against him, Sabre suddenly found himself confronted with, "You know how she hurt her knee, I suppose?"

He knew the tone. "No. My fault, was it?"

"Yes. As it happens, it was your fault—to do with you."

"Good lord! However did I manage to hurt Low Jinks's knee?"

"She did it bringing in your bicycle."

He thought, "Now what on earth is this leading up to?" During the weeks of his separation from Mabel, thinking often of Nona, he had caused himself to think from her to Mabel. His reasoning and reasonable habit of mind had made him, finding extraordinary rest in thought of Nona, accuse himself for finding none in thought of Mabel. She was his wife; he never could get away from the poignancy of that phrase. His wife—his responsibility towards her—the old thought, eight years old, of all she had given up in exchanging her own life for his life—and what was she getting? He set himself, on their reunion, always to remember the advantage he had over her: that he could reason out her attitude towards things; that she could not,—neither his attitude nor, what was more, her own.

Now. What was this leading up to? "She did it bringing in your bicycle." Puzzling sometimes over passages with Mabel that with mysterious and surprising suddenness had plunged into scenes, he had whimsically envisaged how he had been, as it were, led blindfolded to the edge of a precipice, and then, whizz! sent flying over on to the angry crags below.

Bantering protest sometimes averted the disaster. "Well, come now, Mabel, that's not my fault. That was your idea, making Low Jinks come out and meet me every evening as if the old bike was a foam-flecked steed. Wasn't it now?"

"Yes, but not in the dark."

Mysterious manoeuvring! But he felt he was approaching the edge. "In the dark?"

"Yes, not in the dark. What I mean is, I really cannot imagine why you must keep up your riding all through the winter. It was different when there was no other way. Now the railway is running I simply cannot imagine why you don't use it."

"Well, that's easy—because I like the ride."

"You can't possibly like riding back on these pitch dark nights, cold and often wet. That's absurd."

"Well, I like it a jolly sight better than fugging up in those carriages with all that gassing crowd of Garden Home fussers."

And immediately, whizz! he went over the edge.

"That's just it!" Mabel said. And he thought, "Ah!"

"That's just it. And of course you laugh. Why you can't be friendly with people like other men, I never can imagine. There're heaps of the nicest people up at the Garden Home, but from the first you've set yourself against them. Why you never like to make friends like other people!"

He did not answer.

They were at dinner. She made an elaborate business of reaching for the salt. "If you ask me, it's because you don't think they're good enough for you."

He thought, "That's to rouse me. I'm dashed if I'm going to be roused." He thought, "It's getting the devil, this. There's never a subject we start but we work up to something like this. We work on one another like acid on acid. In a minute she'll have another go at it, and then I shall fly off, and then there we'll be. It's my fault. She doesn't think out these things like I do. She just says what comes into her head, whereas I know perfectly well where we're driving to, so I'm really responsible. I rile her. I either rile her by saying something in trying not to fly off, or else I let myself go, and off I fly, and we're at it. Acid on acid. It's getting the devil, this. But I'm dashed if I'll fly off. It's up to me."

He tried in his mind for some matter that would change the subject. Extraordinary how hard it was to find a new topic when some other infernal thing hung in the air. It was like, in a nightmare, trying with leaden limbs to crawl away from danger.

And then she began:

She resumed precisely at the point where she had left off. While his mind had journeyed in review all around and about the relations between them, her mind had remained cumbrously at the thought of her last words. There, he told himself, was the whole difference between them. He was intellectually infinitely more agile (he did not put it higher than that) than she. She could not get away from things as he could. They remained in her mind and rankled there. To get impatient with her, to proceed from impatience to loss of temper, was flatly as cruel as to permit impatience and anger with one bedridden and therefore unable to join in robust exercises. He thought, "I'll not do it."

She said, actually repeating her last words, "Yes, if you ask me, it's because you don't think they're good enough for you. As it happens, there're all sorts of particularly nice men up there, only you never take the trouble to know them. And clever—the only thing you pretend to judge by; though what you can find clever in Mr. Fargus or those Perches goodness only knows. There're all sorts of Societies and Circles and Meetings up there that I should have thought were just what would have attracted you. But, no. You prefer that pottering Mr. Fargus with his childish riddles and even that young Perch without spirit enough to go half a yard without that everlasting old mother of his—"

It was longer and fiercer than he had expected. He intercepted. "I say, Mabel, what's the point of all this, exactly?"

"The point is that it makes it rather hard for me, the way you go on. I've made many, many friends up at the Garden Home. Do you suppose it doesn't seem funny to them that my husband is never to be seen, never comes near the place, never meets their husbands? Of course they must think it funny. I know I feel it very awkward."

He thought, "Girding! Sneering! Can't I get out of this?" Then he thought, "Dash it, man, it's only just her way. What is there in it?" He said, "Yes, but look here, Mabel, we started at my riding home in the dark—or rather at old Low Jinks's muffin knee. Let's work out the trouble about that."

"That's what I'm talking about. I think it's extraordinary of you to go riding by yourself all through the winter just to avoid people I'd like you to be friendly with. I ask you not to and you call it 'fugging up in railway carriages with them.' That was the elegant expression you used."

"Elegant." That was the word Nona had said she was going to have for her own.

He sat up in his chair. He was glad he had kept his mind detached all through this business. He was going to make an effort.

He said, "Well, listen, Mabel. I'll explain. This is me explaining. Behind this fork. I see what you mean. Perfectly well. I'm sorry. I'm absolutely rotten at meeting new people. I always have been. I never seem to have any conversation. They always think I'm just a fool— which, as a matter of fact, I always feel in a crowd. But apart from that. You've no idea how much I enjoy the bike ride. I wouldn't give it up for anything. I've tried to explain to you sometimes. It gets me away from things, and I like getting away from things. I feel—it's hard to explain a stupid thing like this—I feel as if I were lifted out of things and able to look at things from a sort of other-world point of view. It's jolly. Don't you remember I suggested to you, oh, years ago, when we were first—when we first came here, suggested you might ride in part of the way with me of a morning, and told you the idea of the thing? You didn't quite understand it—"

She pushed back her chair. "I don't understand it now," she said.

His eyes had been shining as they shone when he was interested or eager. He threw himself back in his seat. "Oh, well!"

She got up. She said in a very loud, very thin and edged voice, the little constrictions on either side of her nose extraordinarily deep:

"I never can understand any of your ideas, except that no one else ever seems to have them. Except your Fargus friends perhaps. I should keep them for them if I were you. Anyway, all I wanted to say I've said. All I wanted to say was that, if you persist in riding home in the dark, I really cannot allow Rebecca to go out and bring in your bicycle. After this leg of hers is over, if it ever is over, I really cannot allow it any more. That's all I wanted to say."

She left the room.

He began to fumble with extraordinary intensity in the pocket of his dinner jacket for his cigarette case. He could feel it, but his fingers seemed all thumbs. He got it out and it slipped through his fingers on to the table. His hands were shaking.

CHAPTER VI

I

A draper occupied the premises opposite Fortune, East and Sabre's. On the following afternoon, just before five o'clock, Sabre saw Nona alight from her car and go into the draper's. He put on his hat and coat and descended into the street. As he crossed the road she came out.

"Hullo, Marko!"

"Hullo. Well, there's evidently one woman in the world who can get out of a draper's in under an hour. You haven't been in a minute."

"Did you see me go in? As a matter of fact I didn't want anything. As a matter of fact, I was making up my mind—"

"Whether to come in and see me?"

She nodded.

"What about having some tea somewhere?"

"I think that's a good idea."

He suggested the Cloister Tea Rooms. She spoke to the chauffeur and accompanied him.

II

The Cloister Tea Rooms were above a pastry cook's on the first floor of one of the old houses in The Precincts. The irregularly shaped room provided several secluded: tables, and they took one in a remote corner. But their conversation would have suffered nothing in a more central and neighboured situation. Nona began some account of her summer visitations. Sabre spoke a little of local businesses: had she seen the new railway? Had he been round the Garden Home since her return? But the subjects were but skirmishers thrown out before dense armies of thoughts that massed behind; met, and trifled, and rode away. When pretence of dragging out the meal could no longer be maintained, Nona looked at her watch. "Well, I must be getting back. We haven't had a particularly enormous tea, but the chauffeur's had none."

Sabre said, "Yes, let's get out of this." It was as though the thing had been a strain.

He put her into the car. She was so very, very quiet. He said, "I've half a mind to drive up with you. I'd like a ride, and a walk back."

She said the car could run him back, or take him straight over to Penny Green. "Yes, come along up, Marko. They have rather fun in the billiard room after tea."

He got in and she shared with him the heavy fur rug. "Not that I want fun in the billiard room," he said.

She asked him lightly, "Pray what can we provide for you, then?"

"I just want to drive up with you."

III

It was only three miles to Northrepps. It seemed to Sabre an incredibly short time before a turn in the road fronted them with the park gates. And they had not spoken a word! He said, "By Jove, this car travels! I'll get down at the gates, Nona. I'm not coming in. I want the walk back."

She made no attempt to dissuade him. She leaned forward and called to the chauffeur; but as the car began to slow down, she gave a little catch of emotion and said, "Well, we have had a chatty drive. You'd better change your mind and come along up, Marko."

He disengaged the rug from about him. "No, I think I'll get out here." He turned towards her. "Look here, Nona. Get out here and walk up." He echoed the little sound of feeling she had given, pretended laughter. "It will do you good after that enormous tea."

She said something about the tea being too enormous for exertion.

The car drew up. He got out and turned to her. "Look here. Please do."

He saw the colour fade away upon her face. "What for?"

"To talk." It was all he could say.

She put away the rug and gave him her hand. Warm, and she said, "How dreadfully cold your hand is! Go on and get your tea, Jeffries. I'm going to walk up."

133

The man touched his cap. The car slid away and left them.

IV

They were within the gates. It had been a dull day. Evening stood mistily far up the long avenue of the drive and in the distances about the park on either hand. Among October's massing leaves, a small disquiet stirred. The leaves banked orderly between their parent trunks. Sabre noticed as a curious thing how, when they stirred, they only trembled in their massed formations, not broke their ranks, as if some live thing ran beneath them.

He said, "Do you know what this seems to me? It seems as though it was only yesterday, or this morning, that you came to see me at the office and we talked. Well, I want it to be only yesterday. I want to go on from there."

She said, "Yes."

He hardly could hear the word. He looked at her. She was as tall as he. Not least of the contributions to her beauty in his eyes was the slim grace of her stature. But her face was averted; and he wanted most terribly to see her face. "Stand a minute and look at me, Nona." He touched her arm. "I want to see your face."

She turned towards him and raised her eyes to his eyes. "Oh, what is it you want to say, Marko?"

There was that which glistened upon her lower lids; and about her mouth were trembling movements; and in her throat a pulse beating.

He said, "It's you I want to say something. I want you to explain some things. Some things you said. Nona, when you came into my room that day and shook hands you said, 'There!' when you gave me your hand. You took off your glove and said, 'There!' I want to know why you said 'There!' And you said, 'Well, I had to come.' And you said you were flotsam. And that night—when we'd been up to you—you said, 'Oh, Marko, do write to me.' I want you to explain what you meant."

She said, "Oh, how can you remember?"

He answered, "Because I remember, you must explain."

"Please let me sit down, Marko." She faltered a little laugh. "I can explain better sitting down."

A felled trunk had been placed against the trees facing towards the parkland. They went to it and he sat beside her. She sat upright but bending forward a little over her crossed knees, her hands clasped on them, looking before her across the park.

"No, you must look at me," he said.

She very slowly turned her body towards him. He thought her most beautiful and the expression of her beautiful face was most terrible to him in all his emotions.

V

She spoke very slowly; almost with a perceptible pause between each word. She said, "Well, I'll tell you. I said 'flotsam', didn't I? If I explain that—you know what flotsam is, Marko. Have you ever looked it up in the dictionary? The dictionary says it terribly. 'Goods shipwrecked and found floating on the sea.' I'm twenty-eight, Marko. I suppose that's not really very old. It seems a terrible age to me. You see, you judge age by what you are in contrast with what you were. If you're very happy I think it can't matter how old you are. If you look back to when you were happy and then come to the now when you're not, it seems a most terrible and tremendous gulf—and you see yourself just floating—drifting farther and farther away from the happy years and just being taken along, taken along, to God knows where, God knows to what." She put out the palms of her hands towards where misty evening banked sombrely across the park. "That's very frightening, Marko."

The live thing ran beneath the leaves banked at their feet. A stronger gust came in the air. A scattering of leaves clustered together and moved with sudden agitation across the sward before them; paused and seemed to be trying to flutter a hold into the ground; rushed aimlessly at a tangent to their former direction; paused again; and again seemed to be holding on. Before a sudden gust they were spun helplessly upward, sported aloft in mazy arabesques, scattered upon the breeze.

"Those leaves!" she said. And as if she had not made the interjection she went on, "Most awfully frightening. Well, all the time there was you, Marko. You were always different from anybody I ever knew. Long ago I used to chaff you because you were so different. In those two years when we were away it got awful. In those two years I knew I was flotsam. One day—in India—I went and looked at it in the little dictionary in my writing case, and I knew I was. Do you know what I did? I crossed out flotsam in the dictionary and wrote Nona. There it was, and it was the most exact thing—'Nona: goods shipwrecked and found floating in the sea.' I meant to have torn out the page. I forgot. I left it there and Tony saw it."

Sabre said, "What did he say?" In all she had told him there was something omitted. He knew that his question approached the missing quantity. But she did not answer it.

She went on, "Well, there was you. And I began to want you most awfully. You were always such a dear, slow person; and I wanted that most awfully. You were so steady and good and you had such quiet old ideas about duty and rightness and things, and you thought about things so, and I wanted that most frightfully. You see, I'd known you all my life—well, that's how it was, Marko. That explains all the things you asked. I said 'There'; and I said I had to come; because I'd wanted it so much, so long. And I wanted you to write to me because I did want to go on having the help I had from you—"

He had desired her to look at him, but it was he who had turned away. He sat with his head between his hands, his elbows on his knees.

She repeated, with rather a plaintive note, as though in his pose she saw some pain she had caused him, "You see, I had known you all my life, Marko—"

He said, still looking upon the ground between his feet, "But you haven't explained anything. You've only told me. You haven't explained why."

She said with astounding simplicity, "Well, you see, Marko, I made a mistake. I made a most frightful mistake. I chose. I chose wrong. I ought to have married you, Marko."

And his words were a groan. "Nona—Nona—"

CHAPTER VII

I

He was presently walking back, returning to Tidborough.

He was trying very hard, all his life's training against sudden unbridling of his bridled passions, to grapple his mind back from its wild and passionate desires and from its amazed coursings upon the immense prairies, teeming with hazards, fears, enchantments, hopes, dismays, that broke before this hour as breaks upon the hunter's gaze, amazingly awarded from the hill, savannas boundless, new, unpathed,—from these to grapple back his mind to its schooled thought and ordered habit, to its well-trodden ways of duty, obligation, rectitude. He had not left them. But for that cry of her name wrung from him by sudden application of pain against whose shock he was not steeled, he had answered nothing to her lamentable disclosure. This which he now knew, these violent passions which now he felt, but lit for him more whitely the road his feet must take. If he had ever tried consciously to see his life and Mabel's from Mabel's point of view, now, when his mind threatened disloyalty to her, he must try. And would! The old habit, the old trick of seeing the other side, acted never so strongly upon him as when unkindness appeared to lie in his own attitude. Unkindness was unfairness and unfairness was above all qualities the quality he could not tolerate. And here was unfairness, open, monstrous, dishonourable.

Mabel should not feel it.

But he was aware, he was informed as by a voice in his ears, "You have struck your tents. You are upon the march."

II

He approached the town. The school lay in this quarter and his way ran through its playing fields and its buildings. Nature in her moods much fashioned his thoughts when he walked the countryside or rode his daily journey on his bicycle. He now carried his thoughts into her mood that stood about him.

Nature was to him in October, and not in spring, poignantly suggestive, deeply mysterious, in her intense and visible occupation. She was enormously busy; but she was serenely busy. She was stripping her house of its deckings, dismantling her habitation to the last and uttermost leaf; but she stripped, dismantled, extinguished, broke away, not in despair, defeat, but in ordered preparation and with

137

exquisite certitude of glory anew. That, in October, was her voice to him, stirring tremendously that faculty of his of seeing more clearly, visioning life more poignantly, with his mind than with his eye. She spoke to him of preparation for winter, and beyond winter with ineffable assurance for spring, bring winter what it might. He saw her dismantling all her house solely to build her house again. She packed down. She did not pack up, which is confusion, flight, abandonment. She packed down, which is resolve, resistance, husbandry of power to build and burst again; and burst again,—in stout affairs of outposts in sheltered banks and secret nooks; in swift, amazing sallies of violet and daffodil and primrose; in multitudinous clamour of all her buds in May; and last in her resistless tide and flood and avalanche of beauty to triumph and possession.

That was October's voice to him; that he apprehended and tingled to it, as the essence of its strange, heavy odours; secret of its veiling mists; whisper of its moisture-laden airs; song of its swollen ditches, brooks and runnels. It was not "Take down. It is done." It was "Take down. It is beginning."

Mankind, frail parasite of doubt, seeks ever for a sign, conceives no certainty but the enormous certitude of uncertainty. A sign! In death: "Take down, then; but leave me this—and this—for memory. Perhaps—who knows?—it may be true.... But leave me this for memory." In promise: "So be it, then—but give me some pledge, some proof, some sign." Not thus October. October spoke to Sabre of Nature's sublime imperviousness to doubt; of her enormous certainty, old as creation, based in the sure foundations of the world. "Take down. It is beginning."

Sabre used to think, "It gets you—terrifically. It's stupendous. It's too big to bear." He had this thought out of October: "You can't, can't walk along lanes or in woods in October and see all this mysterious business going on without knowing perfectly well that this astounding certainty must apply equally to human life. I'd wish the death of any one I loved to be in early autumn. No one can possibly doubt in early autumn. In winter, perhaps; and in spring and in summer you can know, cynically, it will pass. But in October—no. Impossible then. And not only death, Life. Life as one lives it. You can't, can't feel in autumn that in the lowest depths there is lower yet. You only can feel, know, that the thing will break, that there's an uplift at the bottom of it all. There must be."

III

Take down: it is beginning. The spirit and the message of the season
(as they communicated themselves to him) began, as opiate among
enfevered senses, to steal about his thoughts. Had anything happened?
His feeling was rather that he was at the beginning of something; or at
the end of something, which was the same thing. The place whereon
he stood entered into his thoughts. He had left the main road and was
skirting through the school precincts. He was crossing The Strip,
historic sward whereon were played the First XV football matches.
Impossible to be upon The Strip without peopling it again with the
tremendous battles that had been here, the giants of football who here
had made their fame and the school's fame; the crowded, tumultuous
touch lines; the silent, tremendous combat in between. Memories
came to him of his own two seasons in the XV; his own name from a
thousand throats upon the wintry air. His muscles tautened as again he
fought some certain of those enormous moments when the whole of
life was bound up solely in the unspeakable necessity to win.
Astounding trick of thought from what beset him! He was alone upon
The Strip, in an overcoat, on the way to forty, not a sound, not a soul,
and with that brooding sense of being upon the edge and threshold of
something vast, dark, threatening, unfathomable.

IV

Down the steep hill flanked by masters' houses. Twilight merging now
into darkness. Boys passing in and out of the gateways. Past Telfer's
which had been his own house. All this youth was preparing for life;
all these houses eternally, generation after generation, pouring boys
out into life as at Shotley iron foundry he had seen molten metal
poured out of a cauldron. And every boy, poured out, imagined he was
going to live his own life. O hapless delusion! Lo, as the same moulds
awaited and confined the metal, so the same moulds awaited and
confined the living stuff. Mysterious conventions, laws, labours;
imperceptibly receiving; implacably binding and shaping. The last day
he had come down the steps of Telfer's—jumped down—how
distinctly he remembered it! It was his own life he was coming down,
eagerly jumping down, into.—Well, here he was, passing those very
steps, and whose life was he living? Mabel's? Old Fortune's? And to
what end?

V

Whose life was Nona living?

He had asked her, "Tell me about you and Tybar."

With pitiable gentleness of voice she had approached that quantity which had been missing from her first statement of her position. And she had done tribute to her husband's parts with generosity, nay with pride. "Tony does everything better than any one else." She had said it on that occasion of their first reëncounter; its burthen had been the opening of her recital of what else she had for him.

"Marko, I think Tony's the most wonderful person that ever was. He does everything that men do and he does everything best. And everybody admires him and everybody likes him. You've no idea. You've no idea how he wins everybody he meets. People will do anything for him. They love him. Well, you've only got to look at him, haven't you? Or hear him talk? I think there's never been any one so utterly captivating as Tony is to look at and to hear."

Most engagingly, with such words, she had presented him: one that passed through life airily, exquisitely; much fairy-gifted at his cradle with gifts of beauty, charm, preëminence in all he touched; knowing no care, knowing no difficulty, knowing no obstacle, or danger, or fear, or illness, or fatigue, or anything in life but gay and singing things, which touching, he made more bright, more tuneful yet; meeting no one, of whatever age or degree, but his charm was to that age or degree exactly touched; captivating all, leading all, by all desired in leadership. Fortune's darling!

"And, Marko," she at last had come to. "And Marko—this is the word—graceless. Utterly, utterly graceless. Without heart, Marko, without conscience, without morals, without the smallest scrap of an approach to any moral principle. Marko, that's an awful, a wicked, an abominable thing for a wife to say of her husband. But he wouldn't mind a bit my telling you. Not a bit. He'd love it. He'd laugh. He'd utterly love to know he had stung me so much. And he'd utterly love to know he'd driven me to tell you. He'd think—he'd love like anything to drive me to do awful things. He's tried—especially these two years. He'd love to be able to point a finger at me and laugh and say, 'Ah! Ha-ha! Ah!' You know, he hasn't got any feelings at all— love or hate or anything else; and it simply amuses him beyond anything to arouse feeling in anybody else. There have been women all the time we've been married and he simply amuses himself with them until he's tired of them, and until the next one takes his fancy, and he does it quite openly before me, in my house, and tells me what I can't see before my own eyes just for the love of seeing the suffering it gives me. You saw that Mrs. Winfred. He's done with her now. And he's as shameless about me with them as he is about them with me. And what he loves above all is the way I take it; and I can take it in no other way. You see I won't, I simply will not, Marko, let these women of his see—or let any one in the world suspect—that I—that I suffer. So when we are together before people I keep up the gay way we always show together. He loves it; it's delicious to him, because it's a game played over the torture underneath. And I won't do any other way, Marko. I will keep my face to the world—I won't have any one pity me."

"I pity you," he had said.

"Ah, you...."

VI

And he was suddenly shot into an encounter of extraordinary incongruity with his thoughts and of extraordinary intensity. A voice accosted him. He was astounded, as if suddenly awakened out of heavy sleep, to see to where he had come. He was in the narrow old ways of Tidborough Old Town, approaching The Precincts, by the ancient Corn Exchange. A keen-looking young man, particularly well set up and wearing nice tweeds, was accosting him. Sabre recognised Otway, captain and adjutant of the depot, up at the barracks, of the county regiment, one of the crack regiments, famous as "The Pinks."

Otway said, "Hullo, Sabre. How goes it? Are you going to this show to-morrow?"

He was pointing with his stick to a poster displayed against the Corn Exchange. Sabre read it. It announced that Field Marshal Lord Roberts was speaking there, under the auspices of the National Service League, on Home Defence—a Citizen Army.

"I hadn't thought about going," Sabre said. He wanted to get away.

Otway was staring at the poster as though he had never seen it before; but he had been staring at it when Sabre came along the street. "You ought to," Otway said. "You ought to hear old Bobs. Of course the little chap's all wrong."

He seemed to be talking to himself, staring at the poster, more than to Sabre. Sabre, despite his preoccupation, was surprised. "All wrong?

141

Good lord, I should have thought you of all people—" And immediately a torrent of Otway was let loose upon him, bursting into his thoughts like a stone chucked through a study window.

Otway spun around in his keen, quick way to face him. "All wrong in the way he's putting his case, I mean. All these National Service chaps are. Home defence they talk about, nothing but Home Defence. It's like chucking sawdust into a fire—the fire being all the bloody fools who are opposed to military training. Any fool can knock the bottom out of this Home Defence business. The Blue Water fools are champions at it. They say the only defence against invasion is the Navy and that half a million spent on the Navy is worth untold millions chucked away on this 'Nation in Arms' shout. And they're damn right."

"Well, then?" said Sabre. "What's the argument? What's the harm in knocking the bottom out of—this?" he nodded towards the poster.

Otway spoke with astonishing intensity. "Why, good God alive, man, don't you see, we do want a nation in arms; we want it like hell. But we don't want it for here, at home; we want it to fight on the Continent. That's where we've got to fight,—out there. And that's where we're going to fight before we're many years older."

In his intensity he had extended his left hand and was beating his points into it with the handle of his stick. "See that?"

Sabre was not in the mood to see anything. He only wanted to be away.

"No, I'm dashed if I do. What are we going to fight on the Continent for—supposing we ever do have to fight anywhere?"

The stick hammered away again. "Because we've got obligations there. We've got to defend Belgium, for one. And if we hadn't—if we hadn't any obligations we'd pretty soon, we'd damn soon find them as soon as ever Germany breaks loose. That's what these National Service Johnnies ought to tell the people, that's what Bobs ought to tell them, that's what these blasted politicians ought to tell them: you don't want National Service to defend your perishing homes. The Navy's going to do that. You want it like hell because you've got to defend your lives—out there." He waved his stick towards "out there." "My

God!" he said. He was consumed with the intensity of his own emotions. "My God!"

Despite himself, Sabre was impressed. The man would have impressed anybody. His eyes were extraordinarily penetrating. There actually were tiny little points of perspiration about his nose.

"I never thought about that," Sabre said doubtfully. "I never thought there were any obligations. I doubt any member of the Government would admit there were any."

"I know damn well they wouldn't," Otway declared. "And they'd be helped to deny it, or to evade it, by the howl of laughter there'd be in the Commons if any one had the guts to get up and ask if we had any obligations. There's no joke goes down like that sort of joke. Well—" His manner changed. He tucked his stick under his arm and took out a silver cigarette case. "Cigarette? Well—they'll laugh the other side of their chuckle heads one of these days."

Sabre took a cigarette. "You're pretty sure there's going to be a war, aren't you?"

The extraordinary man, who had become smiling and airy, immediately became extraordinary again. He had struck a match, held it to Sabre's cigarette, and was applying it to his own. He extinguished it with violent jerks of his arm and dashed it on to the pavement. "Sure? My God, sure? I tell you, Sabre, you won't be five years, I don't believe you'll be two years, one year, older before you'll not only be sure—you'll know! I've just finished a course at the Staff College, you know. We finished up with a push over to Belgium to do the battlefields. We went into Germany, some of us. They fed us in some of their messes. Do you know, those chaps in those messes there talked about fighting us as naturally and as certainly as you talk with your opponents about a coming footer match. They talked about 'When we fight you'—not 'if we fight you'—'when', as if it was as fixed as Christmas. And they didn't talk any of this bilge about fighting us in England; they knew, as I know, and every soldier knows—every soldier who's keen—that it's going to be out there. In Europe." He had not taken two puffs at his cigarette before he wrenched it from his mouth and dashed it after the match. "Sabre, why the hell aren't people here told that? Why are they stuck up with this rot about defending their shores when they can see for themselves that only the Navy can defend their shores? What are they going to do when the war comes? Are they going to lynch these bloody politicians who haven't told them they've got to fight for their lives? Are they going to turn around and say they never knew it so they'll be damned if they'll fight for their lives? Are they going to follow any of these politicians who will have betrayed them? Do you suppose any man who's been party to this betrayal is going to be found big enough to run a war? I tell you that's another thing. Do you suppose a chap who's been a miserable vote-snatcher all his life is going to turn round suddenly and be a heaven-sent administrator in a war? You can take your oath Heaven doesn't send out geniuses on that ticket. What you've lived and done in fat times—that's what you're going to live and do in lean. Heaven's chucked stocking divine fire."

"I'm with you there," Sabre said. He did not believe half this intense man said, but he conceived a sudden and great admiration for his intensity. And he had had no idea that a soldier ever thought so far away from his own subject—which was sport and one chance in a million of fighting—as to produce aphorisms on habit and development. "But you know, Otway," he said, "it's jolly hard to believe all this inevitableness of war stuff that chaps like you put up. Do you read the articles in the reviews and the quarterlies? They all pretty well prove that, apart from anything else, a big European war is impossible by the—well, by the sheer bigness of the thing. They say these modern gigantic armies couldn't operate, couldn't provision themselves. And there's the finance. They prove you can't fight without money and that credit would go and the thing would stop before it had begun, pretty well. I don't know anything about that sort of thing, but the arguments strike me as absolutely sound."

Otway was waiting with fidgety impatience. "I've heard all that. I don't give a damn for it. Of course you don't know anything about it. No one does. Least of all those writing chaps. It's all theory. Every one thought that with modern this, that and the other you were as safe on the last word in liners as in your own bedroom. Then comes along that Titanic business in April, and where the hell are you with your modern conditions? Fifteen hundred people done in. I tell you it isn't that things that used to happen can't happen now; it's simply that they'll happen a million times worse. What's the good of theories when you've got facts? Look at the things there've been with Germany just this year alone. Old Haldane over in Germany in February for 'unofficial discussions', Churchill threatening two keels to one if the German Navy law is exceeded. That was March. In April the Germans whack up their Navy Law Amendment, twelve more big ships. That chap Bertrand Stewart getting three and a half years for espionage in Germany; and two German spies caught by us here,—that chap Grosse over at Winchester Assizes, three years, and friend Armgaard Graves up at Glasgow, eighteen months. An American cove at Leipzig taking four years' penal for messing around after plans of the Heligoland fortifications. Those five yachting chaps in July arrested for espionage at Eckernforde. War, too, skits of it. Turkey and Italy hardly done when all these Balkan chaps set to and slosh Turkey. Have you seen to-day's papers? I'll bet you they'll send Turkey to hell at Kirk Kilisse or thereabouts before the week's out."

He had been ticking these points off on his fingers, much astonishing Sabre by his marshalling of scattered incidents that had been merely rather pleasing newspaper sensations of a couple of days. He presented the ticked-off fingers bunched up together. "There, there's concrete facts for you, Sabre. Can you say things aren't tightening up? Why, if war—when war comes people will look back on this year, 1912, and wonder where in hell their eyes were that they didn't see it. What are they seeing?—" He threw his fingers apart. "None of these things. Not one. All this doctors and the Insurance Bill tripe, Marconi Inquiry, Titanic, Suffragettes smashing up the West End, burning down Lulu Harcourt's place, trying to roast old Asquith in the Dublin Theatre, Seddon murder, this triangular cricket show. Hell's own excitement because there's so much rain in August and people in Norwich have to go about in boats, and then hell's own hullaballoo because there's no rain for twenty-two days in September and people get so dry they can't spit or something." His keen face wrinkled up into laughter. "Eh, didn't you read that?" He laughed but was immediately intense again. "That's all that really interests the people. By God, they'll sit up and take notice of the real stuff one of these days. Pretty soon. Tightening up, I tell you. Well, I'm off, Sabre. When are you coming up to the Mess again? Friday? Well, guest night the week after. I'll drop you a line. So long." He was off, carrying his straight back alertly up the street.

VII

His going was somehow as sudden and startling as his appearance had been sudden and tumultuous. He had carried away Sabre's thoughts as a jet from a hosepipe will spin a man out of a crowd; smashed into his preoccupation as a stone smashing through a window upon one deep in study; galloped across his mind as a cavalcade thundering through a village street,—and the effect of it, and the incongruity of it as, getting his bicycle from the office, he rode homewards, kept returning to

Sabre's mind, as an arresting dream will constantly break across daylight thoughts.

Nona had said that Tybar knew she thought often of him. "He knows I think of you." That was the way she had put it. It explained that mock in his eyes when they met that day on the road, and Mrs. Winfred's remark and her look, and Tybar's, that day outside the office. Extraordinary, Otway bursting in like that with all those ridiculous scares. Here he was riding along with all this reality pressing enormously about him, and with this strange and terrible feeling of being at the beginning of something or at the end of something, with this voice in his ears of, "You have struck your tents and are upon the march"; and there was Otway, up at the barracks, miles away from realities, but as obsessed with his impossible stuff as he himself with these most real and pressing dismays. What would he, with his apprehension of what might lie ahead, be saying to a chap like Otway in two or three years and what would Otway with his obsessions be saying to him? Ah, two or three years...!

But Nona loved him.... But his duty was here.... And he could have taken her beautiful body into his arms and held her beloved face to his.... But he had said not a word of love to her, only his cry of "Nona—Nona...." His duty was here.... But what would the years bring...? But what might have been! What might have been!

VIII

He finished his ride in darkness. The Green, as he passed along it on the free-wheel run, merged away through gloom into obscurity. Points of light from the houses showed here and there. The windows of his home had lamplight through their lattices. The drive was soft with leaves beneath his feet.

Lamplight, and the yielding undertread and all around walled about with obscurity. It was new. It had shown thus now for some nights on his return. But it was the first time he had apprehended it. New. Different. A commencement. An ending.

He left his bicycle in the roomy porch. He missed Low Jinks with her customary friendly greeting. It was very lonely, this. He opened the hall door and entered. Absolute silence. He had grown uncommonly accustomed to Low Jinks being here.... Absolute silence. It was like coming into an empty house. And he had got to go on coming into it, and living in it, and tremendously doing his duty in it.

146

Like an empty house. He stood perfectly still in the perfect stillness. Take down: it is beginning. You have struck your tents and are upon the march.

PART THREE

EFFIE

CHAPTER I

I

But life goes on without the smallest regard for individual preoccupations. You may take up what attitude you like towards it or, with the majority, you may take up no attitude towards it but immerse yourself in the stupendous importance of your own affairs and disclaim any connection with life. It doesn't matter tuppence to life. The ostrich, on much the same principle, buries its head in the sand; and just as forces outside the sand ultimately get the ostrich, so life, all the time, is massively getting you.

You have to go along with it.

And in October of the following year, October, 1913, life was going along at a most delirious and thrilling and entirely fascinating speed. There never was such a delicious and exciting and progressive year as between October, 1912, and October, 1913.

And it certainly took not the remotest notice of Sabre.

In February, Lord Roberts, at Bristol, opened a provincial campaign for National Service. The best people—that is to say those who did not openly laugh at it or, being scaremongers, rabidly approve it— considered it a great shame and a great pity that the poor old man should thus victimise those closing years of his life which should have been spent in that honourable retirement which is the right place for fussy old people of both sexes and all walks of life.

Sabre, reading the reports of the campaign—two or three lines—could not but reflect how events were falsifying, and continued to falsify the predictions of the intense Otway in this regard. Deliciously pleasant relations with Germany were variously evidenced throughout 1913. The King and Queen attended in Berlin the wedding of the Kaiser's daughter, and the popular Press, in picture and paragraph, told the genial British public what a thoroughly delightful girl the Kaiser's daughter was. The Kaiser let off loud "Hochs!" of friendly pride, and the Press of the world responded with warm "Hochs" of admiration and tribute; and the Kaiser, glowing with generous warmth, celebrated the occasion by releasing and handsomely pardoning three of those very British "spies" to whose incarceration in German fortresses (Sabre recalled) the intense Otway had attached such deep significance. This was a signal for more mutual "Hochs." Later the Prince of Wales visited Germany and made there an extended stay of nine weeks; and in June the twenty-fifth anniversary of the Emperor William's accession was "Hoch'd" throughout the German Empire and admiringly "Hoch'd" back again from all quarters of the civilised globe.

It was all splendid and gratifying and deeply comforting. So many "Hochs!" and such fervent and sincere "Hochs!" never boomed across the seas of the world, and particularly the North Sea or (nice and friendly to think) German Ocean, in any year as in the year 1913.

II

Not that relations with Germany counted for anything in the whirl of intensely agreeable sensations of these excellent days. Their entirely pleasing trend prevented the scaremongers from interfering with full enjoyment of the intensely agreeable sensations; otherwise they were, by comparison with more serious excitements, completely negligible. The excitements were endless and of every nature. At one moment the British Public was stirred to its depths in depths not often touched (in 1913) by reading of Scott's glorious death in the Antarctic; at another it was unspeakably moved by the disqualification of the Derby winner for bumping and boring. In one week it was being thrilled with sympathy by the superb heroism and the appalling death-roll, four hundred twenty-nine, in the Welsh colliery disaster at Senghenydd; in another thrilled with horror and indignation at the baseness of a sympathetic strike. In one month was immense excitement because the strike of eleven thousand insufferable London taxi-drivers drove everybody into the splendid busses; and in another month immense excitement because the strike of all the insufferable London bus-drivers drove everybody into the splendid taxis. M. Pegond accomplished the astounding feat of flying upside down at Juvisy without being killed and then came and flew upside down without being killed at Brooklands. One man flew over the Simplon Pass and another over the Alps. Colonel Cody flew to his death in one waterplane, and Mr. Hawker made a superb failure to fly around Great Britain in another waterplane. The suffragists threw noisome and inflammable matter into the letter boxes, bombs into Mr. Lloyd

George's house at Walton and into other almost equally sacred shrines of the great, stones into windows, axes into pictures, chained their misguided bodies to railings and gates, jammed their miserable bodies into prisons, hunger-struck their abominable bodies out again, and hurled their outrageous bodies in front of the sacred race for the Derby at Epsom, and the only less sacred race for the Gold Cup at Ascot.

It was terrific!

At one moment the loyal public were thrilled by the magnificent enrolment of the Ulster Volunteers, and at another moment outraged by the seditious and mutinous enrolment of the Nationalist Volunteers; in one month the devoted Commons read a third time the Home Rule Bill, the Welsh Church Disestablishment Bill and the Plural Voting Bill, and in the very same month the stiff-necked and abominable Lords for the third time threw out the Home Rule Bill, the Welsh Church Disestablishment Bill and the Plural Voting Bill. It was terrific. The newspapers could scarcely print it—or anything— terrifically enough. Adjectives and epithets became exhausted with overwork and burst. The word crisis lost all meaning. There was such a welter of crises that the explosions of those that came to a head were unnoticed and pushed away into the obscurest corners of the newspapers, before the alarming swelling of those freshly rushing to a head. It was magnificent. It was a deliciously thrilling and emotional year. A terrific and stupendous year. Many well-known people died.

III

It was naturally a year of strong partisanship. A year of violent feelings violently expressed; and amidst them, and because of them, Sabre found with new certainty that he had no violent feelings. Increasingly he came to know that he had well expressed his constitutional habit, the outstanding trait in his character, when, on the day of that talk in the office with Nona, he had spoken of his disastrous inability—disastrous from the point of view of being satisfactory to single-minded persons, or of pulling out that big booming stuff called success—to see a thing, whatever it might be, from a single point of view and go all out for it from that point of view. "Convictions," he had said, and often in the welter of antagonistic convictions of 1913 thought again, "Convictions. If you're going to pull out this big booming stuff they call success, if you're going to be satisfactory to anybody or to anything, you must shut down on everybody's point of view but your own. You must have convictions. And narrower than that—not only convictions but conviction. Conviction that your side is the right side and that the other side is wrong, wrong to hell."

And he had no such convictions. Above all, and most emphatically, he had never the conviction that his side, whichever side it might be in any of the issues daily tabled for men's discussion, was the right side and the other side the wrong and wicked and disastrous side.

He used to think, "I can't stand shouting and I can't stand smashing. And that's all there is. These newspapers and these arguments you hear—it's all shouting and smashing. It's never thinking and building. It's all destructive; never constructive. All blind hatred of the other views, never fair examination of them. You get some of these Unionists together, my class, my friends. They say absolutely nothing else but damning and blasting and foaming at Lloyd George and Asquith and the trade-unionists. Absolutely nothing else at all. And you get some of these other chaps together, or their newspapers, and it's exactly the same thing the other way about. And yet we're all in the same boat. There's only one life—only one living—and we're all in it. Come into it the same way and go out of it the same way; and all up against the same real facts as we are against the same weather. That fire the other night in High Street. All sorts of people, every sort of person, lent a hand in putting it out. And that frightful railway disaster at Aisgill; all sorts of people worked together in rescuing. No one stopped to ask whether the passengers were first class or third. Well, that's the sort of thing that gets me. Fire and disaster—those are facts and everybody gets to and deals with them. And if there was a big war everybody would get to and fight it. And yet all these political and social things are just as much facts that affect everybody, and all anybody can do is to shout and smash up the other man's rights in them. They all do it—in everything. Religion's as bad as any—worse. Here's one of these bishops saying he can't countenance Churchmen preaching in chapels or dissenters being invited to preach in churches because the Church must stand by the rock principles of its creed, and to preach in a chapel would mean politely not touching on those principles. You'd think heaven didn't come into the business at all. And you'd think that life doesn't come into the business of living at all. All smashing.... Well, I can't stick shouting and I can't stick smashing."

IV

Something of these views he one day expressed to Pike, the Editor of the Tidborough County Times. He was taken into the County Times office by business connected with an error in the firm's standing account for advertisement notices and, encountering Pike outside his room, entered with him and talked.

Pike was a man of nearly sixty with furiously black and luxuriant hair. He had been every sort of journalist in America and in London, and some years previously had been brought into the editorship of the County Times. The Press, broad-based on the liberty of the English people and superbly impervious to whatever temptation to jump in the direction the cat jumps, is, on the other hand, singularly sensitive to apparently inconsequent trifles in the lives of its proprietary. Pike, with his reputation, was brought into the editorship of the County Times solely because the proprietor late in life suddenly married. The wife of the proprietor desiring to share a knighthood with her husband, the proprietor, anxious to please but unwilling to pay, incontinently sacked the tame editor who was beguiling an amiable dotage with the County Times and looked about for a wild editor, whom unquestionably he found in Mr. Pike.

The breath of the County Times became as the breath of life to the Tory tradition and burst from its columns as the breath of a fiery furnace upon all that was opposed to the Tory tradition. The proprietor felt that his knighthood was assured as soon as the tide of liberalism turned; and the County Times, which could not notice even a Baptist harvest festival without snorting fire and brimstone upon it, said that the tide of radicalism—it did not print the words Liberal or Liberalism—was turning every day. About once a week the County Times said that the tide of radicalism "definitely turned last night."

Pike was a man of extraordinarily violent language. Consequent, no doubt, on the restraint of having to write always in printable language, his vocal discussion of the subjects on which he wrote was mainly in unprintable. He spoke of trade-unionists always as "those swine and dogs" and of the members of the Government as "those dogs and swine",—swine and dogs being refined and temperate euphuisms for the epithets Mr. Pike actually employed.

However he heard Sabre's stumbling periods tolerantly out and tolerantly dealt with him.

"Excuse me, Sabre, but that sort of stuff's absolutely fatal—fatal. It's simply compromise. Compromise. The most fatal defect in the English character."

Sabre happened to be stout enough on this particular point. "That's just what it isn't. Precisely what it isn't. I loathe compromise. More than anything. Compromise is accepting a little of what you know to be wrong in order to get a little of what you imagine to be right."

Pike made a swift note in shorthand on his blotting pad. "Exactly. Well?"

"Well, that's just the opposite to what I mean. I mean accepting, admitting, what you know to be right."

Pike smote his hand upon the blotting pad. "But, damn it, those dogs and swine never are right."

"There you are!" said Sabre.

And there they were, shouting, smashing; and Sabre could not do either and retired dismayed from the arenas of both.

CHAPTER II

I

It much affected his relations with those nearest to him,—with Mabel, with Mr. Fortune, and with Twyning. In those months, and in the months following, the year changing and advancing in equal excitements and strong opinions through winter into spring, he found himself increasingly out of favour at The Precincts and increasingly estranged in his home. And it was his own fault. Detached and reflective in the fond detachment of the daily bicycle ride, awake at night mentally pacing about the assembled parts of his puzzles, he told himself with complete impartiality that the cause of these effects was entirely of his own making. "I can't stick shouting and smashing"—"I can't help seeing the bits of right in the other point of view": those were the causes. He was so difficult to get on with: that was the effect of the complaint.

"Really, Sabre, I find it most difficult to get on with you nowadays," Mr. Fortune used to say. "We seem never to agree. We are perpetually at loggerheads. Loggerheads. I do most strongly resent being perpetually bumped and bruised by unwilling participation in a grinding congestion of loggerheads."

And Twyning, "Well, I simply can't hit it off with you. That's all there is to it. I try to be friendly; but if you can't hear Lloyd George's name without taking up that kind of attitude, well, all I can say is you're trying to put up social barriers in a place where there's no room for social barriers, and that's in business."

And Mabel: "Well, if you want to know what I think, I think you're getting simply impossible to get on with. You simply never think the same as other people think. I should have thought it was only common decency at a time like this to stand up for your own class; but, no. It's always your own class that's in the wrong and the common people who are in the right."

"Always." He began to hate the word "always." But it was true. In those exciting and intensely opinionated days it seemed there was never a subject that came up, whether at The Precincts or at home, but he found himself on the other side of the argument and giving intense displeasure because he was on the other side. In Mabel's case—he did not particularly trouble himself about what Twyning and Fortune thought—but in Mabel's case, much set on his duty to give her happiness, he came to prepare with care for the dangerous places of

154

their intercourse. But never with success. Places whose aggravations drove her to her angriest protestations of how utterly impossible he was to get on with never looked dangerous as they were approached: he would ride in to them with her amicably or with a slack rein,—and suddenly, mysteriously, unexpectedly, he would be floundering, the relations between them yet a little more deeply foundered.

Such utterly harmless looking places:

"And those are the people, mind you," said Mabel—not for the first time "those are the people that we have to lick stamps for Lloyd George for!"

This was because High Jinks had been seen going out for her afternoon with what Mabel described to Sabre as a trumpery, gee-gaw parasol.

The expression amused him. "Well, why in heaven's name shouldn't High Jinks buy a trumpery, gee-gaw parasol?"

"I do wish you wouldn't call her High Jinks. Because she can't afford a trumpery, gee-gaw parasol."

He spoke bemusedly. No need for caution that he could see. "Well, I don't know—I rather like to see them going out in a bit of finery."

Mabel sniffed. "Well, your taste! Servants look really nice in their caps and aprons and their black, if they only knew it. In their bit of finery, as you call it, they look too awful for words."

Signs of flying up. He roused himself to avert it. "Oh, rather. I agree. What I meant was I think it's rather nice to see them decking themselves out when they get away from their work. Rather pathetic."

"Pathetic!"

She had flown up!

He said quickly, "No, but look here, Mabel, wait a bit. I ought to have explained. What I mean is they have a pretty rotten time, all that class. When High Jinks puts up a trumpery, gee-gaw parasol, she's human. That's pathetic, only being human once a week and alternate Sundays.

And when you get a life that finds pleasure in a trumpery, gee-gaw parasol, well that's more pathetic still. See?"

Real anxiety in his "See?" But the thing was done. "No. I absolutely don't. Pathetic! You really are quite impossible to get on with. I've given up even trying to understand your ideas. Pathetic!" She gave her sudden laugh.

"Oh, well," said Sabre.

Deeper foundered!

II

And precisely the same word—pathetic—came up between them in the matter of Miss Bypass. Miss Bypass was companion to Mrs. Boom Bagshaw, the mother of Mr. Boom Bagshaw. Mabel hated Miss Bypass because Miss Bypass was, she said, the rudest creature she ever met. And "of course" Sabre took the opposite view—the ridiculous and maddening view—that her abominably rude manner was not rude but pathetic.

The occasion was an afternoon call paid at the vicarage. Of all houses in the Garden Home Sabre most dreaded and feared the vicarage. He paid this call, with shuddering, in pursuance of his endeavour to do with Mabel things that gave her pleasure. (And in the most uncongenial of them, as this call at the vicarage, he used to think, characteristically, "After all, I haven't got the decency to do what she's specially asked—give up the bike ride.")

The Vicarage drawing-room was huge, handsomely furnished, much adorned with signed portraits of royal and otherwise celebrated persons, and densely crowded with devoted parishioners. Among them the Reverend Boom Bagshaw moved sulkily to and fro; amidst them, on a species of raised throne, Mrs. Boom Bagshaw gave impressive audience. The mother of the Reverend Boom Bagshaw was a massive and formidable woman who seemed to be swaddled in several hundred garments of heavy crêpe and stiff satin. She bore a distinct resemblance to Queen Victoria; but there was stuff in her and upon her to make several Queen Victorias. About the room, but chiefly, as Sabre thought, under his feet, fussed her six very small dogs. There were called Fee, Fo and Fum, which were brown toy Poms; and Tee, To, Tum, which were black toy Poms, and the six were the especial care and duty of Miss Bypass. Every day Miss Bypass, who was tall and pale and ugly, was to be seen striding about Penny Green and the Garden Home in process of exercising the dogs; the dogs, for their part, shrilling their importance and decorating the pavements in accordance with the engaging habits of their lovable characteristics. In the drawing-room Miss Bypass occupied herself in stooping about after the six, extracting bread and butter from their mouths—they were not allowed to eat bread and butter—and raising them for the adoring inspection of visitors unable at the moment either to adore Mr. Boom Bagshaw or to prostrate themselves before the throne of Queen Victoria Boom Bagshaw.

Few spoke to Miss Bypass. Those who did were answered in the curiously defiant manner which was her habit and which was called by Mabel abominably rude, and by Sabre pathetic. As he and Mabel were taking their leave, he had Miss Bypass in momentary conversation, Mabel standing by.

"Hullo, Miss Bypass. Haven't managed to see you in all this crowd. How're things with you?"

"I'm perfectly well, thank you."

"Been reading anything lately? I saw you coming out of the library the other day with a stack of books."

Miss Bypass gave the impression of bracing herself, as though against suspected attack. "Yes, and they were for my own reading, thank you. I suppose you thought they were for Mrs. Boom Bagshaw."

Certainly her manner was extraordinarily hostile. Sabre took no notice.

"No, I bet they were your own. You're a great reader, I know."

Her tone was almost bitter. "I suppose you think I read nothing but Dickens and that sort of thing."

"Well, you might do a good deal worse, you know. There's no one like Dickens, taking everything together."

She flushed. You could almost see she was going to say something rude. "That's a very kind thing to say to uneducated people, Mr. Sabre. It makes them think it isn't education that prevents them enjoying more advanced writers. But I don't suffer from that, as it so happens. I daresay some of my reading would be pretty hard even for you."

Sabre felt Mabel pluck at his sleeve. He glanced at her. Her face was very angry. Miss Bypass, delivered of her sharp words, was deeper flushed, her head drawn back. He smiled at her. "Why, I'm sure it would, Miss Bypass. I tell you what, we must have a talk about reading one day, shall we? I think it would be rather jolly to exchange ideas."

An extraordinary and rather alarming change came over Miss Bypass's hard face. Sabre thought she was going to cry. She said in a thick voice, "Oh, I don't really read anything particularly good. It's only— Mr. Sabre, thank you." She turned abruptly away.

When they were outside, Mabel said, "How extraordinary you are!"

"Eh? What about?"

"Making up to that girl like that! I never heard such rudeness as the way she spoke to you." Sabre said, "Oh, I don't know."

"Don't know! When you spoke to her so politely and the way she answered you! And then you reply quite pleasantly—"

He laughed. "You didn't expect me to give her a hard punch in the eye, did you?"

"No, of course I didn't expect you to give her a hard punch in the eye. But I should have thought you'd have had more sense of your own dignity than to take no notice and invite her to have a talk one day."

He thought, "Here we are again!" He said, "Well, but look, Mabel. I don't think she means it for rudeness. She is rude of course, beastly rude; but, you know, that manner of hers always makes me feel frightfully sorry for her."

"Sorry!"

"Yes, haven't you noticed many people like her with that defiant sort of way of speaking—people not very well educated, or very badly off, or in rather a dependent position, and most frightfully conscious of it. They think every one is looking down on them, or patronising them, and the result is they're on the defensive all the time. Well, that's awfully pathetic, you know, all your life being on the defensive; back against the wall; can't get away; always making feeble little rushes at the mob. By Jove, that's pathetic, Mabel."

She said, "I'm not listening, you know."

He was startled. "Eh?"

"I say I'm not listening. I always know that whenever I say anything about any one I dislike, you immediately start making excuses for them, so I simply don't listen."

He mastered a sudden feeling within him. "Well, it wasn't very interesting," he said.

"No, it certainly wasn't. Pathetic!" She gave her sudden burst of laughter. "You think such extraordinary things pathetic; I wonder you don't start an orphanage!"

He halted and faced her. "Look here, I think I'll leave you here. I think I'll go for a bit of a walk."

Pretty hard, sometimes, not to—

III

At The Precincts the increasing habit of seeing the other side of things was confined, in its increasing exemplifications of how impossible he was to get on with, to the furiously exciting incidents of public affairs; but the result was the same; the result was that, just as, on opening his door on return home at night, he had that chill and rather eerie feeling of stepping into an empty house, so, on entering the office of a morning, he came to have again that sensation that it was a deserted habitation into which he was stepping; no welcome here; no welcome there. He began to look forward with a new desire for the escape and detachment of the bicycle ride; he began to approach its termination at either end with a sense of apprehension, gradually of dismay.

They were as unexpected, the conflicts of opinion, in the office as they were at home. The subject would come up, he would enter it according to his ideas and without foreseeing trouble, and suddenly he would find himself in acute opposition and giving acute offence because he was in acute opposition.

159

The Suffragettes! The day when Mr. Fortune received through the post letters upon which militancy had squirted its oppression and its determination in black and viscid form through the aperture of the letter box. "And you're sticking up for them!" declared Mr. Fortune in a very great passion. "You're deliberately sticking up for them. You—pah!—pouff!—paff! I have got the abominable stuff all over my fingers."

Sabre displayed the "wrinkled-up nut" of his Puzzlehead boyhood. "I'm not sticking up for them. I detest their methods as much as you do. I think they're monstrous and indefensible. All I said was that, things being as they are, you can't help seeing that their horrible ways are bringing the vote a jolly sight nearer than it's ever been before. Millions of people who never would have thought about woman suffrage are thinking about it now. These women are advertising it as it never could be advertised by calmly talking about it, and you can't get anything nowadays except by shouting and smashing and abusing and advertising. I only wish you could. No one listens to reason. It's got to be what they call a whirlwind campaign or go without. That's not sticking up for them. It's simply recognising a rotten state of affairs."

"And I say to you," returned Mr. Fortune, scrubbing furiously at his fingers with a duster, "and I say to you what I seem to be perpetually forced to say to you, that your ideas are becoming more and more repugnant to me. There's not a solitary subject comes up between us but you adopt in it what I desire to call a stubborn and contumacious attitude towards me. Whoof!" He blew a cyclonic blast down the speaking tube. "Send Parker up here. Parker! Send Parker up here! Parker! Parker! Parker! Pah! Pouff! Paff! Now it's all over the speaking tube! I am by no means recovered yet, Sabre, I am very far from being yet recovered, from your remarks yesterday on the Welsh Church Disestablishment Bill. Let me remind you again that your attitude was not only very painful to me in my capacity of one in Holy Orders, it was also outrageously opposed to the traditions and standing of this firm. We are out of sympathy, Sabre. We are seriously out of sympathy; and let me tell you that you would do well to reflect whether we are not dangerously out of sympathy. Let me—"

The door porter entered in the venerable presence of the summoned Parker, much agitated.

Sabre began, "If you can't see what I said about the Disestablishment Bill—"

"I did not see; I do not see; I cannot see and I shall not see. I—"

Sabre moved towards his door. "Well, I'd better be attending to my work. If anything I've said annoyed you, it certainly was not intended to."

And there followed him into his room, "Pumice stone! Pumice stone! Pumice stone! Go to the chemist's and get some pumice stone.... Very well then, sir, don't stand there staring at me, sir!"

IV

Like living in two empty houses: empty this end; empty that end. More frequently, for these estrangements, appealed to him the places of his refuge: the room of his mind, that private chamber wherein, retired, he assembled the parts of his puzzles; that familiar garment in which, invested, he sat among the fraternity of his thoughts; the evenings with Young Perch and old Mrs. Perch; the evenings with Mr. Fargus.

Most strongly of all called another refuge; and this, because it called so strongly, he kept locked. Nona.

They met no more frequently than, prior to her two years' absence, they had been wont to meet in the ordinary course of neighbourly life; and their lives, by their situations, were much detached. Northrepps was only visited, never resided at for many months together.

His resolution was not to force encounters. Once, very shortly after that day of her disclosure, he had said to her, "Look here, we're not going to have any arranged meetings, Nona. I'm not strong enough—not strong enough to resist. I couldn't bear it."

She answered, "You're too strong, Marko. You're too strong to do what you think you ought not to do; it isn't not being strong enough."

He told her she was very wrong. "That's giving me strength of character. I haven't any strength of character at all. That's been my failing all my life. I tell you what I've got instead. I've got the most frightfully, the most infernally vivid sense of what's right in my own

161

personal conduct. Lots of people haven't. I envy them. They can do what they like. But I know what I ought to do. I know it so absolutely that there's no excuse for me when I don't do it, certainly no credit if I do. I go in with my eyes open or I stay out merely because my eyes are open. There's nothing in that. If it's anything it's contemptible."

She said, "Teach me to be contemptible."

V

In those words he had expressed his composition. What he had not revealed—that very vividness of sense of what was right (and what was wrong) in his conduct forbidding it—was the corroding struggle to preserve the path of his duty. Because of that struggle he kept locked the refuge that Nona was to him in his dismays. He would have no meetings with her save only such as thrice happy chance and most kind circumstance might apportion. That was within the capacity of his strength. He could "at least" (he used to think) prevent his limbs from taking him to her. But his mind—his mind turned to her; automatically, when he was off his guard, as a swing door ever to its frame; frantically, when he would abate it, as a prisoned animal against its bars. By day, by night, in Fortune's company, in Mabel's company, in solitude, his mind turned to her. This was the refuge he kept locked, using the expression and envisaging it.

He used to think, "Of course I fail. Of course she's always in my mind. But while I make the effort to prevent it, while I do sometimes manage to wrench my mind away, I'm keeping fit; I'm able to go on putting up some sort of a fight. I'm able to help her."

To help her! But helping her, unfolding before her in his own measured words, as one pronouncing sentence, rectitude's austere asylum for their pains, watching her while she listened, hearing her gentle acquiescence,—these were most terrible to his governance upon himself.

VI

He said one day, "You see, there's this, Nona. Life's got one. We're in the thing. All the time you've got to go on. You can't go back one single second. What you've done, you've done. It may take only a minute in the doing, or in the saying, but it's done, or said, for all your life, perhaps for the whole of some one else's life as well. That's terrific, Nona.

"Nona, that's how life gets us; there's just one way we can get life and that's by thinking forward before we do a thing. By remembering that it's going to be there for always. What's in our hearts for one another, Nona, is no hurt to to-morrow or to next year or to twenty years hence, either to our own lives or to any one else's—no hurt while it's only there and not expressed, or acted on. I've never told you what's in my heart for you, nor you told me what's in your heart for me. It must remain like that. Once that goes, everything goes. It's only a question of time after that. And after that, again, only a question of time before one of us looks back and wishes for the years over again."

She made the smallest motion of dissent.

He said, "Yes. There's right and wrong, Nona. Nothing else in between. No compromise. No way of getting round them or over them. You must be either one thing or the other. Once we took a step towards wrong, there it is for ever, and all its horrible things with it—deceit, concealment, falsehood, subterfuge, pretence: vile and beastly things like that. I couldn't endure them; and I much less could endure thinking I had caused you to suffer them. And then on through that mire to dishonour.—It's easy, it sounds rather fine, to say the world well lost for love; but honour, honour's not well lost for anything. You can't replace it. I couldn't—"

The austere asylum of their pains. He looked back upon it as he had unfolded it. He looked forward across it as, most stern and bleak, it awaited them. He cried with a sudden loudness, as though he protested, not before her, but before arbitrament in the high court of destiny, "But I cannot help you upward; I can only lead you downward."

She said, "Upward, Marko. You help me upward."

Her gentle acquiescence!

There swept upon him, as one reckless in sudden surge of intoxication, most passionate desire to take her in his arms; and on her lips to crush to fragments the barriers of conduct he had in damnable sophistries erected; and in her ears to breathe, "You are beloved to me! Honour, honesty, virtue, rectitude—words, darling, words, words, words! Beloved, let the foundations of the world go spinning, so we have love."

163

He called most terribly upon himself, and his self answered him; but shaken by that most fierce onset he said thickly, "I'll have this. If ever it grows too hard for you, tell me—tell me."

VII

It must be kept locked. In grievous doubt of his own strength, in loneliness more lonely for his doubt, more deeply, as advancing summer lengthened out his waking solitude, he explored among his inmost thoughts; more eagerly, in relief from their perplexities, turned to the companionship of Fargus and the Perches. How very, very glad they always were to see him! It was the strong happiness they manifested in greeting him that most deeply gave the pleasure he had in their company. He often pondered the fact. It was, in their manifestation of it, as though he brought them something,—something very pleasurable to them and that they much wanted. Certainly he, for his own part, received such from them: a sense of warmth, a kindling of the spirit, a glowing of all his affections and perceptions.

His mind would explore curiously along this train of thought. He came to determine that infinitely the most beautiful thing in life was a face lighting up with the pleasure of friendship: in its apotheosis irradiating with the wonder of love. That frequent idea of his of the "wanting something" look in the faces of half the people one saw: he thought that the greeting of some one loved might well be a touching of the quality that was to seek. The weariest and the most wistful faces were sheerly transfigured by it. But he felt it was not entirely the secret. The greeting passed; the light faded; the wanting returned. But he determined the key to the solution lay within that ambit. The happiness was there. It was here in life, found, realised in loving meeting, as warmth is found on stepping from shadow into the sun. The thing lacking was something that would fix it, render it permanent, establish it in the being as the heart is rooted in the body.—Something? What?

He thought, "Well, why is it that children's faces are always happy? There's something they must lose as they grow out of childhood. It's not that cares and troubles come; the absurd troubles of childhood are just as terrific troubles to them as grown-ups' cares are to grown-ups. No, it is that something is lost. Well, what had I as a child that I have not as a man? Would it be hope? Would it be faith? Would it be belief?"

He thought, "I wonder if they're all the same, those three—belief, faith, hope? Belief in hope. Faith in hope. It may be. Is it that a child knows no limitation to hope? It can hope impossible things. But a man hopes no further than he can see—I wonder—"

And suddenly, in one week, life from its armoury discharged two events upon him. In the next week one upon the world.

CHAPTER III

I

Towards the end of July there was some particularly splendid excitement for the newspaper-reading public. Ireland provided it; and the newspapers, as the events enlarged one upon the other, could scarcely find type big enough to keep pace with them. On the twenty-first, the King caused a conference of British and Irish leaders to assemble at Buckingham Palace. On the twenty-fourth, the British and Irish leaders departed from Buckingham Palace in patriotic halos of national champions who had failed to agree "in principle or detail." Deadlock and Crisis flew about the streets in stupendous type; and though they had been doing so almost daily for the past eighteen months, everybody could see, with the most delicious thrills, that these were more firmly locked deadlocks and more critical crises than had ever before come whooping out of the inexhaustible store where they were kept for the public entertainment. Austria, and then Germany, made a not bad attempt on public attention by raking up some forgotten sensation over a stale excitement at a place called Sarajevo; but on the twenty-sixth, Ireland magnificently filled the bill again by the far more serious affair of Nationalist Volunteers landing three thousand rifles and marching with them into Dublin. Troops fired on the mob, and the House of Commons gave itself over to a most exciting debate on the business; the Irish Party demanded a large number of brutal heads to be delivered on chargers; and Unionist politicians, Press, and public declared that the heads were not brutal heads but loyal and devoted heads and should not be delivered; on the contrary they should be wreathed. It was delicious.

II

It was delicious and it was, moreover, reassuring. In these same days between the summoning of the Buckingham Palace Conference and the landing of the Nationalist guns, Continental events arising out of the stale Sarajevo affair reared their heads and looked towards Great Britain in a presumptuous and sinister way to which the British public was not accustomed, and which it resented. The British public had never taken any interest in international affairs and it did not wish to take any interest in international affairs. It certainly did not wish to be disturbed by them, and at this moment of the exciting Irish deadlock the Wilhelmstrasse, the Ball Platz, the Quai d'Orsay and similar stupid, meaningless and unpronounceable places intruded themselves disturbingly in British homes, much as the writing on the wall vexatiously disturbed Belshazzar's feast, and were similarly resented. Belshazzar probably ordered in a fresh troupe of dancers to remove

166

the chilly effect of the stupid, meaningless and unpronounceable writing, and in the same way the British public turned with relief and with thrills to the gun-running and the shooting.

It was characteristically intriguing in the nature of its excitement. It was characteristically intriguing because, like all the domestic sensations to which the British Public had become accustomed, it in no way interfered with the lives of those not directly implicated in it. Like them all, it entertained without inconveniencing. They knew their place, the deadlocks, the crises and the other sensations of those glowing days. They caused no member of their audience to go without his meals. They interfered neither with pleasure nor with business.

III

Sometimes this was a little surprising. Fresh from newspaper instruction of the deadness of the deadlock, the poignancy of the crisis, or the stupendity of the achievement, one rather expected one's own personal world to stand still and watch it. But one's own personal world never did stand still and watch it.

Sabre, coming into his office on the day reporting the affray in Dublin, was made to experience this.

In the town, on his arrival, he purchased several of the London newspapers to read other accounts and other views of the gun-running and its sensational sequel. His intention was to read them the moment he got to his room. He put them on a chair while he hung up his straw hat and filled a pipe.

They remained there unopened till the charwoman removed them in the evening. On his desk, as he glanced towards it, was a letter from Nona.

He turned it over in his hands—the small neat script. She never before had written to him at the office. It bore the London postmark. She would be writing from their town house. It would be to say she was coming back.... But she never wrote on the occasions of her return; they just met.... And she had never before written to the office.

Mr. Fortune appeared at the communicating door. Sabre put the letter into his pocket and turned towards him.

Mr. Fortune came into the room. With him was a young man, a youth, whose face was vaguely familiar to Sabre; Twyning behind.

"Ah, Sabre," said Mr. Fortune. "Good morning, Sabre. This is rather a larger number of visitors than you would commonly expect, but we are a larger staff this morning than we have heretofore been. I am bringing in to you a new member of our staff." He indicated the young man beside him. "A new member but bearing an old name. A chip of the old block—the old Twyning block." He smiled, stroking his whale-like front rather as though this pleasantry had proceeded from its depths and he was congratulating it. The young man smiled. Twyning, edging forward from the background, also smiled. All the smiles were rather nervous. This was natural in the new member of the staff but in Twyning and Mr. Fortune gave Sabre the feeling that for some reason they were not entirely at ease. His immediate thought had been that it was an odd thing to have taken on young Twyning without mentioning it even casually to him. It was significant of his estrangement in the office; but their self-conscious manner was even more significant: it suggested that he had been kept out of the plan deliberately.

He gave the young man his hand. "Why, that's very nice," he said. "I thought I knew your face. I think I've seen you with your father. You've been in Blade and Parson's place, haven't you?"

Young Twyning replied that he had. He had his father's rather quick and stiff manner of speaking. He was fair-haired and complexioned, good-looking in a sharp-featured way, a juvenile edition of his father in a different colouring.

Mr. Fortune, still stroking the whale-like front, produced further pleasantry from it. "Yes, with Blade and Parson. Twyning here has snatched him from the long arm of the law before he has had time to develop the long jaw of the legal shark. In point of fact, Sabre"—Mr. Fortune ceased to stroke the whale-like front. He moved a step or two out of the line of Sabre's regard, and standing before the bookshelves, addressed his remarks to them as though what else he had to say were not of particular consequence—"In point of fact, Sabre, this very natural and pleasing desire of Twyning to have his son in the office, a desire which I am most gratified to support, is his first—what shall I say?—feeling of his feet—establishing of his position—in his new—er—in his new responsibility, duty—er—function. I like this deeper tone in the 'Six Terms' binding, Sabre. I distinctly approve it. Yes.

What was I saying? Ah, yes, Twyning is now in partnership, Sabre. Yes. Good."

He came abruptly away from the shelves and directed the whale-like front towards his door in process of departure. "A little reorganisation. Nothing more. Just a little reorganisation. I think you'll find we shall all work very much the more comfortably for it." He paused before young Twyning. "Well, young man, now you've made your bow before our literary adviser. I think we decided to call him Harold, eh, Twyning? Avoid confusion, don't you agree, Sabre?"

"If that's his name," Sabre said. He had remained standing looking towards father and son precisely as he had stood and looked at the party's entry.

Mr. Fortune glanced sharply at him and compressed his lips. "It is," he said shortly. He left the room.

IV

Twyning spoke his first words since his entry. "Well, there we are, old man." He smiled and breathed strongly through his nose, as if tensing himself against some emergency that might arise.

Sabre said, "Yes, well done, Twyning. Of course he promised you this long ago."

"Yes, didn't he? Glad you remember my telling you. Of course it won't make the least difference to you, old man. What I mean is, if anything I hope I shall be able to give you a leg up in all sorts of ways. I've been telling Harold what a frightfully smart man you are, haven't I, Harold?"

Harold smiled assent to this tribute, and Sabre said, "I suppose we shall go on much as before?"

"Oh, rather, old man."

"Harold be working in your room, eh?"

"Yes, that's the idea, for a start, anyway. They're just shoving up a desk for him. Come along in and see how we're fixing it, old man."

"I'll look in presently."

"Righto, old man. Come along, Harold." At the door he turned and said, "Oh, by the way. I want you to show Harold through the work of this side of the business a bit later on."

Sabre looked quickly at him. "You want me to?"

Twyning flushed darkly. "Well, he may as well get the hang of the whole business, mayn't he? That's what I mean."

"Oh, certainly he should. I quite agree. Send him along any time you like."

"Thanks awfully, old man."

But outside the door Twyning added to himself: "You thought that was an order, my lord; and you didn't like it. Pretty soon you won't think. You'll know."

V

Sabre remained standing at his desk. He had a tiny ball of paper in his hand and he rolled it round between his finger and thumb, round and round and round and round.... In his mind was a recollection: "You have struck your tents and are upon the march."

He thought, "This has been coming a long time.... It's my way of looking at things has done this. I'm getting so I've got nowhere to turn. It's no good pretending I don't feel this. I feel it most frightfully.... I've let down the books. They'll take a back place in the business now. Twyning's always been jealous of them. Fortune's never really liked my success with them. They'll begin interfering with the books now.... My books.... It was rottenly done. Behind my back. Plotted against me, or they wouldn't have sprung it on me like that. That shows what it's going to be like.... It's all through my way of looking at things.... I've no one here I can take things to. This frightful feeling of being alone in the place. And it's going to be worse. And nowhere to get out of it. More empty at home.... And now there's this. And I've got to go back to that.... 'You have struck your tents and are upon the march' ... Yes. Yes...."

He suddenly recollected Nona's letter. He took it from his pocket and opened it; and the second event was discharged upon him.

She wrote from their town house:

"Marko, take me away—Nona."

His emotions leapt to her with most terrible violence. He felt his heart leap against his breast as though, engine of his tumult, it would burst its bonds and to her. He struck his hand upon the desk. He said aloud, "Yes! Yes!" He remembered his words, "If ever you feel you can't bear it, tell me.—Tell me."

VI

He began to write plans to her. He would come to London to-morrow.... She should come to the station if she could; if not, he would be at the Great Western Hotel. She would telephone to him there and they could arrange to meet and discuss what they should do.... He would like to go away with her directly they met, but there were certain things to see to. He wrote, "But I can only take you—"

His pen stopped. Familiar words! He repeated them to himself, and their conclusion and their circumstance appeared and stood, as with a sword, across the passage of his thoughts. "But I can only lead you downwards. I cannot lead you upwards ..."

As with a sword—

He sat back in his chair and gazed upon this armed intruder to give it battle.

VII

The morning passed and the afternoon while still he sat, no more moving than to sink lower in his seat as the battle joined and as he most dreadfully suffered in its most dreadful onsets. Towards five o'clock he put out his hand without moving his position and drew towards him the letter he had begun. The action was as that of one utterly undone. He very slowly tore it across, and then across again, and so into tiniest fragments till his fingers could no more fasten upon them. He dropped his arm away and opened his hand, and the white pieces fluttered in a little cloud to the floor.

Presently he drew himself up to the table and began to write, writing very slowly because his hand trembled so. In half an hour he blotted the few lines on the last sheet:

"...So, simply what I want to do is to let our step—if we take it—be mine, not yours. We shall forget absolutely that you ever wrote. It's as though it had never been written. On Tuesday I will write and ask you, 'Shall I come up to you?' So if you say 'Yes' the action will have been entirely mine. It will start from there. This hasn't happened. And during these days in between, just think like anything over what I've said. Honour can't have any degree, Nona, any more than truth can have any degree: whatever else the world can quibble to bits it can't partition those: truth is just truth and honour is just honour. And a marriage vow is a pledge of honour like any other pledge of honour, and if one breaks it one breaks one's honour, never mind what the excuse is. There's no conceivable way of arguing out of that. That's what I shall ask you to do on Tuesday and I'm just warning you so you shall have time to think beforehand."

He took his pen, and steadied his hand, and wrote:

"And your reply, when I ask you, whichever it is, shall bring me light into darkness, unutterable darkness.—M."

He could hear the homeward movements about the office. It was time to go. He wheeled his bicycle to the letter box at the corner of The Precincts. As he dropped in his letter, the evening edition of Pike's paper came bawling around the corner.

AUSTRIA
DECLARES WAR
ON SERVIA

He shook his head at the paper the boy held out to him and rode away. What had that kind of thing to do with him?

VIII
Unutterable darkness! He lived within it during the days that followed while he awaited the day appointed to write to Nona again. He had put away that for which, with a longing that was almost physical in its pain, his spirit craved; and craved the more terribly for his denial of it. Whatever she said when he asked, whichever way she answered him, he would be brought relief from his intolerable stress. If she maintained honour above love, his weakness, he knew, would be welded into strength, as the presence of another brings enormous support to timidity; if she declared for love,—his mind surged within him at the imagination of bursting away once and for ever the

squeamish principles which for years, hedging about his conduct on this side and on that, had profited nothing those on whose behalf they had been erected and his own life had desolated into barrenness.

He was little disposed, in these dismays and in this darkness, to divert attention to the international disturbances which now were rumbling across the newspapers in portentous and enormous headlines. Ireland was pressed away. It was all Europe now—thrones, chancelleries, councils, armies. He tried to say, "What of it?" Many in Great Britain tried to say, "What of it?" Crises and deadlocks again! Meaningless and empty words, for months and years past worked to death and rendered hollow as empty vessels. Some one would climb down. Some one always climbed down.

Nobody climbed down.

The cauldron whose seething and bubbling had entertained some, fidgeted some, some nothing at all concerned, suddenly boiled over, and poured in boiling fat upon the flames, and poured in flames upon the hearth of every man's concerns.

On Friday the Stock Exchange closed. On Saturday Germany declared war on Russia. In Sunday's papers Sabre read of the panic run on the banks, people fighting to convert their notes into gold. One London bank had suspended payment. Many had shut out failure only by minutes when midday permitted them to close their doors. People were besieging the provision shops to lay in stores of food.

And poured in flames upon the hearth of every man's concerns....

All his concerns, the crisis with Nona, with his honour and his love, that awaited determination, were disputed their place in his mind by the incredible and enormous events that each new hour discharged upon the world. He watched them as one might be watching a burning building and feeling at every moment that the roof will crash in, yet somehow feeling that it cannot and will not fall in. The thing was gone beyond possibility of recovery, there terribly arose now the urgency for Great Britain to declare for honour, yet somehow he felt that it could not and would not fail to be averted. It could not happen.

It did happen. On Tuesday the mounting amazements burst amain. On Tuesday the roof that could not fall in fell in. On Tuesday, the day appointed for his letter to Nona, he uttered in realisation that which, uttered in speculation, had been meaningless as an unknown word spoken in a foreign tongue: "War!"

IX

The news of Tuesday morning caused him at six o'clock in the evening to have been standing two hours in the great throng that filled Market Square gazing towards the offices of the County Times. Our mobilisation, our resolve to stand by France if the German Fleet came into the Channel, lastly, most awfully pregnant of all, our obligations to Belgium,—that had been the morning's news, conveyed in the report of Sir Edward Grey's statement in the House of Commons. That afternoon the Prime Minister was to make a statement.

A great murmur swelled up from the waiting crowd, a great movement pressed it forward towards the County Times offices. On the first-floor balcony men appeared dragging a great board faced with paper, on the paper enormous lettering. The board was pulled out endways. The man last through the window took a step forward and swung the letters into view.

PREMIER'S STATEMENT
_____

ULTIMATUM TO GERMANY
EXPIRES MIDNIGHT

Sabre said aloud, "My God! War!"

As a retreating wave harshly withdrawing upon the reluctant pebbles, there sounded from the crowd an enormous intaking of the breath. An instant's stupendous silence, the wave poised for return. Down! A shattering roar, tremendous, wordless. The figure of Pike appeared upon the balcony, in his shirt sleeves, his long hair wild about his face, in his hands that which caught the roar as it were by the throat, stopped it and broke it out anew on a burst of exultant clamour. A Union Jack. He shook it madly with both hands above his head. The roar broke into a tremendous chant. "God Save the King!"

Sabre pressed his way out of the Square. He kept saying to himself, "War.... War...." He found himself running to the office; no one was in the office; then getting out his bicycle with frantic haste, then riding home,—hard.

And he kept saying, "War!"

He thought, "Otway!" and before his eyes appeared a vision of Otway with those little beads of perspiration on his nose.

War—he couldn't get any further than that. Like the systole and diastole of a slowly beating pulse, the word kept on forming in his mind and welling away in a tide of confused and amorphous scenes; and forming again; and again oozing in presentments of speculations, scenes, surmises, and in profound disturbances of strange emotions. War.... And there kept appearing the face of Otway with the little points of perspiration about his nose. Otway had predicted this months ago.—And he was right. It had come.

War....

CHAPTER IV

I

He approached Penny Green and realised for the first time the hard pace at which he had been riding. And realised also the emotions which subconsciously had been driving him along. All the way he had been saying "War!" What he wanted, most terribly, was to say it aloud to some one. He wanted to say it to Mabel. He had a sudden great desire to see Mabel and tell her about it and talk to her about it. He felt a curiously protective feeling towards her. For the first time in his life he pedalled instead of free-wheeling the conclusion of the ride. He ran into the house and into the morning room. Mabel was not there. It was almost dinner time. She would be in her room. He ran upstairs. She was standing before her dressing table and turned to him in surprise.

"Whatever—"

"I say, it's war!"

She echoed the word. "War?"

"Yes, war. We've declared war!"

"Declared war?"

"Yes, declared war. We've sent Germany an ultimatum. It ends to-night. It's the same thing. It means war."

He was breathless, panting. She said, "Good gracious! Whatever will happen? Have you brought an evening paper? Do you know the papers didn't come this morning till—"

He could not hear her out. "No, I didn't wait. I simply rushed away." He was close to her. He took her hands. "I say, Mabel, it's war." His emotions were tumultuous and extraordinary. He wanted to draw her to him and kiss her. They had not kissed for longer than he could have remembered; but now he held her hands hard and desired to kiss her. "I say, it's war."

She gave her sudden burst of laughter. "You are excited. I've never seen you so excited. Your collar's undone."

He dropped her hands. He said rather stupidly, "Well, it's war, you know," and stood there.

She turned to her dressing table. "Well, I do wish you'd stayed for a paper. Now we've got to wait till to-morrow and goodness only knows—" She was fastening something about her throat and held her breath in the operation. She released it and said, "Just fancy, war! I never thought it would be. What will happen first? Will they—" She held her breath again. She said, "It's too annoying about those papers coming so late. If they haven't arrived when you go off to-morrow you can tell Jones he needn't send them any more. He's one of those independent sort of tradesmen who think they can do just what they like. Just fancy actually having war with Germany. I can't believe it." She turned towards him and gave her sudden laugh again. "I say, aren't you ever going to move?"

He went out of the room and along the passage. As he reached his own room he realised it again. "War—" He went quickly back to Mabel. "I say—" He stopped. His feelings most frightfully desired some vent. None here. "Look here. Don't wait dinner for me. You start. I'm going round to Fargus to tell him."

At the hall door he turned back and went hurriedly into the kitchen. "I say, it's war!"

"Well, there now!" cried High Jinks.

"Yes, war. We've sent an ultimatum to Germany. It ends to-night."

Low Jinks threw up her hands. "Well, if that isn't a short war!"

"Girl alive, the ultimatum ends, not the war. Don't you know what an ultimatum is?"

Outside he ran down the drive and ran to Fargus's door. It stood open. In the hall the eldest Miss Fargus appeared to be maintaining the last moment before dinner by "doing" a silver card salver.

"Hullo, Miss Fargus. I say, is your father about? I say, it's war. We've declared war!"

The eldest Miss Fargus lifted her head to another Miss Fargus also "doing" something on the stairs above her, and in a very high voice called, "Papa! War!"

The staircase Miss Fargus took it up immediately. "Papa! War!" and Sabre heard it go echoing through the house, "Papa! War! Papa! War! Papa! War!"

"How terrible, how dreadful, how frightful, how awful," said the eldest Miss Fargus. "You must excuse me shaking hands, but as you see I am over pink plate powder. I'm not surprised. We were discussing it only at breakfast; and for my part, though Julie, Rosie, Poppy and Bunchy were against me, I—" She broke off to turn and take her portion in a new chorus now filling the house. Sounds of some one descending the stairs at break-neck speed were heard, and the chorus shrilled, "Papa, take care! Papa, take care! Papa, take care!"

Mr. Fargus's grey little figure came terrifically down the last flight and up the hall, a cloud of female Farguses in his wake. He ran to Sabre with hands outstretched and grasped Sabre's hands and wrung them. "Sabre! Sabre! What's this? Really? Truly? War? We've declared war? Well, I say, thank God! Thank God! I was afraid. I was terribly afraid we'd stand out. But thank God, England is England still.... And will be, Sabre; and will be!" He released Sabre's hands and took out a handkerchief and wiped his eyes. "I prayed for this," he said. "I prayed for God to be in Downing Street last night."

The chorus, unpleasantly shocked at the idea of God being asked to go to Downing Street, said in a low but stern tone, "Papa, hush. Papa, hush. Papa, hush"; but Sabre had come for this excited wringing of his hands and for this emotion. It was what he had been seeking ever since Pike's notice board had swung the news before his eyes. When presently he left he carried with him that which, when his mind would turn to it, caused his heart to swell enormously within him. Through the evening, and gone to bed and lying awake long into the night, he was at intervals caught up from the dark and oppressive pictures of his mind by surging onset of the emotions that came with Mr. Fargus's emotion. War.... His spirit answered, "England!"

II

Lying awake, he thought of Nona. He had not written the letter to her. The appointed day was past and he had not written. He would have said, during that unutterable darkness in which he had awaited it, that not the turning of the world upside down would have prevented him writing; but the world had turned upside down. It was not a board Pike's men had swung around in that appalling moment when he had watched them appear on the balcony. It was the accustomed and imponderable world, awfully unbalanced. Nona would understand. Nona always understood everything. He wondered how she had maintained this terrific day. He was assured that he knew. She would have felt just as he had felt. He thought, with a most passionate longing for her, that he would have given anything to have been able to turn to her when he had exclaimed, "My God, war", and to have caught her hands and looked into her beautiful face. To-morrow he would send the letter. To-morrow? Why, yes, to-day, like all to-days in the removed and placid light of all to-morrows, would be shown needlessly hectic. Ten to one something would have happened in the night to make to-day look foolish. If nothing had happened, if it still was war, it could only be a swiftly over business, a rapid and general recognition of the impossibility of war in modern conditions.

Disturbingly upon these thoughts appeared the face of Otway, the little beads of perspiration about his nose.

His consciousness stumbled away into the mazy woods of sleep, and turned, and all night sought to return, and stumbled sometimes to its knees among the drowsy snares, and saw strange mirages of the round world horrifically tilted with "War" upon its face, of Nona held away and not approachable, of intense light and of suffocating darkness; and rousing and struggling away from these, and stumbling yet, rarely succumbing.

III

When he went down into Tidborough in the morning it was to know at once that this to-morrow gave no lie to its precedent day. It intensified it. The previous day foreshadowed war. The new day presented it.

The papers, as it happened, did not arrive before he left, and Mabel had more to say of her annoyance with the insufferable Jones than of what his withheld wares might contain. Her attitude towards the international position was—up to this point of its development— precisely this: she had been following the crisis day by day with appreciation of its sensational headlines while these were in the paper before her, but without further interest when the paper was read. She folded up the thrones, the chancelleries, the councils, the armies and the peoples and put them away in the brass newspaper rack in the morning room and proceeded about her duties and her engagements. But she liked unfolding them and she was thoroughly annoyed with the insufferable Jones for preventing her from unfolding them. She said she would come down into Tidborough and speak to Jones herself.

"Yes, do," said Sabre. "There'll be things to see."

There were things to see. As he rode into the town people were standing about in little groups, excitedly talking; every one seemed to have a newspaper. In a row, as he approached the news agent's, were hugely printed contents bills, all with the news, in one form or another, "War Declared."

It was war. Yesterday no dream. He could not stop to rest his bicycle against the curb. He leant it over and dropped it on the pavement with a crash and hurried into the shop and bought and read.

War.... He looked out into the street through the open doorway. All those knots of people standing talking. War.... A mounted orderly passed down the street at a brisk trot, his dispatch bag swaying and bumping across his back. Every one turned and stared after him, stepped out into the roadway and stared after him. War.... He bought all the morning papers and went on to the office. Outside a bank a small crowd of people waited about the doors. They were waiting to draw out their money. Lloyd George had announced the closing of the banks for three days; but they didn't believe it was real. Was it real? He passed Hanbury's, the big grocer's. It seemed to be crammed. People outside waiting to get in. They were buying up food. A woman struggled her way out with three tins of fruit, a pot of jam and a bag of flour. She seemed thoroughly well pleased with herself. He heard her say to some one, "Well, I've got mine, anyway." He actually had a sense of reassurance from her grotesque provisioning. He thought, "You see, every one knows it can't last long."

IV

No one in the office was pretending to do any work. As in the street, all were in groups eagerly talking. The clerks' room resounded with excited discussion. Everybody wanted to talk to somebody. He went into Mr. Fortune's room. Mr. Fortune and Twyning and Harold were gathered round a map cut from a newspaper, all talking; even young Harold giving views and being attentively listened to. They looked up and greeted him cordially. Everybody was cordial and communicative to everybody. "Come along in, Sabre." He joined them and he found their conversation extraordinarily reassuring, like the woman who had sufficiently provisioned with three tins of fruit, a pot of jam and a bag of flour. They knew a tremendous lot about it and had evidently been reading military articles for days past. They all showed what was going to be done, illustrating it on the map. And the map itself was extraordinarily reassuring: as Twyning showed—his fingers covering the whole of the belligerent countries—while the Germans were delivering all their power down here, in Belgium, the Russians simply nipped in here and would be threatening Berlin before those fools knew where they were!

He thought, "By Jove, yes."

"And granted," said Mr. Fortune—Mr. Fortune was granting propositions right and left with an amiability out of all keeping with his normal stubbornness—"and granted that Germany can put into the field the enormous numbers you mention, Twyning, what use are they to her? None. No use whatever. I was talking last night to Sir James Boulder. His son has been foreign correspondent to one of the London papers for years. He's attended the army manoeuvres in Germany, France, Austria everywhere. He knows modern military conditions through and through, as you may say. Well, he says—and it's obvious when you think of it—that Germany can't possibly use her enormous masses. No room for them. Only the merest fraction can ever get into action. Where they're coming in is like crowding into the neck of a bottle. Two thirds of them uselessly jammed up behind. A mere handful can hold them up—"

Harold put in, "Yes, and those terrific fortresses, sir."

"Precisely. Precisely. Liége, Namur, Antwerp—absolutely impregnable, all the military correspondents say so. Impregnable. Well, then. There you are. It's like sending a thousand men to fight in a street. Look here—" He went vigorously to the window. They all went to the window; Sabre with them, profoundly impressed. Mr. Fortune pointed into the street. "There. That's what it is. Here comes your German army down this way from the cathedral. Choked. Blocked. Immovable mob. How many do you suppose could hold them up? Thirty, twenty, a dozen. Hold them up and throw them into hopeless and utter disorder. Pah! Simple, isn't it? I don't suppose the thing will last a month. What do you say, Sabre?"

Sabre was feeling considerably more at ease. He felt that the first shock of the thing had made him take an exaggerated view. "I don't see how it can," he said, "now I'm hearing a bit more about it. I was thinking just now what a dramatic thing it would be if it lasted—of course it can't—but if it lasted till next June and the decisive battle was fought in June, 1915, just a hundred years after Waterloo. That would be dramatic, eh?"

They all laughed, and Sabre, realising the preposterousness of such a notion, laughed with them. Twyning said, "Next June! Imagine it! At the very outside it will be well over by Christmas."

And they all agreed, "Oh, rather!"

V

It was all immensely reassuring, and Sabre gathered up his bundle of papers and went into his room, feeling on the whole rather pleasurably excited than otherwise. But as he read, column after column and paper after paper, measures that had been taken by the Government, orders to Army and Naval reservists, the impending call for men, the scenes in the streets of London, and with these the deeply grave tone of the leading articles, the tremendous statistics and the huge foreshadowing of certain of the military correspondents, the breathless news already from the seats of war,—as his mind thus received there returned to it its earlier sense of enormous oppression and tremendous conjecture. War.... England.... The first sentence of his history, now greatly advanced, came tremendously into his mind: "This England you live in is yours...." And now at war—challenged—threatened—

It surged enormously within him. He got up. He must go out into the streets and see what was happening.

The day wore on. He felt extraordinarily shy and self-conscious about the performance of a matter that had entered his mind with that surging uplift of his feelings. It was four o'clock in the afternoon before he took himself to it and then, leaving its place, he unexpectedly encountered Mabel. She was just going into the station. She had come in, as she had proposed, and she told him what she had said to Jones and what Jones had said to her. "Abominably rude man."

Then she asked him, "Was that Doctor Anderson's gate you came out of just now?"

"Yes."

"Whatever had you been to see him about?"

He flushed. He never could invent an excuse when he wanted one. "I'd been asking him to have a look at me."

"Whatever for?"

"Oh, nothing particular."

"You couldn't have been to see him for nothing."

"Well, practically nothing. You remember when I increased my life insurance some time ago they said my heart was a bit groggy and made a bit of a fuss? Well, I thought I'd just see again so as to get out of paying that higher premium."

"Oh, that. What nonsense it was. What did he say?"

"Said I had a murmur or some rot. I say, if you're going back now, don't wait dinner for me to-night. I'll get something here. The Evening Times is bringing out a special edition at nine o'clock. I'd like to wait for it."

She assented, "Yes, bring home the paper."

He went into the office. The afternoon post had brought letters to his desk. He turned them over without interest, then caught up one,—from Nona.

Marko, this frightful war! I have thanked God on my knees for you that last week you prevented me. If I had done it with this! Tony has rejoined the Guards, he was in the Reserve of Officers. And you see that whatever has been, and is, dear, he's my man to stand by in this. Marko, it would have been too awful if I couldn't, and I thank God for you, again and again and again. Nona.

Twyning appeared. "Hullo, old man, heard the latest? I say, you look as if you're ready to take on the whole world."

CHAPTER V

I

The enormous and imponderable world awfully unbalanced. Upside down. Extraordinarily unreal. Furiously real.

Life, which had been a thing of the clock and of the calendar, became a thing of events in which there was no time,—only events.

Things began one day very shortly after the declaration of war when, passing the barracks on his way home, Sabre was accosted and taken into the Mess by Cottar, a subaltern of the Pinks.

"You must come along in and have a cup of tea," young Cottar urged. "We've got a hell of a jamborino on. At least we shall have to-night. We're just working up for it. I can't tell you why. You can guess."

Sabre felt a sudden catch at his emotions. "Is the regiment going?"

They were at the door of the anteroom. Cottar swung it open. The room was full of men and tobacco smoke and noise. A very tall youth, one Sikes, was standing on the table, a glass in his hand. "Hullo, Sabre! Messman, one of those very stiff whiskies for Mr. Sabre—go on, Sabre, you must. Because—" He had not Cottar's reticence. He burst into song, waving his glass—"Because—

"We shan't be here in the morning—"

They all took it up, bawling uproariously:

We shan't be here in the morning,

We shan't be here in the morning,

We shan't be here in the mor-or-ning,

Before the break of day!

Otway came in. "Shut up, you noisy young fools. What the—"

Sikes from the table. "Ah, Papa Otway! Three cheers for Papa Otway in very discreet whispers. Messman, one of those very stiff whiskies for Captain Otway."

Otway laughed pleasantly. "No, chuck it, I'm not drinking. Hood, I want you; and you, Carmichael, and you, Bullen." He saw Sabre and came to him. "Hullo, Sabre. You've heard now. We've managed to keep it pretty close, but it's all over the place now. Yes, we entrain at daybreak."

Sabre felt frightfully affected. He could hardly speak. "Good Lord. I can't realise it. I say, Otway, do you remember predicting this nearly two years ago? You said this would find us all unawares. You were one of the people every one laughed at."

Precisely the same Otway who had spoken with such extraordinary intensity outside the Corn Exchange eighteen months before began to speak with extraordinary intensity now. "That? Oh, I don't give a damn for any of that now. This is our show now, Sabre. The Army's show. I don't give a damn for what happens at home now. This is our show. Sabre, you don't know what this is for me. I've lived for this, dreamt about it, thought about it, eaten it, drunk it ever since I was a kid at Sandhurst. Now it's come. By God, it's come at last!"

The same Otway! Positively the little beads of perspiration were shining about his nose. His eyes scintillated an extraordinary light. He said, "By God, Sabre, you ought to have seen the battalion on parade this morning! By God, they were magnificent. They're the finest thing that ever happened. There's nothing in the Army List to touch us. When I think I'll be in action with them perhaps inside a week—I—"

An orderly approached and spoke to him. "Right. Right. I'll come along at once." He was swiftly away. "Patterson, I want you too. There's a man in your company says his wife—"

And, stilled during his presence, babel broke out anew with his departure. Some one, standing on a sofa, caught up Otway's last word into a bawling song—

I've got a wife and sixteen kids,

I've got a wife and sixteen kids,

I've got a wife and—

A cushion whizzed across the room into his face. A tag began. Sikes on the table was laying down laws of equipment at the top of his voice. "Well, I'm going to take nothing but socks. I'm going to stuff my pack absolutely bung full of socks. Man alive, I tell you nothing matters except socks. If you can keep on getting clean socks every— I'm going to stuff in socks enough to last me—"[1]

[1] A very short time afterwards, while the incident was fresh in his memory, Sabre heard that Sikes took out eleven pairs of socks and was killed, at Mons, in the pair he landed in.

II

The blessed gift in the war was to be without imagination. The supreme trial, whether in endurance on the part of those who stayed at home, or in courage on the part of those who took the field, was upon those whose mentality invested every sight and every happening with the poignancy of attributes not present but imagined. For Sabre the war definitely began with that visit to the Mess on the eve of the Pinks' departure. The high excitement of the young men, their eager planning, the almost religious ecstasy of Otway at the consummation of his life's dream, moved Sabre, visioning what might await it all, in depths profound and painful in their intensity. His mind would not abandon them. He sat up that night after Mabel had gone to her room. How on earth could he go to bed, be hoggishly sleeping, while those chaps were marching out?

He could not. At two in the morning he went quietly from the house and got out his bicycle and rode down into Tidborough.

He was just in time. The news had been well kept, or in those early days had not the meaning it came to have. Nevertheless a few people stood about the High Street in the thin light of the young morning, and when, almost immediately, the battalion came swinging out of the Market Place, many appeared flanking it, mostly women.

"Here they come!"

Frightful words! Sabre caught them from a young woman spoken to a very old woman whose arm she held a few paces from where he stood. Frightful words! He caught his breath, and, more dreadfully upon his emotions, as the head of the column came into sight, the band, taking them to the station, burst into the Pinks' familiar quickstep.

The Camp Town races are five miles long,

Doo-da! Doo-da!

The Camp Town races are five miles long,

Doo-da! Doo-da! Day!

Gwine to run all night. Gwine to run all day.

I bet my money on the bob-tail nag,

Somebody bet on the bay!

He never in his life had experienced anything so utterly frightful or imagined that anything could be so utterly frightful. His throat felt bursting. His eyes were filled. They were swinging past him, file by file. Doo-da! Doo-da! Day! He scarcely could see them. They were marching at ease, their rifles slung. They seemed to be appallingly laden with stupendous packs and multitudinous equipment. A tin mug and God knows what else beside swung and rattled about their thighs. The women with them were running to keep up, and dragging children, and stretching hands into the ranks, and crying—all crying.

...Doo-da! Doo-da!

The Camp Town races are five miles long,

Doo-da! Doo-da! Day!

He thought, "Damn that infernal music." He wiped his eyes. This was impossible to bear ... Doo-da! Doo-da! A most frightful thing happened. A boy broke out of the ranks and came running, all rattling and jingling with swinging accoutrements, to the old woman beside Sabre, put his arms around her and cried in a most frightful voice, "Mother! Mother!" And a sergeant, also rattling and clanking, dashed up and bawled with astounding ferocity, "Get back into the bloody ranks!" And the boy ran on, rattling. And the old woman collapsed prone upon the pavement. And the sergeant, as though his amazing ferocity had been the buttress of some other emotions, bent over the old woman and patted her, rattling, and said, "That's all right, Mother. That's all right. I'll look after him. I'll bring him back. That's all right, Mother." And ran on, jingling. Doo-da! Doo-da! Day!

III

187

He turned away. He absolutely could not bear it. He walked a few paces and equally could not forbear to stop and look again. The men were nearly all laughing and whistling and singing.... This bursting sensation in all his emotions! It was beyond anything he had ever experienced before. But he had experienced something like it before. His mind threw back across the years and presented the occasion to him. It was when he was a very small boy in his first term at Tidborough. The Christmas term and he was on the Strip, trying frantically behind a crowd of boys to get a glimpse of the match in progress,—one of the great matches of the season, vs. Tidborough Town. One of the boys against whose waist his frantic head was butting turned and said in a lordly way, "Let that kid through," and he was roughly bundled to a front position. The boy who had commanded his presence jolted him in the back with his knee and said, using the school argot for to cheer or shout, "Swipe up, you ghastly young ass! Swipe up! Can't you see they're pressing us?"

Couldn't he see! He felt that the end of the world was coming at what he saw. The enormous, full-grown town men were almost on the school goal-line; the school team clinging to them and battling with them like tiger-cats. He had only been at Tidborough a month, but he felt he would die if the line was crossed. He swiped till he thought his throat must crack. When his cracking throat incontinently took intervals of rest, he prayed to God for the school, visioning God on his throne on the school goalposts and mentioning to Him the players whose names he knew:

"Oh, let Barnwell get in his kick! Oh, do let Harris see they're heeling the ball! Oh, help Tufnell to get that man! Help him! Help him! Schoo-o-ool! Schoo-oo-ool! Schoo-oo-ool!"

Doo-da! Doo-da! Day!

His bursting heart was now saying, "England! England!"

IV

The column passed and was gone. He was left with his most frightful feelings. He could do nothing now. Four o'clock in the morning. But he must do something now. He could not go home till he had. He must. He followed to the station. The men were entraining in the goods yard. He waited about, not trusting himself to speak to Otway or any of the others who were going. Presently his opportunity came in a sight of Colonel Rattray, who commanded the depot and was not

188

going, standing for a minute alone. Sabre went quickly to him and they exchanged greetings and said the obvious things proper to the occasion. Then Sabre said, feeling extraordinarily embarrassed, "I say, Colonel, I want to get into this. I absolutely must get into this."

"Eh? Into what?"

"The war." It was easier after the plunge, and he went on quickly, "I see in the papers that civilians are being given commissions, getting them by recommendation. Can you get me a commission? Can you?"

Colonel Rattray showed surprise. He turned squarely about and faced Sabre and looked him up and down, but not in the way in which soldiers looked civilians up and down rather later on. "Well, I don't know. I might. I've no doubt I could, if you're eligible. How old are you, Sabre?"

"Thirty-six."

Colonel Rattray said doubtfully, "It's a bit on the steep side for a commission."

"Well, I'd go in the ranks. I must get in. I absolutely must."

The soldier smiled pleasantly. "Oh, I wouldn't get thinking about the ranks, Sabre. There're heaps before you, you know. Still, I wouldn't stop any man getting into the Army if I could help him. I'll see what I can do. Certainly I will. Mind you, I'm doubtful. Are you fit?"

"I think I am. I'm supposed to have a bit of a heart. But it's absolute rot. It never affects me in the slightest degree. I can do anything."

"Well, that's the first thing, you know. Look here, I'm wanted. Come up to the Mess in the morning and I'll get our doctor to have a look at you. Then we'll see what can be done. All right, eh?"

V

He rode home much relieved from the stresses he had suffered in that awful business of watching the regiment march out. He felt that if only he could be "in it" he could equably endure any of these things that were happening and that would get worse; if he had just to stand by and watch them his portion would be insupportable. England! Other

189

people whom he knew could not possibly feel it in the way he felt it. His history with its opening sentence, "This England you live in is yours", had arisen out of his passionate love for all that England meant to him. In all Shakespeare there was no passage that moved him in quite the same way whenever he recalled it as Richard the Second's

Dear earth, I do salute thee with my hand....

Mock not my senseless conjuration, lords,

This earth shall have a feeling....

Stooping and touching the soil of England as one might bend and touch a beloved face. That was what England for years had meant to him. And now.... It was upon these emotions, vaguely, "in case", that he had gone to Doctor Anderson on the morning of the frightful news. Anderson had told him he couldn't possibly be passed for the Army, but at the moment the idea of ever wanting to go into the Army had only been an almost ridiculously remote contingency, and what did Anderson know about the Army standard, anyway?

VI

He said nothing to Mabel of his intention. It was just precisely the sort of thing he could not possibly discuss with Mabel. Mabel would say, "Whyever should you?" and of all imaginable ordeals the idea of exposing before Mabel his feeling about England ... he would tell her when it was done, if it came off. He could say then, in what he knew to be the clumsy way in which he had learnt to hide his ideas from her, he could say, "Well, I had to."

And his thought was, when a few hours later he was walking slowly away from his interview with Major Earnshaw, the doctor at the barracks, "Thank God, I never said anything to Mabel about it."

The very few officers left behind at the depot were at breakfast when he arrived to keep Colonel Rattray to his word. Major Earnshaw had very pleasantly got up from the table to "put him out of his misery" there and then without formality and had "had a go at this heart of yours" in the billiard room. Withdrawn his stethoscope and shaken his head. It was "no go; absolutely none, Sabre."

"Well, but that's for a commission. I'll go into the ranks. Isn't that any different?"

190

No different. "You can't possibly go in as you are—now. In time, if this thing goes on, the standards will probably be reduced. But they'll have to be reduced a goodish long way before you'll get in, I don't mind telling you."

Sabre wheeled his bicycle slowly away across the barrack square. "Thank goodness, I never said anything to Mabel about it." A cluster of young men of various degrees of life were waiting outside the door of the recruiting office. The rush of the first few days was thinning down but recruits were still pouring in. They were all laughing and talking noisily. He had the wish that he could take the thing in that spirit. Why couldn't he? After all, what did it really matter that he was not able to get "in it"? Even if he had been accepted it would only have been pretending. He never would have got really "in it"; none of those chaps would; every one knew the war couldn't last long; it would be over long before any of these recruits could be trained.

VII

This "common sense" argument carried him through following days; then came another of the frightful undoings of his emotions; and just as the war definitely began for him with the glimpse of the beginnings of that "jamborino" in the Mess, so from this new occasion began, unceasingly and increasingly, and with shocking effect upon his sensitiveness, a dreadful oppression by the war and, adding to its darkness, a gnawing and unreasonable self-accusation that he was not "in it."

The occasion was that of his meeting with Harkness outside the County Times office. Harkness was a captain of the battalion that had gone out who had been left behind owing to some illness. The British Expeditionary Force had been in action. There had been scraps of news of some heavy fighting. Harkness said dully, "Hullo, Sabre. I've just been in to see that chap Pike to see if he'd got anything. We've had some news, you know." He stopped. His face was twitching.

Sabre said, "News? Anything about the Pinks?"

Harkness nodded. He seemed to be swallowing. Then he said, "Yes, the regiment. Pretty bad."

Sabre said, "Any one—?" and also stopped.

Harkness looked, not at Sabre, but straight across the top of his head and began an appalling, and as it seemed to Sabre, an endless recitative. "The Colonel's killed. Bruce is killed. Otway's killed—"

"Otway...."

"Cottar's killed. Bullen's killed—"

Endless! The names struck Sabre like successive blows. Were they never going to end?

"Carmichael's killed. My young brother's—" his voice cracked— "killed. Sikes is killed."

"Sikes killed.... And your brother...."

Harkness said in a very thin, squeaking voice, "Yes, the regiment's pretty well—The regiment's—" He looked full at Sabre and said in a very loud, defiant voice, "I bet they were magnificent. By God, I bet you they were magnificent. Oh, my God, why the hell wasn't I there?" He turned abruptly and went away, walking rather funnily.

This was the moment at which there descended upon Sabre, never to leave him while he remained not "in it", the appalling sense of oppression that the war exercised upon him. On his brain like a weight; on his heart like a pressing hand. He thought of Otway's intense, gleaming face. "My God, Sabre, you ought to have seen the battalion on parade this morning." He saw Otway's face cold and stricken. He thought of Sikes, on the table. "Well, I'm going to take nothing but socks. I'm going to stuff my pack absolutely bung full of socks." He saw Sikes flung like a disused thing in some field....

VIII

And still events; still, and always, now, disturbing things.

While he stood there he was suddenly aware of Young Rod, Pole or Perch, rather breathlessly come up.

"I say, Sabre, have you heard this frightful news about the Pinks?—I say, Sabre, I want your help most frightfully. I want you to talk to my mother. She likes you. She'll listen to you. I'm going to enlist. I've been putting it off day after day, trying to fix up things for my mother and trying to persuade her; but I haven't done much and I absolutely can't wait any longer."

Sabre said, "Good Lord, are you, Perch? Must you? Your mother, why, what on earth will she do without you? She'll—"

Young Perch winced painfully. "I know. I know. It pretty well kills me to think of it and I'm having the most frightful scenes with her. But I've thought it all out, Sabre, and I know I'm doing the right thing. I've looked after my mother all my life, and a month ago the idea of leaving her even for a couple of nights would have been unthinkable. But this is different. This is—" He flushed awkwardly—"you can't talk that sort of patriotic stuff, you know, but this is, well this is a chap's country, and I've figured it out it's got to come before my mother. It's got to. She says it will kill her if I go. I believe it will, Sabre. And my God, if it does—but I can't help it. I know what's the right thing. I'll tell you something else." His face, which had been red and cloudy as with tears, became dark and passionate. "I'll tell you something else. People are saying things about me and to me because I'm young and unmarried and haven't got a wife to support. Curse them, Sabre—what do they know about it? Aren't their wives young, strong, able to take care of themselves? My mother can't come downstairs without me and can't let any one else—"

He rubbed a hand across his eyes and broke off. "Never mind about that; I know what I've got to do. Look here, Sabre, I tell you where I want your help, like anything. You know lots of people. I don't. Well, I want to get hold of some nice girl to live with my mother and take care of her in my place while I'm away. A sort of companion, aren't they called? Like that Bypass person up at old Boom Bagshaw's, only much nicer and younger and friendlier than she is. You see, I know my mother. If it was any one of any age, she wouldn't have her in the house at any price, and she'd send her flying out of the window in about two days if she did have her. She swears no power on earth will induce her to have any one at all as it is. But I'm going to manage it if I can get the right person. I want some one who my mother will indignantly call a chit of a child"—he gave rather a broken little laugh—"can't I hear her saying it! But she'll instantly begin to mother her because she is a chit of a child, and to fuss over her and tell her what she ought to eat and what she ought to wear, and does she wear a flannel binder, and all that, just as she does to me. And in about a week she'll be as right as rain and writing me letters all day and arguing with the girl how to spell 'being' and 'been'—you know what my mother is. I say, Sabre, do for God's sake help me, if you can. Do you know any one?"

Sabre, during this greatly troubled outpouring, had the feeling that this was all of a part with the calamitous news he had just had from Harkness,—a direct continuation of it. This frightful war! Was it going to attack even that pathetic little old woman at Puncher's Farm with her fumbling hands and her frail existence centred solely in her son? He said, "I'm awfully sorry, Perch. Frightfully sorry for your mother and for you. You know best what you ought to do. I won't say anything either way. I think a man's only judge in this ghastly business is himself. Of course, I'll help you. I'll help you all I can. It's a funny coincidence but I believe I do know just the very girl that would be what you want—"

Young Perch grasped his hand in delighted relief. "Oh, Sabre, if you do! I felt you would help. You've always been a chap to turn to!"

"I've turned to you, Perch, you and your mother, a good deal more than you might imagine. I'm glad to help if I can. The chance I'm thinking about I was hearing of only a few days ago. The works' foreman in my office, an old chap called Bright. He's got a daughter about eighteen or thereabouts, and I was hearing he wanted to get her into some kind of post like yours. I've spoken to her once or twice when she's been about the place for her father and I took a tremendous fancy to her. She's as pretty as a picture. Effie, she's called. I believe your mother would take to her no end. And she'd just love your mother."

Young Perch said rather thickly, "Any one would who takes her the right way."

Sabre touched him encouragingly on the shoulder. "This girl Effie will if only we can get her. She's that sort, I know. I'll see about it at once. Buck up, old man."

"Thanks most frightfully, Sabre. Thanks most awfully."

IX

It was from Twyning that Sabre had heard that a post of some sort was being considered for Effie Bright. Her father, as he had told young Perch, was works' foreman at Fortune, East and Sabre's. "Mr. Bright." A massive old man with a massive, rather striking face hewn beneath

194

a bald dome and thickly grown all about and down the throat with stiff white hair. He had been in the firm as long as Mr. Fortune himself and appeared to Sabre, who had little to do with him, to take orders from nobody. He was intensely religious and he had the deep-set and extraordinarily penetrating eyes that frequently denote the religious zealot. He was not liked by the hands. They called him Moses, disliked his intense religiosity and feared the cold and heavy manner that he had. He trod heavily about the workshops, looking into the eyes of the young men as if far more concerned to search their souls than their benches; and Sabre, when speaking to him, always had the feeling that Mr. Bright was penetrating him with the same intention.

Extraordinary that such a stern and hard old man should have for daughter such a fresh and lovable slip of a young thing as his Effie! Bright Effie, Sabre always called her, inverting her names. Mr. Bright had a little cupboard called his office at the foot of the main stairway and Bright Effie came often to see her father there. Sabre had spoken to her in the little cupboard or just outside it. He had delight in watching the most extraordinary shining that she had in her eyes. It was like reading an entertaining book, he used to think, and he had the idea that humor of that rarest kind which is unbounded love mingled with unbounded sense of the oddities of life was packed to bursting within her. All that she saw or heard seemed to be taken into that exhaustless fount, metamorphosed into the most delicious sensations, and shone forth in extraordinarily humorous delight through her eyes. Somewhere in the dullest day light is found and thrown back by a bright surface. It was just so, Sabre used to think, with Effie. All things were fresh to her and she found freshness in all things.

Some such apprehension of her Sabre had expressed to Twyning on the occasion that came to his mind during young Perch's entreaty for some one to live with his mother. Sabre had been standing with Twyning at Mr. Fortune's window, Mr. Bright and Effie leaving the office and crossing the street together beneath them. Twyning, who was on intimate terms with Mr. Bright, had given a short laugh and said, "Hullo, you seem to have been thinking a lot about the fair Effie!"

The kind of laugh and the kind of remark that Sabre hated and he gave a slight gesture which Twyning well knew meant that he hated it. This was what Twyning called "stuck-uppishness" and equally hated, and he chose words expressive of his resentment,—the class insistence.

"Well, she's got to earn her living, however jolly she is. She's not one of your fine ladies, you know."

Sabre recognised the implication but ignored it. "What's old Bright going to do with her?"

"He doesn't quite know. He was talking to my missus about it the other day. He's as good as we are, you know. He's an idea of getting her out as a sort of lady's companion somewhere."

This was what Sabre had remembered; and he went straight from young Perch to Twyning and recalled the conversation.

Twyning said, "Hullo, still interested in the fair Effie?"

"It's for young Perch over at Penny Green I'm asking. For his mother. He's a young man"—Sabre permitted his eyes to rest for a moment on Harold, seated at his desk—"and he feels he ought to join the army. He wants the girl to be with his mother while he's away."

Twyning, noting the glance, changed his tone to one of much friendliness. "Oh, I see, old man. No, Effie's got nothing yet. She was over to our place to tea last Sunday."

"Good. I'll go and talk to old Bright. I'm keen about this."

"Yes, you seem to be, old man."

X

Mr. Bright received the suggestion with a manner that irritated Sabre. While he was being told of the Perches he stared at Sabre with that penetrating gaze of his as though in the proposal he searched for some motive other than common friendliness. His first comment was, "They'll want references, I suppose, sir?"

Sabre smiled. "Oh, scarcely, Mr. Bright. Not when they know who you are."

The old man was standing before Sabre in the little cupboard bending his head close towards him as though he would sense out, if he could not see, some hidden motive behind all this. He contracted his great brows as if to squeeze more penetration into his gaze. "Yes, but I'll want references, Mr. Sabre. My girl's been well brought up. She's not going here, there, nor anywhere."

Extraordinary the intensity of his searching, suspicious stare! Hard, stupid old man, Sabre thought. "Dash it, does he suppose I've got designs on the girl?" He would have returned an impatient answer had he not been so anxious on the Perches' behalf. Instead he said pleasantly, "Of course she's not, Mr. Bright. You may be sure I wouldn't suggest this if I didn't know it was in every way desirable. Mrs. Perch is a very old friend of mine and a very simple and kind old lady. There'll be only herself for Effie to meet. And she'll make a daughter of her."

Nothing, of the penetration abated from the deep-set eyes, nor came any expression of thanks from the stern, pursed mouth. "I'll take my girl over and see for myself, Mr. Sabre."

Surly, stupid old man! However, poor young Perch! Poor old Mrs. Perch! The very thing, if only it would come off.

XI

It came off. Sabre went up to Puncher's Farm on the evening of the day Mr. Bright, "to see for himself", had called with Effie. Young Perch greeted him delightedly in the doorway and clasped his hand in gratitude. "It's all right. It's fixed. She's coming. I've had the most frightful struggle with my mother. But it's only her way, you know." He stopped and Sabre heard him gulp. "Only her way. I could see she took to the girl from the start. My mother's started knitting me a pair of socks and old man Bright—I say, he's rather an alarming sort of person, Sabre—had hardly opened his mouth when they arrived when the girl, in the most extraordinary, making-a-fuss-of-her kind of way, told her she was using the wrong size needles or something. And my mother, as if she had known her all her life, said, 'There you are, I knew I was. It's simply useless asking Freddie to do any shopping for me. He simply lets them give him anything they like.' And she told the girl she thought she had some other needles in one of those gigantic old boxes of ours. And they went off together to look, and heaven only knows what they got up to; they were away about half an hour and came back with about three hundredweight of old wools and nine pounds of needles, and talking about how they were going through all the other boxes, 'now I've got some one to help me', as my mother said. By Jove, the girl's wonderful. D'you know, she actually kissed my mother when she was leaving and said, 'Now be sure to try that

197

little pillow just under your side to-night. Just press it in as you're falling asleep.' By Jove, you can't think how grateful I am to you, Sabre."

"I am glad," Sabre told him. "I felt she'd be just like that. But why have you been having a frightful struggle over it with your mother if she's taken to her so?"

Young Perch gave the fond little laugh with which Sabre had so often heard him conclude his enormous arguments with his mother. "Oh, you know what my mother is. She's now made up her mind that the girl is coming here to do what she calls 'catch me.' She'll forget that soon. Anyway, the girl's coming. She's coming the day after to-morrow, the day I'm going. Come along in and see my mother and keep her to it."

The subject did not require bringing up. "I suppose Freddie's told you what he's forcing me into now, Mr. Sabre," old Mrs. Perch greeted him. "It's a funny thing that I should be forced to do things at my time of life. Of course she's after Freddie. Do you suppose I can't see that?"

"Well, but she won't see Freddie, Mrs. Perch. He won't be here."

"She'll catch him," declared Mrs. Perch doggedly. "Any girl could catch Freddie. He's a positive fool with one of these girls after him. Now she's got to have his uncle Henry's armchair in her room, if you please. That's a nice thing, isn't it?"

"Now look here, Mother, you know perfectly well that was your own idea. You said you felt sure she had a weak back and that—"

"I never supposed she was going to have your uncle Henry's chair for her weak back or for any other back. Ask Mr. Sabre what he thinks. There he is. Ask him."

Sabre said, "But you do like the girl, don't you, Mrs. Perch?"

Mrs. Perch pursed her lips.

"I don't say I don't like her. I merely ask what I'm going to do with her in the house. When Freddie said he wanted to bring some one in to be with me, I never supposed he was going to bring a chit of a child into the house. I assure you I never supposed that was going to be done to me."

And then quite suddenly Mrs. Perch dropped into a chair and said in a horribly weak voice, "I don't mind who comes into the house, now. I can't contend like I used to contend." Immense tears gathered in her eyes and began to run swiftly down her cheeks. "I'm not fit for anything now. I can't live without Freddie. I like the girl; but all this house where we've been so happy ... without Freddie ... I shall see his dear, bright face everywhere. Why must he go, Mr. Sabre? Why must he go? I don't understand this war at all." Her voice trailed off. Her hands fumbled on her lap. A tear fell on them. She brushed at it with a fumbling motion but it remained there.

Young Perch took her hand and fondled it. Sabre saw the wrinkled, fumbling old hand between the strong brown fingers. "That's all right, Mother. Of course, you don't understand it. That's just it. You think I'm going out to fighting and all that. And I'm just going into a training camp here in England for a bit. And before Christmas it will all be over and I shall come flying back and we'll send Miss Bright toddling off home and—Don't cry, Mother. Don't cry, Mother. Isn't that so, Sabre? Just training in England. Isn't that so? Now wherever's your old handkerchief got to? Look here; here's mine. Look, this is the one I chose that day with you in Tidborough. Do you remember what a jolly tea we had that day? Remember what a laugh we had over that funny teapot. There, let me wipe them, Mother...."

Sabre turned away. This frightful war....

CHAPTER VI

I

This frightful war! On his brain like a weight. On his heart like a pressing hand.

Came Christmas by which, at the outset, everybody knew it would be over, and it was not over. Came June, 1915, concerning which, at the outset, he had joined with Mr. Fortune, Twyning and Harold in laughter at his own grotesque idea of the war lasting to the dramatic effect of a culminating battle on the centenary of Waterloo, and the war had lasted, and was still lasting.

"This frightful war!" The words were constantly upon his lips, ejaculated to himself in reception of new manifestations of its eruptions; forever in his mind, like a live thing gnawing there. Other people seemed to suffer the war in spasms, isolated amidst the round of their customary routines, of dejection or of optimistic reassurance. The splendid sentiment of "Business as usual" was in many valiant mouths. The land, in so far as provisions and prices were concerned, continued to flow in milk and honey as the British Isles had always flowed in milk and honey. In July a rival multiple grocer's shop opened premises opposite the multiple grocer's shop already established in the shopping centre of the Garden Home and Mabel told Sabre how very exciting it was. The rivals piled their windows, one against the other, with stupendous stacks of margarine and cheese at sevenpence the pound each; and then one day, "Whatever do you think?" the new man interspersed his mountains of margarine and cheese with wooden bowls running over with bright new pennies, and flamed his windows with announcements that this was "The Money-back Shop." You bought a pound of margarine for sevenpence and were handed a penny with your purchase! And the next day, "Only fancy!" the other man also had bright new pennies (in bursting bags from the bank) and also bellowed that he too was a Money-back Shop.

"The fact is the war really hasn't mattered a bit," Mabel said. "I think it's wonderful. And when you remember at the beginning how people rushed to buy up food and what awful ideas of starvation went about; you were one of the worst."

And Sabre agreed that it really was wonderful: and agreed too with Mabel's further opinion that he really ought not to get so fearfully depressed.

But he remained fearfully depressed. The abundance of food, and such manifestations of plenty as the bowls and bags of bright new pennies meant nothing to him. He knew nothing about war. Very possibly the prophecies of shortage and restrictions and starvation were, in the proof, to be refuted as a thousand other prophecies of the early days, optimistic and pessimistic, were being refuted. What had that to do with it? Remained the frightful facts that were going on out there in Belgium and in Gallipoli and in Russia. Remained the increasing revelation of Germany's enormous might in war and the revelation of what war was as she conducted it. Remained the sinister revelation that we were not winning as in the past we had "always won." Remained his envisagement of England—England!—standing four-square to her enemies, but standing as some huge and splendid animal something bewildered by the fury of the onset upon it. Shaking her head whereon had fallen stunning and unexpected blows, as it might be a lion enormously smashed across the face; roaring her defiance; baring her fangs; tearing up the ground before her; dreadful and undaunted and tremendous; but stricken; in sore agony; in heavy amazement; her pride thrust through with swords; her glory answered by another's glory; her dominion challenged; shaken, bleeding.

England.... This frightful war!

II

Remained also, blowing about the streets, in the newspapers and at meetings, in the mouths of many, and in the eyes of most, the new popular question, "Why aren't you in khaki?" The subject of age, always shrouded in a seemly and decorous modesty in England, and especially since, a few years previously, an eminent professor of medicine had unloosed the alarming theory of "Too old at forty", was suddenly ripped out of its prudish coverings. One generation of men began to talk with thoroughly engaging frankness and largeness about their age. They would even announce it in a loud voice in crowded public conveyances. It was nothing, in those days, to hear a man suddenly declare in an omnibus or tramway car, "Well, I'm thirty-eight and I only wish to heaven I was a few years younger." Other men would heartfully chime in, "Ah, same thing with me. It's hard." And all these men, thus cruelly burdened with a few more years than the age limit, would look with great intensity at other men, apparently not thus burdened, who for their part would assume attitudes of physical unfitness or gaze very sternly out of the window.

Several of the younger employees of Fortune, East and Sabre's joined up (as the current phrase had it) in the first weeks of the war. In the third month Mr. Fortune assembled the hands and from across the whale-like front indicated the path of duty and announced that the places of all those who followed it would be kept open for them. "Hear, hear!" said Twyning. "Hear, hear!" and as the men were filing out he took Sabre affectionately by the arm and explained to him that young Harold was dying to go. "But I feel a certain duty is due to the firm, old man. What I mean is, that the boy's only just come here and I feel that in my position as a partner it wouldn't look well for me practically with my own hand to be paying out unearned salary to a chap who'd not been four months in the place. Don't you agree, old man?"

Sabre said, "But we wouldn't be paying him, would we? Fortune said salaries of married men."

"Ah, yes, old man, but between you and me he's going to do it for unmarried men as well, as the cases come up."

"Why didn't he tell them so?"

Twyning's genial expression hardened under these questions, but he said, still on his first note of confidential affection, "Ah, because he thinks they ought to do their duty without being bribed. Quite right, too. No, it's a difficult position for me. My idea is not to give way to the boy's wishes for a few months while he establishes his position here, and then, if men are still wanted, why of course he'll go. Sound, don't you think, old man?"

Sabre disengaged his arm and turned into his own room. "Well, I think this is a business in which you can't judge any one. I think every man is his own judge."

An astonishing rasp came into Twyning's voice. "How old are you?"

"Thirty-six. Why?"

Twyning laughed away the rasp. "Ah, I'm older. I daresay you'll have a chance later on, if the Times and the Morning Post and those class papers have their way. And you've got no family, have you, old man?"

III

That was in the third month of the war. But by June, 1915, the position on these little points had hardened. In June, "Why aren't you in khaki?" was blowing about the streets. Questions looked out of eyes. Certain men avoided one another. And in June young Harold joined up. Sabre greeted the news with very great warmth. Towards Harold he had none of the antipathy that was often aroused in him by Harold's father. He shook the good-looking young man very heartily by the hand. "By Jove, I'm glad. Well done, Harold. That's splendid. Jolly good luck to you."

Later in the morning Twyning came in. He entered abruptly. His air, and when he spoke, his manner, struck Sabre as being deliberately aggressive. "Well, Harold's gone," he said.

"Yes, I'm jolly glad for the boy's sake. I was just congratulating him. I think it's splendid of him."

Twyning breathed heavily through his nose. "Splendid? Hur! He wanted to go long ago. Well, he's gone now and I hope you're satisfied."

Sabre turned in his chair and questioned Twyning with puckered brows. "Satisfied? What on earth do you mean—satisfied?"

"You always thought he ought to go. You're one of those who've sent him off. My boy saw it."

"You're talking nonsense. I've never so much as mentioned the subject to Harold. I told you long ago that I think every man's his own judge, and sole judge, in this business."

Twyning always retracted when Sabre showed signs of becoming roused. "Ah, well, what does it matter? He's gone now. He'll be in this precious khaki to-night. No one can point at him now." He drew out a handkerchief and wiped his eyes slowly. He stared inimically at Sabre. "I'll tell you one thing, Sabre. You wait till you've got a son, then you'll think differently, perhaps. You don't know what my boy means to me. He's everything in the world to me. I got him in here so as to have him with me and now this cursed war's taken him. You don't know what he is, my boy Harold. He's a better man than his father, I'll tell you that. He's a good Christian boy. He's never had a bad thought or said a bad word."

He broke off. He rammed his handkerchief into his trouser pocket. As though the sight of Sabre sitting before him suddenly infuriated him he broke out, "It's all right for you sitting there. You're not going. Never mind. My boy Harold's gone. You're satisfied. All right."

Sabre got up. "Look here, Twyning, I'm sorry for you about Harold. I make allowances for you. But—"

When Twyning was angry his speech sometimes betrayed that on which he was most sensitive. "I don't want you to make no allowances for me. I don't—"

"You've repeated the stupid implication you made when you first came in."

Twyning changed to a hearty laugh. "Oh, I say, steady, old man. Don't let's have a row. Nothing to have a row about, old man. I made no implication. Whatever for should I? No, no, I simply said 'All right.' I say people have sent my boy Harold off, and I'm merely saying 'All right. He's gone. Now perhaps you're satisfied.' Not you, old man. Other people." He paused. His tone hardened. "All right. That's all, old man. All right."

IV

Not very long after this incident occurred another incident. In its obvious aspect it was also related to the "Why aren't you in khaki?" question; Sabre apprehended in it a different bearing.

One morning he stepped suddenly from his own room into Mr. Fortune's in quest of a reference. Twyning and Mr. Fortune were seated together in deep conversation. They were very often thus seated, Sabre had noticed. At his entry their conversation abruptly ceased; and this also was not new.

Sabre went across to the filing cabinet without speaking.

Mr. Fortune cleared his throat. "Ah, Sabre. Ah, Sabre, we were just saying, we were just saying—" His hesitation, and the pause before he had begun quite clearly informed Sabre that what he was now about to say was not going to be—precisely—what he had just been saying. "We were just saying what a very unfortunate thing, what a very deeply unfortunate thing it is that none of us principals are of an age to do the right thing by the Firm by joining the Army. I'm afraid we've got one or two shirkers downstairs, and we were just saying what a splendid, what an entirely splendid thing it would be if one of us were able to set them an example."

Sabre faced about from the cabinet towards them. Twyning in the big chair had his elbow on the arm and was biting his nails. Mr. Fortune, revolved to face the room, was exercising his watch chain on his whale-like front.

"Yes, it's a pity," Sabre said.

"I'm glad you agree. I knew you would. Indeed, yes, a pity; a very great pity. For myself, of course, I'm out of the question. Twyning here is getting on for forty and of course he's given his son to the war; moreover, there's the business to be thought of. I'm afraid I'm not quite able to do all I used to do. You—of course, you're married too, and there we are! It does, as you say, seem a great pity." The watch chain, having been generously exercised, was put to the duty of heavy tugs at its reluctant partner. Mr. Fortune gazed at his watch and remarked absently, "I hear young Phillips of Brown and Phillips has persuaded his wife to let him go. You were at the school with him, Sabre, weren't you? Isn't he about your age?"

Sabre spoke very slowly. Most furious anger had been rising within him. It was about to burst when there had suddenly come to its control the thought, "These two aren't getting at you for any love of England, for any patriotic reason. That's not it. Don't bother about that. Man alive, don't mix them up in what you feel about these things. Don't go cheapening what you think about England. Theirs is another reason." He said very slowly, "I never told you, perhaps I ought to have told you at the time, that I was refused for the Army some while ago."

Mr. Fortune's watch slipped through his fingers to the full length of his chain. Twyning got up and went over to a bookcase and stared at it.

Mr. Fortune heaved in the line with an agitated hand over hand motion. "I'd no idea! My dear fellow, I'd no idea! How very admirable of you! When was this? After that big meeting in the Corn exchange the other day?"

"Don't tell them when it was," said Sabre's mind. He said, "No, rather before that. I was rejected on medical grounds."

"Well, well!" said Mr. Fortune. "Well, well!" He gave the suggestion of being unable to array his thoughts against this surprising turn of the day. "Most creditable. Twyning, do you hear that?"

Twyning spun around from the bookcase and came forward. "Eh? Sorry, I'm afraid I wasn't listening."

"Our excellent Sabre has offered himself for enlistment and been rejected."

Twyning said, "Have you, by Jove! Jolly good. What bad luck being turned down. What was it?"

Sabre moved across to his room. "Heart."

"Was it, really? By Jove, and you look fit enough, too, old man. Fancy, heart! Fancy—Jolly sporting of you. Fancy—Oh, I say, old man, do let's have a look at your paper if you've got it on you. I want to see one of those things."

Sabre was at his door. "What paper?"

"Your rejection paper, old man. I've never seen one. Only if you've got it on you."

"I haven't got one."

"Not got one! You must have, old man."

"Well, I haven't. I was seen privately. I'm rather friendly with them up at the barracks."

"Oh, yes, of course. Wonder they didn't give you a paper, though."

"Well, they didn't."

"Quite so, old man. Quite so. Funny, that's all."

Sabre paused on the threshold. He perfectly well understood the villainous implication. Vile, intolerable! But of what service to take it up?—To hear Twyning's laugh and his "My dear old chap, as if I should think such a thing!" He passed into his room. The thought he had had which had arrested his anger at Mr. Fortune's hints, revealing this incident in another light, was, "They want to get rid of me."

V

In August, the anniversary month of the war, he again offered himself for enlistment and was again rejected, but this time after a longer scrutiny: the standard was not at its first height of perfection. Earnshaw, Colonel Rattray, all the remnant of his former friends, were gone to the front: Sabre submitted himself through the ordinary channels and this time received what Twyning had called his "paper." He did not show it to Twyning, nor mention either to him or to Mr. Fortune that he had tried again. "Again! most creditable of you, my dear Sabre." "Again, have you, though? By Jove, that's sporting of you. Did they give you a paper this time, old man?" No. Not much. Feeling as he felt about the war, acutely aware as he was of the partners' interest in the matter, that, he felt, could not be borne.

But on this occasion he told Mabel.

The war had not altered his relations with Mabel. He had had the feeling that it ought to bring them closer together, to make her more susceptible to his attempts to do the right thing by her. But it did not bring them closer together: the accumulating months, the imperceptibly increasing strangeness and tension and high pitch of the war atmosphere increased, rather, her susceptibility to those characteristics of his which were most impossible to her. He felt things with draught too deep and with burthen too capacious for the navigability of her mind; and here was an ever-present thing, this (in her phrase) most unsettling war, which must be taken (in her view) on a high, brisk note that was as impossible to him as was his own attitude towards the war to her. The effect of the war, in this result, was but to sunder them on a new dimension: whereas formerly he had learned not to join with her on subjects his feelings about which he had been taught to shrink from exposing before her, now the world contained but one subject; there was no choice and there was no upshot but clash of incompatibility. His feelings were daily forced to the ordeal; his ideas daily exasperated her. The path he had set himself was not to mind her abuse of his feelings, and he tried with some success not to mind; but (in his own expression, brooding in his mind's solitude) they riled her and he had nothing else to offer her; they riled her and he had set himself not to rile her. It was like desiring to ease a querulous invalid and having in the dispensary but a single—and a detested—palliative.

Things were not better; they were worse.—But he made his efforts. The matter of telling her (when he tried in August) that he thought he ought to join the Army was one, and it came nearest to establishing pleasant relations. That it revealed a profound difference of sensibility was nothing. He blamed himself for causing that side to appear.

Her comment when, on the eve of his attempt, he rather diffidently acquainted her with his intention, was, "Do you really think you ought to?" This was not enthusiastic; but he went ahead with it and made a joke, which amused her, about how funny it would be if she had to start making "comforts" for him at the War Knitting League which she was attending with great energy at the Garden Home. He found, as they talked, that it never occurred to her but that it was as an officer that he would be going, and something warned him not to correct her assumption. He found with pleased surprise quite a friendly chat afoot between them. She only began to fall away in interest when he, made forgetful by this new quality in their contact, allowed his deeper feelings to find voice. Once started, he was away before he had realised it, in how one couldn't help feeling about England and how utterly glorious would be his own sensations if he could actually get into uniform and feel that England had admitted him to be a part of her.

She looked at the clock.

His face was reddening in its customary signal of his enthusiasm. He noticed her glance, but was not altogether checked. He went on quickly, "Well, look here. I must tell you this. I'll tell you what I'll say to myself first thing if I really do get in. A thing out of the Psalms. By Jove, an absolutely terrific thing, Mabel. In the Forty-fifth. Has old Bag—has Boom Bagshaw told you people up at the church what absolutely magnificent reading the Psalms are just now, in this war?"

She shook her head. "We sing them every Sunday, of course. But I don't see how the Psalms—you mean the Bible Psalms, don't you?—can have anything to do with war."

"Oh, but they have. They're absolutely hung full of it. Half of them are the finest battle chants ever written. You ought to read them, Mabel; every one ought to be reading them these days. Well, this verse I'm telling you about. I say, do listen, I won't keep you a minute. It's in that one where there comes in a magnificent chant to some princess who was being brought to marriage to some foreign king—"

Mabel's dispersing attention took arms. "To a princess! However can it be? It's the Psalms. You do mean the Bible Psalms, don't you?"

He said quickly, "Oh, well, never mind that. Look here, this is it. I shall say it to myself directly I get in, and then often and often again. It ought to be printed on a card and given to every recruit. Just listen:

"Good luck have thou with thine honour; ride on, because of the word of truth, of meekness and of righteousness: and thy right hand shall show thee terrible things.

"Isn't that terrific? Isn't it tremendous? By Jove, it—"

For the first time in her married life she looked at him, in this humour, not distastefully but curiously. His flushed face and shining eyes! Whatever about? He was perfectly incomprehensible to her. She got up. She said, "Yes—but 'Ride on'—of course you're not going in the cavalry, are you?"

He said, "Oh, well. Sorry. It's just a thing, you know. Yes, it's your bedtime, I'm afraid. I've kept you up, gassing. Well, dream good luck for me to-morrow."

His thoughts, when she had gone from the room, went, "A better evening! That's the way! I can do it, you see, if I try. That other thing doesn't matter. I was a fool to drag that in. She doesn't understand. Yes, that's the way!"

He sat late, happily. If only he could get past the doctor to-morrow!

VI

That's the way! But on the following evening the way was not to be recaptured. The old way was restored. He was enormously cast down by his rejection. When he got back that night he went straight in to her. "I say, they've rejected me. They won't have me." His face was working. "It's that cursed heart."

She slightly puckered her brows. "Oh—d'you know, for the minute I couldn't think what on earth you were talking about. Were you rejected? Well, I must say I'm glad. Up at the Knitting League Mrs. Turner was saying her son saw you at the recruiting office after you were rejected and that it was into the ranks you were going. You never told me that. I must say I don't think you ought to have thought about the ranks without telling me. And I wouldn't have liked it. I wouldn't have liked it at all. I think you ought to be very thankful you were rejected. I'm sure I am."

He said flatly, "Why are you? Thankful—good lord—you don't know—what do you mean, I ought to be thankful?"

"Because you ought to be an officer, if you go at all. It's not the place for you in your position. And apart from anything else—" She gave her sudden burst of laughter.

He felt arise within him violent and horrible feelings about her. "What are you laughing at?"

"Well, do just imagine what you'd look like in private soldier's clothing!" She laughed very heartily again.

He turned away.

CHAPTER VII

I

Up in his room he began a long letter to Nona, pouring out to her all his feelings about this second rejection. He was writing to her—and hearing from her—regularly and frequently now. It was his only vent in the oppression of these frightful days. She said that it was hers, too.

After that letter of hers, at the outbreak of the war, in which she had said that she thanked God for him that he had delayed her decision to unchain their chains and to join their lives, no further reference had been made by either to that near touch of desire's wand. It was, as he had said it should be, as though her letter had never been written. And in her letters she always mentioned Tony. She wrote to Tony every day, she told him; and there were few of her letters but mentioned a parcel of some kind sent to her husband. Tony never wrote. Sometimes, she said, there came a scrap from him relative to some business matter she must see to; but never any response to her daily budget of gossip—"the kind of news I know he likes to hear"—or any news of himself and his doings.

She once or twice said, without any comment, "But he is writing often to Mrs. Stanley and Lady Grace Heddon and Sophie Basildon and I hear bits of him from them and know he is keeping well. Of course, I pretend to them that their news is stale to me." Another time, "I've just finished my budget to Tony," she wrote, "and have sent him two sets of those patent rubber soles for his boots. Do you think he can get them put on? Every day I try to think of some new trifle he'd like; and you'd be shocked, and think I care nothing about the war, at the number of theatres I make time to go to. You see, it makes something bright and amusing to tell him, describing the plays. I feel most frightfully that, although of course my canteen work is useful, the real best thing every woman can do in this frightful time is to do all she can for her man out there; and Tony's mine. When this is all over—oh, Marko, is it ever going to be over?—things will hurt again; but while he's out there the old things are dead and Tony's mine and England's— my man for England: that is my thought; that is my pride; that is my prayer."

And a few lines farther on, "And he's so splendid. Of course you can imagine how utterly splendid he is. Lady King-Warner, his colonel's wife, told me yesterday her husband says he's brave beyond anything she could imagine. He said—she's given me his letter—'the men have picked up from home this story about angels at Mons and are

211

beginning to believe they saw them. Tybar says he hopes the angels were near him, because he thought he was in hell, the particular bit he got into, and he thinks it must be good for angels, enlarging for their minds, to know what hell is like! As a matter of fact, Tybar himself is nearer to the superhuman than anything I saw knocking about at Mons. His daring and his coolness and his example are a byword in a battalion composed, my dear, with the solitary exception of the writer, entirely of heroes. In sticky places Tybar is the most wonderful thing that ever happened. I like to be near him because his immediate vicinity is unquestionably a charmed circle; and I shudder to be near him because his is always the worst spot.'

"Can't you imagine him, Marko?"

II

And always her letters breathed to Sabre his own passionate love of England, his own poignant sense of possession in her and by her, his own intolerable aching at the heart at his envisagement of her enormously beset. They reflected his own frightful oppression and they assuaged it, as his letters, she told him, assuaged hers, as burdens are assuaged by mingling of distress. "There is no good news," he told her, "and for me who can do nothing—and sometimes things are a little difficult with me here and I suppose that makes it worse—there seems to be no way out. But your letters are more than good news and more than rescue; they are courage. Courage is like love, Nona: it touches the spirit; and the spirit, amazing essence, is like a spring: it is never touched but it—springs!"

She was working daily at a canteen at Victoria station. She had been on the night shift "but I can't sleep, I simply cannot sleep nowadays"; and so, shortly before he wrote to her of his second rejection, she had changed on to the day shift and at night took out the car to run arriving men from one terminus to another. "And about twice a week I get dog-tired and feel sleepy and send the chauffeur with the car and stay at home and do sleep. It's splendid!"

Northrepps had been handed over to the Red Cross as a military hospital. Her answer to his letter telling of his second rejection at the recruiting office—most tender words from her heart to his heart, comforting his spirit as transfusion of blood from health to sickness maintains the exhausted body—her reply told him that on that day fortnight she was coming down to say of his disappointment what she could so inadequately express in writing. She was going out to war work in France—in Tony's name she had presented a fleet of ambulance cars to a Red Cross unit and she was going out to drive one—and she was coming down to look at things at Northrepps before she left.

On the following day Tidborough, opening its newspapers, shook hands with itself in all its houses, shops and offices on its own special and most glorious V.C.,—Lord Tybar.

III

Tybar's V.C. was the first thing Sabre spoke of to Nona when, a fortnight later, she came down and he went up to her at Northrepps in the afternoon. Its brilliant gallantry, rendered so vivid to him by the intimacy with which he could see that thrice attractive figure engaged in its performance, stirred him most deeply. He had by heart every line of its official record in the restrained language of the Gazette.

...The left flank of the position was insecure, and the post, when taken over, was ill prepared for defence.... When the battalion was suffering very heavy casualties from a 77mm. field gun at very close range, Captain Lord Tybar rushed forward under intense machine gun fire and succeeded in capturing the gun single-handed after killing the entire crew.... Later, when repeated attacks developed, he controlled the defence at the point threatened, giving personal assistance with revolver and bombs.... Single-handed he repulsed one bombing assault.... It was entirely owing to the gallant conduct of this officer that the situation was relieved....

Oh, rare and splendid spirit! Fortune's darling thrice worthy of her dowry!

Nona had written of it in ringing words. She flushed in beautiful ardour of the enthusiasm she joined with Sabre's at his opening words of their meeting; but she ended with a sad little laugh. "And then!" she said.

"What do you mean, Nona, 'And then'?"

She took a letter from her bag. "I only got this this morning just as I was coming away. It's in reply to the one I wrote him about his V.C.

213

Oh, Marko, so splendid, so utterly splendid as he is, and then to be like this. Look, he says he's just got leave and he's going to spend it in Paris! One of his women is there. That Mrs. Winfred. He's taken up with her again. He says, 'Poor thing. She's all alone in Paris. I know how sorry you will feel for her, and I feel I ought to go and look after her. I know you will agree with me. I'll tell her you sent me. That will amuse and please her so.'"

She touched her eyes with her handkerchief. "It rather hurts, Marko. It's not that I mind his going. It's just what he would do. But it's the way he tells me. He just says it like that deliberately to be cruel because he knows it will hurt. So utterly splendid, Marko, and so utterly graceless." She gave her little note of sadness again. "Utterly splendid! Look, this is all he says about his V.C. Isn't this fine and isn't it like him? He says, 'P.S. Yes, that V.C. business. You know why I got it, don't you? It stands for Very Cautious, you know.'"

They laughed together. Yes, like him! Tybar exactly! Sabre could see him writing the letter. Delighting in saying words that would hurt; delighting in his own whimsicality that would amuse. Splendid; airy, untouched by fear; untouched by thought; fearless, faithless, heedless, graceless. Fortune's darling; invested in her robe of mockery.

Nona's laughter ended in a little catch at her breath. He touched her arm. "Let's walk, Nona."

IV

He thought she was looking thin and done up. Her face had rather a drawn look, its soft roundness gone. He thought she never had looked so beautiful to him. She spoke to him of what she had tried to say in her letters of his disappointments in offering himself for service. Never had her sweet voice sounded so exquisitely tender to him. They spoke of the war. Never, but in their letters, had he been able thus to give his feelings and receive them, touched with the same perceptions, kindled and enlarged, back into his sympathies again. With others the war was all discussion of chances and circumstances, of this that had happened and that that might happen, of this that should be done and that that ought not to have been done. Laboratory examination of means and remedies. The epidemic everything and the patient upstairs nothing. The wood not seen for the trees. With Nona he talked of how he felt of England:

Dear earth, I do salute thee with my hand.

He told her that.

She nodded. "I know. I know. Say it all through, Marko."

He stumbled through it. At the end, a little abashed, he smiled at her and said, "Of course, no one else would think it applies. Richard was saying it in Wales where he'd just landed, and it's about civil war, not foreign; but where it comes to me is the loving of the soil itself, as if it were a living thing that knew it was being loved and loved back in return. Our England, Nona. You remember Gaunt's thing in the same play:

"This royal throne of kings, this sceptre'd isle,

This other Eden, demi-paradise....

This happy breed of men, this little world,

This precious stone set in the silver sea....

This blessed plot, this earth, this realm, this England...."

She nodded again. He saw that her dear eyes were brimming. She said, "Yes—yes.—Our England. Rupert Brooke said it just perfectly, Marko:

"And think, this heart, all evil shed, away....

Gives somewhere back the thoughts by England given;

Her sights and sounds; dreams happy as her day;

And laughter, learnt of friends; and gentleness,

In hearts at peace, under an English heaven."

She touched his hand. "Dear Marko—" She made approach to that which lay between them. "'This heart, all evil shed away.' Marko, in this frightful time we couldn't have given back the thoughts by England given if we had.—And that was you, Marko."

He shook his head, not trusting himself to look at her. He said, "You. Not I. Any one can know the right thing. But strength to do it— Strength flows out of you to me. It always has. I want it more and more. I shall want it. Things are difficult. Sometimes I've a frightful feeling that things are closing in on me. There's Shelley's 'Ode to the West Wind.' It makes me—I don't know—wrought up. And sometimes I've the feeling that I'm being carried along like that and towards that frightful cry at the end, 'O Wind, if winter comes-'"

He stopped. He said, "Give me your handkerchief to keep, Nona. Something of your own to keep. There will be strength in it for me— to help me hold on to the rest—to believe it—'If Winter comes—Can Spring be far behind?'"

She touched her handkerchief to her lips and gave it to him.

V

After October, especially, he spent never less than two evenings a week with old Mrs. Perch. In October Young Perch went to France and on his draft-leave took from Sabre the easy promise to "keep an eye on my mother." Military training, which to most gave robustness, gave to Young Perch, Sabre thought, a striking enhancement of the fine-drawn expression that always had been his. About his eyes and forehead Sabre apprehended something suggestive of the mystic, spiritually-occupied look that paintings of the Huguenots and the old Crusaders had; and looking at him when he came to say good-by, and while he spoke solely and only of his mother, Sabre remembered that long-ago thought of Young Perch's aspect,—of his spirit being alighted in his body as a bird on a twig, not engrossed in his body; a thing death would need no more than to pluck off between finger and thumb.

But unthinkable, that. Not Young Perch....

Old Mrs. Perch was very broken and very querulous. She blamed Sabre and she blamed Effie that Freddie had gone to the war. She said they had leagued with him to send him off. "Freddie I could have managed," she used to say; "but you I cannot manage, Mr. Sabre; and as for Effie, you might think I was a child and she was mistress the way she treats me."

Bright Effie used to laugh and say, "Now, you know, Mrs. Perch, you will insist on coming and tucking me up at night. Now does that look as if she's the child, Mr. Sabre?"

Mrs. Perch in her dogged way, "If Mr. Sabre doesn't know that you only permit me to tuck you up one night because I permit you to tuck me up the next night, the sooner he does know how I'm treated in my own establishment the better for me."

Thus the initial cause of querulousness would bump off into something else; and in an astonishing short number of moves Bright Effie would lead Mrs. Perch to some happy subject and the querulousness would give place to little rays of animation; and presently Mrs. Perch would doze comfortably in her chair while Sabre talked to Effie in whispers; and when she woke Sabre would be ready with some reminiscence of Freddie carefully chosen and carefully carried along to keep it hedged with smiles. But all the roads where Freddie was to be found were sunken roads, the smiling hedges very low about them, the ditches overcharged with water, and tears soon would come.

She used to doze and murmur to herself, "My boy's gone to fight for his country. I'm very proud of my boy gone to fight for his country."

Effie said Young Perch had taught her that before he went away.

While they were talking she used to doze and say, "Good morning, Mrs. So-and-So. My boy's gone to fight for his country. I'm very proud of my boy gone to fight for his country. Good morning, Mr. So-and-So. My boy's gone to—He didn't want to go, but I said he must go to fight for his country.... But that's not true, Freddie.... Oh, very well, dear. Good morning, Mrs. So-and-So.—"

She used to wake up with a start and say, "Eh, Freddie? Oh, I thought Freddie was in the room." Tears.

She said she always looked forward to the evenings when Sabre came. She liked him to sit and talk to Effie and to smoke all the time and knock out his pipe on the fender. She said it made her think Freddie was there. Effie said that every night she went into Young Perch's room and tucked up the bed and set the alarm clock and put the candle and the matches and one cigarette and the ash-tray by the bed; and every night in this performance said, "He said he's certain to come in quite unexpectedly one night, and he will smoke his one cigarette before he goes to sleep. It's no good my telling him he'll set the house on fire one night. He never listens to anything I tell him." And every morning, when Effie took her in a cup of tea very early (as Freddie used to), she always said, "Has Freddie come home in the night, Effie, dear? Now just go and knock on his door very quietly and then just peep your head in."

VI

Sabre had always thought Bright Effie would be wonderful with old Mrs. Perch. He wrote long letters to Young Perch, telling him how much more than wonderful Bright Effie was. Effie mothered Mrs. Perch and managed her and humoured her in a way that not even Young Perch himself could have bettered. In that astounding fund of humour of hers, reflected in those sparkling eyes, even Mrs. Perch's most querulously violent attacks were transformed into matter for whimsical appreciation, delightfully and most lovingly dealt with. When the full, irritable, inconsequent flood of one of Mrs. Perch's moods would be launched upon her in Sabre's presence, she would turn a dancing eye towards him and immediately she could step into the torrent and would begin, "Now, look here, Mrs. Perch, you know perfectly well—"; and in two minutes the old lady would be mollified and happy.

Marvellous Effie! Sabre used to think; and of course it was because her astounding fund of humour was based upon her all-embracing capacity for love. That was why it was so astounding in its depth and breadth and compass. Sabre liked immensely the half-whispered talks with her while Mrs. Perch dozed in her chair. Effie was always happy. Nothing of that wanting something look was ever to be seen in Effie's shining eyes. She had the secret of life. Watching her face while they talked, he came to believe that the secret, the thing missing in half the faces one saw, was love. But—the old difficulty—many had love; himself and Nona; and yet were troubled.

One evening he asked her a most extraordinary question, shot out of him without intending it, discharged out of his questing thoughts as by a hidden spring suddenly touched by groping fingers.

"Effie, do you love God?"

Her surprise seemed to him to be more at the thing he had asked than at its amazing unexpectedness and amazing irrelevancy. "Why, of course I do, Mr. Sabre."

"Why do you?"

She was utterly at a loss. "Well, of course I do."

He said rather sharply, "Yes, but why? Have you ever asked yourself why? Respecting, fearing, trusting, that's understandable. But love, love, you know what love is, don't you? What's love got to do with God?"

She said in simple wonderment, as one asked what had the sun to do with light, or whether water was wet, "Why, God is love."

He stared at her.

VII

The second Christmas of the war came. The evening before the last day of the Old Year was to have given Sabre a rare pleasure to which he had been immensely looking forward. He was to have spent it with Mr. Fargus. The old chess and acrostic evenings hardly ever happened now. Mr. Fargus, most manifestly unfitted for the exposures of such a life, had become a special constable. He did night duty in the Garden Home. He chose night duty, he told Sabre, because he had no work to do by day and could therefore then take his rest. Younger men who were in offices and shops hadn't the like advantage. It was only fair he should help in the hours help was most wanted. Sabre said it would kill him in time, but Mrs. Fargus and the three Miss Farguses still at home replied, when Sabre ventured this opinion to them, that Papa was much stronger than any one imagined, also that they agreed with Papa that one ought to do in the war, not what one wanted to do, but what was most required to be done; finally that, being at home by day, Papa could help, and liked helping, in the many duties about the house now interfered with by the enlistment of the entire battalion of female Farguses in work for the war. One detachment of female Farguses had leapt into blue or khaki uniforms and disappeared into the voracious belly of the war machine; the remainder of the battalion thrust their long legs into breeches and boots and worked at home as land girls. Little old Mr. Fargus in his grey suit, and the startled child Kate with one hand still up her back in search of the errant apron string "did" what the battalion used to do and were nightly, on the return of the giant land girls, shown how shockingly they had done it.

Rare, therefore, the old chess and acrostic evenings and most keenly anticipated, accordingly, this—the first for a fortnight—on the eve of New Year's Eve. It was to have been a real long evening; but it proved not very long. It was to have been one in which the war should be shut out and forgotten in the delights of mental twistings and slowly puffed pipes; it proved to be one in which "this frightful war!" was groaned out of Sabre's spirit in emotion most terrible to him.

At ten o'clock profound gymnastics of the mind in search of a hidden word beginning with e and ending with l were interrupted by the entry of the startled Kate. One hand writhed between her shoulders for the apron string, the other held a note. "Please, Mr. Sabre, I think it's for you, Mr. Sabre. A young boy took it to your house and said you was to have it most particular, and please, your Rebecca sent him on here, please."

"For me? Who on earth—?"

He opened it. He did not recognise the writing on the envelope. He had not the remotest idea—It was a jolly evening.... could Enamel be that word in e and l? He unfolded it. Ah!

"Freddie's killed. Please do come at once. I think she's dying.—E.B."

CHAPTER VIII

I

He was alone in the room where Mrs. Perch lay,—not even Effie. One o'clock. This war! He had thought to shut it away for a night, and here was the inconceivable occupation to which it had brought him: alone in here—

The doctor had been and was coming again in the morning. There was nothing to be done, he had said; just watch her.

Watch her? How long had he been standing at the foot of the huge bed—the biggest bed he had ever seen—and what was there to watch? She gave no sign. She scarcely seemed to breathe. He would not have recognised her face. It had the appearance of a mask. "Sinking," the doctor had said. In process here before his eyes, but not to be seen by them, awful and mysterious things. Death with practised fingers about his awful and mysterious surgery of separating the spirit from the flesh, the soul from the body, the incorruptible from the corruptible.

It could not be! There was not a sign; there was not a sound; and what should he be doing to be alone here, blind watcher of such a finality? It was not real. It was an hallucination. He was not really here. The morning—and days and weeks and years—would come, and he would know that this never had really happened.

But Young Perch was dead. Young Perch was killed. It was real. He was here. This war!

II

He had gone downstairs with the doctor and had remained there some little time after his departure. Effie had been left kneeling by the bed. When he came back she was sound asleep where she knelt, worn out. The news had come on the previous evening. This was Effie's second night without sleep. Now she was overcome; collapsed; suffocated and bound and gagged in the opiates and bonds she had for thirty hours resisted. He touched her. She did not stir. He shook her gently; still no response. He lifted her up and carried her along the passage to the room he knew to be hers; laid her on her bed and covered her with a quilt. Inconceivable occupation. Was all this really happening?

Two o'clock. He went to look at Effie, still in profound slumber. Why awaken her? Nothing could be done; only watch. He returned to his vigil.

Yes, Mrs. Perch was sinking. More pronounced now that masklike aspect of her face. Yes, dying. He spoke the word to himself. "Dying." As of a fire in the grate gone to one dull spark among the greying ashes.—It is out; it cannot burn again. So life here too far retired, too deeply sunk to struggle back and vitalise again that hue, those lips, that masklike effigy.

Profound and awful mystery. Within that form was in process a most dreadful activity. The spirit was preparing to vacate the habitation it had so long occupied. It gave no sign. The better to hide its preparations it had drawn that mask about the face. Seventy years it had sojourned here; now it was bound away. Seventy years it had been known to passers-by through the door and windows of this its habitation; now, deeply retired within the inner chambers, it set its house in order to be gone. Profound and awful mystery. Dreadful and momentous activity. From the windows of her eyes turning off the lights; from the engines of her powers cutting off its forces; drawing the furnaces; dissevering the contacts. A lifetime within this home; now passenger into an eternity. A lifetime settled; now preparing to be away on a journey inconceivably tremendous, unimaginably awful. Did it shrink? Did it pause in its preparations to peer and peep and shudder?

III

He felt very cold. He moved from the bed and replenished the fire and crouched beside it.

This war! He said beneath his breath, "Young Perch! Young Perch!" Young Perch was killed. Realise the thing! He was never going to see Young Perch again. He was never going to see old Mrs. Perch again. He was never to come into Puncher's again. Another place of his life was to be walled up. His home like an empty house; the office like an empty house; now no refuge here. Things were crowding in about him, things were closing in upon him. And he was just to live on here, out of the war, yet insupportably beset by the war. Beset by the war yet useless in the war. Young Perch! How in pity was he to go on living out of the war, now that the war had taken Young Perch and killed old Mrs. Perch and shut this refuge from its oppression? He must get in. He could not endure it. He could not, could not....

Ten minutes past three. There was perceptible to him no change in that face upon the pillow. He brought a lamp from the dressing table and looked at her, shading the light with his hand. Impenetrable mask! Profound and awful mystery. Much more than a house that dreadfully engrossed spirit was preparing to leave. This meagre form, scarcely discernible beneath the coverlet, had been its fortress, once new, once strong, once beautiful, once by its garrison proudly fought, splendidly defended, added to, enlarged, adorned. Then past its glory, past attention. Then crumbling, then decaying. Now to be abandoned. It had known great stresses and abated them; sieges and withstood them; assaults and defeated them. O vanity! It had but temporised with conquest. Time's hosts had camped these many years about its walls, in ceaseless investment, with desultory attacks, but with each attack investing closer. Now a most terrible assault had breached the citadel. The garrison was stricken amain. The fortress no longer could be defended. Its garrison was withdrawing from that place and handing it over to destruction.

IV

There was some strange sound in the room. He had dozed in a chair. Some strange sound, or had he imagined it? He sat up tensely and listened. It was her breathing, a harsh and laboured sound. He stepped quickly to the bed and looked and then ran into the passage and called loudly, "Effie! Effie!"

Frightening, terrible, agonising. He was kneeling on one side of the bed, Effie at the other. The extreme moment was come to her that lay between them. She was moaning. He bowed his face into his hands. The sound of her moaning was terrible to him. That inhabitant of this her body had done its preparations and now stood at the door in the darkness, very frightened. It wanted to go back. It had been very accustomed to being here. It could not go back. It did not want to shut the door. The door was shutting. It stood and shrank and whimpered there.

Oh, terrible! Beyond endurance, agonising. It was old Mrs. Perch that stood there whimpering, shrinking, upon the threshold of that huge abyss, wide as space, dark as night. It was no spirit. It was just that very feeble Mrs. Perch with her fumbling hands and her moving lips. Look here, Young Perch would never allow her even to cross a road without him! How in pity was she to take this frightful step? He twisted up all his emotions into an appeal of tremendous intensity. "Young Perch! Come here! Your mother! Young Perch, come here!"

Telling it, once, to Nona, he said, "I don't know what happened. They talk about self-hypnotism. Perhaps it was that. I know I made a most frightful effort saying 'Young Perch.' I had to. I could see her—that poor terrified thing. Something had to be done. Some one had to go to her. I said it like in a nightmare, bursting to get out of it, 'Young Perch. Come here.' Anyway, there it is, Nona. I heard them. It was imagination, of course. But I heard them."

He heard, "Now then, Mother! Don't be frightened. Here I am, Mother. Come on, Mother. One step, Mother. Only one. I can't reach you. You must take just one step. Look, Mother, here's my hand. Can't you see my hand?"

"It's so dark, Freddie."

"It's not, Mother. It's only dark where you are. It's light here. Don't cry, Mother. Don't be frightened. It's all right. It's quite all right."

That tall and pale young man, with his face like one of the old Huguenots! That very frail old woman with her fumbling hands and moving lips!

"It's so cold."

"Now, Mother, I tell you it isn't. Do just trust me. Do just come."

"I daren't, Freddie. I can't, Freddie. I can't. I can't."

"You must. Mother, you must. Look, look, here I am. It's I, Freddie. Don't cry, Mother. Just trust yourself entirely to me. You know how you always can trust me. Look, here's my hand. Just one tiny step and you will touch it. I know you feel ill, darling Mother. You won't any, any more, once you touch my hand. But I can't come any nearer, dearest. You must. You—. Ah, brave, beloved Mother—now!"

He heard Effie's voice, "Oh, she's dead! She's dead!"

Dead? He stared upon her dead face. Where was gone that mask? Whence had come this glory? That inhabitant of this her body, in act of going had looked back, and its look had done this thing. It had closed the door upon a ruined house, and looked, and left a temple. It had departed from beneath a mask, and looked, and that which had been masked now was beatified.

Young Perch!

V

In the morning a mysterious man with a large white face, crooked spectacles and a crooked tie, and a suggestion of thinking all the time of something else, or of nothing at all, mysteriously drifted into the house, drifted about it with apparent complete aimlessness of purpose, and presently showed himself to Sabre as about to drift out of it again. This was the doctor, a stranger, one of those new faces which the war, removing the old, was everywhere introducing, and possessed of a mysterious and astounding faculty of absorbing, resolving, and subjugating all matters without visibly attending to any matter. "Leave everything to me," it was all he seemed to say. He did nothing yet everything seemed to come to his hand with the nicety and exactness of a drawing-room conjurer. He bewildered Sabre.

His car left and returned during his brief visit. Sabre, who had thought him upstairs, and who had a hundred perplexities to inquire of him, found him in the hall absorbed in adjusting the weights of a grandfather's clock.

He remarked to Sabre, "I thought you'd gone. You'd better get off and get a bath and some breakfast. Nothing you can do here. Leave everything to me."

"But, look here, I can't leave—"

"That's all right. Just leave everything to me. I'm taking Miss Bright back to my wife for breakfast and a rest. After lunch I'll run her to her home. She can't stay here. Have you any idea how this thing hooks on?"

"But what about—"

The extraordinary man seemed to know everything before it was said. "That's all right. I've sent for a woman and her daughter. Leave everything to me. Here's the car. Here they are."

Two women appeared.

"But about—"

"Yes, that's all right. The poor old lady's brother is coming down. He'll take charge. I found his name in her papers last night. Telegraphed." He was looking through the door. "Here's the answer."

A telegraph messenger appeared.

Astounding man!

He read the telegram. "Yes, that's all right. He'll be here by the eleven train at Tidborough. I'll take Miss Bright now."

Effie appeared.

Sabre had the feeling that if he opened the next thought in his mind, an undertaker would rise out of the ground with a coffin. This astonishing man, coming upon his overwrought state, made him feel hysterical. He turned to Effie and gave her both his hands. "The doctor's taking you, Effie. It's been dreadful for you. It's all over now. Try to leave it out of your mind for a bit."

She smiled sadly. "Good-by, Mr. Sabre. Thank you so much, so very much, for coming and staying. What I should have done without you I daren't think. I've never known any one so good as you've been to me."

"I've done nothing, Effie, except feel sorry for you."

He saw her into the car. No, he would not take a lift.

"Well, leave everything to me," said the doctor. The chauffeur spoke to him about some engine trouble. "Yes, I'll see to that. Leave everything to me, Jenkins."

Even his car!

VI

Sabre, passed on from the ordeal of the night to the ordeal of the day by this interlude of the astonishing doctor, did not know how overwrought he was until he was at home again and come to Mabel seated at breakfast. The thought in his mind as he walked had been the thought in his mind as he had sat on after the death, waiting for morning. After this, after the war had done this, how was he to go on enduring the war and refused part in it? He dreaded meeting Mabel.

He dreaded going on to the office and meeting Fortune and Twyning. To none of these people, to no one he could meet, could he explain how he felt about Young Perch and what he had gone through with Mrs. Perch, nor why, because of what he felt, more poignant than ever was his need to get into the war. And yet with these feelings he must go on facing these people and go on meeting the war in every printed page, in every sight, in every conversation. Unbearable! He could not.

Mabel looked up from her breakfast. "Well, I do think—"

This was the beginning of it. He felt himself digging his nails into the palms of his hands. "I've been up with old Mrs. Perch—"

"I know you have. I sent around to the Farguses. I must say I do think—"

He felt he could not bear it. "Mabel, look here. For goodness' sake don't say you do think I ought to have let you know. I know I ought but I couldn't. And I'm not in a state to go on niggling about it. Young Perch is killed and his mother's dead. Now for goodness' sake, for pity's sake, let it alone. I couldn't send and there's the end of it."

He went out of the room. He thought, "There you are! Now I've done it!" He went back. "I say, I'm sorry for bursting out like that; but I've had rather a night of it. It's terrible, isn't it, both of them like that? Aren't you awfully sorry about it, Mabel?"

She said, "I'm very sorry. Very sorry indeed. But you can't expect me to say much when you speak in that extraordinary manner."

"I was with her when she died. It's upset me a bit."

"I don't wonder. If you ask me, I think it was very extraordinary your being there. If you ask me, I think it was very funny of that Miss Bright sending for you at that hour of the night. Whyever should she send for you of all people?"

"I was their greatest friend."

"Yes, I know you always liked them. But you couldn't be of any use. I must say I do think people are very funny sometimes. If Miss Bright had done the right thing, as we are their nearest neighbors, she would have sent and asked me if I could let one of the maids go over and be with her. Then you could have gone up too if you'd wished and could have come back again. I don't think she had any right to send for you."

He had sat down and was about to pour himself out some tea. He put down the teapot and got up. "Look here, do me a favour. They're dead, both of them. Don't say anything more about them. Don't mention the subject again. For God's sake."

He went out of the house and got his bicycle and set out for the office. At the top of the Green he passed young Pinnock, the son of Pinnock's Stores. Some patch of colour about young Pinnock caught his eye. He looked again. The colour was a vivid red crown on a khaki brassard on the young man's arm. The badge of the recruits enrolled under the Derby enlistment scheme. He dismounted. "Hullo, Pinnock. How on earth did you get that armlet?"

"I've joined up."

"But I thought you'd been rejected about forty times. Haven't you got one foot in the grave or something?"

Young Pinnock grinned hugely. "Don't matter if you've got both feet in, or head and shoulders neither, over at Chovensbury to-day, Mr. Sabre. It's the last day of this yer Derby scheme, an' there's such a rush of chaps to get in before they make conscripts of 'em they're fair letting anybody through."

Sabre's heart—that very heart!—bounded with an immense hope. "D'you think it's the same at Tidborough?"

"They're saying it's the same everywhere. They say they're passing you through if you can breathe. I reckon that's so at Chovensbury anyway. Why, they didn't hardly look at me."

Sabre turned his front wheel to the Chovensbury road. "I'll go there."

VII

At Chovensbury the recruiting station was in the elementary schools. Sabre entered a large room filled with men in various stages of dressing, odorous of humanity, very noisy. It was a roughish collection: the men mostly of the labouring or artisan classes. At a table in the centre two soldiers with lance corporal's stripes were filling up blue forms with the answers to questions barked out at the file of men who shuffled before them. As each form was completed, it was pushed at the man interrogated with "Get undressed."

Sabre took his place in the chain. In one corner of the room a doctor in uniform was testing eyesight. Passed on from there each recruit joined a group wearing only greatcoat or shirt and standing about a stove near the door. At intervals the door opened and three nude men, coat or shirt in hand, entered, and a sergeant bawled, "Next three!"

Sabre was presently one of the three. Of the two who companioned him one was an undersized little individual wearing a truss, the other appeared to be wearing a suit of deep brown tights out of which his red neck and red hands thrust conspicuously. Sabre realised with a slight shock that the brown suit was the grime of the unbathed. Across the passage another room was entered. The recruits dropped their final covering and were directed, one to two sergeants who operated weights, a height gauge and a measuring tape; another to an officer who said, "Stand on one leg. Bend your toes. Now on the other. Toes. Stretch out your arms. Work your fingers. Squat on your heels." The third recruit went to an officer who dabbed chests with a stethoscope and said, "Had any illnesses?" When the recruit had passed through each performance he walked to two officers seated with enrolment forms at a table, was spoken to, and then recovered his discarded garment and walked out. The whole business took about three minutes. They were certainly whizzing them through.

Sabre came last to the officer with the stethoscope. He was just polishing off the undersized little man with the truss. "Take that thing off. Cough. How long have you had this? Go along." He turned to Sabre, dabbed perfunctorily at his lungs, then at his heart. "Wait a minute." He applied his ear to the stethoscope again. Then he looked up at Sabre's face. "Had any illnesses?" "Not one in my life." "Shortness of breath?" "Not the least. I was in the XV at school." Sabre's voice was tremulous with eagerness. The doctor's eyes appeared to exchange a message with him. They gave the slightest twinkle. "Go along."

He went to the table where sat the two officers with the paper forms. "Name?" "Sabre." The officer nearer him drew a form towards him and poised a fountain pen over it. Sabre felt it extraordinarily odd to be standing stark naked before two men fully dressed. In his rejection at Tidborough the time before this had not happened.

229

"Any complaints?"

Sabre was surprised at such consideration. He thought the reference was to his treatment during examination. "No."

The officer, who appeared to be short-tempered, glanced again at the form and then looked quickly at him. "Absolutely nothing wrong with you?"

"Oh, I thought you meant—"

The officer was short-tempered. "Never mind what you thought. You hear what I'm asking you, don't you?"

It was Sabre's first experience of a manner with which he was to become more familiar. "Sorry. No, nothing whatever."

The fountain pen made a note. "Get off."

He could have shouted aloud. He thought, "By God!"

In the dressing room a sergeant bawled, "All recruits!"—paused and glared about the room and drew breath for further discharge. This mannerism Sabre was also to become accustomed to: in the Army, always "the cautionary word" first when an order was given. The sergeant then discharged: "All recruits past the doctor proceed to the room under this for swearing in. When sworn, to office adjoining for pay, card and armlet. And get a move on with it!"

VIII

The most stupendously elated man in all England was presently riding to Penny Green on Sabre's bicycle. On his arm blazed the khaki brassard, in the breast pocket of his waistcoat, specially cleared to give private accommodation to so glorious a prize, were a half-crown and two pennies, the most thrillingly magnificent sum he had ever earned,—his army pay. His singing thought was, "I'm in the Army! I'm in the Army! I don't care for anything now. By gad, I can't believe it. I'm in the war at last!" His terrific thought was, "Good luck have thee with thine honour; ride on ... and thy right hand shall show thee terrible things."

He burst into the house and discharged the torrent of his elation on to Mabel. "I say, I'm in the Army. They've passed me. Look here! Look at my Derby armlet! And look at this. That's my pay! Just look, Mabel—two and eightpence."

He extended the coins to her in his hand. "Look!"

She gave her sudden burst of laughter. "How perfectly ridiculous! Two and eightpence! Whyever did you take it?"

"Take it? Why, it's my pay. My army pay. I've never been so proud of anything in my life. I'll keep these coins forever. Where shall I put them?" He looked around for a shrine worthy enough. "No, I can't put them anywhere yet. I want to keep looking at them. I say, you're glad I'm in, aren't you? Do say something."

She gave her laugh. "But you're not in. You do get so fearfully excited. After all, it's only this Lord Derby thing where they call the men up in age classes, the papers say. Yours can't come for months. You may not go at all."

He dropped the coins slowly into his pocket,—chink, chink, chink. "Oh, well, if that's all you've got to say about it."

"Well, what do you expect? You just come rushing in and telling me without ever having said a word that you were going. And for that matter you seem to forget the extraordinary way in which you went off this morning. I haven't."

"I had forgotten. I was upset. I went off, I know; but I don't remember—"

"No, you only swore at me; that's all."

"Mabel, I'm sure I didn't."

"You bawled out, 'For God's sake.' I call that swearing. I don't mind. It's not particularly nice for the servants to hear, but I'm not saying anything about that."

His brows were puckered up. "What is it you are saying?"

"I'm simply saying that, behaving like that, it's not quite fair to pretend that I'm not enthusiastic enough for you about this Lord Derby thing. It isn't as if you were really in the Army—"

He wished not to speak, but he could not let this go. "But I am in."

"Yes, but not properly in—yet. And perhaps you won't ever be. It doesn't seem like being in to me. That's all I'm saying. Surely there's no harm in that?"

He was at the window staring out into the garden. "No, there's no harm in it."

"Well, then. What are we arguing about it for?"

He turned towards her. "Well, but do understand, Mabel. If you think I was a fool rushing in like that, as you call it. Do understand. It's a Government scheme. It's binding. It isn't a joke."

"No, but I think they make it a joke, and I can't think why you can't see the funny side of it. I think giving you two and eightpence like that—a man in your position—is too lovely for words."

He took the coins from his pocket, and jerked them on the table before her. "Here, pay the butcher with it."

IX

But as he reached the door, his face working, the tremendous and magnificent thought struck into his realisation again. "I'm in the Army! By gad, I'm in the Army. I don't care what happens now." He strode back, smiling, and took up the money. "No, I'm dashed if I can let it go!" He went out jingling it and turned into the kitchen. "I say, High, Low, I'm in the Army! I've got in. I'll be off soon. Look at my badge!"

They chorused, "Well, there now!"

He said delightedly, "Pretty good, eh? Isn't it fine! Look at this—that's my pay. Two and eightpence!"

The chorus, "Oh, if ever!"

High Jinks said, "That armlet, sir, that's too loose. It don't half show down on your elbow, sir. You want it up here."

"Yes, that's the place. Won't it stay?"

"I'll put a safety pin in, sir; and then to-night shift the buttons. That's what it wants."

"Yes, do, High. That's fine."

He held out his arm and the two girls pinned to advantage the splendid sign of his splendid triumph.

"There, sir. Now it shows. And won't we be proud of you, just, in khaki and all!"

He laughed delightedly. "I'm jolly proud of myself, I tell you! Now, then, Thumbs, I don't want bayonets in me yet!"

Glorious! Glorious! And what would not Nona say!

CHAPTER IX

I

Life, when it takes so giant a hand in its puppet show as to upturn a cauldron of world war upon the puppets, may be imagined biting its fingers in some chagrin at the little result in particular instances. As vegetation beneath snow, so individual development beneath universal calamity. Nature persists; individual life persists. The snow melts, the calamity passes; the green things spring again, the individual lives are but approached more nearly to their several destinations.

Sabre was called up in his Derby Class within eight weeks of his enrolment,—at the end of February, 1916. He was nearly two years in the war; but his ultimate encounter with life awaited him, and was met, at Penny Green. It might have been reached precisely as it was reached without agency of the war, certainly without participation in it. Of the interval only those few events ultimately mattered which had connection with his life at home. They seemed in the night of the war transient as falling stars; they proved themselves lodestars of his destiny. They seemed nothing, yet even as they flashed and passed he occupied himself with them as the falling star catches the attention from all the fixed and constant. They were of his own life: the war life was life in exile.

And, caught up at last in the enormous machinery of the war, his feelings towards the war underwent a great change. First in the training camp in Dorsetshire, afterwards, and much more so, in the trenches in Flanders, it was only by a deliberate effort that he would recapture, now and then, the old tremendous emotions in the thought of England challenged and beset. He turned to it as stimulant in moments of depression and of dismay, in hours of intense and miserable loathing of some conditions of his early life in the ranks, and later in hours when fatigue and bodily discomfort reached degrees he had not believed it possible to endure—and go on with. He turned to it as stimulant and it never failed of its stimulation. "I'm in it. What does this matter? This is the war. It's the war. Those infernal devils.... If these frightful things were being done in England! Imagine if this was in England! Thank God I'm in it. There you are! I'm absolutely all right when I remember why I'm here." And enormous exaltation of spirit would lift away the loneliness, remove the loathing, banish the exhaustion, dissipate the fear. The fear—"And thy right hand shall show thee terrible things"—He was more often than once in situations in which he knew he was afraid and held fear away only because, with his old habit of introspection, he knew it for fear,—a horrible thing that sought mastery of him and by sheer force of mental detachment must be held away where it could be looked at and known for the vile thing it was. In such ordeals, in Flanders, he got the habit of saying to himself between his teeth, "Six minutes, six hours, six days, six months, six years. Where the hell will I be?" It somehow helped. The six minutes would go, and one could believe that all the periods would go,—and wonder where they would find one.

But more than that: now, caught up in the enormous machinery of the war, he never could accept it, as other men seemed to accept it, as normal and natural occupation that might be expected to go on for ever and outside of which was nothing at all. His life was not here; it was at home. He got the feeling that this business in which he was caught up was a business apart altogether from his own individual life,—a kind of trance in which his own life was held temporarily in abeyance, a kind of transmigration in which he occupied another and a very strange identity: from whose most strange personality, often so amazingly occupied, he looked wonderingly upon the identity that was his own, waiting his return.

And it was when, in thought or fleeting action, he came in touch with that old, waiting identity, that there happened the things that seemed transient as falling stars but moved into his horoscope as planets,— and remained.

II

He first went to France, in one of the long string of Service battalions that had sprung out of the Pinks, in the June following his enlistment. Mabel had not wished to make any change in her manner of life while he was still in England in training and she did not wish to when, at home three days on his draft leave, he discussed it with her. She much preferred, she said, to go on living in her own home. She was altogether against any idea of going to be with her father at Tidborough, and there was no cousin "or anybody like that" (her two sisters were married and had homes of their own) that she would care to have in the house with her. Relations were all very well in their right place but sharing the house with you was not their right place. She had plenty to do with her war work and one thing and another; if, in the matter of obviating loneliness, she did make any change at all, it might be to get some sort of paid companion: if you had any one permanently in the house it was much better to have some one in a dependent position, not as your equal, upsetting things.

The whole of these considerations were advanced again in a letter which Sabre received in July and which gave him great pleasure. Mabel had decided to get a paid companion—it was rather lonely in some ways—and she had arranged to have "that girl, Miss Bright." Sabre, reading, exclaimed aloud, "By Jove, that's good. I am glad." And he thought, "Jolly little Effie! That's splendid." He somehow liked immensely the idea of imagining Bright Effie about the house. He thought, "I wish she could have been in long ago, when I was there. It would have made a difference. Some one between us. We used to work on one another's nerves. That was our trouble. Pretty little Effie! How jolly it would have been! Like a jolly little sister."

He puckered his brows a little as he read on to Mabel's further reflections on the new enterprise: "Of course she's not our class but she's quite ladylike and on the whole I think it just as well not to have a lady. It might be very difficult sometimes to give orders to any one of one's own standing."

He didn't quite like that; but after all it was only just Mabel's way of looking at things. It was the jolliest possible idea. He wrote back enthusiastically about it and always after Effie was installed inquired after her in his letters.

But Mabel did not reply to these inquiries.

III

He was writing regularly to Nona and regularly hearing from her. He never could quite make out where she was, addressing her only to her symbol in the Field post-office. She was car driving and working very long hours. There was one letter that he never posted but of the existence of which he permitted himself to tell her. "I carry it about with me always in my Pay-book. It is addressed to you. If ever I get outed it will go to you. In it I have said everything that I have never said to you but that you know without my saying it. There'll be no harm in your hearing it from my own hand if I'm dead. I keep on adding to it. Every time we come back into rest, I add a little more. It all could be said in the three words we have never said to one another. But all the words that I could ever write would never say them to you as I feel them. There! I must say no more of it. I ought not to have said so much."

And she wrote, "Marko, I can read your letter, every line of it. I lie awake, Marko, and imagine it to myself—word by word, line by line;

and word by word, line by line, in the same words and in the same lines, I answer it. So when you read it to yourself for me, read it for yourself from me. Oh, Marko—

"That I ever shall have cause to read it in actual fact I pray God never to permit. But so many women are praying for so many men, and daily—. So I am praying beyond that: for myself; for strength, if anything should happen to you, to turn my heart to God. You see, then I can say, 'God keep you—in any amazement.'"

IV

Early in December he wrote to Mabel:

"A most extraordinary thing has happened. I'm coming home! I shall be with you almost on top of this. It's too astonishing. I've suddenly been told that I'm one of five men in the battalion who have been selected to go home to an Officer Cadet battalion for a commission. Don't jump to the conclusion that I'm the Pride of the Regiment or anything like that. It's simply due to two things: one that this is not the kind of battalion with many men who would think of taking commissions; the other that both my platoon officer and the captain of my company happen to be Old Tidburians and, as I've told you, have often been rather decent to me. So when this chance came along the rest was easy. I know you'll be glad. You've never liked the idea of my being in the ranks. But it's rather wonderful, isn't it? I hope to be home on the third and I go to the Cadet battalion, at Cambridge, on the fifth."

Two days later he started, very high of spirit, for England. As he was leaving the village where the battalion was resting—his immediate programme the adventure of "lorry-jumping" to the railhead—the mail came in and brought him a letter from Mabel. It had crossed his own and a paragraph in it somehow damped the tide of his spirits.

"I was very much annoyed with Miss Bright yesterday. I had been kept rather late at our Red Cross Supply Depot owing to an urgent call for accessories and when I came home I found that Miss Bright had actually taken what I consider the great liberty of ordering up tea without waiting for me. I considered it great presumption on her part and told her so. I find her taking liberties in many ways. It's always the way with that class,—once you treat them kindly they turn on you. However, I have, I think, made it quite clear to her that she is not here for the purpose of giving her own orders and being treated like a princess."

It clouded his excitement. His thought was, "Damn it, I hope she isn't bullying Effie."

He had the luck almost at once to jump a lorry that would lift him a long bit on his road, and the driver felicitated him with envious cheerfulness on being off for "leaf." He would have responded with immense heartiness before reading that letter. With Mabel's tart sentences in his mind a certain gloom, a rather vexed gloom, bestrode him. Her words presented her aspect and her attitude and her atmosphere with a reminiscent flavour that took the edge off his eagerness for home. On the road when the lorry had dropped him, on the interminable journey in the train, on the boat, the feeling remained with him. England—England!—merged into view across the water, and he was astonished, as his heart bounded for joy at Folkestone coming into sight, to realise from what depression of mind it bounded away. He was ashamed of himself and perturbed with himself that he had not more relished the journey: the journey that was the most glorious thing in the dreams of every man in France. He thought, "Well, what am I coming home to?"

The train went speeding through the English fields,—dear, familiar, English lands, sodden and bare and unspeakably exquisite to him in their December mood. He gazed upon them, flooding all his heart out to them. He thought, "Why should there be anything to make me feel depressed? Why should things be the same as they used to be? But dash that letter.... Dash it, I hope she's not been bullying that girl."

V

He made rather a boisterous entry into the house on his arrival, arriving in the morning before breakfast. He entered the hall just after eight o'clock and announced himself with a loud, "Hullo, everybody!" and thumped the butt of his rifle on the floor. An enormous crash in the kitchen and a shriek of "It's the master!" heralded the tumultuous discharge upon him of High Jinks and Low Jinks. Effie appeared from the dining room. He was surrounded and enthusiastically shaking hands. "Hullo, you Jinkses! Isn't this ripping? By Jove, High—and Low—it's famous to see you again. Hullo, Effie! Just fancy you being here! How jolly fine, eh? High Jinks, I want the most enormous breakfast you've ever cooked. Got any kippers? Good girl. That's the stuff to give the troops. Where's the Mistress? Not down yet? I'll go up. Low Jinks—Low Jinks, I'm dashed if you aren't crying! Well, it is jolly nice to see you again, Low. How's the old bike? Look here, Low, I want the most boiling bath—"

He broke off. "Hullo, Mabel! Hullo! Did you get my letter? I'm coming up."

Mabel was in a wrapper at the head of the stairs. He ran up. "I'm simply filthy. Do you mind?" He took her hand.

She said, "I never dreamt you'd be here at this hour. How are you, Mark? Yes, I got your letter. But I never expected you till this evening. It's very annoying that nothing is ready for you. Sarah, something is burning in the kitchen. I shouldn't stand there, Rebecca, with so much to be done; and I think you've forgotten your cap. Miss Bright,—oh, she's gone."

Just the same Mabel! But he wasn't going to let her be the same! He had made up his mind to that as he had come along with eager strides from the station. She turned to him and they exchanged their greetings and he went on, pursuing his resolution, "Look here, I've got a tremendous idea. When I get through this cadet business I shall have quite a bit of leave and my Sam Browne belt. I thought we'd go up to town and stick up at an hotel—the Savoy or somewhere—and have no end of a bust. Theatres and all the rest of it. Shall we?"

That chilly, vexed manner of hers, caused as he well knew by the uproar of his arrival, disappeared. "Oh, I'd love to. Yes, do let's. Now you want a bath, don't you? I'm annoyed there was all that disturbance just when I was meeting you. I've been having a little trouble lately—"

"Oh, well, never mind that now, Mabel. Come and watch me struggle out of this pack. Yes, look here, as soon as ever I know for certain when the course ends we'll write for rooms at the Savoy. I hear you have to do it weeks ahead. We'll spend pots of money and have no end of a time."

She reflected his good spirits. Ripping! He splashed and wallowed in the bath, singing lustily one of the songs out there:

"Ho, ho, ho, it's a lovely war!"

VI

But the three days at home were not to go on this singing note. They were marred by the discovery that his suspicion was well founded; she was bullying Effie. He began to notice it at once. Effie, with whom he had anticipated a lot of fun, was different: not nearly so bright; subdued; her eyes, not always, but only by occasional flashes, sparkling that intense appreciation of the oddities of life that had so much attracted him in her. Yes, dash it, Mabel was treating her in a rotten way. Bullying. No, it was not exactly bullying, it was snubbing, a certain acid quality always present in Mabel's voice when she addressed her,—that and a manner of always being what he thought of as "at her." The girl seemed to have an astonishing number of quite trivial duties to perform—trivial; there certainly was no suggestion of her being imposed upon as he had always felt Miss Bypass up at the vicarage was imposed upon, but Mabel was perpetually and acidly "at her" over one trivial thing or another. It was forever, "Miss Bright, I think you ought to be in the morning room, oughtn't you?" "Miss Bright, I really must ask you not to leave your door open every time you come out of your room. You know how I dislike the doors standing open." "Miss Bright, if you've finished your tea, there's really no need for you to remain."

He hated it. He said nothing, but it was often on the tip of his tongue to say something, and he showed that he intensely disliked it, and he knew that Mabel knew he disliked it. On the whole it was rather a relief when the three days were up and he went down to the Cadet battalion at Cambridge.

In March he came back, a second lieutenant; and immediately, when in time to come he looked back, things set in train for that ultimate encounter with life which was awaiting him.

The projected visit to town did not come off. While he was at Cambridge Mabel wrote to say that the Garden Home Amateur Dramatic Society was going to do "His Excellency The Governor" in aid of the Red Cross funds at the end of March. She was taking part, she was fearfully excited about it, and as rehearsals began early in the month she naturally could not be away. She was sure he would understand and would not mind.

He did not mind in the least. They were years past the stage when it would have so much as crossed his mind that she might give up this engagement for the sake of spending his leave on a bit of gaiety in town; he had only suggested the idea on her account; personally he much preferred the prospect of doing long walks about his beloved countryside now passing into spring.

VII

Arriving, he began at once to do so. He went over for one visit to the office at Tidborough. Not so much enthusiasm greeted him as to encourage a second. Twyning and Mr. Fortune were immersed in adapting the workshops to war work for the Government. Normal business was coming to a standstill. Now Twyning had conceived the immense, patriotic, and profitable idea of making aeroplane parts, and it was made sufficiently clear to Sabre that, so long away and immediately to be off again, there could be no interest for him in the enterprise.

"You won't want to go into all we are doing, my dear fellow," said Mr. Fortune. "Your hard-earned leave, eh? We mustn't expect you to give it up to business, eh, Twyning?"

And Twyning responded, "No, no, old man. Not likely, old man. Well, it's jolly to see you in the office again"; and he looked at his watch and said a word to Mr. Fortune about "Meeting that man" with an air which quite clearly informed Sabre that it would be jollier still to see him put on his cap and walk out of the office again.

Well, it was only what he had expected; a trifle pronounced, perhaps, but the obvious sequel to their latter-day manner towards him: they had wanted to get him out; he was out and they desired to keep him out.

He rose to go. "Oh, that's all right. I'm not going to keep you. I only called in to show off my officer's uniform."

Twyning said, "Yes, congratulations again, old man." He laughed. "You mustn't think you're going to have Harold saluting you though, if you ever meet. He's getting a commission too." His manner, directly he began to speak of Harold, changed to that enormous affection and admiration for his son which Sabre well remembered on the occasion of Harold joining up. His face shone, his mouth trembled with loving pride at what Harold had been through and what he had done. And he was such a good boy,—wrote twice a week to his mother and once when he was sick in hospital the Padre of his battalion had written to say what a good and sterling boy he was. Yes, he had been

241

recommended for a commission and was coming home that month to a Cadet battalion at Bournemouth.

When Sabre made his congratulations Twyning accompanied him downstairs to the street and warmly shook his hand. "Thanks, old man; thanks most awfully. Yes, he's everything to me, my Harold. And of course it's a strain never knowing.... Well, well, he's in God's hands; and he's such a good, earnest boy."

Extraordinarily different Twyning the father of Harold, and Twyning in daily relations.

VIII

His leave drew on. He might get his orders any day now. Mabel was much occupied with her rehearsals. He spent his time in long walks alone and, whenever they were possible, in the old evenings with Mr. Fargus. In Mabel's absence he and Effie were much thrown together. Mabel frequently came upon them thus together, and when she did she had a mannerism that somehow seemed to suggest "catching" them together. And sometimes she used that expression. It would have been uncommonly jolly to have had Bright Effie as companion on the walks, and once or twice he did. But Mabel showed very clearly that this was very far from having her approval and on the second occasion said so. There was the slightest possible little tiff about it; and thenceforward—the subject having been opened—there were frequent little passages over Effie, arising always out of his doing what Mabel called "forever sticking up for her." How frequent they were, and how much they annoyed Mabel, he did not realise until, in the last week of his leave, and in the midst of a sticking up for her scene, Mabel surprisingly announced, "Well, anyway I'm sick and tired of the girl, and I'm sick and tired of having you always sticking up for her, and I'm going to get rid of her—to-morrow."

He said, "To-morrow? How can you? I don't say it's not the best thing to do. She's pretty miserable, I should imagine, the way you're always picking at her, but you can't rush her off like that, Mabel."

"Well, I'm going to. I'm going to pay her up and let her go."

"But, Mabel—what will her people think?"

"I'm sure I don't care what they think. If you're so concerned about the precious girl, I'll tell her mother that I was going to make other arrangements in any case and that as this was your last week we thought we'd like to be alone together. Will that satisfy you?"

"I hope it will satisfy them. And I hope very much indeed that you won't do it."

IX

But she did do it. On the following day Effie left. Sabre, pretending to know nothing about it, went for a long walk all day. When he returned Effie had gone. He said nothing. Her name was not again mentioned between him and Mabel. It happened that the only reference to her sudden departure in which he was concerned was with Twyning.

Setting out on his return to France—his orders were to join a Fusilier battalion, reporting to 34th Division—he found Twyning on the platform at Tidborough station buying a paper.

"Hullo, old man," said Twyning. "Just off? I say, old man, old Bright's very upset about Effie getting the sack from your place like that. How was it?"

He felt himself flush. Beastly, having to defend Mabel's unfairness like this. "Oh, I fancy my wife had the idea of getting some relation to live with her, that's all."

Twyning was looking keenly at him. "Oh, I see. But a bit sudden, wasn't it? I mean to say, I thought you were on such friendly terms with the girl. Why, only a couple of days before she left I saw you with her having tea in the Cloister tea rooms. I don't think you saw me, did you, old man?"

"No, I didn't. Yes, I remember; we were waiting for my wife. There'd been a dress rehearsal of this play down at the Corn Exchange."

"Oh, yes, waiting for your wife, were you?" Twyning appeared to be thinking. "Well, that's what I mean, old man. So friendly with the girl—both of you—and then sending her off so suddenly like that."

Sabre essayed to laugh it off. "My wife's rather a sudden person, you know."

Twyning joined very heartily in the laugh. "Is she?" He looked around. "She's seeing you off, I suppose?"

"No, she's not. She's not too well. Got a rotten cold."

Twyning stared again in what struck Sabre as rather an odd way. "Oh, I'm sorry, old man. Nothing much, I hope. Well, you'll want to be getting in. I'll tell old Bright what you say about Effie. Nothing in it. I quite understand. Seemed a bit funny at first, that's all. Good-by, old man. Jolly good luck. Take care of yourself. Jolly good luck."

He put out his hand and squeezed Sabre's in his intensely friendly grip; and destiny put out its hand and added another and a vital hour to Sabre's ultimate encounter with life.

X

His leave ended with the one thing utterly unexpected and flagrantly impossible. One of those meetings so astounding in the fact that the deviation of a single minute, of half a minute, of what one has been doing previously would have prevented it; and out of it one of those frightful things that ought to come with premonition, by hints, by stages, but that come careering headlong as though malignity, bitter and wanton, had loosed a savage bolt.

He arranged to spend the night at the Officers' Rest House near Victoria station. Arriving about nine and disinclined for food, he strolled up to St. James's Park and walked about a little, then back to the station and into the yard to buy a paper. He stood on a street refuge to let by a cab coming out of the station. As it passed he saw its occupants—two women; and one saw him—Nona! Of all incredible things, Nona!

She stopped the cab and he hurried after it.

"Nona!"

"Marko!"

She said, "I'm hurrying to Euston to catch a train. Tony's mother is with me."

He could not see her well in the dim light, but he thought she looked terribly pale and fatigued. And her manner odd. He said, "I'm just going back. But you, Nona? I thought you were in France?"

"I was—this morning. I only came over to-day."

How funny her voice was. "Nona, you look ill. You sound ill. What's up? Is anything wrong?"

She said, "Oh, Marko, Tony's killed."

"Nona!"

... That came careering headlong, as though malignity, bitter and wanton, had loosed a savage bolt.

Tybar killed! The cab was away and he was standing there. Tybar killed. She had said they were hurrying to Scotland, to Tony's home. Tybar killed! He was getting in people's way. He went rather uncertainly to the railings bounding the pavement where he stood, and leaned against them and stared across into the dim cavern of the station yard. Tybar dead....[2]

[2] At a much later date Nona told Sabre of Tony's death:

"It was in that advance of ours. Just before Vimy Ridge. At Arras. Marko, he was shot down leading his men. He wouldn't let them take him away. Re was cheering them on. And then he was hit again. He was terribly wounded. Oh, terribly. They got him down to the clearing station. They didn't think he could possibly live. But you know how wonderful he always was. Even in death that extraordinary spirit of his.... They got him to Boulogne. I was there and I heard quite by chance."

"You saw him, Nona?"

She nodded. "Just before he died. He couldn't speak. But he'd been speaking just before I came. He left a message with the nurse."

She drew a long breath. "Marko, the nurse gave me the message. She thought it was for me—and it wasn't."

She wiped her eyes. "He was watching us. I know he knew she was telling me, and his eyes—you know that mocking kind of look they used to have? Poor Tony! It was there. He died like that.... Marko, you know I'm very glad he just had his old mocking way while he died. Now it's over I'm glad. I wouldn't have had him sorry and unhappy just when he was dying. He was just utterly untouched by anything all his life, not to be judged as ordinary people are judged, and I know perfectly well he'd have wished to go out just his mocking, careless self to the last. He was utterly splendid. All that was between us, that was nothing once the war came. Always think kindly of him, Marko."

Sabre said, "I do. I've never been able but to admire him." She said, "Every one did Poor Tony. Brave Tony!"

XI

On the following morning he crossed to France, there to take up again that strange identity in whose occupancy his own self was held in abeyance, waiting his return. Seven months passed before he returned to that waiting identity and he resumed it then permanently,—done with the war. The tremendous fighting of 1917—his participation in the war—his tenancy of the strange personality caught up in the enormous machinery of it all—ended for him in the great break through of the Hindenburg Line in November. On top of a recollection of sudden shock, then of whirling giddiness in which he was conscious of some enormous violence going on but could not feel it—like (as he afterwards thought) beginning to come to in the middle of a tooth extraction under gas—on the top of these and of extraordinary things and scenes and people he could not at all understand came some one saying:

"Well, it's good-by to the war for you, old man."

He knew that he was aware—and somehow for some time had been aware—that he was in a cot in a ship. He said, "I got knocked out, didn't I?"

... Some one was telling him some interminable story about some one being wounded in the shoulder and in the knee. He said, and his voice appeared to him to be all jumbled up and thick, "Well, I don't care a damn."

... Some one laughed.

Years—or minutes—after this he was talking to a nurse. He said, "What did some one say to me about it being good-by to the war for me?"

The nurse smiled. "Well, poor thing, you've got it rather badly in the knee, you know."

He puzzled over this. Presently he said, "Where are we?"

The nurse bent across the cot and peered through the port; then beamed down on him:

"England!"

She said, "Aren't you glad? What's the matter?"

His face was contracted in intensity of thought, extraordinary thought: he felt the most extraordinary premonition of something disastrous awaiting him: there was in his mind, meaninglessly, menacingly, over and over again, "Good luck have thee with thine honour ... and thy right hand shall show thee terrible things...."

"Terrible things!"

PART FOUR

MABEL—EFFIE—NONA

CHAPTER I

I

Said Hapgood—that garrulous Hapgood, solicitor, who first in this book spoke of Sabre to a mutual friend—said Hapgood, seated in the comfortable study of his fiat, to that same friend, staying the night:

"Well, now, old man, about Sabre. Well, I tell you it's a funny business—a dashed funny business, the position old Puzzlehead Sabre has got himself into. Of course you, with your coarse and sordid instincts, will say it's just what it appears to be and a very old story at that. Whereas to me, with my exquisitely delicate susceptibilities.... No, don't throw that, old man. Sorry. I'll be serious. What I want just to kick off with is that you know as well as I do that I've never been the sort of chap who wept he knows not why; I've never nursed a tame gazelle or any of that sort of stuff. In fact I've got about as much sentiment in me as there is in a pound of lard. But when I see this poor beggar Sabre as he is now, and when I hear him talk as he talked to me about his position last week, and when I see how grey and ill he looks, hobbling about on his old stick, well, I tell you, old man, I get—well, look here, here it is from the Let Go.

"Look here, this is April, April, 1918, by all that's Hunnish—dashed nearly four years of this infernal war. Well, old Sabre got knocked out in France just about five months ago, back in November. He copped it twice—shoulder and knee. Shoulder nothing much; knee pretty bad. Thought they'd have to take his leg off, one time. Thought better of it, thanks be; patched him up; discharged him from the Army; and sent him home—very groggy, only just able to put the bad leg to the ground, crutches, and going to be a stick and a bit of a limp all his life. Poor old Puzzlehead. Think yourself lucky you were a Conscientious Objector, old man.... Oh, damn you, that hurt.

"Very well. That's as he was when I first saw him again. Just making first attempts in the stick and limp stage, poor beggar. That was back in February. Early in February. Mark the date, as they say in the detective stories. I can't remember what the date was, but never you mind. You just mark it. Early in February, two months ago. There was good old me down in Tidborough on business—good old me doing the heavy London solicitor in a provincial town—they always put down a red carpet for me at the station, you know; rather decent, don't you think?—and remembering about old Sabre having been wounded and discharged, blew into Fortune, East and Sabre's (business wasn't with them this time) for news of him.

"Of course he wasn't there. Saw old Fortune and the man Twyning and found them in regard to Sabre about as genial and communicative as a maiden aunt over a married sister's new dress. Old Fortune looking like a walking pulpit in a thundercloud—I should say he'd make about four of me round the equator; and mind you, a chap stopped me in the street the other day and offered me a job as Beefeater outside a moving-picture show: yes, fact, I was wretchedly annoyed about it— and the man Twyning with a lean and hungry look like Cassius, or was it Judas Iscariot? Well, like Cassius out of a job or Judas Iscariot in the middle of one, anyway. That's Twyning's sort. Chap I never cottoned on to a bit. They'd precious little to say about Sabre. Sort of handed out the impression that he'd been out of the business so long that really they weren't much in touch with his doings. Rather rotten, I thought it, seeing that the poor beggar had done his bit in the war and done it pretty thoroughly too. They said that really they hardly knew when he'd be fit to get back to work again; not just yet awhile, anyway. And, yes, he was at home over at Penny Green, so far as they knew,—in the kind of tone that they didn't know much and cared less: at least, that was the impression they gave me; only my fancy, I daresay, as the girl said when she thought the soldier sat a bit too close to her in the tram.

"Well, I'd nothing to do till my train pulled out in the afternoon, so I hopped it over to Penny Green Garden Home on the railway and walked down to old Sabre's to scoop a free lunch off him. Found him a bit down the road from his house trying out this game leg of his. By Jove, he was no end bucked to see me. Came bounding along, dot and carry one, beaming all over his old phiz, and wrung my honest hand as if he was Robinson Crusoe discovering Man Friday on a desert island. I know I'm called Popular Percy by thousands who can only admire me from afar, but I tell you old Sabre fairly overwhelmed me. And talk! He simply jabbered. I said, 'By Jove, Sabre, one would think you hadn't met any one for a month the way you're unbelting the sacred rites of welcome.' He laughed and said, 'Well, you see, I'm a bit tied to a post with this leg of mine.'

"'How's the wife?' said I.

"'She's fine,' said he. 'You'll stay to lunch? I say, Hapgood, you will stay to lunch, won't you?'

"I told him that's what I'd come for; and he seemed no end relieved,—so relieved that I think I must have cocked my eye at him or something, because he said in an apologetic sort of way, 'I mean, because my wife will be delighted. It's a bit dull for her nowadays, only me and always me, crawling about more or less helpless.'

"It struck me afterwards—oh, well, never mind that now. I said, 'I suppose she's making no end of a fuss over you now, hero of the war, and all that sort of thing?'

"'Oh, rather!' says old Sabre, and a minute or two later, as if he hadn't said it heartily enough, 'Oh, rather. Rather, I should think so.'"

II

"Well, we staggered along into the house, old Sabre talking away like a soda-water bottle just uncorked, and he took me into a room on the ground floor where they'd put up a bed for him, him not being able to do the stairs, of course. 'This is my—my den,' he introduced it, 'where I sit about and read and try to do a bit of work.'

"There didn't look to be much signs of either that I could see, and I said so. And old Sabre, who'd been hobbling about the room in a rather uncomfortable sort of way, exclaimed suddenly, 'I say, Hapgood, it's absolutely ripping having you here talking like this. I never can settle down properly in this room, and I've got a jolly place upstairs where all my books and things are.'

"'Let's go up then,' I said.

"'I can't get up.'

"'Well, man alive, I can get you up. Come on. Let's go.'

"He seemed to hesitate for some reason I couldn't understand. 'It's got to be in a chair,' he said. 'It's a business. I wonder—' That kind of thing, as though it was something he oughtn't to do. 'But it would be fine,' he said. 'I've not been up for days. I could show you some of my history I'm going to take up again one of these days—one of these days,' said he, with his nut rather wrinkled up. And then suddenly, 'Come on, let's go!'

"At the door he called out, 'I say, you Jinkses!' and two servant girls came tumbling out rather as if they were falling out of a trap and each trying to fall out first. 'I say,' old Sabre says, 'Mistress not back yet, is she?' and when they told him No, 'Well', d'you think you'd like to get me upstairs on that infernal chair?' he says.

"'Oh, we will, sir,' and they got out one of those invalid chairs and started to lift him up. Course I wanted to take one end, but they wouldn't hear of it. 'If you please, we like carrying the master, sir,' and all that kind of thing; and they fussed him in and fiddled with his legs, snapping at one another for being rough as if they were the two women taking their disputed baby up to old Solomon.

"They'd scarcely got on to the stairs when the front door opened and in walks his wife. My word, I thought they were going to drop him. She says in a voice as though she was biting a chip off an ice block, 'Mark, is it really necessary—' Then she saw me and took her teeth out of the ice. 'Oh, it's Mr. Hapgood, isn't it? How very nice! Staying to lunch, of course? Do let's come into the drawing-room.' Very nice and affable. I always rather liked her. And we went along, I being rather captured and doing the polite in my well-known matinée idol manner, you understand; and I heard old Sabre saying, 'Well, let me out of the damned thing, can't you? Help me out of the damn thing'; and presently hobbled in and joined us, and soon after that lunch, exquisitely cooked and served and all very nice, too.

"Well, as I say, old man, I always rather liked his wife. I—always—rather—liked—her. But somehow, as we went on through lunch, and then on after that, I didn't like her quite so much. Not—quite—so—much. I don't know. Have you ever seen a woman unpicking a bit of sewing? Always looks rather angry with it, I suppose because it's got to be unpicked. They sort of flip the threads out, as much as to say, 'Come out of it, drat you. That's you, drat you.' Well, that was the way she spoke to old Sabre. Sort of snipped off the end of what he was saying and left it hanging, if you follow me. That was the way she spoke to him when she did speak to him. But for the most part they hardly spoke to one another at all. I talked to her, or I talked to him, but the conversation never got triangular. Whenever it threatened to, snip! she'd have his corner off and leave him floating. Tell you what it was, old man, I jolly soon saw that the reason old Sabre was so jolly anxious for me to stay to lunch was because meals without dear old me or some other chatty intellectual were about as much like a feast of reason and a flow of soul as a vinegar bottle and a lukewarm potato on a cold plate. Similarly with the exuberance of his greeting of me. I hate to confess it, but it wasn't so much splendid old me he had been so delighted to see as any old body to whom he could unloose his tongue without having the end of his nose snipped off.

"Mind you, I don't mean that he was cowed and afraid to open his mouth in his wife's presence. Nothing a bit like that. What I got out of it was that he was starved, intellectually starved, mentally starved, starved of the good old milk of human kindness—that's what I mean. Everything he put up he threw down, not because she wanted to snub him, but because she either couldn't or wouldn't take the faintest interest in anything that interested him. Course, she may have had jolly good reason. I daresay she had. Still, there it was, and it seemed rather rotten to me. I didn't like it. Damn it, the chap only had one decent leg under the table and an uncommonly tired-looking face above it, and I felt rather sorry for him."

III

"After lunch I said, 'Well, now, old man, what about going up to this room of yours and having a look at this monumental history?' Saw him shoot a glance in his wife's direction, and he said, 'Oh, no, not now, Hapgood. Never mind now.' And his wife said, 'Mark, what can there be for Mr. Hapgood to see up there? It's too ridiculous. I'm sure he doesn't want to be looking at lesson books.'

"I said, 'Oh, but I'd like to. In fact, I insist. None of your backing out at the last minute, Sabre. I know your little games.'

"Sort of carried it off like that, d'you see; knowing perfectly well the old chap was keen on going up, and seeing perfectly clearly that for some extraordinary reason his wife stopped him going up.

"By Jove, he was pleased, I could see he was. We got in the maids and upped him, to a room he used to sleep in, I gathered, and up there he hobbled about, taking out this book and dusting up that book, and fiddling over his table, and looking out of the window, for all the world like an evicted emigrant restored to the home of his fathers.

"He said, 'Forgive me, old man, just a few minutes; you know I haven't been up here for over three weeks.'

"I said, 'Why the devil haven't you, then?'

"'Oh, well,' says he. 'Oh, well, it makes a business in the house, you know, heaving me up.'

"Well, that didn't cut any ice, you know, seeing that I'd seen the servants rush to the job as if they were going to a school treat. It was perfectly clear to me that the reason he was kept out of the room was because his wife didn't want him being lugged up there; and for all I knew never had liked him being there and now was able to stop it.

"However, his wife was his funeral, not mine, and I said nothing and presently he settled himself down and we began talking. At least he did. He's got some ideas, old Sabre has. He didn't talk about the war. He talked a lot about the effect of the war, on people and on institutions, and that sort of guff. Devilish deep, devilishly interesting. I won't push it on to you. You're one of those soulless, earth-clogged natures.

"Tell you one thing, though, just to give you an idea of the way he's been developing all these years. He talked about how sickened he was with all this stuff in the papers and in the pulpits about how the nation, in this war, is passing through the purging fires of salvation and is going to emerge with higher, nobler, purer ideals, and all that. He said not so. He quoted a thing at me out of one of his books. Something about (as well as I can remember it) something about how 'Those waves of enthusiasm on whose crumbling crests we sometimes see nations lifted for a gleaming moment are wont to have a gloomy trough before and behind.' And he said:

"'That's what it is with us, Hapgood. We've been high on those crests in this war and already they're crumbling. When the peace comes, you look out for the glide down into the trough. They talk about the nation, under this calamity, turning back to the old faiths, to the old simple beliefs, to the old earnest ways, to the old God of their fathers. Man,' he said, 'what can you see already? Temples everywhere to a new God—Greed—Profit—Extortion. All out for it. All out for it,' I remember him saying, 'all out to get the most and do the least.'

"He got up and hobbled about, excited, flushed, and talked like a man who uses his headpiece for thinking. 'Where's that making to, Hapgood?' he asked. 'I'll tell you,' he said. 'You'll get the people finding there's a limit to the high prices they can demand for their labour: apparently none to those the employers can go on piling up for their profits. You'll get growing hatred by the middle classes with fixed incomes of the labouring classes whose prices for their labour they'll see—and feel—going up and up; and you'll get the same growing hatred by the labouring classes for the capitalists. We've been nearly four years on the crest, Hapgood,—on the crest of the war—and it's been all classes as one class for the common good. I tell you, Hapgood, the trough's ahead; we're steering for it; and it's rapid and perilous sundering of the classes.

"'The new God,' old Sabre said. 'High prices, high prices: the highest that can be squeezed. Temples to it everywhere. Ay, and sacrifices, Hapgood. Immolations. Offering up of victims. No thought of those who cannot pay the prices. Pay the prices, or get them, or go under. That's the new God's creed.'

"I said to him, 'What's the remedy, Sabre?'

"He said to me, 'Hapgood, the remedy's the old remedy. The old God. But it's more than that. It's Light: more light. The old revelation was good for the old world, and suited to the old world, and told in terms of the old world's understanding. Mystical for ages steeped in the mystical; poetic for minds receptive of nothing beyond story and allegory and parable. We want a new revelation in terms of the new world's understanding. We want light, light! Do you suppose a man who lives on meat is going to find sustenance in bread and milk? Do you suppose an age that knows wireless and can fly is going to find spiritual sustenance in the food of an age that thought thunder was God speaking? Man's done with it. It means nothing to him; it gives nothing to him. He turns all that's in him to get all he wants out of this world and let the next go rip. Man cannot live by bread alone, the churches tell him; but he says, "I am living on bread alone, and doing well on it." But I tell you, Hapgood, that plumb down in the crypt and abyss of every man's soul is a hunger, a craving for other food than this earthy stuff. And the churches know it; and instead of reaching down to him what he wants—light, light—instead of that, they invite him to dancing and picture shows, and you're a jolly good fellow, and religion's a jolly fine thing and no spoilsport, and all that sort of latter-day tendency. Damn it, he can get all that outside the churches and get it better. Light, light! He wants light, Hapgood. And the padres come down and drink beer with him, and watch boxing matches with him, and sing music-hall songs with him, and dance Jazz with him, and call it making religion a Living Thing in the Lives of the People. Lift the hearts of the people to God, they say, by showing them that religion is not incompatible with having a jolly fine time. And there's no God there that a man can understand for him to be lifted up to. Hapgood, a man wouldn't care what he had to give up if he knew he was making for something inestimably precious. But he doesn't know. Light, light—that's what he wants; and the longer it's withheld the lower he'll sink. Light! Light!'"

IV

"Well, I make no extra charge for that (said Hapgood, and helped himself to a drink). That's not me. That's Sabre. And if you'd seen him as I saw him, and if you'd heard him as I heard him, you'd have been as impressed as I was impressed instead of lolling there like a surfeited python. I tell you, old Sabre was all pink under his skin, and his eyes shining, and his voice tingling. I tell you, if you were a real painter instead of a base flatterer of bloated and wealthy sitters, and if you'd seen him then, you'd have painted the masterpiece of your age and called it The Visionary. I tell you, old Sabre was fine. He said he'd been thinking all round that sort of stuff for years, and that now, for one reason and another, it was beginning to crystallize in him and take form and substance.

"I asked him, 'What reasons, Sabre?' and he said, 'Oh, I don't know. The war; and being out there; and thinking about the death of an old woman I attended once; and things I picked up from a slip of a girl; and things from a woman I know—oh, all sorts of things, Hapgood; and I tell you what chiefly—loneliness, my God, loneliness....'

"I didn't say anything. What could I say? When a chap suddenly rips a cry out of his heart like that, what the devil can you say if you weigh fourteen stone of solid contentment and look it? You can only feel you weren't meant to hear and try to look as if you hadn't.

"Well, anyway, time came for me to go and I went. Sabre stayed where he was. Would I mind leaving him up there? It was so seldom he got up; and talking with me had brought back old feelings he thought he'd never recapture again, and he was going to see if he couldn't start in and do a bit of writing again. So I pulled out and left him; and that was old Sabre as I saw him two months ago; and one way and another I thought a good deal coming back in the train of what I had seen. Those sort of ideas in his head and that sort of life with his wife. D'you remember my telling you years—oh, years ago—

that he looked like a chap who'd lost something and was wondering where he'd put it? Well, the Sabre I left down there two months ago had not only lost it, but knew it was gone for good and all. That was Sabre—except when the pink got under his skin when he got talking.

"All right. All right. Now that's just the prologue. That's just what you're supposed to know before the Curtain goes up. Now, am I going on to the drama or are we going to bed.... The drama? Right. You're a lewd fellow of the baser sort, but you occasionally have wise instincts. Right. The drama."

CHAPTER II

I

Continued Hapgood:

"All right. That was two months ago. Last week I was down at Tidborough again. Felt I'd got rather friendly with old Sabre on my last visit so as soon as I could toddled off to the office to look him up. Felt quite sure he'd be back there again by now. But he wasn't. He wasn't, and when I began inquiring for him found there seemed to be some rummy mystery about his absence. Like this. Some sort of a clerk was in the shop as I went in. 'Mr. Sabre upstairs, eh?' I asked. 'No. No, Mr. Sabre's not—not here,' says my gentleman, with rather an odd look at me.

"'What, not still laid up, is he?'

"The chap gave me a decidedly odd look. 'Mr. Sabre's not attending the office at present, sir.'

"'Not attending the office? Not ill, is he?'

"'No, not ill, I think, sir. Not attending the office. Perhaps you'd like to see one of the partners?'

"I looked at him. He looked at me. What the devil did he mean? Just then I caught sight of an old bird I knew slightly coming down the stairs with a book under his arm. Old chap called Bright. Sort of foreman or something. Looked rather like Moses coming down the mountain with the Tables of Stone in his fist. I said in my cheery way, 'Hullo, Mr. Bright. Good morning. I was just inquiring for Mr. Sabre.'

"By Jove, I thought for a minute the old patriarch was going to heave the tables of stone at my head. He caught up the book in both his hands and gave a sort of choke and blazed at me out of his eyes—by gad, I might have been poor old Aaron caught jazzing round the golden calf.

"'Let me tell you, sir, this is no place to inquire after Mr. Sabre,' said he. 'Let me tell you—'

"Well, I'd ha' let him tell me any old thing. That was what I was there for. But he shut himself up with a kind of gasp and cannoned himself into his tabernacle under the stairs and left me there, wondering if I was where I thought I was, or had got into a moving-picture show by mistake. The clerk had fallen through the floor or something. I was alone. Friendless. Nobody wanted me. I thought to myself, 'Percival, old man, you're on the unpopular side of the argument. You're nonsuited, old man.' And I thought I wouldn't take any more chances in this Biblical film, not with old father Abraham Fortune or Friend Judas Iscariot Twyning; I thought I'd push out to Penny Green and see old Sabre for myself.

"So I did. I certainly did....

"You can imagine me, old man, in my natty little blue suit, tripping up the path of Sabre's house and guessing to myself that the mystery wasn't a mystery at all, but only the office perhaps rather fed up with Sabre for staying away nursing his game leg so long. By Jove, it wasn't that. House had rather a neglected appearance, I thought. Door knob not polished, or blinds still down somewhere or something. I don't know. Something. And what made me conscious of it was that I was kept a long time waiting after I'd rung the bell. In fact, I had to ring twice. Then I heard some one coming, and you know how your mind unconsciously expects things and so gives you quite a start when the thing isn't there; well, I suppose I'd been expecting to see one of Sabre's two servants, 'my couple of Jinkses' as he calls them, and 'pon my soul I was quite startled when the door opened and it wasn't one of them at all, but a very different pair of shoes.

"It was a young woman; ladylike, dressed just in some ordinary sort of clothes; I don't know; uncommonly pretty, or might have been if she hadn't looked so uncommonly sad; and—this was what knocked me carrying a baby. 'Pon my soul, I couldn't have been more astonished if the door had been opened by the Kaiser carrying the Crown Prince.

"I don't know why I should have imagined she was the kid's mother, but I did. I don't know why I should have looked at her hands, but I did. I don't know why I should have expected to see a wedding ring, but I did. And there wasn't one.

"Well, she was saying 'Yes?' in an inquiring, timid sort of way, me standing there like a fool, you understand, and I suddenly recovered from my flabbergasteration and guessed the obvious thing—that the Sabres had let their house to strangers and gone away. Still more obvious, you might say, that Mrs. Sabre had produced a baby, and that the girl was her sister or some one, but that never occurred to me. No,

I guessed they'd gone away, and I said, 'I was calling to see Mr. Sabre. Has he gone away?'

"I'd thought her looking timid. She was looking at me now decidedly as if she were frightened of me. 'No, no, Mr. Sabre's not gone away. He's here. Are you a friend of his?'

"I smiled at her. 'Well, I used to be,' I said. She didn't smile. What the dickens was up? 'I used to be. I always thought I was. My name's Hapgood.'

"'Perhaps you'd better come in.'

"You know, it was perfectly extraordinary. Her voice was as sad as her face. I stepped in. What on earth was I going to hear? Sabre dying? Wife dying? Air-raid bomb fallen on the house and everybody dead? 'Pon my soul, I began to feel creepy. Scalp began to prick. Then suddenly there was old Sabre at the head of the stairs. 'What is it, Effie?' Then he saw me. 'Hullo, Hapgood!' His voice was devilish pleased. Then he said again, rather in a thoughtful voice, 'Hullo, Hapgood,' and he began to come down, slowly, with his stick.

"Well, he wasn't dead, anyway; that was something to go on with. I took his hand and said, 'Hullo, Sabre. How goes it, old man? Able to do the stairs now, I see. I was down to Tidborough and thought I'd come and look you up again.'

"'Fine,' he said, shaking my hand. 'Jolly nice of you.' Then he said, 'Did you go to the office for me, Hapgood?'

"'Just looked in,' I said offhandedly. 'Saw a clerk who said you weren't down to-day, so I came along up.'

"He was doing some thinking, I could see that. He said, 'Jolly good of you. I am glad. You'll stay a bit, of course.' The girl had faded away. He went a bit along the passage and called out, 'Effie, you can scratch up a bit of lunch for Mr. Hapgood?'

"I suppose she said Yes. 'Lunch'll be on in about two minutes,' he came back to me with. 'You're later than when you came up last time. Come along in here.'

"Led me into the morning room and we sat down and pretended to talk. Very poor pretence, I give you my word. Both of us manifestly straining to do the brisk and hearty, and the two of us producing about as much semblance of chatty interchange as a couple of victims waiting their turn in a dentist's parlour. The door was open and I could hear some one moving about laying the lunch. That was all I could hear (bar Sabre's spasmodic jerks of speech) and I don't mind telling you I was a deal more interested in what I could hear going on outside than in anything we could put up between us. Or rather in what I couldn't hear going on outside. No voices, none of those sounds, none of that sort of feeling that tells you people are about the place. No, there was some mystery knocking about the place somewhere, and it was on the other side of the door, and that was where my attention was.

"Presently I heard the girl's voice outside, 'Lunch is ready.'

"We jumped up like two schoolboys released from detention and went along in. More mystery. Lunch at Sabre's place was always a beautifully conducted rite, as I was accustomed to it. Announced by two gongs, warning and ready, to begin with, and here we'd been shuffled in by a girl's casual remark in the passage; and beautifully appointed and served when you got there and here was—Well, there were places laid for two only and a ramshackle kind of cold picnic scattered about the cloth. Everything there, help yourself kind of show. Bit of cold meat, half a cold tart, lump of cheese, loaf of bread, assortment of plates, and so on.

"Sabre said, 'Oh, by the way, my wife's not here. She's away.'

"I murmured the polite thing. He was staring at the two places, frowning a bit. 'Half a minute,' he said and hopped off on his old stick. Then I heard him talking to this mysterious girl. At least I heard her voice first. 'Oh, I can't! I can't!'

"Then Sabre: 'Nonsense, Effie. You must. You must. I insist. Don't be silly.'

"Then a door slammed.

"Well, I ask you! If I didn't say to myself, 'The plot thickens,' if I didn't say it, I can promise you I thought it. I did. And it proceeded to curdle. The door that had slammed opened and presently in comes

Sabre with the girl. And the girl with the baby in her arms. Sabre said in his ordinary, easy voice—he's got a particularly nice voice, has old Sabre—'This is a very retiring young person, Hapgood. Had to be dragged in. Miss Bright. Her father's in the office. Perhaps you've met him, have you?'

"Well, I don't know what I said, old man. I know what I thought. I thought just precisely what you're thinking. Yes, I had a furiously vivid shot of a recollection of old Bright as I'd seen him a couple of hours before, of his blazing look, of his gesture of wanting to hurl the Tables of Stone at me, and of his extraordinary remark about Sabre,— I had that and I did what you're doing: I put two and two together and found the obvious answer (same as you) and I jolly near fell down dead, I did. Jolly near.

"But Sabre was going on, pleasant and natural as you please. 'Miss Bright was here as companion to my wife while I was in France. Now she's staying here a bit. Put the baby on the sofa, Effie, and let's get to work. I'd like you two to be friends. Hapgood and I were at school together, you know, about a thousand years ago. They used to call him Porker because he was so thin.'

"The girl smiled faintly, I put up an hysterical sort of squeak, and we sat down. The meal wasn't precisely a banquet. We helped ourselves and stacked up the soiled plates as we used them. No servants, d'you see? That was pretty clear by now. No wife, no servants, no wedding ring; nothing but old Bright's daughter and old Bright's daughter's baby—and—and—Sabre.

"I suppose I talked. I heard my voice sometimes. The easy flow Sabre had started with didn't last long. The girl hardly spoke. I watched her a lot. I liked the look of her. She must have been uncommonly pretty in a vivacious sort of way before she ran up against her trouble, whatever it was. I say Whatever it was. I'd no real reason to suppose I knew; though mind you, I was guessing pretty shrewdly it was lying there on the sofa wrapped up in what d'you call 'ems—swaddling clothes. Yes, uncommonly pretty, but now sad—sad as a young widow at the funeral, that sort of look. It was her eyes that especially showed it. Extraordinary eyes. Like two great pools in a shadow. If I may quote poetry, at you,

Her eyes were deeper than the depth

Of waters stilled at even.

And all the sorrow in them of all the women since Mary Magdalen. All the time but once. Once the baby whimpered, and she got up and went to it and stooped over it the other side of the sofa from me, so I could see her face. By gad, if you could have seen her eyes then! Motherhood! Lucky you weren't there, because if you've any idea of ever painting a picture called Motherhood, you'd ha' gone straight out and cut your throat on the mat in despair. You certainly would.

"Well, anyway, the banquet got more and more awkward to endure as it dragged on, and mighty glad I was when at last the girl got up— without a word—and picked up the baby and left us. Left us. We were no more chatty for being alone, I can promise you. I absolutely could not think of a word to say, and any infernal thing that old Sabre managed to rake up seemed complete and done to death the minute he'd said it.

"Then all of a sudden he began. He fished out some cigarettes and chucked me one and we smoked like a couple of exhaust valves for about two minutes and then he said, 'Hapgood, why on earth should I have to explain all this to you? Why should I?'

"I said, a tiny bit sharply—I was getting a bit on edge, you know—I said, 'Well, who's asked you to? I haven't asked any questions, have I?'

"Sabre said, 'No, I know you haven't asked any, and I'm infernally grateful to you. You're the first person across this threshold in months that hasn't. But I know you're thinking them—hard. And I know I've got to answer them. And I want to. I want to most frightfully. But what beats me is this infernal feeling that I must explain to you, to you and to everybody, whether I want to or not. Why should I? It's my own house. I can do what I like in it. I'm not, anyway, doing anything wrong. I'm doing something more right than I've ever done in my life, and yet everybody's got the right to question me and everybody's got the right to be answered and—Hapgood, it's the most bewildering state of affairs that can possibly be imagined. I'm up against a code of social conventions, and by Jove I'm absolutely down and out. I'm absolutely tied up hand and foot and chucked away. Do you know what I am, Hapgood—?'

"He gave a laugh. He wasn't talking a bit savagely, and he never did talk like that all through what he told me. He was just talking in a tone of sheer, hopeless, extremely interested puzzlement—bafflement—amazement; just as a man might talk to you of some absolutely baffling conjuring trick he'd seen. In fact, he used that very expression. 'Do you know what I am, Hapgood?' and he gave a laugh, as I've said. 'I'm what they call a social outcast. A social outcast. Beyond the pale. Unspeakable. Ostracized. Blackballed. Excommunicated.' He got up and began to stump about the room, hands in his pockets, chin on his collar, wrestling with it,—and wrestling, mind you, just in profoundly interested bafflement.

"'Unspeakable,' he said. 'Excommunicated. By Jove, it's astounding. It's amazing. It's like a stupendous conjuring trick. I've done something that isn't done—not something that's wrong, something that's incontestably right. But it isn't done. People don't do it, and I've done it and therefore hey, presto, I'm turned into a leper, a pariah, an outlaw. Amazing, astounding!'

"Then he settled down and told me. And this is what he told me."

II

"When he was out in France this girl I'd seen—this Effie, as he called her, Effie Bright—had come to live as companion to his wife. It appears he more or less got her the job. He'd seen her at the office with her father and he'd taken a tremendous fancy to her. 'A jolly kid,' that was the expression he used, and he said he was awfully fond of her just as he might be of a jolly little sister. He got her some other job previously with some friends or other, and then the old lady there died and the girl came to his place while he was away. Something like that. Anyway, she came. She came somewhere about October, '15, and she left early in March following, just over a year ago. His wife got fed up with her and got rid of her—that's what Sabre says—got fed up with her and got rid of her. And Sabre was at home at the time. Mark that, old man, because it's important. Sabre was at home at the time—about three weeks—on leave.

"Very well. The girl got the sack and he went back to France. She got another job somewhere as companion again. He doesn't quite know where. He thinks at Bournemouth. Anyway, that's nothing to do with it. Well, he got wounded and discharged from the Army, as you know, and in February he was living at home again with his wife in the conditions I described to you when I began. He said nothing to me about the conditions—about the terms they were on; but I've told you what I saw. It's important because it was exactly into the situation as I then saw it that came to pass the thing that came to pass. This:

"The very week after I'd been down there, his wife, reading a letter at breakfast one morning, gave a kind of a snort (as I can imagine it) and chucked the letter over to him and said, 'Ha! There's your wonderful Miss Bright for you! What did I tell you? What do you think of that? Ha!'

"Those were her very words and her very snorts and what they meant—what 'Your wonderful Miss Bright for you' meant—was, as he explained to me, that when he was home on leave, with the girl in the house, they were frequently having words about her, because he thought his wife was a bit sharp with her, and his wife, for her part, said he was forever sticking up for her.

"'What do you think of that? Ha!' and she chucked the letter over to him, and from what I know of her you can imagine her sitting bolt upright, bridling with virtuous prescience confirmed, watching him, while he read it.

"While he read it.... Sabre said the letter was the most frightfully pathetic document he could ever have imagined. Smudged, he said, and stained and badly expressed as if the writer—this girl—this Effie Bright—was crying and incoherent with distress when she wrote it. And she no doubt was. She said she'd got into terrible trouble. She'd got a little baby. Sabre said it was awful to him the way she kept on in every sentence calling it 'a little baby'—never a child, or just a baby, but always 'a little baby,' 'my little baby.' He said it was awful. She said it was born in December—you remember, old man, it was the previous March she'd got the sack from them—and that she'd been living in lodgings with it, and that now she was well enough to move, and had come to the absolute end of her money, she was being turned out and was at her wits' end with despair and nearly out of her mind to know what to do and all that kind of thing. She said her father wouldn't have anything to do with her, and no one would have anything to do with her—so long as she kept her little baby. That was her plight: no one would have anything to do with her while she had the baby. Her father was willing to take her home, and some kind people had offered to take her into service, and the clergyman where she was had said there were other places he could get her, but only, all of them, if she would give up the baby and put it out to nurse somewhere: and she said, and underlined it about fourteen times,

Sabre said, and cried over it so you could hardly read it, she said: 'And, oh, Mrs. Sabre, I can't, I can't, I simply can not give up my little baby.... He's mine,' she said. 'He looks at me, and knows me, and stretches out his tiny little hands to me, and I can't give him up. I can't let my little baby go. Whatever I've done, I'm his mother and he's my little baby and I can't let him go.'

"Sabre said it was awful. I can believe it was. I'd seen the girl, and I'd seen her stooping over her baby (like I told you) and I can well believe awful was the word for it. Poor soul.

"And then she said—I can remember this bit—then she said, 'And so, in my terrible distress, dear Mrs. Sabre, I am throwing myself on your mercy, and begging you, imploring you, for the love of God to take in me and my little baby and let me work for you and do anything for you and bless you and ask God's blessing for ever upon you and teach my little baby to pray for you as—' something or other, I forget. And then she said a lot of hysterical things about working her fingers to the bone for Mrs. Sabre, and knowing she was a wicked girl and not fit to be spoken to by any one, and was willing, to sleep in a shed in the garden and never to open her mouth, and all that sort of thing; and all the way through 'my little baby,' 'my little baby.' Sabre said it was awful. Also she said,—I'm telling you just what Sabre told me, and he told me this bit deliberately, as you might say—also she said that she didn't want to pretend she was more sinned against than sinning, but that if Mrs. Sabre knew the truth she might judge her less harshly and be more willing to help her. Yes, Sabre told me that....

"All right. Well, there was the appeal, 'there was this piteous appeal', as Sabre said, and there was Sabre profoundly touched by it, and there was his wife bridling over it—one up against her husband who'd always stuck up for the girl, d'you see, and about two million up in justification of her own opinion of her. There they were; and then Sabre said, turning the letter over in his hands, 'Well, what are you going to do about it?'

"You can imagine his wife's tone. 'Do about it! Do about it! What on earth do you think I'm going to do about it?'

"And Sabre said, 'Well, I think we ought certainly to take the poor creature in.'

"That's what he said; and I can perfectly imagine his face as he said it—all twisted up with the intensity of the struggle he foresaw and with the intensity of his feelings on the subject; and I can perfectly well imagine his wife's face as she heard him, by Jove, I can. She was furious. Absolutely white and speechless with fury; but not speechless long, Sabre said, and I dare bet she wasn't. Sabre said she worked herself up in the most awful way and used language about the girl that cut him like a knife—language like speaking of the baby as 'that brat.' It made him wince. It would—the sort of chap he is. And he said that the more she railed, the more frightfully he realised the girl's position, up against that sort of thing everywhere she turned.

"He described all that to me and then, so to speak, he stated his case. He said to me, his face all twisted up with the strain of trying to make some one else see what was so perfectly clear to himself, he said, 'Well, what I say to you, Hapgood, is just precisely what I said to my wife. I felt that the girl had a claim on us. In the first place, she'd turned to us in her abject misery for help and that alone established a claim, even if it had come from an utter stranger. It established a claim because here was a human creature absolutely down and out come to us, picking us out from everybody, for succour. Damn it, you've got to respond. You're picked out. You! One human creature by another human creature. Breathing the same air. Sharing the same mortality. Responsible to the same God. You've got to! You can't help yourself. You're caught. If you hear some one appealing to any one else you can scuttle out of it. Get away. Pass by on the other side. Square it with your conscience any old how. But when that some one comes to you, you're done, you're fixed. You may hate it. You may loathe and detest the position that's been forced on you. But it's there. You can't get out of it. The same earth as your earth is there at your feet imploring you; and if you've got a grain, a jot of humanity, you must, you must, out of the very flesh and bones of you, respond to that cry of this your brother or your sister made as you yourself are made.

"'Well, Hapgood,' he went on, 'that's one claim the girl had on us, and to my way of thinking it was enough. But she had another, a personal claim. She'd been in our house, in our service; she was our friend; sat with us; eaten with us; talked with us; shared with us; and now, now, turned to us. Good God, man, was that to be refused? Was that to be denied? Were we going to repudiate that? Were we going to say, "Yes, it's true you were here. You were all very well when you were of use to us; that's all true and admitted; but now you're in trouble and you're no use to us; you're in trouble and no use, and you can get to hell out of it." Good God, were we to say that?'

"You should have seen his face; you should have heard his voice; you should have seen him squirming and twisting in his chair as though this was the very roots of him coming up out of him and hurting him. And I tell you, old man, it was the very roots of him. It was his creed, it was his religion, it was his composition; it was the whole nature and basis and foundation of the man as it had been storing up within him all his life, ever since he was the rummy, thoughtful sort of beggar he used to be as a kid at old Wickamote's thirty years ago. It got me, I can tell you. It made me feel funny. Yes, and the next thing he went on to was equally the blood and bones of him. In a way even more characteristic. He said, 'Mind you, Hapgood, I don't blame my wife that all this had no effect on her. I don't blame her in the least, and I never lost my temper or got angry over the business. I see her point of view absolutely. And I see absolutely the point of view of the girl's father and of every one else who's willing to take in the girl but insists she must give up the baby. I see their point of view and understand it as plain as I see and understand that calendar hanging on the wall. I see it perfectly,' and he laughed in a whimsical sort of way and said, 'That's the devil of it.'

"Characteristic, eh? Wasn't that just exactly old Sabre at school puzzling up his old nut and saying, 'Yes, but I see what he means'?

"Well, wait a bit. He came to that again afterwards. It seems that, if you please, the very next day the girl herself follows up her letter by walking into the house. Eh? Yes, you can well say 'By Jove.' In she walked, baby and all. She'd walked all the way from Tidborough, and God knows how far earlier in the day. Sabre said she was half dead. She'd been to her father's house, and her father, that terrific-looking old Moses coming down the mountain that I've described to you, had turned her out. He'd take her—he had cried over her, the poor crying creature said—if she'd send away her baby, also if she'd say who the father was, but she wouldn't. 'I can't let my little baby go,' she said. Sabre said it was awful, hearing her. And so he drove her out, the old Moses man did, and the poor soul tried around for a bit—no money— and then trailed out to them.

"Sabre wouldn't tell me all that happened between his wife and himself. I gather that, in his quiet way, perfectly seeing his wife's point of view and genuinely deeply distressed at the frightful pitch things were coming to, in that sort of way he nevertheless got his back up against his sense of what he ought to do and said the girl was not to be sent away, that she was to stop.

"His wife said, 'You're determined?'

"He said, 'Mabel' (that's her name) 'Mabel, I'm desperately, poignantly sorry, but I'm absolutely determined.'

"She said, 'Very well. If she's going to be in the house, I'm going out of it. I'm going to my father's. Now. You'll not expect the servants to stay in the house while you've got this—this woman living with you—' (Yes, she said that.) 'So I shall pay them up and send them off, now, before I go. Are you still determined?'

"The poor devil, standing there with his stick and his game leg, and his face working, said, 'Mabel, Mabel, believe me, it kills me to say it, but I am, absolutely. The girl's got no home. She only wants to keep her baby. She must stop.'

"His wife went off to the kitchen.

"Pretty fierce, eh?

"Sabre said he sat where she'd left him, in the morning room in a straight-backed chair, with his legs stuck out in front of him, wrestling with it—like hell. The girl was in the dining room. His wife and the servants were plunging about overhead.

"In about two hours his wife came back dressed to go. She said, 'I've packed my boxes. I shall send for them. The maids have packed theirs and they will send. I've sent them on to the station in front of me. There's only one more thing I want to say to you. You say this woman—' ('This woman, you know!' old Sabre said when he was telling me.) 'You say this woman has a claim on us?'

"He began, 'Mabel, I do. I—'

"She said, 'Do you want my answer to that? My answer is that perhaps she has a claim on you!'

"And she went."

III

"Well, there you are, old man. There it is. That's the story. That's the end. That's the end of my story, but what the end of the story as Sabre's living it is going to be, takes—well, it lets in some pretty wide guessing. There he is, and there's the girl, and there's the baby; and he's what he says he is—what I told you: a social outcast, beyond the pale, ostracized, excommunicated. No one will have anything to do with him. They've cleared him out of the office, or as good as done so. He says the man Twyning worked that. The man Twyning—that Judas Iscariot chap, you remember—is very thick with old Bright, the girl's father. Old Bright pretty naturally thinks his daughter has gone back to the man who is responsible for her ruin, and this Twyning person—who's a partner, by the way—wrote to Sabre and told him that, although he personally didn't believe it—'not for a moment, old man,' he wrote—still Sabre would appreciate the horrible scandal that had arisen, and would appreciate the fact that such a scandal could not be permitted in a firm like theirs with its high and holy Church connections. And so on. He said that he and Fortune had given the position their most earnest and sympathetic thought and prayers—and prayers, mark you—and that they'd come to the conclusion that the best thing to be done was for Sabre to resign.

"Sabre says he was knocked pretty well silly by this step. He says it was his first realisation of the attitude that everybody was going to take up against him. He went off down and saw them, and you can imagine there was a bit of a scene. He said he was dashed if he'd resign. Why on earth should he resign? Was he to resign because he was doing in common humanity what no one else had the common humanity to do? That sort of thing. You can imagine it didn't cut much ice with that crowd. The upshot of it was that Twyning, speaking for the firm, and calling him about a thousand old mans and that sort of slush, told him that the position would be reconsidered when he ceased to have the girl in his house and that, in the interests of the firm, until he did that he must cease to attend the office.

"And then old Sabre said he began to find himself in exactly the same position with every one. Every door closed to him. No one having anything to do with him. Even an old chap next door, a particular friend of his called Fungus or Fargus or some such name—even this old bird's house and his society is forbidden him. Sabre says old Fungus, or whatever his name is, is all right, but it appears he's ruled by about two dozen ramping great daughters, and they won't let their

269

father have anything to do with Sabre. No, he's shut right out, everywhere.

"And Sabre, mind you—this is Sabre's extraordinary point of view: he's not a bit furious with all these people. He's feeling his position most frightfully; it's eating the very heart out of him, but he's working up not the least trace of bitterness over it. He says they're all supporting an absolutely right and just convention, and that it's not their fault if the convention is so hideously cruel in its application. He says the absolute justice and the frightful cruelty of conventions has always interested him, and that he remembers once putting up to a great friend of his as an example this very instance of society's attitude towards an unmarried girl who gets into trouble,—never dreaming that one day he was going to find himself up against the full force of it. He said, 'If this poor girl, if any girl, didn't find the world against her and every door closed to her, just look where you'd be, Hapgood. You'd have morality absolutely gone by the hoard. No, all these people are right, absolutely right—and all conventions are absolutely right—in their principle; it's their practice that's sometimes so terrible. And when it is, how can you turn round and rage? I can't.'

"Well, I said to him what I say to you, old man. I said, 'Yes, that's all right, Sabre. That's true, though there're precious few would take it as moderately as you; but look here, where's this going to end? Where's it going to land you? It's landed you pretty fiercely as it is. Have you thought what it may develop into? What are you doing about it?'

"He said he was writing round, writing to advertisers and to societies and places, to find a place where the girl would be taken in to work and allowed to have her baby with her. He said there must be hundreds of kind-hearted people about the place who would do it; it was only a question of finding them. Well, as to that, kind hearts are more than coronets and all that kind of thing, but it strikes me they're a jolly side harder than coronets to find when it comes to a question of an unmarried mother and her baby, and when the kind hearts, being found, come to make inquiries and find that the person making application on the girl's behalf is the man she's apparently living with, and the man with Sabre's extraordinary record in regard to the girl. I didn't say that to poor old Sabre. I hadn't the face to. But I say it to you. You're no doubt thinking it for yourself. All that chain of circumstances, eh? Went out of his way to get her her first job. Got her into his house. In a way responsible for her getting the sack. Child born just about when it must have been born after she'd been sacked.

Girl coming to him for help. Writing to his wife, 'If only you knew the truth.' Wife leaving him. Eh? It's pretty fierce, isn't it? And I don't believe he's got an idea of it. I don't believe he realises for a moment what an extraordinary coil it all is. God help him if he ever does.... He'll want it.

"No, I didn't say a word like that to him. I couldn't. The nearest I got to it was I said, 'Well, but time's getting on, you know, old man. It's a—a funny position on the face of it. What do you suppose your wife's thinking all this time?'

"He said his wife would be absolutely all right once he'd found a home for the girl and sent her away. He said his wife was always a bit sharp in her views of things, but that she'd be all right when it was all over.

"I said, 'H'm. Heard from her?'

"He had—once. He showed me the letter. Well, you know, old man, every fox knows what foxes smell like; and I smelt a dear brother solicitor's smell in that letter. Smelt it strong. Asking him to make a home possible for her to return to so they might resume their life together. I recognised it. I've dictated dozens.

"I handed it back. I said, 'H'm' again. I said, 'H'm, you remember, old man, there was that remark of hers just as she was leaving you—that remark that perhaps the girl might have a claim on you. Remember that, don't you?'

"By Jove, I thought for a minute he was going to flare up and let me have it. But he laughed instead. Laughed as if I was a fool and said, 'Oh, good Lord, man, that's utterly ridiculous. That was only just my wife's way. My wife's got plenty of faults to find with me—but that kind of thing! Man alive, with all my faults, my wife knows me.'

"Perhaps—I say, my holy aunt, it's nearly two o'clock! Come on, I'm for bed. Perhaps his wife does know him. What I'm thinking is, does he know his wife? I'm a solicitor. I know what I'd say if she came to me."

CHAPTER III

I

On a day a month later—in May—Hapgood said:

"Now, I'll tell you. Old Sabre—by Jove, it's frightful. He's crashed. The roof's fallen in on him. He's nearly out of his mind. I don't like it. I don't like it a bit. I've only just left him. Here, in London. A couple of hours ago. I oughtn't to have left him. The chap's not fit to be left. But I had to. He cleared me off. I had to go. He wasn't in a state to be argued with. I was frightened of irritating him. To tell you the truth, I'm frightened now about him. Dead frightened.

"Look here, it's in two parts, this sudden development. Two parts as I saw it. Begins all right and then works up. Two parts—morning and afternoon yesterday and a bit to-day. And of all extraordinary places to happen at—Brighton.

"Yes, Brighton. I was down there for a Saturday to Monday with my Missus. This absolutely topping weather, you know. We were coming back Monday evening. Yesterday. Very well. Monday morning we were sunning on the pier, she and I. I was reading the paper, she was watching the people and making remarks about them. If Paradise is doing in the next world what you best liked doing in this, my wife will ask Peter if she can sit at the gate and watch the demobilised souls arriving and pass remarks about them. She certainly will.

"Well, all of a sudden she began, 'Oh, what a frightfully interesting face that man's got!' That's the way she talks. 'What a most interesting face. Do look, Percy.'

"I said, 'Well, so have I got an interesting face. Look at mine.'

"'Oh, but do, Percy. You must. On that seat by himself just opposite. He's just staring at nothing and thinking and thinking. And his face looks so worn and tired and yet so very kind and such a wistful look as though he was thinking of—'

"I growled, still reading: 'He's probably thinking what he's going to have for lunch. Oh, dash it, do stop jogging me. Where is he?'

"And then I looked across. Old Sabre! By Jove, you might have pushed me over with one finger. Old Sabre in a tweed suit and a soft hat, and his game leg stuck out straight, and his old stick, and his hands about a thousand miles deep in his pockets, and looking—yes, my wife said the true thing when she said how he was looking. Any one would have taken a second squint at old Sabre's face as I saw it then—taken a second squint and wondered what he'd been through and what on earth his mind could be on now. They certainly would.

"I knew. I knew; but I tell you this, I could see he'd been through a tough lot more, and thought a considerable number of fathoms deeper, in the month since I'd seen him last. Yes, by Jove, I could see that without spectacles.

"I went over to him. You could have pushed him off the seat with one finger when he saw me. Except that you wouldn't have had any fingers worth using as fingers, after he'd squeezed your hands as he squeezed mine. Both of them. And his face like a shout on a sunny morning. Yes, he was pleased. I like to think how jolly pleased the old chap was.

"I took him over to my wife, and my wife climbed all over him, and we chatted round for a bit, and then I worked off my wife on a bunch of people we knew and I got old Sabre on to a secluded bench and started in on him. What on earth was he doing down at Brighton, and how were things?

"He said 'Things...? Things are happening with me, Hapgood. Not to me—with me. Happening pretty fierce and pretty quick. I'm right in the middle of the most extraordinary, the most astounding, the most amazing things. I had to get away from them for a bit. I simply had to. I came down here for a week-end to get away from them and go on wrestling them out when they weren't right under my eyes. I'm going back to-morrow. Effie was all right—with her baby. She was glad I should go—glad for me, I mean. Poor kid, poor kid. Top of her own misery, Hapgood, she's miserable to death at what she says she's let me in for. She's always crying about it. Crying. She's torn between knowing my house is the only place where she can have her baby, between that and seeing what her coming into the place has caused. She spends her time trying to do any little thing she can to make me comfortable, hunts about for any little thing she can do for me. It's pathetic, you know. At least, it's pathetic to me. Jumped at this sudden idea of mine of getting away for a couple of days. Said it would please her more than anything in the world to know I was right away from it all for a bit. Fussed over me packing up and all that, you know. Pathetic. Frightfully. Look, just to show you how she hunts about for anything to do for me—said my old straw hat was much too shabby for Brighton and would I get her some stuff, oxalic acid, and let her clean it up for me. That sort of little trifle. As a matter of fact she made such a shocking mess of the hat that I hardly liked to wear it. Couldn't hurt her feelings, though. Chucked it into the sea when I got here and bought this one. Make a funny story for her when I get back about how it blew off. That's the sort of life we lead together, Hapgood. She always trying to do little things for me and I trying to think out little jokes for her to try and cheer her up. Give you another example. Just when I had brought her the stuff for my hat. Met me with, Had I lost anything? Made a mystery of it. Said I was to guess. Guessed at last that it must be my cigarette case. It was. She'd found it lying about and took me to show where she'd put it for safety—in the back of the clock in my room. Said I was always to look there for any little valuables I might miss, and wanted me to know how she liked to be careful of my things like that. Fussing over me, d'you see? Trying to make it seem we were living normal, ordinary lives.

"'That's the sort of life we lead together, Hapgood—together; but the life I'm caught up in, the things that are happening with me, that I'm right in the middle of, that I felt I had to get away from for a bit—astounding, Hapgood, astounding, amazing....'

"I'm trying to give you exactly his own words, old man. I want you to get this business just exactly as I got it. Old Sabre turned to me with that—with that 'astounding, amazing'—turned and faced me and said:

"'Hapgood, I'm finding out the most extraordinary things about this life as we've made it and as we live it. Hapgood, if I kept forty women in different parts of London and made no secret of it, nothing would be said. People would know I was rather a shameless lot, my little ways would be an open secret, but nothing would be said. I should be received everywhere. But I'm thought to have brought one woman into my house and I'm banned. I'm unspeakable. Forty, flagrantly, outside, and I'm still a received member of society. People are sorry for my wife, or pretend to be, but I'm still all right, a bit of a rake, you know, but a decent enough chap. But I take pity on one poor girl because she clings to her motherhood although she's unmarried, and I'm beyond the pale. I'm unspeakable. Amazing. Do you say it's not absolutely astounding?

"'Hapgood, look here. It's this. This is what I've found. You can do the shocking things, and it can be known you do the shocking things. But you mustn't be seen doing them. You can beat your wife, and it can be known among your friends that you beat your wife. But you mustn't be seen beating her. You mustn't beat her in the street or in your neighbour's garden. You can drink, and it can be known you drink; but you mustn't be seen drunk.

"'Do you see, Hapgood? Do you see? The conventions are all right, moral, sound, excellent, admirable, but to save their own face there's a blind side to them, a shut-eye side. Keep that side of them and you're all right. They'll let you alone. They'll pretend they don't see you. But come out and stand in front of them and they'll devour you. They'll smash and grind and devour you, Hapgood. They're devouring me.

"'That's where they've got me in their jaws, Hapgood; and where they've got Effie in their jaws is just precisely again on a blind, shut-eye side.... They're rightly based, they're absolutely just, you can't gainsay them, but to save their face, again, they're indomitably blind and deaf to the hideous cruelties in their application. They mean well. They cause the most frightful suffering, the most frightful tragedies, but they won't look at them, they won't think of them, they won't speak of them: they mean well....

"Old Sabre put his head in his hands. He might have been praying. He looked to me sort of physically wrestling with what he called the jaws that had got him and had got her. He looked up at me and he said, 'Hapgood, this is where I've got to. This is where I am. Hapgood, life's all wrong, stupid, cruel, blundering, but it means well. We've shaped it to fit us as we think we ought to live and it means well. Means well! My God, Hapgood, the most terrible, the most lamentable self-confession that ears can hear—"I meant well." Some frightful blunder committed, some irreparable harm inflicted, and that piteous, heart-broken, heart-breaking, maddening, infuriating excuse, "I meant well. I meant well. Why didn't some one tell me?" Life means well, Hapgood. It does mean well. It only wants some one to tell it where it's going wrong, where it's blundering, where it's just missing, and why it's just missing, all it means to do.'

"With that he went back to all that stuff I told you he told me when I was down with him last month—that stuff about the need for a new revelation suited to men's minds to-day, the need for new light. I can't tell you all that—it's not in my line, that sort of talk. But he said, his face all pink under his skin, he said, 'Hapgood, I'll tell you a thing. I've got the secret. I've got the key to the riddle that's been puzzling me all my life. I've got the new revelation in terms good enough for me to understand. Light, more light. Here it is: God is—love. Not this, that, nor the other that the intelligence revolts at, and puts aside, and goes away, and goes on hungering, hungering and unsatisfied; nothing like that; but just this: plain for a child, clear as daylight for grown intelligence: God is—love. Listen to this, Hapgood: "He that dwelleth in love dwelleth in God and God in him; for God is love." Ecstasy, Hapgood, ecstasy! It explains everything to me. I can reduce all the mysteries to terms of that. One of these days, perhaps one of these days, I'll be able to write it and tell people.'

"I tell you, old man, you can think what you like about it, but old Sabre, when he was telling me that, was a pretty first-class advertisement for his own revelation. He'd found it all right. The look on him was nearer the divine than anything I've ever come near seeing. It certainly was.

"So you see that was the morning part of this that I'm telling you, what I called the first part, and it was not too bad. He'd been through, he was going through some pretty fierce things, but he was holding up under them. Oh, some pretty fierce things. I haven't told you half. One thing that hit him hard as he could bear was that that old pal of his, Fungus or Fargus, Fargus as a matter of fact, that old chap fell dying and did die—knocked out by pneumonia special constabling—and those dashed ramping great daughters of his wouldn't let poor old Sabre into the house to see him. Fact. He said it hurt him worse, made him realise worse what a ban he was up against, than anything that's happened to him. It would. That chap dying and him too shocking to be admitted.

"They did grant him one squint of his old friend, about five minutes, and stood over him like dragons all the time, five of them. Came to him one morning and said, as though they were speaking to a leper through bars, said, sort of holding their noses, 'We have to ask you to come to see Papa. The doctor thinks there is something Papa wishes to say to you.'

"What it was, apparently, was that the old gentleman had some sort of funny old notion that he was put into life for a definite purpose and when Sabre saw him he could just whisper to Sabre that he was agonised because he was dying before he'd done anything that could possibly be it. Poor old Sabre said it was too terrible for him, because what could he say with that pack of grim daughters standing over him to see he didn't contaminate their papa on his death bed? He said he could only hold his old pal's hand, and had the tears running down his face, and couldn't say a word, and they hustled him out, sort of holding their noses again, and sort of disinfecting the place as they went along. He said to me, brokenly, 'Hapgood, I felt I'd touched bottom. My old friend, you know.' He said he went again next morning, like a tradesman, just to beg for news. They told him, 'Papa has passed away.' He asked them, 'Did he say anything at the last? Do please tell me just that.' They said he suddenly almost sat up and called out something they couldn't understand about, 'Ay, ready!' Sabre said he understood and thanked God for it. He didn't tell me what it meant; it broke him right up even talking about it. There was another thing he mentioned but wouldn't go into. Some other great friend, a woman, whom he said he'd cut right off out of his acquaintance—wouldn't answer her letters: realised how the world was regarding him and felt he couldn't impose himself on any one. He seemed to suffer over that, too."

II

"Well, that was the morning, old man. That was the first part, and you see how it went. He was pretty badly in the depths but he was holding on. He'd got this great discovery of his, and the idea of writing about it after his History, he said. 'If I'm ever able to take up my History again,' he said. Badly down as he was, at least he'd got that and he'd also got to help him the extraordinary, reasonable, reasoning view he took of the whole business: no bitterness against any one, just understanding their point of view as he always has understood the other point of view, just that and puzzling over it all. On the whole, and considering all things, not too bad. Not too bad. Bad, desperately pathetic, I thought, but not too bad. That was the morning. He wouldn't come to lunch with us. He hadn't liked meeting my wife as it was. And of course I could understand how he felt, poor chap. So I left him.

"I left him. When I saw him again was about three o'clock, and I walked right into the middle of the development that, as I told you, has pretty well let the roof down on him.

"I strolled round to his hotel, a one-horse sort of place off the front. He was in the lobby. No one else there. Only a man who'd just been speaking to him and who left him and went out as I came in.

"Sabre had two papers in his hands. He was staring at them and you'd ha' thought from his face he was staring at a ghost. What d'you think they were? Guess. Man alive, the chap I'd seen going out had just served them on him. They were divorce papers. The citation and petition papers that have to be served personally. Divorce papers. His wife had instituted divorce proceedings against him. Naming the girl, Effie.

"Yes, you can whistle....

"You can whistle. I couldn't. I had too much to do. He was knocked out. Right out. I got him up to his room. Tried to stuff a drink into him. Couldn't. Stuffed it into myself. Two. Wanted them pretty badly.

"Well—I tell you. It was pretty awful. He sat on the bed with the papers in his hand, gibbering. Just gibbering. No other word for it. Was his wife mad? Was she crazy? Had she gone out of her mind? He to be guilty of a thing like that? He capable of a beastly thing like that? She to believe, she to believe he was that? His wife? Mabel? Was it possible? A vile, hideous, sordid intrigue with a girl employed in his own house? Effie! His wife to believe that? An unspeakable, beastly thing like that? He tried to show me with his finger the words on the paper. His finger shaking all over the thing. 'Hapgood, Hapgood, do you see this vile, obscene word here? I guilty of that? My wife, Mabel, think me capable of that? Do you see what they call me, Hapgood? What they call me by implication, what my wife, Mabel, thinks I am, what I am to be pointed at and called? Adulterer! Adulterer! My God, my God, adulterer! The word makes me sick. The very word is like poison in my mouth. And I am to swallow it. It is to be me, me, my name, my title, my brand. Adulterer! Adulterer!'

"I tell you, old man ... I tell you....

"I managed to get him talking about the practical side of it. That is I managed to make him listen while I talked. I told him the shop of the business. Told him that these papers had to be served on him personally, as they had been, and on the girl, too. I said I guessed that the solicitor's clerk I'd seen going out had been down to Penny Green the previous day or the day before and served them on Effie and got his address from her. I told him the first step was that within eight days he had to put in an appearance at the Probate and Divorce Registry and enter a defence—just intimate that he intended to defend the action, d'you see? And that the girl would have to too. After that no doubt he'd instruct solicitors, and that of course I'd be glad to take on the job for him.

"Well, of all this jargon—me being mighty glad to have anything to keep talking about, you understand—of all this jargon there were only two bits he froze on to, and froze on hard, I can tell you. I thought he was going mad the way he went on. I still think he may. That's why I'm frightened about him. He just sat there on the bed while I talked and kept saying to himself, 'Adulterer! Adulterer! Me. Adulterer!' It was awful.

"What he caught on to was what I told him about appearing at the Divorce Registry within eight days and about instructing a solicitor afterwards. He said he'd go to the Registry at once—at once, at once, at once! and he said, very impolitely, poor chap, that he'd instruct no infernal solicitors; he'd do the whole thing himself. He had the feeling, I could see, that he must be spurning this horrible thing, and spurning it at once, and spurning it himself. He was like a chap with his clothes on fire, crazy only to rush into water and get rid of it. The stigma of the thing was so intolerable to him that his feeling was that he couldn't sit by and let other people defend him and do the business for him; he must do it himself, hurl it back with his own hands, shout it back with his own throat. He'll calm down and get more reasonable in time, no doubt, and then I'll have another go at him about running the case for him; but anyway, there was the one thing he could do pretty well there and then, and that was enter his defence at the registry. So I took charge of him to help him ease his mind that much.

"I took charge of him. He wasn't capable of thinking of anything for himself. I packed his bag and paid his bill and took him round to our hotel and it wasn't far off then to the train my wife and I had fixed to get back on. I told my wife what had happened and she played the brick. You see, the chap was like as if he was dazed. Like as if he was walking in a trance. Just did what he was told and said nothing. So we played it up on that, my missus and I; we just sort of took him along without consulting him or seeming to take any notice of him. It was too late to do anything that night when we got up to town. He made a bit of a fuss, lost his temper and swore I was trying to hinder him; but my wife managed him a treat; by Jove, she was marvellous with him, and we got him round to our flat and put him up for the night. I pushed him off to bed early, but I heard him walking up and down his room hours after and talking to himself—talking in tones of horror—'Me! Me! Adulterer!'

"It was rather dreadful, hearing the poor chap. You see, what was the matter with him was, being the frightfully clean, intensely refined sort of chap he is, appalling horror at being thought, by his wife who knew him so well, capable of what was so repulsive to his mind. He loathed the very sound of the word that was used against him. Obscene, he kept on calling it. He was like a man fallen in a mire and plucking at the filthy stuff all over him and reeking of it and not able to eat or sleep or think or do anything but go mad with it. That was how it got him. Like that.

"Next morning—that's this morning, you understand—he was a little more normal, able to realise things a bit, I mean: thanked my wife for putting him up and hoped he hadn't been horribly rude or anything last night. More normal, you see: still in a panic fever to be off and state at the Registrar's that he was going to defend the action; but normal enough for me to see it was all right for him to go straight on home immediately after and tell the girl what she had to do and all that. I told him, by the way, that it would pretty well have to come out now, ultimately, who the child's father was: the girl would practically have to give that up in the end to clear him. You know, I told him that in the cab going along down. He ground his teeth over it. It was horrible to hear him. He said he'd kill the chap if he could ever discover him; ground his teeth and said he'd kill him, now—after this.

"Well, he got through his business about twelve—just a formality, you know, declaring his intention to defend. Then a thing happened. Can't think now what it meant. We were waiting for a cab near the Law Courts. I had his bag. He was going straight on to the station. A cab was just pulling in when a man came up, an ordinary enough looking cove, tall chap, and touched Sabre and said, 'Mr. Sabre?' Sabre said, 'Yes' and the chap said very civilly, 'Might I speak to you a minute, sir?'

"They went aside. I wasn't looking at them. I was watching a chap on a bike tumble off in front of a motor bus, near as a toucher run over. Suddenly some one shoved past me and there was old Sabre getting into the cab with this chap who had come up to him. I said, 'Hullo! Hullo, are you off?'

"We'd arranged, d'you see, to part there. I had to get back to my chambers. He turned round on me a face grey as ashes, absolutely dead grey. I'd never seen such a colour in a man's face. He said, 'Yes,

I'm off,' and sort of fell over his stick into the cab. The man, who was already in, righted him on to the seat and said, 'Paddington' to the driver who was at the door, shutting it. I said, through the window, 'Sabre! Old man, are you ill? What's up? Shall I come with you?'

"He put his head towards me and said in the most extraordinary voice, speaking between his clenched teeth as though he was keeping himself from yelling out, he said, 'If you love me, Hapgood, get right away out of it from me and let me alone. This man happens to live at Tidborough. I know him. We're going down together.'

"I said, 'Sabre—'

"He clenched his teeth so they were all bare with his lips contracting. He said, 'Let me alone. Let me alone. Let me alone.'

"And they pushed off.

"I tell you what I'm going to do. I'm going down there to-morrow. I'm frightened about him."

CHAPTER IV

I

Hapgood had said to his friend of the effect on Sabre of Mabel's action against him: "He's crashed. The roof's fallen in on him." And that had been Sabre's own belief. But it was not so. There are degrees of calamity. Dumfounded, stunned, aghast, Sabre would not have believed that conspiracy against him of all the powers of darkness could conceivably worsen his plight. They had shot their bolt. He was stricken amain. He was in the crucible of disaster and in its heart where the furnace is white.

But they had not shot their bolt. The roof had not yet fallen on him. They had discharged but a petard, but a mine to effect a breach. The timbers of the superstructure had but bent and cracked and groaned.

Their bolt was shot, the roof crashed in, the four sides of his world tottered and collapsed upon him, with the words spoken to Sabre by that man who approached and took him aside while he stood to take leave of Hapgood.

The man said, "I daresay you know me by sight, Mr. Sabre. I've seen you about the town. I'm the coroner's officer at Tidborough. You're rather wanted down there. I've been to Brighton after you and followed here and just took a lucky chance on finding you about this part. You're rather wanted down there. The fact is that young woman that's been living with you's been found dead."

Sabre's face took then the strange and awful hue that Hapgood had marked upon it.

"Found dead? Found dead? Where?"

"In your house, Mr. Sabre. And her baby, dead with her."

"Found dead? Found dead? Effie? And her baby? Found dead? Oh, dear God.... Catch hold of my arm a minute. All right, let me go. Let me go, I say. Can't you? Found dead? What d'you mean, found dead?"

"Well, sir, that's rather for the coroner to say, sir. There's to be an inquest to-morrow. That's what you're wanted for."

"Inquest? Inquest?" Sabre's speech was thick. He knew it was thick. His tongue felt enormously too big for his mouth. He could not control it properly. He felt that all his limbs and members were swollen and ponderous and out of his control. "Inquest? Found dead? Inquest? Found dead? Goo' God, can't you tell me something? You come up to me in the street, and all the place going round and round, and you say to me, 'Found dead.' Can't you say anything except 'Found dead'? Can't you tell me what you mean, found dead? Eh? Can't you?"

The man said, "Now look here, sir. I say that's for the coroner. Least said best. And least you say best, sir, if you understand me. Looks as if the young woman took poison. That's all I can say. Looks as if she took poison. Oxalic acid."

"Oxalic acid!"

"Now, see here, sir. You've no call to say anything to me and I've no call to say more to you than I've told you. Is that your cab, sir? Because if so—"

They went to the cab.

II

One of two questions is commonly the first words articulated by one knocked senseless in a disaster. Recovering consciousness, or recovering his scattered wits, "What's happened?" he asks; or "Where am I?" In the first shock he has not known he was hurt. He recovers his senses. He then is aware of himself mangled, maimed, delivered to the torturers.

In that day and through the night Sabre was numb to coherent thought, numb to any realisation of the meaning to himself of this that had befallen him. The roof had crashed in upon him; but he lay stunned. As one pinned beneath scaffolding knows not his agony till the beams are being lifted from him, so stupefaction inhibited his senses until, on the morrow, he was dug down to in the coroner's court and there awakened.

He could not think. Through the day and through the night his mind groped with outstretched arms as one groping in a dark room, or as a blind man tapping with a stick. He could not think. He could attend to things; he could notice things; he could perform necessary actions; but "Effie is dead." "Effie has killed herself." "Effie has killed herself and her child—now what?" In pursuit of these his mind could only grope with outstretched hands; these, in the dark room of his calamity, eluded his mind. He groped and stumbled after them. They stole and slipped away.

In the train going down to Tidborough the man who had accosted him permitted himself to be more communicative. A policeman, observing lights burning in the house at midday on Sunday, had knocked, and getting no answer had gone in. He had found the young woman dead on her bed, the baby dead beside her. A tumbler was on a small table and a bottle of oxalic acid, "salts of lemon, as they call it," said the man.

Sabre stared out of the window. "Effie has killed herself. Effie has killed herself and her baby." No, he could not fasten upon it. "Effie has killed herself." That was what this man was telling him. It circled and spun away from him as from the rushing train the fields circled and spun before his vision.

He was able to attend to things and to do things. At Tidborough he took a cab and drove home, and dismissing it at the gate was able to give normal attention to the requirements of the morrow and instruct the man to come out for him at half-past eleven; the inquest was at twelve.

He was able to notice things. For years turning the handle and entering this house had been like entering an empty habitation. It struck cold now. It was like entering a tomb. He went into the morning room. No one was there. He went into the kitchen. No one was there. He stood still and tried to think. Of course no one was here. Effie had killed herself. He climbed to his room, still awkward on stairs with his leg and stick, and went in and stood before his books and stared at them. He was still staring when it occurred to him that it had grown dusk since he first entered and stared. Effie had killed herself.... He went out and along the passage to her room and entered and stared upon the bed. Effie had been found dead. This was where they had found her— dead. No, it was gone; he could not get hold of it. He turned and stared about the room. Things seemed to have been taken out of the room. The man had said something about a glass and a bottle. But there was no glass or bottle here. They had taken things out of the room. And they had taken Effie out of the room—picked up Effie and carried her out like a—an orgasm of terrible emotion surged enormously within him; a bursting thing was in his throat—No, it was gone. What phenomenon had suddenly possessed him? What was the matter? Effie had killed herself. No, he could not get hold of it. He turned away and began to wander from room to room. In some he lit lights because you naturally lit lights when it was dark. All night he wandered from room to room, rarely sitting down. All night his mind groped with outstretched hands for that which all night eluded it.

III

In the morning, in the mortuary adjoining the coroner's court, his mind suddenly and with shock most terrible made contact with the calamity it had pursued.

In the mortuary....

When he arrived and alighted from his cab he found a small crowd of persons assembled about the yard of the court. Some one said, "There he is!" Some one said, "That's him!" A kind of threatening murmur went up from the people. A general movement was made towards him. What was the matter? What were they looking at? They stood in his way. He seemed to be wedged among a mass of dark and rather beastly faces breathing close to his own. He could not get on. He was being pushed. He was caused to stagger. He said, "Look out, I've got a game leg." That threatening sort of murmur arose more loudly in answer to his words. Some one somewhere threw a piece of orange peel at some one. It almost hit his face. What was up? What were they all doing?

A policeman and the coroner's officer came shouldering through the press and helped him towards the court. He thought it was rather decent of them.

The policeman said, "You'd better get inside. They're a bit rough."

At the door of the court Sabre looked across to where on the other side of the yard some men were shuffling out of a detached building. The coroner's officer said, "Jury. They've been viewing the corpse."

"Corpse!" The rough word stabbed through his numbness. He thought, "Corpse! Viewing the corpse! Obscene and horrible phrase! Corpse! Effie!" He made a movement in that direction.

The man said, "Yes, perhaps you'd better."

They took him across and into the detached building.

He was against a glass screen, misty with breaths of those who had stared and peered through it. The policeman wiped his sleeve across the glass. "There you are."

Ah, ...! Now, suddenly and with shock most terrible, his mind made contact with that which it had pursued. It had groped as in a dark room with outstretched hands. Now, suddenly and with shock most terrible, it was as if those groping hands had touched in the darkness a face.

Ah, insupportable! This was Effie. This was Bright Effie. This was that jolly little Effie of the old, million-year-old days. This! This!

She lay on a slab inclined towards the glass. She was swathed about in cerements. Only her face was visible. Within the hollow of her arm reposed a little shape, all swathed. She had brought it into the world. She had removed it from the world that would have nothing of it. She had brought a thousand smiles into the world, but she had given offence to the world and the offended world had thrown back her smiles and she now had expressed her contrition to the world. This was her contrition that she lay here for men to breathe upon the glass, and stare, and rub away the dimness with their sleeves, and breathe, and stare again.

Oh, insupportable calamity! Oh, tragedy beyond support! He thought of her as oft and again he had seen her,—those laughing lips, those shining eyes. He thought of her alone when he had left her, planning and preparing this frightful dissolution of her body and her soul. He thought of her in the stupendous moment while the glass paused at her lips. He thought of her in torment of inward fire by that which had blistered her poor lips.

A very terrible groan was broken out of him.

They took him along.

IV

The court was crammed. In two thirds of its space were crowded benches. At the upper end of the room was a dais, a schoolmaster's desk. Flanking it on one hand were forms occupied by the men Sabre had seen shuffling out of the mortuary. On the other hand a second dais stood. Facing the central dais was a long table at which men were seated on the side looking towards the dais. Two men sat also at the head of this table, facing the jury. As Sabre entered they were in deep conversation with a stunted, hunchbacked man who sat next them at the corner.

Every face in the room turned towards the door as Sabre entered. They might have belonged to a single body and they appeared to have a single expression and a single thought: a dark and forbidding expression and a thought dark and hostile. There was again that murmur that had greeted him when he stepped from the cab. At the sight of him one of the two men at the head of the table started to his feet. A very big man, and with a very big and massive face and terrific eyes who started up and raised clenched fists and had his jaws working. Old Bright. His companion at the head of the table restrained him and drew him down again. A tall, spare, dark man with a thin mouth in a deeply lined face,—Twyning. The hunchbacked man beside them twisted about in his chair and stared long and narrowly at Sabre, a very faint smile playing about his mouth; a rather hungry sort of smile, as though he anticipated a bit of a game out of Sabre.

They led Sabre to a seat on the front of the benches.

V

From a door behind the central dais a large, stout man entered and took his seat. Whispers about the court said, "Coroner." Some one bawled "Silence."

The coroner fiddled with some papers, put pince-nez on his nose and stared about the court. He had a big, flat face. He stared about. "Is the witness Sabre in attendance?"

The coroner's officer said, "Yes, sir."

Some one jogged Sabre. He stood up.

The coroner looked at him. "Are you legally represented?"

Sabre's mind played him the trick of an astoundingly clear recollection of the officer at the recruiting station who had asked him, and at whom he had wondered, "Any complaints?" He wondered now. He said, "Represented? No. Why should I be represented?"

The coroner turned to examine some papers. "That you may perhaps discover," he remarked drily.

287

The court tittered. The hunchbacked man, little more than whose huge head appeared above the table, laughed out loud and rubbed his hands between his knees and made a remark to Twyning. He seemed pleased that Sabre was not legally represented.

A man seated not far from the hunchback rose and bowed and said, "I am watching the interests of Mrs. Sabre."

Sabre started. Mrs. Sabre! Mabel!

The hunchback sprang to his feet and jerked a bow. "I represent Mr. Bright, the father of the deceased."

The coroner bowed to each. The hunchback and the solicitor representing the interests of Mrs. Sabre leaned back in their chairs and exchanged whispers behind the men seated between them.

The jury shuffled up from their seats and were sworn in and shuffled back again.... The coroner was speaking. "... and you will hear the evidence of the witnesses who will be brought before you ... and I propose to take first the case of the deceased child ... two deaths ... and it will be found more convenient to dispose first of the case of the child.... First witness!"

CHAPTER V

I

Hapgood said:

"Did I say to you last time, after that Brighton business, that the man had crashed, that the roof had fallen in on him? Did I say that? May I never again use superlatives till I've turned over the page to make sure they weren't comparatives. Eh, man, sitting on his bed there at Brighton and gibbering at me, Sabre was a whole man, a sane man; he was a fortunate and happy man, compared with this that I saw come at him down at Tidborough yesterday.

"I've told you that chap that came up to him outside the Law Courts evidently told him the girl had killed herself and that he was wanted for the inquest. Next day I went down, knowing nothing about it, of course. I hit up Tidborough about twelve. No train out to Penny Green for an hour, so I went to take a fly. Old chap I went to charter, when he heard it was Sabre's place I was looking for, told me Sabre was at this inquest; said he'd driven him in to it. And told me what inquest. Inquest! You can guess how I felt. It was the first I'd heard about it. Hopped into the cab and drove down to it.

"By Jove, old man.... By Jove, old man, how I'm ever going to tell you. That poor chap in there baited by those fiends.... By Jove.... By Jove.... You know, old man, I've told you before, I'm not the sort of chap that weeps, he knows not why; I never nursed a tame gazelle and all that sort of thing. I can sit through a play thinking about my supper while my wife ruins her dress and my trousers crying over them—but this business, old Sabre up in that witness box with his face in a knot and stammering out 'Look here—. Look here—'; that was absolutely all he ever said; he never could get any farther—old Sabre going through that, and the solicitor tearing the inside out of him and throwing it in his face, and that treble-dyed Iscariot Twyning prompting the solicitor and egging him on, with his beastly spittle running like venom out of the corners of his mouth—I tell you my eyes felt like two boiled gooseberries in my head: boiled red hot; and a red-hot potato stuck in my throat, stuck tight. I tell you....

"When I crept into that infernal court, that infernal torture chamber, they were just finishing the case of the child. This solicitor chap—chap with a humped back and a head as big as a house—was just finishing fawning round a doctor man in the box, putting it up to him that there was nothing to suggest deliberate suffocation of the baby.

289

Oxalic acid poisoning—was it not the case that the girl would have died in great agony? Writhed on the bed? Might easily have overlaid the child? The doctor had seen the position in which she was found lying in regard to the child—would he not tell the jury that she almost certainly rolled on to the child while it slept—that sort of rather painful stuff. Doctor chap rather jibbed a bit at being rushed, but humpback kept him to it devilish cleverly and the verdict was as good as given. The doc. was just going out of the box when Humpo called him back. 'One moment more, Doctor, if you please. Can you tell me, if you please, approximately the age of the child—approximately, but as near as you possibly can, Doctor?'

"The doctor said about five months—four to five months.

"'Five months,' says Humpo, mouthing it. 'Five months.' He turned deliberately round and looked directly at Sabre, sitting sort of huddled up on the front bench. 'Five months. We may take it, then, the child was born in December last. In December last.' Still with his back to the witness and staring at Sabre, you understand, and the jury all staring with him and people standing up in the court to see what the devil he was looking at. 'We may take that, may we, Doctor?' He was watching Sabre with a sort of half smile. The doctor said he might take it. The chap snapped up his face with a jerk and turned round. 'Thank you, Doctor. That will do.' And he sat down. If ever I saw a chap playing a fish and suddenly strike and hook it, I saw it then, when he smiled towards Sabre and then snapped up his face and plumped down. And the jury saw it. He'd got 'em fixed from that moment. Fixed. Oh, he was clever—clever, my word!

"That ended that. The coroner rumbled out a bit of a summary, practically told the jury what to say, reminded them, if they had any lingering doubts, that the quality of mercy was not strained—him showing before the morning was out that he knew about as much about mercy as I know about Arabic—and the jury without leaving the box brought in that the child had died of suffocation due to misadventure.

"The court drew a long breath; you could hear it. Everybody settled himself down nice and comfortably. The curtain-raiser was over, and very nice too; now for the drama.

"They got it."

II

"Look here, get the hang of the thing. Get a bearing on some of these people. There was the coroner getting off his preamble—flavouring it with plenty of 'distressings' and 'painfuls' and 'father of the deceased well known to and respected by many of us-es.' Great big pudding of a chap, the coroner. Sat there impassive like a flabby old Buddha. Face like a three-parts deflated football. Looked as if he'd been poured on to his seat out of a jug and jellified there. There was old Bright, the girl's father, smouldering like inside the door of a banked-up furnace; smouldering like if you touched him he'd burst out into roaring flame and sparks. There was Mr. Iscariot Twyning with his face like a stab—in the back—and his mouth on his face like a scar. There was this solicitor chap next him, with his hump, with his hair like a mane, and a head like a house, and a mouth like a cave. He'd a great big red tongue, about a yard long, like a retriever's, and a great long forefinger with about five joints in it that he waggled when he was cross-examining and shot out when he was incriminating like the front nine inches of a snake.

"That chap! When he was in the full cry and ecstasy of his hunt after Sabre, the perspiration streamed down his face like running oil, and he'd flap his great red tongue around his jaws and mop his streaming face and chuck away his streaming mane; and all the time he'd be stooping down to Twyning, and while he was stooping and Twyning prompting him with the venom pricking and bursting in the corners of his mouth, all the time he was stooping this chap would leave that great forefinger waggling away at Sabre, and Sabre clutching the box, and his face in a knot, and his throat in a lump and choking out, 'Look here—. Look here—'

"I tell you, old man ... I tell you....

"Sabre, when they started to get at it, was sitting on the front bench braced up forwards and staring towards what he was hearing like a man watching his brother balancing across a narrow plank stretched over a crater. He had his hands on the crook of his old stick and he was working at the crook as if he was trying to tear it off. I wonder he didn't, the way he was straining at it. And every now and then while Humpo was leading on the witnesses, and when Sabre saw what they were putting up against him, he'd half start to his feet and open his mouth and once or twice let fly that frightful 'Look here—' of his; and old Buddha would give him, 'Be silent, sir!' and he'd drop back like a

291

man with a hit in the face and sit there swallowing and press his throat.

"I tell you....

"I was standing right across the court at right angles to him. I was wedged tight. Scarcely breathe, let alone move. I wrote on a bit of paper to Sabre that I was here and let him get up and ask for me; and I wrapped it round half-a-crown and pushed it across the heads of the mob to a police sergeant. He gave it to Sabre. Sabre snatched the thing as if he was mad at it, and read it, and buzzed it on the floor and ground his heel on it. Just to show me, I suppose. Nice! Poor devil, my gooseberry eyes went up about ten degrees. Bit later I had another shot. I—well, I'll come to that in a minute."

III

"They pushed off the case with the obvious witnesses—police, doctor, and so on. Then the thing hardened down. Then Sabre saw what was coming at him—saw it at a clap and never had remotely dreamt of it; saw it like a tiger coming down the street to devour him; saw it like the lid of hell slowly slipping away before his eyes. Saw it! I was watching him. He saw it; and things—age, greyness, lasting and immovable calamity—I don't know what—frightful things—came down on his face like the dust of ashes settling on a polished surface.

"You see, what this Humpo fiend was laying out for was, first that Sabre was the father of the girl's child, second that he'd deliberately put the poison in her way, and brutally told her he was done with her, and gone off and left her so that she should do what she had done and he be rid of her. Yes. Yes, old man. And he'd got a case! By the living Jingo, he'd got such a case as a Crown prosecutor only dreams about after a good dinner and three parts of a bottle of port. There wasn't a thing, there wasn't an action or a deed or a thought that Sabre had done for months and months past but bricked him in like bricking a man into a wall, but tied him down like tying a man in a chair with four fathoms of rope. By the living Jingo, there wasn't a thing.

"Listen. Just listen and see for yourself. Worked off the police evidence and the doctor, d'you see? Then—'Mr. Bright!' Old man comes up into the box. Stands there massive, bowed with grief, chest heaving, voice coming out of it like an organ in the Dead March. Stands there like Lear over the body of Cordelia. Stands there like the father of Virginia thinking of Appius Claudius.

292

"Like this, his evidence went: Was father of the deceased woman (as they called her). Was employed as foreman at Fortune, East and Sabre's. Had seen the body and identified it. So on, so on.

"Then Humpo gets on to him. Was his daughter the sort of girl to meditate taking her life?—'Never! Never!' Great rending cry that went down to your marrow.

"Touching the trouble that befell her, the birth of her child—had she ever betrayed signs of loose character while living beneath his roof?—'Never! Never!'

"How came she first to leave his house? Was any particular individual instrumental in obtaining for her work which first took her from beneath his roof?—'There! There!' Clenched fist and half his body over the box towards Sabre.

"'Look here!' bursts out old Sabre. 'Look here—!'

"They shut him up.

"'Answer the question, please, Mr. Bright.'—'Mr. Sabre led to her first going from me. Mr. Sabre!'

"Had this Mr. Sabre first approached him in the matter or had he solicited Mr. Sabre's help?—'He came to me! He came to me! Without rhyme, or reason, or cause, or need, or hint, or suggestion he came to me!'

"Was the situation thus obtained for the girl nearer her father's house or nearer Mr. Sabre's?—'Not a quarter of an hour, not ten minutes, from Mr. Sabre's house.'

"Had the witness any knowledge as to whether this man Sabre was a frequent visitor at the place of the girl's situation?—'Constantly, constantly, night after night he was there!'

"'Was he, indeed?' says Humpo, mightily interested. 'Was he, indeed? There were perhaps great friends of his own standing there, one or two men chums, no doubt?'—'No one! No one!' cries the old man. 'No one but an old invalid lady, nigh bedridden, past seventy, and my daughter, my daughter, my Effie.'

293

"That was all very well, all very well, says Humpo. Mr. Bright's word was of course accepted, but had the witness any outside proof of the frequency of these visits to this bedridden old lady old enough to be the man Sabre's grandmother? Had the witness recently been shown a diary kept by Mr. Twyning at that period?—'Yes! Yes!'

"And it contained frequent reference to Sabre's mention in the office of these visits?—'Yes! Yes!'

"Did one entry reveal the fact that on one occasion this Sabre spent an entire night there?

"'Look here—' bursts out old Sabre. 'Look here—'

"Can't get any farther. Buddha on the throne shuts him up if he could have got any farther. 'Yes,' groans old Bright out of his heaving chest. 'Yes. A night there.'

"And on the very next day, the very next day, did this man Sabre rush off and enlist?—'Yes. Yes.'

"Viewed in light of the subsequent events, did that sudden burst of patriotism bear any particular interpretation?—'Running away from it,' heaves the old man. 'Running away from it.'

"'Look here—' from Sabre again. 'Look here—' Same result.

"So this Humpo chap went on, piling it up from old Bright like that, old man; and all the time getting deeper and getting worse, of course. Sabre getting the girl into his own house after the old lady's death removes the girl from the neighbourhood; curious suddenness of the girl's dismissal during Sabre's leave; girl going straight to Sabre immediately able to walk after birth of child, and so on. Blacker and blacker, worse and worse.

"And then Humpo ends, 'A final question, Mr. Bright, and I can release you from the painful, the pitiable ordeal it has been my sad duty to inflict upon you. A final question: 'Have you in your own mind suspicions of the identity of this unhappy woman's betrayer?' Old man cannot speak for emotion. Only nods, hands at his breast like a prophet about to tear his raiment. Only nods.

"'Do you see him in this court?'

"Old man hurls out his arms towards Sabre. Shouts, 'There! There!'

"Warm-hearted and excellent Iscariot leaps up and leads him tottering from the box; court seethes and groans with emotion; Humpo wipes his streaming face, Sabre stammers out, 'Look here—Look here—' Case goes on."

IV

"Next witness. Chemist. Funny little chap with two pairs of spectacles, one on his forehead and one on his nose. From Alton. Remembers distinctly sale of oxalic acid (produced) on Friday before the Saturday of the girl's death. Remembers distinctly the purchaser, could identify him. Does he see him in court? Yes, there he is. Points at Sabre. Anything odd about purchaser's manner? Couldn't say exactly odd. Remembered he sat down while making the purchase. Ah, sat down, did he? Was it usual for customers to sit down when making a trifling purchase? No, not in his shop it wasn't usual. Ah, it struck him then as peculiar, this sitting down? As if perhaps the purchaser was under a strain? No, not for that reason—customers didn't as a rule sit in his shop, because he didn't as a rule have a chair in front of the counter for them to sit on. Court howls with laughter in relief from tension. Humpo says sternly, 'This is no laughing matter, sir. Stand down, sir.' Glares after him as he goes to his seat. Jury glares. Buddha glares. General impression that little chemist has been trying to shield Sabre.

"Next witness. Chap I'd seen serve the divorce papers on Sabre at Brighton. Solicitor's clerk. Humpo handles him very impressively— also very carefully. Informs him no need to tell the court on what business he went down to Sabre's house on the fatal Saturday. 'Sufficient,' says Humpo, 'that it was legal business of a deeply grave nature implicating the deceased and the man Sabre?' Witness agrees. Court nearly chokes itself whispering conjectures. 'And you saw the deceased but not the man Sabre?' Witness agrees again. Goes on, led by Humpo, to state that he served certain papers on the deceased. That she looked noticeably unhappy, frightened, lonely, deserted, when she opened the door to him. Had great difficulty in obtaining from her the whereabouts of the man Sabre. At first refused to tell. No, didn't actually say she had been told not to tell; but, yes, certainly gave that impression. Extracted from her at last that he was probably at Brighton. Couldn't get anything more definite out of her.

"'Look here—', cries Sabre. 'Look here—look here, she didn't know!'

"'I am not surprised,' says Humpo, 'I am not at all surprised.' Court laughs cynically. 'You have interrupted us a great deal,' says Humpo. 'It is time we saw if you will be equally informative in the witness box.'

"Some one bawls, 'Next witness. Mark Sabre.'

"Court draws an enormous breath and gets itself ready for butchery to make a Tidborough holiday."

CHAPTER VI

I

Hapgood went on:

"I'm telling you, old man, that after the coroner had done with him, and after this Humpo, with his viprous forefinger, and his retriever tongue, and his perspiration streaming down his face, and Twyning tugging him down by the coat and putting him on the trail afresh— after the coroner, and after this Humpo like that, had been on to him for a bit, Sabre absolutely couldn't speak. He was like he had a constriction in his throat. There was nothing he could say but begin all his sentences with, 'Look here—Look here—'; and nine times out of ten incapable of anything to follow it up with.

"He was distraught. He was speechless. He was clean crazed.

"At the very beginning, with the coroner, he wouldn't use the word 'the deceased.' Insisted on keeping calling her Effie. Coroner kept pulling him up over it, and about the twentieth time pulled him up hard.

"Poor chap threw out his arms like he was throwing the word away and then hammered on the ledge. 'I won't say deceased. I won't call her the deceased. Vile word. Horrible word. Obscene, beastly, hateful word. I won't call her it. Why should I call her the deceased?'

"'Control yourself,' says Buddha. 'Control yourself.'

"He only waved and thumped again. 'I won't. I won't. Why should I call her the deceased? I knew the girl. I was fond of the girl. She was my friend. She was fond of me. I did more for her than any one in this court—her father or any one. When she was in trouble she came to me and I succoured her. She lived in my house. She cooked my meals for me. We went through it together. I've known her for years. I've liked her for years. And now she's dead and you turn around and tell me to call her the deceased. Effie. Effie! Do you hear?—Effie!'

"They couldn't stop him. He was like a sick wolf then, cornered, and Buddha like a big, wary boarhound going in at him and jumping up on the wall out of the way when he made his dashes and then coming down and going in at him again. But they stopped him when Humpo got at him! They wore him down then! He was like that wolf then with a rope round his neck, tied to a post, and every time he'd fly out with,

297

'Look here—Look here—' the rope would catch him and throttle him and over he'd go and Humpo in worrying him again.

"Like this. Link on link of the chain against him and brick by brick of the wall around him. Like this.

"'What date did the deceased leave your wife's employment?'

"'In March. In March last year. Look here—'

"'Did she leave of her own wish or was she dismissed?'

"'Look here—'

"'Was she dismissed because your wife suspected you of relations with her?'

"'Look here—'

"'Answer the question.'

"'Well, but look here—'

"'Answer the question, sir.'

"'Look here—'

"'Very well, sir. Very well. Answer me this question then. Is it the fact that your wife has instituted divorce proceedings against you?'

"'Look here—'

"Court surging with sensation at this dramatic disclosure. Humpo mopping his face, keeping the great forefinger going. Sabre clutching the desk like a man in asthma, Twyning tugging at Humpo's coat. 'Yes, yes,' says Humpo, bending down, then launches at Sabre again.

"'Is it the fact that in these proceedings the deceased woman is named as corespondent?'

"'Look here—'

"'You keep asking me to look here, sir, but you tell me nothing. I ask you plain questions. Have you nothing better than, "Look here"? Is it the fact that these papers were served on you at Brighton on the occasion of your flight?'

"'Flight—flight—Look here—'

"'Is it the fact?'

"'Yes. Brighton, yes. But, look here—flight! flight! Holiday, I tell you. Holiday.'

"'Holiday!' cries Humpo. 'Do you tell me holiday, sir? Holiday! I thank you for that word. We will examine it in a moment. This was at Brighton, then. The business of the witness whom we have recently seen in the box was to serve the papers on you and on the deceased. Now come back a little. Let me ask you to carry back your mind to the summer of 1915—, and with his wagging forefinger, and his sloshing tongue, and his mopping at his face, and his throwing back of his mane as though it were a cloak from under which he kept rushing in to stab home another knife, he takes the unhappy man through all the stuff he had got out of old Bright—Sabre's apparently uncalled-for interest in the girl, first getting her from her father's house to the neighbourhood of his own, then under his own roof, and all the rest of the unholy chain of it. Then he has a chat with Twyning, then mops himself dry, and then hurls in again.

"'Now, sir, this holiday. This pleasant holiday by the sea! Did you make any preparations for it, any little purchases?'

"'No. Purchases? No. Look here—'

"'Never mind about "Look here," sir. No purchases? Did you hear the evidence of the witness—the Alton chemist who declared on oath that you made a purchase in his shop on the very day before you started, a purchase you have admitted? Remembering that, do you still say you made no purchases for your—holiday?'

"'Nothing to do with it. Nothing—'

"'Nothing to do with it? Well, sir, we will accept that for a moment. Do you often go shopping in Alton?'

"The poor beggar shook his head. No voice in his throat.

"'Do you shop there once in a month, once in six months?'

"Shook again.

"'Are there chemists in the Garden House, in Tidborough, in Chovensbury?'

"Nods.

"'Are you known in all these places I have mentioned?'

"Nods.

"'Are you known in Alton?'

"Shakes.

"'Are all these places nearer to you than Alton?'

"Nods.

"Humpo's finger shoots out about two yards long; dashes back his mane with his other hand; rushes in from under it. 'Then, sir, will you tell the jury why, to make this purchase of oxalic acid on the day before you leave home, why you go to a place in which you are unknown and to a place farther away from you than three other centres, one at your very door?'

"Sabre sees like a hit in the face this new thing that's coming to him. Gasps. Puts up his hand to that choked throat of his. Strangles out, 'Look here—'

"'Answer the question, sir.'

"Stammers out like a chap croaking. 'Walk. Walk. Wanted a walk. Wanted to get out. Wanted to get away from it.'

"Back goes the mane and in again like a flash: 'Ah, you wanted to get out of it? The house with its inmates was becoming insupportable to you?'

"'Look here—'

"'I am giving you your own words, sir. Do you tell us that, although you were leaving—for a holiday—on the very next day still, even on the afternoon before, you felt you must get out of it? Is that right, sir?'

"'Look here-'

"'Very well. Let us leave that, sir. We seem to be compelled to leave a great deal, but the jury will acquit me of fault in the matter. Let us come to the purpose of this oxalic acid purchase. Nothing to do with your holiday, you say. With what then? For what purpose?'

"Long pause. Frightful pause. Hours. Whole court holding its breath. Pause like a chunk of eternity. Silent as that. Empty as that. What the devil was he thinking of? Had he forgotten? Was he awake now to the frightful places he kept getting into and wondering if this was another and where exactly it lay? Appalling pause. Dashed woman somewhere in the court goes off into hysterics and dragged out. He didn't hear a scream of it, that poor baited chap in the box. Just stood there. Grey as a raked-out fire. Face twitching. Awful. I tell you, awful. Nearly went into hysterics myself. Humpo slopping his tongue round his jaws, watching him like a dog watching its dinner being cut up. After about two years, slaps in his tongue and demands, 'Come, sir, for what purpose did you buy this oxalic acid?'

"Sabre gives his first clear, calculated words since he had got up there. I guess he had been pulling himself together to look for a trap. He said very slowly, trying each word, like a chap feeling along on thin ice; he said, 'Effie—asked—me—to—get—it—to—clean—my —straw—hat—for—me—for—Brighton.'

"That Humpo! Very gently, very quietly, like a rescuer pushing out a ladder to the man on the ice, 'The deceased asked you to get it to clean your straw hat for you for Brighton.' And then like a trap being sprung he snapped and threw Sabre clean off the balance he was getting. 'Then it was obtained for the purpose of your holiday?'

"'Look here—' All at sea again, d'you see? And the end was quicker than nothing. Twyning pulls Humpo's coat and points at Sabre's hat, soft hat, on the ledge before him. Humpo nods, delighted.

"'And did she carry out her intention, sir? Did she clean your straw hat for you?'

"Nods.

"'You don't appear to be wearing it?'

"Shakes.

"'Pray, where, then, is this straw hat to clean which you obtained the oxalic acid? Is it at your house?'

"Shakes.

"'Not at your house! Odd. Where, then?'

"'Look here—'

"'Where then?'

"'Look here—'

"'Answer the question, sir. Where is this straw hat?'

"'Look here—' Gulps. 'Look here—' Gulps again. 'Look here. I lost it in the sea at Brighton.'

"Humpo draws in his breath. Stares at him for two solid minutes without speaking. Then say, like one speaking to a ghost, 'You lost it in the sea at Brighton! You lost it in the sea at Brighton!' Has an inspiration. Inspired in hell. Turns like a flash to the coroner. 'I have done with this witness, sir.' Sits down. Plump. Court lets go its breath like the four winds round a chimney. Sabre staggers out of the box. Falls across into his seat.

"Too much for me, old man. I bawled out, people in front of me nearly jumping out of their skins with the start, I bawled out, 'Mr. Coroner, I saw the witness at Brighton, and he told me he'd lost his hat in the sea.'

"Buddha, like a talking idol discovering an infidel in his temple, 'Who are you, sir?'

"'I'm a solicitor. I'm Mr. Sabre's solicitor.'

"Buddha to Sabre: 'Have you a solicitor in the court, Sabre?'

"'No! No! Get away! Get out of it! Get away from me!'

"'You have no standing in this court, sir,' says Buddha.

"Awful. Nothing to be done. Sorry I'd spoken. After all, telling me about his hat, what did it prove? Nothing. If anything, easily could be twisted into cunning preparation of his plan beforehand. Useless. Futile.

"Case went on. Presently Twyning in the box. Last witness—put up to screw down the lid on Sabre's coffin, to polish up the argument before it went to the jury. Stood there with the venom frothing at the corners of his mouth, stood there a man straight out of the loins of Judas Iscariot, stood there making his testimony more damning a thousand times by pretending it was being dragged out of him, reluctant to give away his business companion. Told a positively damning story about meeting Sabre at the station on his departure from leave a day after the girl was sacked. Noticed how strange his manner was; noticed he didn't like being asked about circumstances of her dismissal; noticed his wife hadn't come to see him off. Yes, thought it odd. Sabre had explained wife had a cold, but saw Mrs. Sabre in Tidborough very next day. Yes, thought the whole thing funny because had frequently seen Sabre and the girl together during Sabre's leave. Any particular occasion? Well, did it really matter? Must he really answer? Yes, notably in the Cloister tea rooms late one evening. Well, yes, had thought their behavior odd, secretive. Sabre's position in the office? Well, was it really necessary to go into that? Well, had to admit Sabre was no longer a member of the firm. Had been suspended during intimacy with the deceased, now dismissed consequent upon this grave development. Had he ever had occasion in the past, in earlier days, to remonstrate with Sabre concerning attitude towards girl? Well, scarcely liked to say so, hated to say so, but certainly there had been such occasions. Yes, had spoken seriously to Sabre about it.

"There ripped across the court as he said that, old man, a woman's voice from the back. 'It's a lie. It's an abominable lie. And you know it's a lie!'

"By Jove, I tell you! I nearly swallowed my back teeth with the effect of the thing. Give you my word I thought for a minute it was the girl come to life and walked in out of her coffin. That voice! High and clear and fine and true as an Angelus bell across a harvest field. 'It's a lie. It's an abominable lie; and you know it's a lie!'

"Eh? Terrific? I tell you terrific isn't the word. It was the Fairfax business at the trial of King Charles over again. It absolutely was. Buddha nearly had a fit: 'Silence! How dare you, madam! Turn out that woman! Who is that?'

"Commotion. A woman pressed out from the mob behind and walked up the court like a goddess, like Portia, by Jove, like Euphrosyne. 'Let no one dare to touch me,' she said. 'I am Lady Tybar. Every one knows me here. I've just come in. Just heard. This shameful business. All of you killing him between you.' She pointed a hand at Twyning. 'And you. I tell you before all this court, and you may take what steps you like, I tell you that you are a liar, an experienced and calculating liar.' And she went with that to old Sabre and stooped over him and touched him with both her hands and said, 'Marko, Marko.'

"You know she'd got that blooming court stiff and cold. The suddenness and the decision and the—the arrogance of the thing took 'em all ends up and had 'em speechless. She was there by Sabre and stooping over him, mothering him, before Buddha or any of 'em could have found the wits to say what his own name was. Let alone the Iscariot.

"Matter of fact Sabre was the first one to speak. He threw up his arm from where he'd been covering his face, just as he'd thrown it up when I called out, and swung her hands aside and called out, 'Don't touch me. Let me alone. Leave me alone.'

"She motioned to the man beside him, and the chap got up as if her motion had been Circe's and disappeared. Through the roof or somewhere. I don't know. Anyway, he vanished. And she took his place and sat down beside Sabre and poor old Sabre crouched away from her as if he was stung, and old Buddha, reaching out for his dignity, said, 'You may remain there, madam, if you do not interrupt the court.'

"There wasn't much more to interrupt. Twyning had had about as much as he wanted; he'd done what he was out to do, anyway. The case finished. The coroner had a go at the jury. They went out. I suppose they were gone ten minutes. Shuffled in again. Gave their verdict. I was watching Sabre. He took down his hands from his face and stared with all the world's agony in his face, straining himself forward to hear. Verdict. They found suicide while temporarily insane and added their most severe censure of the conduct of the witness Sabre. He jumped up and flung out his hands. 'Look here—Look here—Censure! Censure! Cens—!'

"Dropped back on his seat like he was shot. Twisted himself up. Sat rocking.

"Court cleared in less than no time. Me left in my corner. This Lady Tybar. Sabre, twisted up. Bobby or two. I began to come forward. Sabre looks up. Looks round. Gets his hat. Collects his old stick. Starts to hobble out.

"This Lady Tybar gets in front of him, me alongside of her by then. 'Marko, Marko.' (That was what she called him.) He sort of pushes at her and at me: 'Let me alone. Let me alone. Get right away from me.' Hobbles away down the room.

"A bobby stops him. 'Better go this way, sir. Rough lot of people out there.' Leads him to a side door.

"We followed him up, she and I. Door gave on to a lane running up into the Penny Green road. She tried at him again, gently, very tenderly, 'Marko, Marko, dear.' Would have made your heart squirm. I tried at him: 'Now then, old man.' Swung round on us. 'Let me alone. Get away. Get right away from me!'

"Followed him, the pair of us, up to the main road. She tried again. I tried. He swung round and faced us. 'Let me alone. Won't any one let me alone? Get right away from me. Look here—Look here. If you want to do anything for me, get right away from me and leave me alone. Leave me alone. Do you hear? Leave me alone.'

"Hobbled away out towards Penny Green, bobbing along on his stick fast as he could go.

"She said to me, 'Oh, Oh—' and began to cry. I said I thought the best thing was to leave him for a bit and that I'd go over, or she could, or both of us, a bit later. Clear we were only driving him mad by following him now. There was a cab came prowling by. I gave the chap a pound note and told him to follow Sabre.—'Get up just alongside and keep there,' I said. 'He'll likely get in. Get him in and take him up to Crawshaws, Penny Green, and come back to me at the Royal Hotel and there's another quid for you.'

"Old man, I went along to the Royal with this Lady Tybar. Told her who I was and what I knew. Ordered some tea there (which we didn't touch) and she began to talk to me. Talk to me ... I tell you what I thought about that woman while she talked. I thought, leaving out limelight beauty, and classic beauty and all the beauty you can see in a frame presented as such; leaving out that, because it wasn't there, I thought she was the most beautiful woman I had ever seen. Yes, and I told my wife so. That shows you! You couldn't say where it was or how it was. You could only say that beauty abode in her face as the scent in the rose. It's there and it's exquisite: that's all you can say. If she'd been talking to me in the dark I could have felt that she was beautiful.

"What did she tell me? She talked about herself and Sabre. What did she say? No, you'll have to let that go, old man. It was more what I read into what she said. I'll keep it—for a bit, anyway.

"There's else to tell than that. That cabman I'd got hold of sent in awhile after to see me. Said he'd picked up Sabre a mile along and taken him home. Stopped a bit to patch up some harness or something and 'All of a heap' (as he expressed it) Sabre had come flying out of the house again into the cab and told him to drive like hell and all to the office—to Fortune, East and Sabre's. Said Sabre behaved all the way like as if he was mad—shouting to him to hurry and carrying on inside the cab so the old man was terrified.

"I said, 'To the office! What the devil now?' I ran in to Lady Tybar and we hurried round. We were scared for him, I tell you. And we'd reason to be—when we got there and found him."

CHAPTER VII

I

When that cab which Hapgood had despatched after Sabre from the coroner's court overtook its quest, the driver put himself abreast of the distracted figure furiously hobbling along the road and, his second pound note in view, began, in a fat and comfortable voice, a beguiling monologue of "Keb, sir? Keb? Keb? Keb, sir?"

Sabre at first gave no attention. Farther along he once angrily waved his stick in signal of dismissal. About a mile along his disabled knee, and all his much overwrought body refused longer to be the flogged slave of his tumultuous mind. He stopped in physical exhaustion and rested upon his stick. The cabman also stopped and tuned afresh his enticing and restful rhythm: "Keb, sir? Keb? Keb? Keb, sir?"

He got in.

He did not think to give a direction, but the driver had his directions; nor, when he was set down at his house, to make payment; but payment had been made. The driver assisted him from the cab and into his door—and he needed assistance—and being off his box set himself to the adjustment of a buckle, repair of which he had deferred through the day until (being a man economical of effort) some other circumstance should necessitate his coming to earth.

Sabre stumbled into his house and pushed the door behind him with a resolution expressive of his desire to shut away from himself all creatures of the world and be alone,—be left entirely alone. By habit he climbed the stairs to his room. He collapsed into a chair.

His head was not aching; but there throbbed within his head, ceaselessly and enormously, a pulse that seemed to shake him at its every beat. It was going knock, knock, knock! He began to have the feeling that if this frightful knocking continued it would beat its way out. Something would give way. Amidst the purposeful reverberations, his mind, like one squeezed back in the dark corner of a lair of beasts, crouched shaking and appalled. He was the father of Effie's child; he was the murderer of Effie and of her child! He was neither; but the crimes were fastened upon him as ineradicable pigment upon his skin. His skin was white but it was annealed black; there was not a glass of the mirrors of his past actions but showed it black and reflected upon it hue that was blacker yet. He was a betrayer and a murderer, and every refutation that he could produce turned to a brand in his hands and branded him yet more deeply. He writhed in torment. For ever, in every hour of every day and night, he would carry the memory of that fierce and sweating face pressing towards him across the table in that court. No! It was another face that passed before that passionate countenance and stood like flame before his eyes. Twyning! Twyning, Twyning, Twyning! The prompter, the goader of that passionate man's passion, the instigater and instrument of this his utter and appalling destruction. Twyning, Twyning, Twyning! He ground his teeth upon the name. He twisted in his chair upon the thought. Twyning, Twyning, Twyning! Knock, knock, knock! Ah, that knocking, that knocking! Something was going to give way in a minute. It must be abated. It must. Something would give way else. A feverish desire to smoke came upon him. He felt in his pockets for his cigarette case. He had not got it. He thought after it. He remembered that he had started for Brighton without it, discovered there that he had left it behind. He started to hunt for it. It must be in this room. It was not to be seen in the room. Where? He remembered a previous occasion of searching for it like this. When? Ah, when Effie had told him she had found it lying about and had put it—of all absurd places for a cigarette case—in the back of the clock. Ten to one she had put it there again now. The very last thing she had done for him! Effie! He went quickly to the clock and opened it. Good! It was there. He snatched it up. Something else there. A folded paper. His name pencilled on it: Mr. Sabre.

She had left a message for him!

She had left a message for him! That cigarette case business had been deliberately done!

He fumbled the paper open. He could not control his fingers. He fumbled it open. He began to read. Tears stood in his eyes. Pitiful, oh, pitiful. He turned the page,—knock, knock, knock! The knocking suddenly ceased. He threw up his hand. He gave a very loud cry. A single note. A note of extraordinary exultation: "Ha!"

He crushed the paper between his hands. He cried aloud: "Into my hands! Into my hands thou hast delivered him!"

He opened the paper and read again, his hand shaking, and now a most terrible trembling upon him.

Dear Mr. Sabre,

I wanted you to go to Brighton so I could be alone to do what I am just going to do. I see now it is all impossible, and I ought to have seen it before, but I was so very fond of my little baby and I never dreamt it would be like this. But you see they won't let me keep my little baby and now I have made things too terrible for you. So I see the only thing to do is to take myself out of it all and take my little baby with me. Soon I shall explain things to God and then I think it will be quite all right. Dear Mr. Sabre, when I explain things to God, I shall tell him how wonderful you have been to me. My heart is filled with gratitude to you. I cannot express it; but I shall tell God when I explain everything to him; and my one hope is that after I have been punished I shall be allowed to meet you again, and thank you—there, where everything will be understood.

He turned over.

I feel I ought to tell you now, before I leave this world, what I never was able to tell you or any one. The father of my little baby was Harold Twyning who used to be in your office. We had been secretly engaged a very, very long time and then he was in an officers' training camp at Bournemouth where I was, and I don't think I quite understood. We were going to be married and then he had to go suddenly, and then he was afraid to tell his father and then this happened and he was more afraid. So that was how it all was. I do want you, please, to tell Harold that I quite I forgive him, only I can't quite write to him. And dear Mr. Sabre, I do trust you to be with Harold what you have always been with me and with everybody— gentle, and understanding things. And I shall tell the Perches, too, about you, and Mr. Fargus. Good-by and may God bless and reward you for ever and ever,

Effie.

II

He shouted again, "Ha!" He cried again, "Into my hands! Into my hands!"

He abandoned himself to a rather horrible ecstasy of hate and passion. His face became rather horrible to see. His face became purple and black and knotted, and the veins on his forehead black. He cried aloud, "Harold! Harold! Twyning! Twyning!" He rather horribly mimicked Twyning. "Harold's such a good boy! Harold's such a good, Christian, model boy! Harold's never said a bad word or had a bad thought. Harold's such a good boy." He cried out: "Harold's such a blackguard! Harold's such a blackguard! A blackguard and the son of a vile, infamous, lying, perjured blackguard."

His passion and his hate surmounted his voice. He choked. He picked up his stick and went with frantic striding hops to the door. He cried aloud, gritting his teeth upon it, "I'll cram the letter down his throat. I'll cram the letter down his throat. I'll take him by the neck. I'll bash him across the face. And I'll cram the letter down his throat."

The cab driver, his labour upon the buckle finished, was resting on his box with the purposeful and luxurious rest of a man who has borne the heat and burden of the day. Sabre waved his stick at him, and shouted to him, "Fortune's office in Tidborough. Hard as you can. Hard as you can." He wrenched open the door and got in. In a moment, the startled horse scarcely put into motion by its startled driver, he put his head and arm from the window and was out on the step. "Stop! Stop! Let me out. I've something to get."

He ran again into the house and bundled himself up the stairs and into his room. At his bureau he took a drawer and wrenched it open so that it came out in his hand, swung on the sockets of its handle, and scattered its contents upon the floor. One article fell heavily. His service revolver. He grabbed it up and dropped on his hands and knees, padding eagerly about after scattered cartridges. As he searched his voice went harshly, "He's hounded me to hell. At the very gates of hell I've got him, got him, and I'll have him by the throat and hurl him in!" He broke open the breech and jammed the cartridges in, counting them, "One, two, three, four, five, six!" He sapped up the breech and jammed the revolver in his jacket pocket. He went scrambling again down the stairs, and as he scrambled down he cried, "I'll cram the letter down his throat. I'll take him by the neck. I'll bash him across the face. And I'll cram the letter down his throat. When he's sprawling, when he's looking, perhaps I'll out with my gun and drill him, drill him for the dog, the dog that he is."

All the way down as the cab proceeded, he alternated between shouted behests to the driver to hurry and repetition of his ferocious intention. Over and over again; gritting his teeth upon it; picturing it; in vision acting it so that the perspiration streamed upon his body. "I'll cram the letter down his throat. I'll take him by the neck. I'll bash him across the face, and I'll cram the letter down his throat." Over and over again;

visioning it; in his mind, and with all his muscles working, ferociously performing it. He felt immensely well. He felt enormously fit. The knocking was done in his brain. His mind was tingling clear. "I'll cram ... I'll take ... I'll bash ... I'll cram the letter down his throat."

He was arrived! He was here! "Into my hands! Into my hands." He passed into the office and swiftly as he could go up the stairs. He encountered no one. He came to Twyning's door and put his hand upon the latch. Immediately, and enormously, so that for a moment he was forced to pause, the pulse broke out anew in his head. Knock, knock, knock. Knock, knock, knock. Curse the thing! Never mind. In! In! At him! At him!

He went in.

III

On his right, as he entered, a fire was burning in the grate and it struck him, with the inconsequent insistence of trifles in enormous issues, how chilly for the time of year the day had been and how icily cold his own house. On the left, at the far end of the room, Twyning sat at his desk. He was crouched at his desk. His head was buried in his hands. At his elbows, vivid upon the black expanse of the table, lay a torn envelope, dull red.

Sabre shut the door and leant his stick against the wall by the fire. He took the letter from his pocket and walked across and stood over Twyning. Twyning had not heard him. He stood over him and looked down upon him. Knock, knock, knock. Curse the thing. There was Twyning's neck, that brown strip between his collar and his head, that in a minute he would catch him by.... No, seated thus he would catch his hair and wrench him back and cram his meal upon him. Knock, knock, knock. Curse the thing!

He said heavily, "Twyning. Twyning, I've come to speak to you about your son."

Twyning slightly twisted his face in his hands so as to glance up at Sabre. His face was red. He said in an odd, thick voice, "Oh, Sabre, Sabre, have you heard?"

Sabre said, "Heard?"

"He's killed. My Harold. My boy. My boy, Harold. Oh, Sabre, Sabre, my boy, my boy, my Harold!"

He began to sob; his shoulders heaving.

Sabre gave a sound that was just a whimper. Oh, irony of fate! Oh, cynicism incredible in its malignancy! Oh, cumulative touch! To deliver him this his enemy to strike, and to present him for the knife thus already stricken!

No sound in all the range of sounds whereby man can express emotion was possible to express this emotion that now surcharged him. This was no pain of man's devising. This was a special and a private agony of the gods reserved for victims approved for very nice and exquisite experiment. He felt himself squeezed right down beneath a pressure squeezing to his vitals; and there was squeezed out of him just a whimper.

He walked across to the fireplace; and on the high mantle-shelf laid his arms and bowed his forehead to the marble.

Twyning was brokenly saying, "It's good of you to come, Sabre. I feel it. After that business. I'm sorry about it, Sabre. I feel your goodness coming to me like this. But you know, you always knew, what my boy was to me. My Harold. My Harold. Such a good boy, Sabre. Such a good, Christian boy. And now he's gone, he's gone. Never to see him again. My boy. My son. My son!"

Oh, dreadful!

And he went on, distraught and pitiable. "My boy. My Harold. Such a good boy, Sabre. Such a perfect boy. My Harold!"

The letter was crumpled in Sabre's right hand. He was constricting it in his hand and knocking his clenched knuckles on the marble.

"My boy. My dear, good boy. Oh, Sabre, Sabre!"

He dropped his right arm and swung it by his side; to and fro; over the fender—over the fire; over the hearth—over the flames.

"My Harold. Never to see his face again! My Harold."

He stopped his swinging arm, holding his hand above the flames. "He that dwelleth in love dwelleth in God and God in him; for God is love." He opened his fingers, and the crumpled letter fell and was consumed. He pushed himself up from the mantlepiece and turned and went over to Twyning and stood over him again. He patted Twyning's heaving shoulders. "There, there, Twyning. Bad luck. Bad luck. Hard. Hard. Bear up, Twyning. Soldier's death.... Finest death.... Died for his country.... Fine boy.... Soldier's death.... Bad luck. Bad luck, Twyning...."

Twyning, inarticulate, pushed up his hand and felt for Sabre's hand and clutched it and squeezed it convulsively.

Sabre said again, "There, there, Twyning. Hard. Hard. Fine death.... Brave boy...." He disengaged his hand and turned and walked very slowly from the room.

He went along the passage, past Mr. Fortune's door towards that which had been his own, still walking very slowly and with his hand against the wall to steady himself. He felt deathly ill....

He went into his own room, unentered by him for many months, now his own room no more, and dropped heavily into the familiar chair at the familiar desk. He put his arms out along the desk and laid his head upon them. Oh, cumulative touch! He began to be shaken with onsets of emotion, as with sobs. Oh, cumulative touch!

The communicating door opened and Mr. Fortune appeared. He stared at Sabre in astounded indignation. "Sabre! You here! I must say—I must admit—"

Sabre clutched up his dry and terrible sobbing. He turned swiftly to Mr. Fortune and put his hands on the arms of the chair to rise.

A curious look came upon his face. He said, "I say, I'm sorry. I'm sorry. I—I can't get up."

Mr. Fortune boomed, "Can't get up!"

"I say—No. I say, I think something's happened to me. I can't get up."

The door opened. Hapgood came in, and Nona.

313

Sabre said, "I say, Hapgood—Nona—Nona! I say, Nona, I think something's happened to me. I can't get up."

A change came over his face. He collapsed back in the chair.

"Marko! Marko!"

She who thus cried ran forward and threw herself on her knees beside him, her hands stretched up to him. Hapgood turned furiously on Mr. Fortune. "Go for a doctor! Go like hell! Sabre! Sabre, old man!"

"Hemorrhage on the brain," said the doctor. "...Well, if there's no more effusion of blood. You quite understand me. I say if there isn't.... Has he been through any trouble, any kind of strain?

"Trouble," said Hapgood. "Strain. He's been in hell—right in."

When he was removed and they had left him, Nona said to Hapgood as they came down the steps of the County Hospital, "There was a thing he was so fond of, Mr. Hapgood:

"...O Wind,

If Winter comes, can Spring be far behind?

"It comes to me now. There must be a turning now. If he dies ... still, a turning."

CHAPTER VIII

I

Hapgood across the coffee cups, the liqueur glasses and the cigarettes, wagged a solemn head at that friend of his, newly returned from a long visit to America. He wagged a solemn head:

"She's got her divorce, that wife of his....

"Eh?... Well, man alive, where do you expect me to begin? You insinuate yourself into a Government commission to go to America to lecture with your 'Sketchbook on the Western Front', and I write you about six letters to every one I get out of you, and you come back and expect me to give you a complete social and political and military record of everything that's happened in your absence. Can't you read?...

"Well, have it your own way. I've told you in my letters how he went on after that collapse, that brain hemorrhage. I told you we got Ormond Clive on to him. I told you we got him up here eventually to Clive's own nursing home in Welbeck Place. Clive was a friend of that Lady Tybar. She was with Sabre all the time he was in Queer Street— and it was queer, I give you my word. Pretty well every day I'd look in. Every day she'd be there. Every day Ormond Clive would come. Time and again we'd stand around the bed, we three,—watching. Impenetrable and extraordinary business! There was his body, alive, breathing. His mind, his consciousness, his ego, his self, his whatever you like to call it—not there. Away. Absent. Not in that place. Departed into, and occupied in that mysterious valley where those cases go. What was he doing there? What was he seeing there? What was he thinking there? Was he in touch with this that belonged to him here? Was he sitting in some fastness, dark and infinitely remote, and trying to rid himself of this that belonged to him here? Was he trying to get back to it, to resume habitation and possession and command? It was rummy. It was eerie. It was creepy. It was like staring down into a dark pit and hearing little tinkling sounds of some one moving there, and wondering what the devil he was up to. Yes, it was creepy....

"Process of time he began to come back. He'd struck a light down there, as you might say, and you could see the dim, mysterious glimmer of it, moving about, imperceptibly coming up the side. Now brighter, now fainter; now here, now there. Rummy, I can tell you. But he was coming up. He was climbing up out of that place where he had been. What would he remember? Yes, and what was he coming up to?

315

"What was he coming up to? That was what began to worry me. This divorce suit of his wife's was climbing up its place in the list. He was climbing up out of the place where he had been and this case was climbing up towards hearing. Do you get me? Do you get my trouble? Soon as his head emerged up out of the pit, was he going to be bludgeoned down into it again by going through in the Divorce Court precisely that which had bludgeoned him down at the inquest? Was I going to get the case held up so as to keep him for that? Or what was I going to do? I hadn't been instructed to prepare his defence. At Brighton, when I'd suggested it, he'd told me, politely, to go to hell. I hadn't been instructed; no one had been instructed. And there was no defence to prepare. There was only his bare word, only his flat denial—denial flat, unprofitable, and totally unsupported. The only person who could support it was the girl, and she was dead: she was much worse than dead: she had died in atrocious circumstances, his part in which had earned him the severe censure of the coroner's jury. His defence couldn't have been worse. He'd tied himself in damning knots ever since he'd first set eyes on the girl, and all he could bring to untie them was simply to say, 'It wasn't so.' His defence was as bad as if he were to stand up before the Divorce Court and say, 'Before she died the girl wrote and signed a statement exonerating me and fixing the paternity on so-and-so. He's dead, too, that so-and-so, and as for her signed statement, I'm sorry to say I destroyed it, forgetting I should need it in this suit. I was worried about something else at the time, and I quite forgot this and I destroyed it.'

"I don't say his defence would be quite so crudely insulting to the intelligence of the court as that; but I say the whole unsupported twisting and turning and writhing and wriggling of it was not far short of it.

"Well, that was how I figured it out to myself in those days, as the case came along for hearing; and I said to myself: Was I going to put in affidavits for a stay of hearing for the pleasure of seeing him nursed back to life to go through that agony and ordeal of the inquest again and come out with the same result as if he hadn't been there at all? And I decided—no; no, thanks; not me. It was too much like patching up a dying man in a civilised country for the pleasure of hanging him, or like fatting up a starving man in a cannibal country for the satisfaction of eating him.

"And I had this. In further support of my position I had this. My friend, the Divorce Court is a cynical institution. If a respondent and a corespondent have been in places and in circumstances where they might have incriminated themselves, the Divorce Court cynically assumes that, being human, they would have incriminated themselves. 'But,' it says to the petitioner, 'I want proof, definite and satisfactory proof of those places and of those circumstances. That's what I want. That's what you've got to give me.'

"Very well. Listen to me attentively. Lend me your ears. The onus of that proof rests on the petitioner. Because a case is undefended, it doesn't for one single shadow of a chance follow that the petitioner's plea is therefore going to be granted. No. The Divorce Court may be cynical, but it's a stickler for proof. The Divorce Court says to the petitioner, 'It's up to you. Prove it. Never mind what the other side isn't here to deny. What you've got to do is to satisfy me, to prove to me that these places and these circumstances were so. Go ahead. Satisfy me if you can.'

"So I said to myself: now the places and the circumstances of this petition unquestionably were so. All the Sabres in the world couldn't deny that. Let his wife go ahead and prove them to the satisfaction of the Court, if she can. If she can't; good; no harm done that he wasn't there to be bludgeoned anew. If she can satisfy the court, well, I say to you, my friend, as I said then to myself, and I say it deliberately: 'If she can satisfy the court—good again, better, excellent. He's free: he's free from a bond intolerable to both of them.'

"Right. The hearing came on and his wife did satisfy the Court. She got her decree. He's free.... That's that....

"Yesterday I took my courage in both hands and told him. Yesterday Ormond Clive said Sabre might be cautiously approached about things. For three weeks past Clive's not let us—me or that Lady Tybar—see him. Yesterday we were permitted again; and I took steps to be there first. I told him. There was one thing I'd rather prayed for to help me in the telling, and it came off—he didn't remember! He'd come out of that place where he had been with only a confused recollection of all that had happened to him before he went in. Like a fearful nightmare that in the morning one remembers only vaguely and in bits. Vaguely and in bits he remembered the inquest horror, and vaguely and in bits he remembered the divorce matter—and he thought the one was as much over as the other. He thought he had been divorced. I said to him, taking it as the easiest way of breaking my news, I said to him, 'You know your wife's divorced you, old man?' He said painfully, 'Yes, I know. I remember that.'

"I could have stood on my head and waved my heels with relief and joy. Of course it will come back to him in time that the business hadn't happened before his illness. In time he'll begin to grope after detailed recollection, and he'll begin to realise that he never did go through it and that it must have happened while he was ill. Well, I don't funk that. That won't happen yet awhile; and when it does happen I'm confident enough that something else will have happened meanwhile and that he'll see, and thank God for it, that what is is best. There'll be another thing too. He'll find his wife has married again. Yes, fact! I heard in a roundabout way that she's going to marry an old neighbour of theirs, chap called Major Millett, Hopscotch Millett, old Sabre used to call him. However, that's not the thing—though it would be a complication—that I mean will have happened and will make him see, and thank God for, that what is is best. What do I mean? What will have happened meanwhile? Well, that's telling; and I don't feel it's quite mine to tell. Tell you what, you come around and have a look at the old chap to-morrow. I dare bet he'll be on the road towards it by then and perhaps tell us himself. As I was coming away yesterday I passed that Lady Tybar going in, and I told her what I'd been saying to him and what he remembered and what he didn't remember.... What's that got to do with it? Well, you wait and see, my boy. You wait and see. I'll tell you this—come on, let's be getting off to this play or we'll be late—I tell you this, it's my belief of old Sabre that, after all he's been through,

"Home is the sailor, home from the sea

And the hunter home from the hill.

Or jolly soon will be. And good luck to him. He's won out."

II

Sabre, after Hapgood on the visit on which he had begun "to tell him things", had left him, was sitting propped up in bed awaiting who next might come. The nurse had told him he was to have visitors that morning. He sat as a man might sit at daybreak, brooding down upon a valley whence slowly the veiling mists dissolved. These many days they had been lifting; there were becoming apparent to him familiar features about the landscape. He was as one returned after long absence to his native village and wondering to find forgotten things again, paths he had walked, scenes he had viewed, places and people left long ago and still enduring here. More than that: he was to go down among them.

The door opened and one came in. Nona.

She said to him, "Marko!"

He had no reply that he could make.

She slipped off a fur that she was wearing and came and sat down beside him. She wore what he would have thought of as a kind of waistcoat thing, cut like his own waistcoats but short; and opened above like a waistcoat but turned back in a white rolled edging, revealing all her throat. She had a little closefitting hat banded with flowers and a loose veil depended from it. She put back the veil. Beauty abode in her face as the scent within the rose, Hapgood had said; and, as perfume deeply inhaled, her serene and tender beauty penetrated Sabre's senses, propped up, watching her. He had something to say to her.

"How long is it since I have seen you, Nona?"

"It's a month since I was here, Marko."

"I don't remember it."

"You've been very ill; oh, so ill."

He said slowly, "Yes, I think I've been down in a pretty deep place."

"You're going to be splendid now, Marko."

He did not respond to her tone. He said, "I've come on a lot in the last few weeks. I'd an idea you'd been about me before that. I'd an idea you'd be coming again. There's a thing I've been thinking out to tell you."

She breathed, "Yes, tell me, Marko."

But he did not answer.

She said, "Have you been thinking, in these weeks, while you've been coming on, what you are going to do?"

His hands, that had been crumpling up the sheet, were now laid flat before him. His eyes, that had been regarding her, were now averted from her, fixed ahead. "There is nothing I can do, in the way you mean."

She was silent a little time.

"Marko, we've not talked at all about the greatest thing—of course they've told you?—the Armistice, the war won. England, your England that you loved so, at peace, victorious; those dark years done. England her own again. Your dear England, Marko."

He said, "It's no more to do with me. Frightful things have happened to me. Frightful things."

She stretched a hand to his. He moved his hands away. "Marko, they're done. I would not have spoken of them. But shall I.... Your dear England in those years suffered frightful things. She suffered lies, calumnies, hateful and terrible things—not in one little place but across the world. Those who loved her trusted her and she has come through those dark years; and those who know you have trusted you always, and you are coming through those days to show to all. Time, Marko; time heals all things, forgets all things, and proves all things. There's that for you."

He shook his head with a quick, decisive motion.

She went on. "There's your book—your 'England.' You have that to go to now. And all your plans—do you remember telling me all your plans? Such splendid plans. And first of all your 'England' that you loved writing so."

He said, "It can't be. It can't be."

She began again to speak. He said, "I don't want to hear those things. They're done. I don't want to be told those things. They have nothing to do with me."

She tried to present to him indifferent subjects for his entertainment. She could not get him to talk any more. Presently she said, with a movement, "I am not to stay with you very long."

He then aroused himself and spoke and had a firmness in his voice. "And I'll tell you this," he said. "This was what I said I had to tell you. When you go, you are not to return. I don't want to see you again."

She drew a breath, steadying herself, "Why not, Marko?"

"Because what's been has been. Done. I've been through frightful things. They're on me still. They always will be on me. But from everything that belongs to them I want to get right away. And I'm going to."

"What are you going to do?"

"I don't know. Only get right away."

She got up. "Very well. I understand." She turned away. "It grieves me, Marko. But I understand. I've always understood you." She turned again and came close to him. "That's what you're going to do. Do you know what I'm going to do?"

He shook his head. He was breathing deeply.

"I'm going to do what I ought to have done the minute I came into the room. I hadn't quite the courage. This."

She suddenly stooped over him. She encircled him with her arms and slightly raised him to her. She put her lips to his and kissed him and held him so.

"You are never going to leave me, Marko. Never, never, never, till death."

He cried, "Beloved, Beloved," and clung to her. "Beloved, Beloved!" and clung to her....

Postscript.... This went through the mail bearing postmark, September, 1919:

"And seeing in the picture newspaper photograph with printing called 'Lady Tybar, widow of the late Lord Tybar, V.C., who is marrying Mr. Mark Sabre (inset)' and never having been in comfortable situation since leaving Penny Green, have expected you might be wishing for cook and house parlourmaid as before and would be most pleased and obliged to come to you, which if you did not remember us at first were always called by you hi! Jinks and lo! Jinks, and no offence ever taken, as knowing it was only your way and friendly. And so will end now and hoping you may take us and oblige, your obedient servants

"Sarah Jinks (hi!)
"Rebecca Jinks (lo!)"

The End

20813105R00171

Made in the USA
Lexington, KY
19 February 2013